MW01612363

Praise for *Marguerite*

The first book of the 'Merencourt Saga'

"Carol writes with an easy, modern style, breathing life into the true story of one woman's life, sweeping us from the strictures of the French aristocracy, through the confines of a convent in Ireland to the hell of a bad marriage set against the backdrop of British colonial life in the Indian subcontinent. A story of courage, resilience and a free spirit yearning for understanding and true love."
— JENNY SEAGROVE, ACTRESS AND FOUNDER MANE CHANCE SANCTUARY

"A great-aunt with a great story to share."
— JERSEY EVENING POST

"*Marguerite* is superb, enthralling, and an emotional journey. A MUST read. I couldn't put it down. Can't wait for the sequel, *Claire*. Well done to Carol Edgerley for giving us the chance to go on an amazing journey with *Marguerite*."
— MICHELE LEYSHAN, ASSISTANT TRAINER MACAU JOCKEY CLUB

"You will not be disappointed."
— LIVING MAGAZINE

"*Marguerite* runs the full gamut of feelings and the fact that the story is based on true facts makes Carol's tale all the more impressive. Beautifully written and extremely evocative, this is one book we didn't want to end. Part of a trilogy, we look forward to seeing what happens next. We expect great things from Carol."
— WOMAN'S WAY MAGAZINE

CAROL EDGERLEY

SilverWood

Published in 2013 by the author
using SilverWood Books Empowered Publishing®

SilverWood Books
30 Queen Charlotte Street, Bristol, BS1 4HJ
www.silverwoodbooks.co.uk

ISBN 978-1-78132-115-7 (paperback)
ISBN 978-1-78132-116-4 (ebook)

British Library Cataloguing in Publication Data
A CIP catalogue record for this book is available from the British Library

Set in Sabon by SilverWood Books
Printed on responsibly sourced paper

Acknowledgements

As always, I am indebted to my late great-aunt – Christina in the story – who provided me with wonderful tales of life in a bygone age, relationships and destiny.

My thanks to Fiona, my cousin, who nagged me into a better definition of the manuscript. And to Mandy, my sister, who was always there to encourage me should she sense a stumble in self-confidence.

Foreword

Claire was the eldest of the indomitable Marguerite de Merencourt's three daughters. I learned about her from my great-aunt, who related the fascinating story of her sister's life during a long hot summer, when I had thankfully managed to distract her from giving me hours of Maths coaching ordained by my mother.

My great-aunt Christina had always been very close to Claire from their early years in the care of kindly nuns in Simla whilst their mother was absent from their lives. She subsequently remained a presence in Claire's turbulent life, her steadfast loyalty providing an emotional security for Claire's daughters that they would never forget.

Prologue

Calcutta, India 1910

"*Claire*! Stop this bullying of your sister at once!" Minette snapped at her eldest daughter. "If Christina wants to have a pink dress made, who are you to tell her she must wear blue, just because you happen to like the colour."

"Well, she can't!" Claire pushed away her mother's hand holding the pink gingham material, her face darkening. "She always has what I decide is best, so you want the blue, don't you Chrissy?"

"Christina may have whatever colour she wants." Minette struggled to keep her tone neutral. "And don't be so rude! Your sister is perfectly capable of choosing for herself."

"NO!" the older girl shouted in sudden fury. "Mind your own business and leave us alone! After all, you left us alone in Simla for long enough, didn't you? We never argued before you arrived back on the scene."

Minette sighed. It was the same dreary reproach, flung in her face again and again by her eldest son, James, and less frequently by Claire. Nevertheless, this impertinence had to be nipped in the bud. Should her eldest daughter sense her reluctance for confrontation, she would attempt to exploit it.

"Before we go any further," Minette spoke sharply to the glowering girl, "you had better understand, once and for all, I will not tolerate your disgraceful manner of addressing me. For better or for worse, I am your mother, and you will respect that. Neither do I wish to listen to repetitive rubbish about how you were left all by yourselves to suffer alone. It has become tedious to a degree. Do I make myself clear?"

"I suppose so," Claire muttered, "but I'll never forgive you," she added under her breath."

"Yes, *Maman*, if you please," Minette was not finished, "and watch your tone when you speak to me, unless you wish to spend the rest of the day in your room?" Bending down, she picked up the discarded pink and white gingham and turned to her younger daughter. "Here, darling, of course you can have a pink frock if you want." She glanced over at the Sikh tailor seated before his sewing machine on the veranda floor, his

9

bundle of materials alongside. "Look, poor *durzi* is waiting for you to make up your mind."

Casting an agonised glance at her sister's infuriated face, Christina burst into tears and fled from the veranda. Satisfied to have achieved the upper hand, Claire prepared to follow, but found herself swung round by the arm to face her angry mother.

"Claire, I meant what I said about bullying!" Minette maintained a firm grip as the angry girl tried to twist away. "And there is no need to gasp like fish out of water, because that is precisely the correct word for your treatment of Christina. It's no different from what James does to his younger brother – a behaviour you claim to hate. A less than admirable quality in either of you, and I will not have it."

Claire stared at her mother, arrested by the unusual forcefulness of her words. She was quick to realise it was not to her advantage to antagonise her further, as she had always seemed eager to please. Hurriedly, she revised her earlier assessment of her mother's authority.

"Yes, *Maman*," the girl answered sulkily. "May I go now?"

With a resigned sigh, Minette nodded, and watched her eldest daughter toss her mane of dark hair and stalk off. She knew nobody had won that battle, but perhaps Claire would take more care over her treatment of Christina in future. It would also be nice if...

The door opened, interrupting Minette's glum reflections. It was Claire returning, followed by her still-tearful sister. Ignoring her mother, she approached the *durzi*, who had been listening in fascination to the heated exchange between mother and daughter. The English words had not been easy to follow...but tone? Oh, yes! He shook his turbaned head. *Tsk!* Such disrespect from *missy-baba* for her esteemed mother.

"*Durzi*," Claire asked politely, "my sister and I would like two dresses made, please. One pink one and the other blue."

Minette hid an involuntary grin. Wasn't it just like Claire to find a way of not losing face when forced to submit? She would let it go this time. Besides, there were accounts on her desk requiring attention.

Sitting in her office a few minutes later, Minette was unable to concentrate. These frequent and highly unpleasant rows were not only emotionally exhausting, but they were also increasingly difficult to deal with. One would imagine that a boy of sixteen and a girl of twelve should have outgrown such tiresome scenes by now.

Unfortunately, that was not the case. Claire could be an atrocious liar, using blatant untruths as a means to ease herself out of a difficult situation. James was sickeningly avaricious, never satisfied, always bent upon extracting 'compensation' he considered his due after her four-year absence from his life. God in heaven, would they ever stop punishing her? Who did they think paid the bills whilst she was doing her extensive training? Fed and clothed them, ensuring they lacked for nothing?

It certainly wasn't the Angel Gabriel!

Minette ran a hand through her dark hair. Thank God for Charlie, a cheerful and affectionate boy, and never acrimonious towards his mother. Slight in stature, he loved horses and was determined to follow a career in racing a few years hence. Of course, she also had her sweet little Sonia! The youngest of her three girls, Sonia was now six years old. Elfin in appearance, wide pale blue eyes, her head a mass of flaxen curls, she was her mother's constant companion.

Her mouth stretched in a humourless smile. How ironic it was that Sonia happened to possess her own mother's exact colouring. Francine, Marquise de Merencourt...the woman who had rejected her only daughter from the time she was born. That unnatural mother, who tirelessly went out of her way to be rid of her unwanted child – with impressive success. Strange how those pale eyes, once so disdainful, so cold...also belonged to a little girl who gazed up at her with adoration.

And what of nine-year-old Christina? A dumpy, rather plain little thing, she had never really stopped mourning the loss of the nuns she loved so much.

Leaning back in her chair, she wondered where or how she had gone so terribly wrong with James and Claire? It was two years since their arrival in Calcutta, and aside from constant recrimination over their mother's 'abandonment', both never tired of belittling the business that fed and clothed them.

The nursing home.

The establishment had been created in the other half of their large house in Camack Street, and had quickly proved to be a successful venture. Being a fully qualified midwife, and possessing more than a passing knowledge of childish ailments and medication, Minette took up the running of it herself.

Bookings flooded in, not merely for the delivery of a baby, but also as a place of recuperation from the birth in a tranquil environment. The income from the business provided generous living expenses for the family, as well as paying for an excellent education for the four older children at exclusive Calcutta schools.

Minette's personal history was somewhat unorthodox. Marguerite de Merencourt, pet-named "Minette" by her old nurse, had eloped at far too young an age with Patrick O'Hara, an Irish doctor. Shortly thereafter, the couple took part in a clandestine, but nevertheless legal marriage ceremony. To escape prosecution by his bride's father for the abduction of a minor, Patrick was forced abandon his chosen career to join the Indian Cavalry as a doctor-surgeon in northern India. A weak and embittered man, he had rapidly spiralled downward into aggressive alcoholism. Over the years, his young wife had been forced to protect her children from their father's drunken violence.

Subsequent to her husband's sudden assassination, she had made the appalling discovery that she and her family had been left with no means to survive. Patrick had drunk and gambled everything away, leaving nothing but a mountain of debt. It was at this point that she made the decision to train as a nurse and midwife, in order to provide a home and finance her young family's requirements.

Unable to look after the children during her training, she had reluctantly left them with kindly nuns of the Loretto Order in Simla. Her only comfort had been that her family would be healthy and safe in the cool, clean air of the Himalayas.

Marrying again had been an alternative, but in light of her experience with Patrick, it was one she refused to contemplate. Even to her dearest friend, Frederick de Barre. It was this refusal to remarry that lay at the heart of her older children's continued resentment. They adored their Uncle Freddie.

A more recent bone of contention was Minette's decree that the four older children should learn that money did not grow on trees. Although it was largely James's avarice that prompted this, she felt it would not be a bad thing if her children had the opportunity to earn additional pocket money by helping with light duties about the house.

Mailie and Seenta, Minette's two Nepalese *ayahs*, who had been with her for many years, dealt with most tasks about the house including preparation of meals. Unlike most European households, a *bearer* had not been employed, nor a *kensama*. Only a *jamadar* came early each morning to swab the marble floors, and to take out the rubbish. A part-time *mali* maintained the gardens on both sides of a trellis dividing the nursing home from the family residence.

Charlie cheerfully went about his allocated jobs, and even a grumbling Claire complied with the new condition, assisted by her shadow, Christina. At the end of each week, they were gratified to find they had accumulated a substantial sum in addition to their usual pocket money.

James, however, was outraged that he was expected to water potted plants, tidy his bedroom, or sweep the veranda floor. That was servants' work. Waited on hand and foot throughout his life by women, he saw no reason why that should change. He further believed that plenty of pocket money each week was his due, compensating him for what he perceived as his mother's earlier neglect.

Minette ground her teeth in frustration over the older boy's arrogant attitude, but refused to cave in. Thus, he was obliged to watch his siblings counting up their 'wages' every week, sums considerably in excess of what he received. Livid with fury, James vowed revenge on his parsimonious mother, even if it took years...

Chapter One

With a heavy sigh, Claire O'Hara shoved a lock of dark hair back from her perspiring face. She and Christina were sitting on the stone steps from the veranda into the garden, and she leaned back against the wall, her expression mutinous.

"It's really too much," she angrily declared, "that – today of all days – *Maman* has to charge off next door to that blasted nursing home of hers. It's the first of my grown-up birthdays, but we still have to listen to the dreadful racket that woman is making!"

Her party had been ruined, her friends mortified, and she was convinced she would never be able to hold her head up again at school. Only minutes ago, she had been sitting at the dining room table with her mother, two close girlfriends and her younger sisters. Being the birthday girl, she had pride of place at the head of a table laden with festive food, and a chocolate birthday cake resplendent with seventeen flickering candles.

Before she even had a chance to blow out the candles and make a wish, there had been a commotion in the hallway. Agnes, her mother's Anglo-Indian nursing assistant, had come rushing in, babbling about a *breech-birth*...whatever that might be. Her mother and Agnes had hurried away, and moments later, everybody's ears had been assaulted by the most horrific caterwauling coming from next door.

Claire's two girlfriends had exchanged appalled glances, and after fidgeting for a few minutes, they had made a feeble excuse to leave... without even tasting the birthday cake. One could hardly blame them, she thought sourly, as the noise that woman was making completely ruined the spirit of everything.

Claire ground her teeth with frustration over how that nursing home always, *always,* took precedence over family activities. She generally managed to choke down her resentment, as it triggered another boring lecture from her mother about petulance. Not to mention reminders of how they owed their pleasant lifestyle to the awful place.

"I loathe and detest that dratted nursing home!" Claire exploded.

"None of my friends have to share their home with screeching women taking centre stage the whole time."

"*Claire!*" Fourteen-year-old Christina looked fearfully over her shoulder. "You shouldn't swear like that. It's not nice, and *Maman* might hear you from over the trellis."

"Rubbish! I can say what I like now that I'm grown up," the older girl retorted, nevertheless lowering her voice. "After all, James and Charlie can use swear words these days. I hope you aren't getting all holy on me again, are you, Chrissy? Sometimes you sound just like the nuns."

"Well, if I do sound like our nuns...I'm jolly glad." Christina's placid nature was always ruffled by her sister's disrespectful reference to the women she loved and admired. "They are lovely people, and they were awfully kind to us when we lived with them. You ought to remember that."

"Yes, *yes*! Let's drop the subject, shall we?" Claire's prickly reply reduced the younger girl to tight-lipped silence. "Anyway," she added, "it's too hot to argue the toss over rubbish, especially on my birthday."

"Heigh-ho, girls!" came a voice from behind them. Charlie wandered into the veranda and dumped his riding equipment on a nearby rattan chair. "Isn't it your birthday, Claire? What is it now...fourteen? Fifteen?" Grinning, he dodged the cushion hurled at him by his sister. "Any chance of some cake?"

"Plenty," Claire answered grumpily, "since it hasn't even been cut yet." When he threw her a questioning look, she added, "I'll tell you all about it later. Charlie, *do* get your smelly stuff off the chairs, will you? Chrissy and I have to clear up tonight, as it's pocket money pay day tomorrow."

Over the last two years, Claire and Charlie had grown closer, both of them secretly glad for their own reasons to be rid of their surly older brother. James had left home to work for their Uncle Frederick as his personal assistant, and it soon became practical for the young man to move permanently into Frederick's home.

Part of Claire understood James's hostile attitude towards their mother – a bitter resentment that frequently flared into life. Neither she nor James had accepted their mother's reasons for leaving them for all those years, when they were aware she could have married their darling Uncle Freddie.

On the other hand, Charlie had been delighted to be free at last of the person who had made his life utterly miserable for years. The stammer that blighted his life had all but disappeared, and his self-confidence was growing in leaps and bounds. At the age of nineteen he was an apprentice jockey, and leading Calcutta racehorse trainers thought he showed great promise.

His mouth full of chocolate cake, the young man regarded his sister with affection as she fussed over the tack he had thrown on the chair. Recent comments made by his friends sprang to mind, including requests to be introduced to his "gorgeous" sister. With brotherly surprise, he supposed Claire was quite attractive with all that dark curly hair, vivid blue eyes, and her slender figure. He imagined it was how their mother must have looked at one time.

Claire was deceptively dainty – *deceptive* being the operative word – Charlie thought ruefully. Two years ago just after to Christina's Holy Communion, he had thought to amuse his sisters by dressing up in her white Communion dress and veil. Being small in stature, it fitted him to perfection. Prancing about the veranda, Charlie had struck exaggeratedly coy poses – signally failing to notice the horror on Christina's face. Bursting into floods of tears, she had rushed sobbing from the veranda to her bedroom. Sonia had tittered at her brother's antics, but Claire's dark brows had drawn together to see her sister so distressed. With a roar of anger, she had leaped to her feet and chased Charlie out into the garden, yelling dire threats of what she intended to do when she caught him.

Hurriedly shinning up a nearby tree, he had been unaware of an accumulation of bright green stains on the once-pristine muslin dress. Hampered by the white shoes into which he had crammed his feet, he was not quick enough to escape his sister. Halfway up the tree behind her brother, Claire managed to grasp an ankle and give it a good yank. He had slipped, the dress had ripped, and brother and sister froze in consternation.

Charlie hadn't realised that Christina was planning to have a photograph taken clad in Communion attire to send to her dearest nuns. But the dress had been reduced to a filthy rag, so that was out of the question. He had been genuinely contrite, but despite numerous abject apologies, she had refused to speak to him for weeks.

He had finally achieved forgiveness by presenting Christina with a two-month-old puppy. Thrilled by the wriggling ball of mischief, she had christened the puppy Lily, despite the little animal's coat being pitch-black...to everyone's mystification.

Returning home to find her children were gathered on the veranda, Minette interrupted Charlie's amused reminiscences. "Charlie, have you checked on Turka this evening?" she asked. "I thought him to be a little off his feed this morning."

"I was at the stables only a few minutes ago," he replied, "and the old chap was wolfing happily. He probably didn't feel much like eating after being ridden this morning, as it was quite hot. Since the cold weather seems to be on the way out, I'll have to take him out an hour earlier for a gentle walk to stretch his legs."

Everybody loved the little Arab horse Minette had brought from Darjeeling long ago, who remained devoted to her. Although getting on in years, he still enjoyed going out with Charlie a few times a week.

"Before I forget," Minette announced, "Frederick and James are coming round for dinner, as it's your brother's last evening before joining the British Navy. Claire, I do hope you are not going to treat everyone to that sulky face? Oh, and please make sure the table is laid with the best cutlery and glassware."

Briefly nodding, Claire left the veranda, pulling Christina after her. "Why does *Maman* always have to make nasty remarks?" she hissed, once safely out of earshot of her mother. "Even on my blasted birthday! And what's so special about James coming to dinner, I'd like to know?"

"Well, Uncle Freddie is coming, too," Christina offered, trying to smooth troubled waters, "and he deserves the best of everything, doesn't he?"

"I suppose so." Claire's tone was grudging. "After all, he took our vile eldest brother off our hands, praise the Lord!"

Later that evening, Minette and her family were again on the veranda, waiting for Frederick and James to arrive. An hour earlier, Claire had observed her mother in the kitchen putting finishing touches to her eldest brother's favourite meal. Let's hope he appreciates it, she thought acidly, knowing James was quite capable of refusing to eat his mother's carefully prepared dishes.

The guests arrived, and, contrary to Claire's gloomy forebodings, the evening promised to pass pleasantly. Frederick raised his glass in a toast to James's future as a midshipman, and the family joined in to wish him well. The entire meal was perfection itself, and ended with a dessert of rich chocolate mousse.

"James," Minette smiled at her eldest son, "do help yourself, darling!

I know how you love chocolate mousse. Heavens, I can hardly believe you will be leaving Calcutta tomorrow, and I shall miss you dreadfully!"

"Will you now?" James's face took on its habitual sneer. "I would have thought you'd be secretly delighted to see the back of one of us at long last. One down...three yet to go! Of course, one must exclude darling Sonia who is being carefully groomed to become your old-age companion."

"*James*! What a dreadful thing to say!" Minette's face lost every vestige of colour. "Surely you know what my family means to me? How can you—"

"More like a guilty conscience at work, dearest *Maman*!" James interrupted. "We've all noticed your pathetic attempts to appease...trying a shade too hard to make up for your abandonment of us. Why, you even left your newborn infant for others to bring up. You didn't know *that*, did you, Sonia dear?" he added with a curling lip.

Rising furiously to her feet, Minette battled with the sting of her son's words. "How dare you speak to me like—"

"I'll speak as I wish!" barked the young man, standing up to face his mother. "Perhaps you haven't noticed, but I'm no longer a small boy for you to bully. I thank God for Uncle Freddie here, who saved my sanity by allowing me to live with him. The relief of getting away from your hectoring voice and miserable penny-pinching was simply indescribable."

"I really don't think..." Frederick prepared to get up, but seeing Minette shake her head, sank back in his chair.

"Is it necessary to be this unpleasant when you are leaving so soon?" she controlled her anger with an effort. "Heaven knows how hard I've tried to reach you, James, but..."

"Well, you've failed," snarled her son. "*Dismally.* I imagine most people would agree you've been pretty useless as a mother. Not to mention making a laughing stock of us in the eyes of Calcutta society by running that dreadful place next door. And it's hardly helped our family's credibility that you are seen to be doing the filthy job yourself. If your family in France could only see you now, they would die of shame." James laid a hand on Frederick's shoulder. "I'll be off now," he announced. "See you later, Uncle Freddie."

Glancing back at his dumbstruck mother, James gave her a wolfish grin. "Thank you, *Maman*...for a most entertaining evening." With a sarcastic bow, he strode from the dining room and the front door was heard to slam behind him.

Without a word, her movements wooden, Minette also left the dining room, Frederick close behind. The four young people remained frozen at the table, appalled by the scene they had just witnessed.

Sonia broke the silence by jumping up to run wailing after her mother. Although horrified that James should have attacked their mother with such venom, a vengeful aspect of Claire's nature rejoiced to see her hurting. It was unfortunate that Frederick returned to the dining room in time to notice the satisfied expression on her face. Staring at Claire in disgust, his unspoken reproach caused the girl's face to flame with shame and embarrassment.

"Your mother is inordinately upset," he said finally. "She wishes to remain in her room, but asks that you two girls please clear the table for the *ayahs*. Terrible things were said to your mother this evening, and I intend to have words with James about it." Frederick looked round the three young faces.

"I am relying on you to show her that those destructive remarks were far from the truth. You are aware that I have known your mother for a great many years, and I can assure you she has always, *always* had your welfare and happiness at heart. I imagine you will know that already. Is that not so, Claire?" he stared hard at the girl who appeared to have enjoyed her brother's cruelty.

"Y-yes, of course, Uncle Freddie," she stammered. "It's just that *Maman* doesn't always show she loves us, except Sonia, of course."

"Ah, but do *you* show her that you love her?" Frederick raised his eyebrows enquiringly. "I'll bid you goodnight, and do please remember what I said."

"Claire, I saw you smirking just now." Charlie rounded on his sister as soon as the door closed behind their uncle. "How could you? Did you think James's horrid remarks were funny?"

"No," Claire blustered, "I could hardly believe my ears. Poor *Maman*...do you think she's all right?"

"Probably not, but let's leave her in peace as Uncle Freddie suggests," her brother replied. "Come on, I'll help you clear the decks here, and then I must go down to the stables and check that Turka is properly bedded down for the night."

The next day, Minette emerged from her bedroom, composed and unruffled. She did not refer to the previous evening's events, and neither did anybody else. She did, however, have a few sharp words for Claire about a bright red lipstick she had discovered in her dressing table drawer, bought from the local *bazaar* and secreted away.

"I will not have you wandering about Calcutta looking like a lady of the night," she told her glowering daughter. "You may have a lipstick, but a good quality one of my choosing and in a tasteful colour."

"Good Lord, I can't even choose my own makeup!" Claire grizzled later to Christina. "I'm surprised she doesn't insist on supervising my bath time into the bargain."

"That's just as well," the younger girl replied equably, "or she'd see that red ink heart you drew on your bosom. And the one on your right thigh."

"It was only a bit of fun, so don't look so disapproving, Chrissie."

"What's only a bit of fun?" Sonia came in on silent feet, startling both her sisters.

"Mind your own business!" Claire snapped. "And you can stop eavesdropping in the hope of overhearing some tasty morsel you can report to *Maman*."

Sonia stuck out her bottom lip. "I'm going to tell her what you said! She gave me a message for you, so there!"

"Well? What is it?" Claire demanded. "Tell me, and then buzz off!"

"I'll tell her that as well, you horrid thing. Anyway, *Maman* wants to see you in her office straight away."

Claire paused, mentally sifting through recent misdemeanours that might be the reason for this summons. Could her mother have discovered that illicit, if brief visit to the Saturday Club? Swallowing hard, the girl steeled herself for trouble, and with mounting apprehension, tapped on the door of her mother's office and slipped inside.

Minette was standing by the window, in the company of a gentleman unknown to Claire. There was an expression of happiness on her mother's face, such as Claire could not recall ever having seen before.

"Come and meet your Great-Uncle Emile." Minette drew her daughter forward. "Claire is my eldest daughter, only just turned seventeen as a matter of fact."

Demurely casting down her eyes as she had been taught, Claire bobbed a respectful curtsey and extended a slender hand to the visitor. Raising her eyes, she saw the gentleman was staring incredulously at her. Colouring, she wondered what social blunder she might have inadvertently committed?

"*Mais c'est incroyable!*" Emile exclaimed, taking Claire's hand and raising it to his lips. "This child is a replica of yourself at the same age, Minette." He switched back to French. "*Que je suis enchanté de faire la connaissance de Mademoiselle Claire!*"

"*Et de ma part*," replied a fascinated Claire in the same language, "*je suis ravie d'avoir retrouvé un oncle!*"

Smiling in genuine pleasure, Emile turned to his niece. "I see you haven't neglected your daughter's education, *ma chérie*. Do all your children speak French so well?"

"No, only James and Claire found it easy to become bilingual. Charlie and Christina can't do much more than make themselves understood, but in an execrable accent. And my little Sonia has yet to show an interest in a second language."

Claire surreptitiously examined the face of this nice new relative. She hoped to see some family resemblance but disappointingly, none was discernible.

Emile was a tall, elegant man with smiling pale blue eyes, fair hair greying at the temples. Claire felt a *frisson* of pride that such a distinguished gentleman should be related to her, even if he did carry on rather about her resemblance to Minette. In light of her mother's severe expression and thickening waistline, that was hardly flattering!

Emile stayed for dinner that evening, chatting amiably in English with Charlie and Christina about their interests and ambitions for the future. Christina's eyes sparkled as she described the wonderful nuns in Simla who had brought her up. Receiving a sharp kick on the ankle from her sister, the flow of her enthusiasm dried up abruptly. Hoping to cover an awkward moment, Charlie mentioned he was an apprentice flat race jockey.

"No need to look far to discover where the love of horses comes from," Emile grinned. "Although now in a wheelchair, your grandfather is still very much in the business of raising and training thoroughbred horses, as his father was before him."

"Good Lord!" exclaimed the young man in surprise. "I didn't know that. *Maman* used to ride, but not since she became too heavy for our little Arab horse."

Claire's ears had pricked up at the snippet of interesting information Emile had let drop. Their mother had always been annoyingly reticent about her family in France. That her father was a marquis had only been divulged a few years ago, when Claire had come home from school, weeping, two older girls having taunted her about her mother's nursing home. The parents of one of them had been overheard to declare the French woman's business smacked of *trade*…thereby rendering Claire undesirable as a friend.

When she discovered the reason for her daughter's distress, Minette had been furious. "Our family can buy and sell most others in Calcutta," she had snapped. "Not many of those pretentious people can legitimately claim a marquis and a duke as close relatives."

She had then looked squarely at Claire. "Never feel ashamed to take responsibility for your own livelihood, *chèrie*. It's decidedly more admirable than being a useless parasite on some man or the other, examples of which can readily be found at those tiresome lunches thrown by such women. Believe me, I am proud of my achievement."

Hugging this new information about her family to herself, Claire bided her time until the bullies renewed their attack. She did not have long to wait. Delighted by the misery they had managed to inflict on the previous occasion, Claire's tormentors, now a gang of four, intercepted her once again.

"Damned cheek you've got trying to pass yourself off as one of us, Claire O'Hara," one of them accused.

"You and your dreary sister shouldn't be allowed to come to a school like ours," supplied another.

"I can just imagine," said the third, "how your dead common mother must have lied through her teeth to get you accepted here."

The fourth nodded. "It's a disgrace we should be forced to rub shoulders with the likes of someone destined to become a hotel chambermaid!"

"Not that attending our school will her do much good," sniggered the first girl. "After all, you can't make a silk purse from a sow's ear!"

Looking the girls up and down, Claire surprised them by starting to laugh. "Why Cecily," she said, "my mother says she's not surprised you have such a vulgar tongue in your head – in light of that pretentious family you belong to. But before you carry on with your bullying, I think you should know my grandfather is a French marquis of ancient lineage, and my great-grandfather was a duke. Naturally, I speak fluent French. Take my advice and keep your ignorant mouths shut in future, you brainless ninnies."

Giving the gawping foursome a final disdainful glance, she turned on her heel and rejoined her friends a short distance away. Vindicated, she basked in the warmth of their new-found admiration.

Now, with the arrival of Emile, there was the distinct possibility of gleaning even more useful information about her aristocratic grandparents – without attracting her mother's attention, of course. Perhaps she would be called out to the nursing home, leaving the way clear to ask more direct questions? Sadly, however, no such summons occurred. All Claire managed to discover was that the grandparents on her mother's side were both very much alive. The girl ached to know more...

Two days later, Charlie came home, grinning all over his face. "I saw Uncle Emile at the racecourse this morning," he announced, "and he suggested we all go back to France with him for a long holiday. Schools have broken up, so there shouldn't be a problem for you girls."

"What?" Claire jumped to her feet in delight. "Oh, how terrific that would be! What do you think of that, Chrissy?"

"Well, I...I don't really know," Christina looked dazed, as if the idea were too momentous to take in. "Does *Maman* know about it yet?"

Her enthusiasm subsiding, Claire looked at her brother. "*Maman* is bound to find a reason why we can't go," she said despondently, "Besides, she'll never leave that blasted nursing home for any length of time."

"I would suggest," Charlie made an effort to be diplomatic, "that we leave it to Uncle Emile to approach *Maman*. Not you, Claire, you're far too tactless."

Christina clasped her hands in ecstasy. "If we do go to France, maybe we can visit Lourdes whilst we are there. Wouldn't that be wonderful?"

Claire turned on her impatiently. "Do you ever have thoughts that have no religious significance? Not everyone is a pillar of the church, you know."

"Don't be mean, Claire. You know I..." Seeing her sister's attention was already elsewhere, the younger girl's voice trailed to a halt. Sighing, she swallowed her hurt, knowing Claire did not mean half of what she said. She adored her sister, and would do anything for her. Anything, that is, except abandon her beloved nuns in Simla and the religion that always sustained her.

At dinner that evening, the atmosphere was almost buzzing in anticipation of a later visit from Emile, and an excited Claire could scarcely contain herself. Remembering how happy Minette had been to see him, her spirits were buoyant. If anyone could, Emile would somehow persuade her mother to agree. Why, they might even be taken to meet their grandfather, the Marquis de Merencourt. How thrilled he would be to see his grandchildren for the first time! Charlie could talk about horses, and she would ask...

"*Claire!*" Minette's sharp voice broke through the girl's daydream. "Why on earth are you grinning in that ridiculous manner? Get on with your meal before it's congealed."

After dinner, Charlie set up the green baize card table on the veranda, and a game of bridge was soon in progress. Both Claire and Christina excelled at the game, but Charlie played somewhat indifferently, unhappy to sit still for any length of time. Resentful of her mother's attention being diverted by a stupid game, Sonia sulked behind her chair.

"For heaven's sake, Claire," Minette exclaimed in annoyance "*Do* concentrate. What's the matter with you this evening?"

"Sorry! I...er...have a bit of a headache, as a matter of fact," Claire stuttered, caught out in another pleasurable daydream. "But I think it's on its way out now."

Minette frowned. "Why have you got a headache? It's too soon for your time of month, surely?"

"*Maman!*" The girl's face flamed. "Not...not in front of everybody!"

"Don't be silly, we are all females here except Charlie, and since he's family you have no need to be coy." Minette's tone was dismissive. "Now, are you able to go on playing, or not?"

Claire was saved from replying by a peal of the doorbell. Moments later, Emile was shown into the veranda.

"*Bonsoir à tous!* Sorry about being late, but a business meeting went on longer than I had hoped. Am I too late for coffee?"

"No, of course not," Minette rose with a smile to kiss her uncle. "We were just finishing a game of cards. Charlie, be a dear and ask Mailie to make coffee, and bring the drinks tray from the sideboard, will you?"

Emile mopped his perspiring brow with a handkerchief. "*Mon Dieu*, but the hot weather seems to have arrived with a vengeance!" he exclaimed feelingly. "Even your so-called cold weather feels extremely hot to me. How do you stand it, year after year?"

"Oh, one becomes acclimatised," Minette explained with a laugh, "but at least we have electric fans these days, instead of a fellow pulling the string of a *punkah*."

Scarcely able to bear it as her mother continued to reminisce about the bad old days in Lucknow, Claire couldn't prevent herself from fidgeting. Was Emile ever going to mention the holiday? Or had it been a figment of her overwrought imagination after all?

Emile was speaking again. "Where is your eldest son...James, I believe? He is the only one of your children I have yet to meet."

"He left Calcutta a short while ago to join the British Navy," Minette replied. "Of course, we will miss him but he has a wonderful career to look forward to."

"*I* won't miss nasty James one little bit," Sonia piped up. "He shouted at poor *Maman* at dinner, and told horrid lies about her leaving me alone when I was a baby."

"Darling, Uncle Emile isn't interested in silly family arguments." Minette hastened to silence her favourite daughter. "Everyone has them, you know."

"And then James said—"

"*Sonia*!" Charlie barked, "be quiet." His sister lapsed into sulky silence, resentful of his authoritative tone. "You heard what *Maman* said."

With great diplomacy, Emile changed the subject. "*Alors*, Minette, do you happen to have any cognac to offer me with my coffee?"

Glad of the distraction, Charlie went to pour a quantity of the amber liqueur into a balloon glass that he handed to Emile. "I'd join you," he said, "but being a bit of a Philistine, I don't care for the stuff."

Appreciatively breathing in the aroma of fine brandy, the Frenchman leaned back in his chair. "Minette, *ma chèrie*," he began, "I have a suggestion for you to consider. Would it not be an excellent idea for you all to come back to France with me for a holiday? All expenses paid, of course. It would do you a great deal of good to get away from this dreadful heat. And it would be good for the young ones to see something of France."

There was a sudden silence as four faces turned towards Minette, each of her children anxiously awaiting her decision. Flustered, she rose to her feet and wandered over to perch on the veranda wall to consider this unexpected invitation. The brutal rejection she had suffered from her father years ago had gone deep, and had never really healed. She had no wish to see the man who callously refused to take in his homeless grandchildren after their father had been killed.

The silence behind her was almost tangible.

"No." Minette's voice was flat. "It's entirely out of the question. I have bookings for the nursing home, and—"

"Oh, I don't believe this!" Claire leapt to her feet, her face flushing scarlet that her lovely dreams might be crumbling into dust. "It's always, *always* that—"

Charlie seized his sister's wrist in an iron grip. "Claire, sit down!" he hissed in her ear. "You'll ruin everything, so let Emile do the talking."

The girl threw herself back in her chair and stared at the floor. If *Maman* prevented them from taking this wonderful opportunity, she would never forgive her.

Sensing a family drama was about to ignite, Emile took a sip of his cognac and wandered over to join Minette. "*Ma chèrie*, I appreciate that you personally have many commitments to meet, but why don't I take your family off your hands for a couple of months? Think of all those things you would like to do…but don't have the time? Ah, I thought so! And the young ones should see something of the country to which they partly belong, *n'est-ce pas?*"

"*Peut-être.*" Minette's tone was noncommittal. "I'll think about it, but thank you for your generous offer, Emile."

"It would be my pleasure," he replied with a courtly little bow. "I am in Calcutta for another ten days, but remember passages have to be booked if the children are to accompany me." Emile concealed a yawn. "I'd better go now…it's been a very long day. *Bonne nuit, et à bientôt!*"

Chapter Two

Two days later, to Claire's great joy Minette gave her permission for the children to accompany their great-uncle to France. She strongly suspected they had Frederick to thank for persuading their mother to relax her previously rigid stance. For the umpteenth time, she wished he was their real father, for in all but name he most certainly was.

There had been a tense moment when Minette suggested that Sonia should be included in the party. However, Sonia herself had resolved the problem upon the realisation that she would be expected to leave her mother. Screaming and sobbing hysterically to the point of vomiting, Minette had hurriedly taken the girl in her arms, rocking and hushing her as if she were a baby. And so it was settled. Sonia would remain with her mother in Calcutta. Christina and Claire could scarcely hide their jubilation.

Frederick had given the three young travellers a generous sum of money to have new clothes made, in addition to a wallet of francs for pocket money whilst in France. Beside herself with happiness, Claire impatiently waited out the remaining days before taking the train to Bombay, where they would be spending the night. In the early evening of the following day, they would board the liner sailing to France.

One hot afternoon just before they left, Claire and Christina were sitting in their shared bedroom admiring their new purchases, when Sonia looked round the door.

"*Maman* wants to see you in her office right away, Claire," she announced with an air of importance. "Bet you've done something awful again!"

"Well, you don't have to lick your nasty little lips over it," the girl retorted, getting to her feet. "We know how much you enjoy seeing one of us in trouble."

Minette was seated at her desk when Claire tapped on her door and entered her office, and she looked up over her glasses with a frown. "Must you always be so unpleasant to your little sister? Such an unattractive trait in you."

"Is that why you wanted to see me, *Maman*?" Claire asked, casting a venomous glance at Sonia who openly tittered from behind her mother's chair.

"No." Minette removed her glasses. "It's to do with your future after you have left school. Whilst you are away, I want you to think about two suitable careers I have in mind for you. Either you enroll at teachers' training at college here in Calcutta, or you can stay with Aunty Jane in Scotland to undertake nursing training and midwifery." She paused to glare at her daughter. "Kindly don't make that silly face, Claire. Qualifications in nursing and midwifery would mean you could eventually take over the nursing home from me. An established income is not to be sniffed at, my girl."

Claire stared speechlessly at her mother, unable to think of a single diplomatic thing she could say regarding taking over the nursing home. Anything but that. "I'll give it serious thought whilst I am away, *Maman*," she managed at last. "But I still have a school term ahead before I need to decide, don't I?"

"Indeed you do, but this sort of thing has to be arranged well in advance, so I shall expect an answer when you return from France."

"Yes, *Maman*," Claire suppressed an urge to flee. "May I go now, please?"

"You may, but don't dismiss these choices out of hand. Your future is very important. Incidentally I want to see you being kinder to little Sonia." Minette's voice followed her daughter as she left the room.

"It was a blasted nightmare," she later confided to Christina. "Can you imagine me as a midwife, hauling babies out of yowling women? Over my dead body!"

Christina grinned at the image her sister was presenting. "Better be a teacher," she advised, "and have all the school holidays free, I'd have thought."

"Oh, absolutely! Although even that is far from an enticing prospect," Claire grimaced, "but I'll have to think up a diplomatic way of telling *Maman* I don't want her nursing home. Incidentally, I got another flea in my ear for being horrid to darling Sonia. I could actually see the horrible thing sniggering away…well out of *Maman's* sight, of course. I can't stand how she's forever snivelling to her about one or the other of us." Claire suddenly giggled. "*Snivelling-Sonia*…what an appropriate name!"

"Never mind," Christina said. "We'll forget all about dear Sonia when we are far away on the high seas."

The longed-for day of departure arrived at last. The three young O'Haras piled into Frederick's carriage that transported them to Calcutta's Howrah Station, where Emile was waiting to meet them. After a hot and lengthy train journey, the travellers arrived in Bombay, weary and feeling decidedly grubby. As a surprise for his young relatives, Emile had booked rooms for the night at the new and exclusive Taj Mahal Hotel, situated along the seafront.

"What luxury!" Claire sighed ecstatically, bouncing on the wide bed and gazing round the bedroom she was sharing with her sister. "Have you seen that marble bathtub with gold taps shaped like dolphins in our bathroom? And there's a jar of scented pink bath crystals on a ledge. Just think what a lovely soak we are going to have, Chrissy!"

That evening, both girls were awestruck by the grandeur of the hotel's reception rooms and vast expanse of marble flooring. Crystal chandeliers twinkled from vaulted ceilings supported by tall onyx columns, the walls lavishly painted in gold leaf and unusually vibrant colours. The richness of the colour scheme was echoed in the dining room, where they enjoyed a protracted and magnificent dinner. Resplendent in their new clothes, the three O'Haras were relieved to know they were on a par with other elegant people dining at nearby tables.

The following day, Emile and his youthful companions boarded the liner sailing to Marseilles in France. From there, they were to take the train to Bordeaux, where Emile had arranged for his carriage to transport them back to the Dower House, his home on the edge of the Beaurepaire estate in the Périgord.

"Oh, Chrissy, isn't this pure heaven?" Claire lay back in a chaise longue in Emile's garden four weeks later. "Lovely and warm, but without that suffocating Calcutta humidity."

"I could live here forever," Christina sighed. "And I didn't realise France was so religious. Did you notice the statues of Our Lady on almost every crossroad? I must write and tell Mother Clementine about it."

"I don't suppose she was born a nun, so she may have already visited France as well as lots of other countries." Claire yawned. "For all we know, she may be doing penance for doing something very naughty in her youth."

"*Claire*! That's so disrespectful." Christina frowned. "I can't believe you said that about Mother Clementine. She's such a good person, in fact she's—"

"Oh, Chrissy, do belt up! Please tell me you won't bore everyone to tears with religious cant when we have dinner with Uncle Max and Aunt Amélie tomorrow?"

Christina stood up, smoothing down her dress with a hand. "I'm going in. I hate it when you're in one of your horrid moods."

"All right, *all right!* I'm sorry," Claire shaded her eyes to look up at her sister. "It's just that spouting holy stuff isn't everybody's cup of tea."

Christina sat down again. "Yes, I know. I'll keep off the subject if you promise not to pass horrid remarks about our nuns."

"If you aren't carrying on *ad nauseam* about them, I won't feel the need, will I?" Claire grinned. "Why don't we go for a walk? Emile and Charlie won't be back from their ride for ages yet."

"Good idea," Christine agreed, "but I'll have to change my shoes, and you should as well," she glanced at her sister's soft leather slippers, "you can hardly tramp along forest paths in those."

The afternoon was cool, the sun no longer being high in the sky as the girls set off down a winding pathway through the woods. Tall rhododendron bushes grew prolifically on either side, their glossy green leaves interspersed by fading clusters of delicate blooms still scenting the air as the girls strolled along. Startled rabbits bounded away into the bushes, little white tails bobbing as they ran.

At the end of the path, they discovered a small lake, its banks occupied by several ducks nesting among the reeds. Sitting down in the grass beside the water, the two girls laughed to see one up-ending itself to dive under the surface in search of food. A whiskered little face popped up nearby to stare curiously at the girls, before disappearing again into the undergrowth.

"To think *Maman* grew up in this gorgeous environment," Claire sighed. "How could she bear to leave it for a filthy country like India, where one is permanently saturated with sweat?"

"The whole of India isn't like Calcutta," Christina replied. "Simla is clean, pretty, and the climate's cool and fresh."

"I suppose so," Claire conceded, "but here there is so much to do and see. Once round the town in Simla, and you've seen it all."

After a few minutes of relaxed silence, Christina spoke again. "I wonder why *Maman* didn't jump at the chance to come back with us to see her parents?"

"Heaven forbid! We're having a much better time of it without a constant harangue of 'don't do this, don't do that'. In any event, I'm sure Emile will arrange for us to meet our grandparents at some point in time."

Christina looked up at the sky. "I think we had better start going back, especially since Emile and Charlie don't know where we are. They might worry if we aren't at home." She stood up, brushing dry grass from her skirt, and then held out a hand to help her sister up. "It's been a lovely afternoon, hasn't it?"

Hand in hand, the two girls retraced their steps in the direction of the Dower House. Reaching a fork in the path, Claire paused with a frown. "Can you remember which way we came?"

"I think it might have been from the left," Christina guessed, "but I can't be certain. Let's go a little way along and see if we recognise anything."

Minutes later, the girls were convinced they had made a wrong decision. Turning round to retrace their steps, Claire noticed a spiral of smoke coming from over the top of some nearby trees. Peering through the foliage, she saw a little cottage set back from the pathway where an elderly woman was busily sweeping her front doorstep.

"Come on, Chrissy. Let's ask that *vieille femme* to direct us back to the Dower House. She lives here, so she's bound to know the way."

Hearing a rustling, the old woman stopped working and watched as the two girls emerged from the bushes. As they drew nearer, she stared at Claire, her jaw dropping in amazement.

"*Mademoiselle Marguerite?*" she asked tentatively. "*Mais c'est impossible*! She has not been seen in these parts for a great many years."

"Did you hear that?" Claire whispered. "She's talking about *Maman*! I'm supposed to look exactly like her when she was young. The old thing must think she's hallucinating!"

Stepping forward, she addressed the old woman. "*Bonjour Madame*. No, I am not Marguerite…she's my mother. My name is Claire, and this is my sister, Christina."

"*Bonjour,*" the old woman answered, still looking bemused. "I am called Lucie. After Madame la Marquise sacked old Jeanne, I became Mademoiselle Minette's maid until she was sent away from home. I…I accompanied her on the journey to Tours, where an Irish family took charge of her."

"Sent away? *Maman* was sent away?" Christina's schoolgirl French allowed her to follow the gist of what the old woman was saying, and she now prodded her sister. "Ask her why, Claire. And who was Jeanne?"

"Mademoiselle Minette was sent away because she refused to marry the man of her mother's choice," the old woman replied in answer to Claire's question. "He was very much older than she was. Unfortunately, Monsieur, le Marquis agreed she must go. All of us at the château were very sorry to see her leave. She was a nice girl, always polite and thoughtful towards us."

"And Jeanne? Who was she?"

"Jeanne was Mademoiselle Minette's old nurse, who brought her up until she was sixteen. The poor girl was dreadfully upset when old Jeanne suddenly vanished in the middle of the night, during a family holiday at the seaside. Nobody understood why until much later, when Jeanne told us how Madame had summarily sacked her."

Christina pulled at her sister's sleeve. "Claire, we really ought to go. Any longer, and Emile might be furious with us for wandering off."

"One minute more," Claire said. "This is an incredible story. But, Lucie, where was she sent? And it wasn't forever, was it?"

"To Ireland, I believe...for two years. I think Monsieur was sorry he allowed his daughter to be sent away like that, but Madame was insistent."

"*Claire!*" Christina tugged at Claire's arm again. "Do come on."

"One last thing, Lucie...did Minette return home after the two years were up?"

"No, Mademoiselle Claire. Nobody knew what had happened to her."

"Lucie," Claire bobbed a polite little curtsey, "I'm so pleased we took a wrong turning and met you. How amazing that you knew our mother. You may be sure we will tell her when we return to India."

"*India?* Mademoiselle Minette is in India?" The old woman blinked in astonishment. "Please tell her Lucie remembers her *avec beaucoup d'affection*."

The two girls had to run back, arriving out of breath at the Dower House just as Emile and Charlie clattered into the courtyard on their horses. On the way, Claire warned Christina to say nothing to Emile about their encounter with Lucie. Charlie would be told when a private moment could be found. It stood to reason that Emile knew about the drama of those long ago days, but thus far he had chosen to keep silent. It simply would not do to upset their kindly host.

When they went for dinner at the château the following evening, Claire hoped somebody there might enlighten them further about Minette's mysterious background, and the drama of her being sent away from home. But what a laugh to discover their straight-laced mother had once been something of a scapegrace.

However, Claire was destined to be disappointed. Hoping to be regaled with choice anecdotes of her mother's girlhood, nothing remotely titillating was revealed during the course of the evening. Emile's older brother, Maximilian, Comte de Beaurepaire, welcomed his niece's children with great charm. His wife and their middle-aged daughter, Camille, were also present, both ladies greeting the three O'Haras with genuine pleasure. Politely asking after Minette, they hoped she was not suffering too much from the dreadful Indian heat that Emile talked about with so much feeling. And it was inevitable that Claire's close resemblance to her mother was exclaimed over. To the intense relief of Christina and Charlie, English was spoken throughout the evening.

After an excellent dinner, everybody went to sit outside on the terrace in the cool of evening to enjoy tiny cups of coffee and handmade mints. Then, at long last, Minette was mentioned in a more personal way.

"Your mother and I used to see a great deal of each other during our girlhood," Camille confided to the two girls. "In fact, one could say we more or less grew up together. Minette was always such fun!"

Fun? Claire stared incredulously. Their mother...*fun?* Even Christina was looking bemused. "What sort of thing did *Maman* get up to?" she asked with an innocent air.

"Childish mischief in the main." Camille was not about to be drawn. "She used to be very naughty with her governess, I remember – tying shoelaces together, that sort of thing. I believe she once put a live frog in the woman's handbag. But what a horsewoman Minette was! She used to spend a great deal of her day at the Haras schooling Uncle Charles's young horses. Does she still ride?"

"No, not any more," Charlie now joined in the conversation, "but we still have her old Arab horse with us in Calcutta."

"I wonder if she will remember Ariadne, the horse she once had here? I took her over, you know. Minette did a superb job of schooling her for dressage, and for many years Ariadne and I did very well competitively. I lost the lovely old lady only six years ago."

"Camille, why did *Maman*—"

"Charlie," Camille cut across Claire's burning question, "Emile tells us you are a flat race jockey. How wonderful to ride gorgeous thoroughbreds for a living!"

The evening ended an hour later, and Emile and his guests returned to the Dower House. Although dissatisfied not to have discovered more about her mother's youthful misdemeanours, Claire overheard Emile and his brother discussing whether they should be taken to meet their grandparents. Childishly crossing her fingers for luck, Claire hoped so, for maybe then she would find out what the drama had been about.

Privately, Emile was unconvinced that such a visit was appropriate, or even wise. Max thought the intervening years would have blunted remaining animosity their sister might feel towards her daughter. He was certain that neither Charles nor Francine would stoop to rebuff innocent children over their mother's long ago offences. Max also pointed out that it would not be right to deprive their sister and brother-in-law of meeting their only grandchildren. Still not entirely convinced, Emile told his brother he would give it more thought before making a decision. In the meantime, there was a jaunt to the family villa on the Atlantic coast to be arranged.

Emile and his party set off on the relatively short train journey to spend a long weekend at Saint Jean de Luz. Claire had been anxious to visit Paris, but Emile explained the city would soon be empty of people and most shops were closing. It was better to take advantage of the seaside now before hordes of holidaymakers began arriving in another ten days or so. July and August were months when the French left the heat and noise of the cities, in order to relax at country retreats or take trips to the coast.

Even though Claire was accustomed to the sophistication of Calcutta society, Saint Jean de Luz was a revelation to her. The seaside town exceeded all expectations, shops both fabulous and expensive if regretfully beyond her holiday money. She nevertheless dragged Christina to gaze into shop windows, the younger girl shaking her head in horrified disapproval over prices charged for what was, she declared, just a glorified rag!

Resigned to an impecunious state, the two girls sat on the sea wall at eleven o'clock each morning to watch groups of elegantly attired passers-by stroll down the esplanade. At midday, it was customary to enjoy a lingering *déjeuner* in one of the many seafood restaurants that dotted the seafront. Afterwards, the town would be deserted during the hottest hours during the afternoon, people re-emerging at five o'clock for the evening's entertainments. An enviable existence, Claire reflected, and one that she was certain would suit her down to the ground.

Upon their return to Emile's home, the O'Haras learned that they were indeed going to meet their grandparents. Despite his earlier reservations as to the wisdom of such a visit, Emile had decided it would be inadmissible not to allow it. He deemed it better, however, to arrive at the château without advance warning in order to catch Francine off-guard. He only hoped Max had been correct in his assessment of their difficult sister's attitude.

On the morning of the visit, Claire and Christina took great care over their appearance, anxious to make a good impression on their grandparents. Claire wore a layered dress in delicate white muslin, her waist accentuated by a periwinkle blue sash echoing the vivid colour of her eyes. Turning her attention to Christina, she forced her sister to abandon her grey and white dress, for one in pale mauve with matching shoes. Even Charlie was well groomed, his unruly red hair slicked back with water and, Claire suspected, a touch of Emile's brilliantine.

After a brief carriage ride to the Château de Saint Aubrey, the driver turned off the main road and passed through high wrought-iron gates to continue up a winding gravel drive. On either side were neat white-fenced paddocks ringed by clumps of horse chestnut trees, their canopies of lush foliage providing shade for horses grazing beneath.

Beyond the paddocks, a collection of sprawling buildings set back from the driveway could be seen. At a query from Charlie, Emile identified them as the Haras where horses were bred and trained for racing. His eyes shining, the young man voiced the hope that his grandfather might show him around before they left.

Descending from the carriage, the three young people gazed up at the magnificent château that had been their mother's childhood home. A profusion of roses climbed up the walls and over the front door, delicately perfuming the warm spring air. A short distance away, a man with a shock of white hair was sitting in a wheelchair under a tree, a rug over his knees. With an exclamation, Emile walked over to speak to him.

"Charles, are you not well...?" Emile's voice tailed off.

Charles de Merencourt was not listening, mesmerised by something beyond the figure of his brother-in-law. Following his gaze, Emile saw he was staring at Claire – as if he were seeing a ghost. Of course, it had to be the girl's close resemblance to Minette, his daughter.

"Marguerite?" Charles asked in a trembling voice. "Oh, Minette, my darling girl, is it truly you? Have you come back to me at last?"

Emile drew his niece forward. "No Charles," he said in a gentle voice. "This is Claire, Minette's eldest daughter. An amazing resemblance, *n'est-ce pas?*"

Taken aback to see her grandfather's eyes fill with tears, eyes that were still as vivid a blue as her own, Claire leaned down to take his veined hand in both of hers.

"*Gran'père, je suis ravie de vous voir enfin,*" she whispered. "May I introduce my brother, Charles...named after you," she quickly improvised, "and this is Christina, my younger sister."

"*Non! Oh, Non!* Don't let them take you from me again, my darling," cried out the old gentleman. "My beautiful Minette, they sent you away and I thought never to see you again!" Tears trickled down the gaunt cheeks. "Why did they do that? I missed you so much, so very much, my Minette! I don't understand..."

"*Hey!*" came an angry shout from the château. A middle-aged man was standing at the top of a flight of steps leading to the front doors of the house. "What the hell are you up to over there?"

Everybody stared in astonishment as the man came dashing down the steps, and strode across the lawn towards them. "What the devil do you people think you are doing with my father? Are you blind that you can't see how unwell he is?"

"Ah, Jérôme," Emile smoothly greeted the newcomer. "I thought it must be you, judging by the discourteous manner you have of addressing visitors."

Disconcerted, the man paused. "I didn't realise it was you, Uncle Emile, but you should know better than to upset *Papa*! He suffered another stroke two weeks ago, and he can't...." the man's voice trailed to a halt, having suddenly noticed the dark haired girl still holding his father's hand. Losing colour, he took a step backward.

"Jérôme, this is your niece, Claire." Emile grinned without humour. "The eldest daughter of your favourite sister. And this is Christina, another niece, and Charlie is your nephew."

Trying to cover his confusion, Jérôme began rearranging the rug over his father's knees. "I...I didn't know Minette had children," he muttered. "*Maman* never said..."

"I imagine there are quite a few things you don't know," Emile dryly told his nephew. "As a matter of fact, your sister has five children."

"And all of them undoubtedly born out of wedlock!" came a strident voice from behind. "*Shameful!*"

Whirling, Claire came face to face with an older version of Sonia, the same pale eyes with the same spiteful glint. Despite her age, Francine, Marquise de Merencourt, was still a beautiful woman, somewhat offset by an over-rouged slash for a mouth and an embittered expression. Her disdainful glance swept over the three shocked young people standing by her husband's wheelchair. Focusing on Claire, disbelief then incandescent fury contorted the perfect features...and as quickly vanished.

Emile was the first to recover. "Francine, I beg of you," he begged his sister as he drew Claire forward, "This is your eldest grand—"

"I know who the baggage is," snapped the Marquise, "since she has the look of her immoral mother. How dare you take it upon yourself to bring Marguerite's by-blows here, Emile? Can't you see how upsetting it is for Charles?"

"Francine, these young people are your grandchildren! The only ones you are likely to have, since Jérôme rarely leaves your side and Christophe resides in a monastery. Charles became upset because he has always missed his daughter whom you sent away."

"Don't you dare pass judgement on me, Emile!" spat his sister venomously. "You may be my brother, but I draw the line at having Marguerite's illegitimate progeny foisted on us. I suggest you leave at once, and take these...these *people* with you."

"Madame, just a moment if you please," Claire stepped forward, scarlet to the roots of her hair over the insulting terms the Marquise used to describe them. "Why do you say we are illegitimate? You must be aware our parents were married in Scotland?"

"*Pah!* Some outlandish ceremony in a cowshed, I believe." The Marquise's thin lips twisted in scorn. "They were certainly never properly married in the eyes of the Catholic Church. I understand that even the O'Hara fellow's parents were appalled when a litter of little bastards began arriving on the scene with shocking regularity."

Although his French was far from perfect, Charlie picked up on a word – *bâtard*. He had first heard the word as a small boy on the lips of some harridan in Ireland, whom he assumed must have been his father's mother. What in God's name caused these people to refer to them as illegitimate? Bewildered, he looked at Claire who had turned pale with anger, but now drew herself up to look the Marquise in the eye.

"Madame," the girl's tone was icy, "I speak also on behalf of my brother and sister when I tell you how shocking it is to hear our grandmother use such ill-bred language. We were brought up to expect something quite different. I am happy to say the views of other relatives we have met during our visit are not similarly tainted. If *Gran'père* Charles is upset, it is only because of your vile plotting against my mother many years ago." Claire turned to her uncle. "Please may we leave now, Uncle Emile?"

Clearly taken aback, the Marquise's pale eyes were bulging with fury. "How dare you speak to me in that impertinent way, you little hussy?" she grated. "True daughter of your appalling mother."

His face stiff with disgust, Emile nodded an assent to Claire. He truly had not expected his sister to vilify her grandchildren in such a pejorative way. *Mon Dieu!* Minette would be beside herself with fury, should she ever discover her children had been exposed to her mother's brand of vitriol. He should have followed his instincts regarding this visit.

"Suffice it to say, Francine," his voice was frosty, "Claire's assessment of your behaviour is singularly accurate. I am deeply ashamed you happen to be my sister."

Galvanised into action by his uncle's words. Jérôme began to bluster. "Now listen here, I won't allow you to speak to *Maman* like—"

"*Quiet!*" Emile barked. "This has nothing to do with you, Jérôme, so keep your foolish mouth shut, if you please." Turning to the bewildered and visibly upset young people, he added gently, "Come along, my dear ones, I believe we have outstayed our welcome."

Minutes later, he and the three O'Haras were on their way back to the Dower House, each of them silent and preoccupied with the recent unpleasantness.

Christina was the first to break the awkward silence. "My French wasn't good enough to understand everything that woman was saying, but...but she can't be our grandmother, surely? She was looking at us with...with such *hatred*."

"It's *Maman* she hates," Claire answered. "And yes, that was our grandmother. The man in the wheelchair is our grandfather, but the poor man seems a little confused."

"Charles suffered a stroke after a riding accident some years ago," Emile explained. "Although confined to a wheelchair, he was able to get himself about, run his business, and was mentally sound. Unfortunately, he suffered subsequent minor episodes, but this last stroke Jérôme mentioned seems to have tipped the balance of his mind."

"Why was the Marquise calling us illegitimate?" Claire asked. "And what did she mean by saying our parents were married in a cowshed?"

"What?" Christina's head swivelled round to stare at her sister. "Did you say illegitimate? M…married in a cowshed?"

"That," Emile quickly cut in, "is absolute nonsense. I understand your parents were married in a civil ceremony in Scotland, unusual but nevertheless legal."

"But that's not being married in the true sense, is it?" Christina's eyes were glittering with unshed tears. "Was there no proper church ceremony?"

Claire turned on her sister. "Oh, for heaven's sake, don't *you* start! Your darling nuns must have known about it and they didn't make a great fuss!"

Charlie finally spoke up. "She called us *bastards*! And that's what *Papa's* mother called us when we went to see his parents in Ireland."

"Of course, we aren't bastards," Claire said dismissively. "You heard what Uncle Emile just said about our parents' marriage being legal. If there wasn't a religious service, so what?"

"Well, it seems to count with some people," Charlie retorted. "To the point of not recognising that a marriage existed at all. As we already know, awful things are already said about *Maman's* nursing home. Let's hope nobody in Calcutta ever finds out about this latest little gem."

Claire was silent, digesting what her brother had just pointed out. God! What if some of those catty girls at school heard even a whisper of cowsheds and illegitimacy? She would never live it down. How different things would have been if only *Maman* had married Uncle Freddie. That frightful place next door need never have existed, and the stigma of "trade" would not be forever haunting them.

"I think the Marquise must be right," Christina choked out, a sob in her voice. "Illegitimate…that's exactly what we are."

"Shut up, Chrissy," Claire hissed through clenched teeth, "and don't you dare say a word about such a thing when we go home to Calcutta. Especially when you go to Confession with that sneaky old priest, Father O'Donnell."

"But it's Confession, Claire, and Father O'Donnell is strictly bound not to—"

"No! That man is known to be the biggest gossip in Calcutta. There are things one must keep to oneself and this is definitely one of them."

"But if our parents weren't properly married, I mean, not married in the eyes of the Church, then...then we don't even have the right to call ourselves O'Hara. So I don't know who I am anymore..."

"Christina!" Claire interrupted angrily. "I've had more than enough unpleasantness for one day! Just stop it, will you?"

"Christina, *ma chérie*," Emile broke in softly, "do remember, your parents were legally married so you have every right to your surname. Dear girl, please don't upset yourself unnecessarily."

"But that kind of marriage is unrecognised by the Church," Christina muttered obstinately. "I'm never going to marry anyone so I won't have to admit my parents weren't properly married, and I'm—"

"Heavens above!" Claire exploded. "I wouldn't worry, dear girl, since I don't suppose many men will be queuing to marry an over-righteous person such as you!"

Charlie's usually good-natured face flushed with annoyance. "Stop it...both of you! I don't want to hear another word. It all happened a long time a go, and has little to do with us now. We came to France to enjoy ourselves, so let's do just that for the remainder of our holiday, shall we?"

"Suppose so," mumbled his sisters.

Chapter Three

Minette sat at the desk in her office, staring moodily out the window. She had just sent one of the *ayahs* to find Claire and tell her to come to the office at once. That young lady, she told herself, was not going to slide out of making a decision about her future. She had made that plain before the trip to France.

She also intended to have a word about the ridiculous airs and graces her eldest daughter had assumed since her return home. Regularly raiding her mother's linen chest for lace, ruffles and braid, Claire was inventing new ways of adorning the gowns in her wardrobe. A neckline had been cut down far too low in her opinion, and to Claire's outrage, she had promptly confiscated the garment.

Although the holiday had been a clear success for all three of her children, she had noticed odd behaviour in an unexpected quarter.

Christina.

Generally a quiet girl, Christina was now wafting around the house, silent, almost sullen at times. Minette had asked if something was worrying her, but her daughter had denied it whilst avoiding eye contact with her mother. Claire had little to contribute as to why her sister was so withdrawn. Her only suggestion was that perhaps Christina was communing with the Holy Ghost? Really, she thought crossly, that girl is the limit!

A knock at the door interrupted her reverie, and Claire came in, gorgeously clad in one of her latest transformations. Once a simple navy gown, it now sported a navy and white polka dot frill around a neckline that was suspiciously lower than it had originally been. Polka dots also encircled the girl's narrow waist.

Deciding it would serve no purpose to comment on the costume at this point, Minette merely smiled at her daughter,and indicated she should sit down. "*Chèrie*, thank you for coming so quickly. Now, have you given some thought to your future?"

"Oh, *Maman*!" Claire didn't even allow to her finish the question. "Must we talk about that now? I'm going out to tea with Celia and Emma Parkinson in half an hour."

"I'm afraid you aren't going anywhere until we have settled this matter," her mother replied tersely. "I will not allow you to turn into a social butterfly like so many of those foolish empty-headed friends of yours. Have you decided what you want to do? Nursing would be my choice for you."

"I'll go to college to do teacher's training," Claire said. "Surely, *Maman*, you can see I'm not cut out to be a nurse."

"Very well." Minette tried to keep the disappointment from her voice. "If teaching is what you really want to do."

"May I go now, please?"

"Yes, go off to your tea, but make sure you're home by half-past six." Returning to her perusal of the papers on her desk, Minette glanced up briefly. "And no later, if you please!" she added.

"Half-past six?" Claire exploded. "I'm seventeen, remember – not seven."

"Another word, and you won't go at all."

Flouncing out without a reply, Claire retreated to the bedroom she still shared with Christina. The younger girl was sitting on her bed, writing a letter. At her sister's precipitous entrance, she looked up in surprise.

"I thought you were going out for tea?"

"I am. Except I have to be home by half-past six like a baby," Claire raged. "It's so humiliating to have to tell my friends that. When they had tea with us last week, it was easily half-past seven before they went home."

"Maybe *Maman* thinks she's protecting us," Christina offered.

"Protecting us from what? Does she imagine my virtue is likely to be ravaged should I return home an hour later?"

Christina smiled. "Well, you are rather pretty, you know!"

Claire regarded her sister's sweet, if rather plain face with affection. She's got lovely eyes – she suddenly thought. Violet in colour, the younger girl's eyes were framed by thick black lashes. Chrissy must be the most un-jealous selfless creature in the world, which I know I'm not - she admitted to herself with rare frankness.

A few days later, Minette was having a curry lunch with Frederick at the Grand Hotel in Chowringhee. Affectionately regarding her companion, she thought how little he had changed over the years. Slightly heavier perhaps, but still dashing with his black eye-patch, a legacy from active service years ago on the Chinese border.

Twice a year Frederick still asked her to marry him, despite receiving the same answer that their relationship was perfect as it was. It had become something of a bitter-sweet joke between them, but Minette knew it was only partly so for Frederick. He would marry her within the hour, if she would only agree.

Sitting back with a satisfied sigh, she dabbed her mouth that was still pleasurably stinging from the effects of the curry. So odd, she reflected, food that seemed over-spicy at the outset should eventually become positively addictive. All her young ones enjoyed a good curry...except Sonia who always had a fried egg on her *dahl* and rice.

"Freddie," she began, laying her napkin on the table, "I want to talk to you about Claire. She's becoming extremely defiant these days and unwilling to accept normal house rules. Not only that, she seems determined to ape those vapid girls she associates with, whose only interests in life are clothes and parties. I simply won't have it, and if she persists in that attitude, she's going to find herself continually confined to the house."

"*Chèrie*, I don't believe the answer is to further restrict her freedom." Frederick chose his words carefully. "Claire is a lovely, vibrant young girl, and carefully brought up. I think you should allow her space to develop a sense of responsibility. By caging her, all you are likely to achieve is deeper resentment, and I'm sure that would be the last thing you would want."

"Yes." Minette considered his point. "But, Freddie, she's only seventeen. For God's sake, I can't have her running wild in Calcutta."

"I'm not suggesting that you do," he replied. "But let the girl spread her wings a little, perhaps allow her to attend a tea dance at the Saturday Club from time to time. I'm certain Charlie would escort her if you asked him to."

Frederick watched the conflicting expressions crossing Minette's face as she weighed up his suggestion. Sensing that she was about to refute the notion of her daughter attending a club in any sense, he continued before she had an opportunity to speak.

"In my capacity as Attaché to the Brigadier, you know I regularly have to entertain Calcutta businessmen and visiting army personnel. Since you act as my hostess at most of these functions, might it not be an idea to allow Claire to assist you at the dinner party next week? She would have a taste of the social life she craves, but in a situation where we can keep a discreet but watchful eye on her."

Minette gazed down at her folded hands for a moment. "Do you think I am too strict with her?" she finally asked. "I only wish to protect my girls, you know."

Frederick laughed and placed a hand over hers. "My love, cast your mind back to when you were Claire's age. Think how *you* viewed rigid restriction of your preferred activities."

"And look at the catastrophe my rebellious nature landed me in," Minette retorted with an unwilling grin. "Can I be blamed for trying to steer my daughter away from trouble?"

"Of course not," he patted her hand again. "Just try not to bind her too tightly. Think about my suggestion, and let me know about the dinner party next week. I would be surprised if you didn't find Claire to be something of an asset."

Pursing her lips, Minette continued to look dubious but said no more.

Frederick changed the subject. "As a matter of fact, I have a surprise for you, *ma chèrie*. James is due in Calcutta tomorrow for a few days short leave. I promised to pick him up at the docks, and I wondered if you would like to come with me."

Sitting very still, Minette concentrated on wiping her hands with the steaming, rose-scented facecloth proffered by a *bearer*. "I don't know," she said at last. "I didn't part on good terms with my eldest son, as you may recall."

Frederick nodded. "I took him to task about it that same evening," he told her, "so I very much doubt you would be obliged to hear that drivel again." Taking her capable hand once again between both of his, he continued. "Maybe now is the time for you both to come to a better understanding of each other?"

"I'll come," Minette nodded. "I only hope you're right about James behaving in a reasonable manner towards me."

The following Friday, Frederick arrived at Camack Street to collect Minette, and was visibly dismayed to find Sonia in the hallway, expecting to accompany her mother.

"Freddie, you don't mind if Sonia comes with us?" Minette looked rueful. "I tried to persuade her to stay with her sisters, but she became so upset that I thought I had better take her with me."

"If you don't think it's too long a wait for her in the heat, Minette?" Frederick prevaricated. "The ship might be late in, and..."

"Sonia will be fine as long as she's with me," she replied firmly. "If I leave her now, she'll become hysterical and might start vomiting."

"Don't you find that kind of perpetual threat rather daunting?" Frederick asked curiously. "Not being able to go anywhere alone without Sonia threatening to be sick?"

"Of course not." Minette cuddled the child to her. "Sonia's no trouble and, in any event I usually take her everywhere with me."

Frederick concealed his irritation with difficulty. This really was an area where his very dear friend appeared blind. Sonia was a pretty, fairylike child, who ruled her doting mother through emotional blackmail. But Minette could not – would not – see it. The girl was a sly piece of work, and it was hardly surprising that neither Claire nor Christina wanted anything to do with her.

The ship was indeed late, and, true to form, Sonia set up a whine that her legs were tired from standing so long. Picking the girl up bodily, Minette settled her on a hip much as one would carry a baby, seemingly oblivious to the incongruous picture she presented by carrying a ten-year-old in such a manner. Frederick mentally shrugged in resignation. Should Minette detect even a whisper of criticism with regard to her youngest, she became aggressively defensive.

At last, the familiar burnished head of James O'Hara could be seen amongst the crowds milling about on the wharf. Catching sight of Frederick, he grinned in genuine pleasure, the smile slipping a trifle upon noticing his mother standing beside him.

"James, dear boy!" Frederick exclaimed, wrapping his arms about him in a huge hug. "Such a pleasure to see you after such a long time. Give me your other bag so you can say a proper hello to your *Maman*."

Regarding the handsome young man before her with pride, Minette tried to gently detach Sonia's clinging hands from her skirts. Finally, she managed to step forward and kiss her son on both cheeks in the French way.

Unconsciously stiffening, James did not avoid his mother's embrace. "*Maman*, good of you to meet me. I'd forgotten how hot Calcutta can be, and this degree of humidity makes life damnably uncomfortable."

He glanced down irritably at his youngest sister who was still agitating for her mother's attention. "For God's sake, Sonia, do shut up! Why are you blubbering and hanging on to *Maman* like that? No wonder everyone thinks you're..." James shut his mouth with a snap, suddenly aware he was treading on thin ice.

"Just what does everybody think about Sonia?" Minette's voice was deceptively quiet. "James? I asked you a question."

"Don't start, *Maman*, I beg you! I've only just arrived, for God's sake. Let's drop the subject."

"Tell me what you were about to say, if you please."

"If you really want to know, I was about to say that most people have the impression that Sonia is light in the attic," James snapped. "Hardly surprising when you consider how infantile her behaviour is for such a great girl."

"Oh, how cruel." Minette recoiled in outrage. "What none of you seem to understand is that my little Sonia is fragile and needs special care."

"Rubbish." James laughed out loud. "Sonia's only problem is that she's spoiled rotten, and knows exactly how to lead you a merry dance."

"I *won't* listen to any more of this! Why do you have to be so nasty, James? I can see that nothing has changed where you're concerned."

James stared at his mother, scorn evident in his eyes. "No," he said evenly, "certainly nothing has changed as regards your open favouritism for this awful girl. I have never heard you utter the same loving concern for your two other daughters." He turned to his uncle. "May we go now, Uncle Freddie? In the circumstances, I believe it is better for everyone if I stay with you instead of at Camack Street."

"I trust you can bear to stay for dinner with us at least?" Minette enquired acidly. "I assume you will wish to see your two sisters and Charlie?"

"Yes, of course he will," Frederick interceded before James could open his mouth. "And I'm certain they will want to see something of their sailor brother." Giving James a significant look, the young man reluctantly nodded.

The short trip back to Camack Street was undertaken in frosty silence, Sonia continuing to cling to her mother's skirts whilst scowling balefully at her older brother. Frederick sadly reflected that his beloved Minette was sometimes her own worst enemy. In all fairness to James, it was she who had instigated the quarrel. He would have to take her aside for a quiet word at some point.

Both Claire and Christina seemed pleased to see their eldest brother after such a long absence, listening avidly to his descriptions of foreign shores. When Charlie appeared a little later, he greeted James pleasantly enough, if somewhat coolly. Frederick eventually managed to engineer Minette away from the group, anxious to warn her about further unnecessary confrontation with her eldest son.

"But, Freddie," she protested, "James can't be allowed to get away with being nasty to Sonia. It's bad enough that Claire is also horrid to the poor little thing."

"*Chérie*," he said in his most soothing tone, "try to take my advice and leave all uncomfortable subjects alone for tonight. James is here for so short a time, and it would be a pity to ruin his visit."

Minette stared hard at Freddie, but then relaxed with a shrug. "Very well. I'll let it go just this once. But you had better warn that young man to keep unkind remarks about his little sister to himself in future."

The children's visit to France was recounted in detail. The two girls mentioned their encounter with old Lucie, Minette's personal maid from long ago. Noticing the unusual sparkle of tears on her mother's lashes, Claire realised Lucie meant something to her, and she quickly passed on the old woman's message that she had forgotten about. Minette smiled but turned her head away, her lips compressed.

At Emile's earnest request, the visit to their mother's childhood home had not been mentioned upon their return to Calcutta, and was not spoken of now. It would only serve to upset Minette, and might well preclude the possibility of further visits to France. And so the evening passed uneventfully.

A few days later, Claire sat in her bedroom, preparing for the evening ahead at Uncle Freddie's house. She had been astounded when her mother asked if she would care to assist with a formal dinner party there. How wonderful! The dullness of her life was at last beginning to look up, and this *soirée* might well be the precursor to future delightful events.

Taking the usual care with her appearance, Claire chose to wear a dress of rose muslin, its over-modest neckline having been "improved" out of her mother's sight. She fervently hoped the *décolletage* would not be noticed and commented on by her mother. A string of glowing pearls encircled her neck, a birthday present from Uncle Frederick. Brushing her hair into a mass of shining curls, she pinned one side back from her face with a velvet rose. With a satisfied look in the mirror, Claire left the bedroom and went downstairs.

Christina, who was already in the hall, was lost in admiration at the vision her sister presented. At Claire's whispered request, she fetched her own black velvet cloak for her sister to borrow. Although she was certain to die of heat, it concealed the questionable neckline from her mother until it was too late to be sent off to change.

As soon as Sonia realised her mother intended to leave her to at home with Christina and Charlie, she immediately began an altercation in the hall. Fighting like a tigress against Christina's grip on the back of her dress, Sonia screamed and howled as Minette and Claire left the house. Sensing her mother was hesitating and might think of returning to fetch the yelling girl, Claire hustled her into Frederick's new car that departed at once for Alipore.

Closing the front door, Christina released her younger sister who promptly flung herself to the floor, drumming her heels in thwarted fury. With a shrug, Christina stepped over her, and went join Charlie for a glass of wine on the veranda. She doubted that even the *ayahs* would bother to try and console Sonia. The girl was impossible.

Meanwhile, Minette and Claire were deposited under the graceful portico shading the front entrance of Frederick's home. James emerged to greet them, and Claire was struck at how debonair and handsome he looked in his Navy mess uniform. Pity he was leaving so soon, she reflected, as he would have made an impressive escort to Lillian Bayley's birthday party in two weeks' time.

As always, Frederick's dinner party was an unqualified success, this time enhanced by the presence of his protégée, the youthful Claire O'Hara. Party conversation had always been something Minette found difficult, impatient with what she considered foolish inanities or ridiculous pretension. However, this particular social grace came naturally to Claire. Hanging on every word spoken by her elders, the girl conveyed the impression she considered their utterances fascinating. Unconsciously, Claire was learning what constitutes a successful hostess: appeal to the ladies...and the gentlemen would follow like sheep.

Covertly watching her daughter, Minette was torn between being proud that she was so well received by Frederick's guests...and annoyance that the girl had butchered a perfectly good dress to the brink of 'tartiness'. She promised herself to have words about it with that young lady afterwards. Nevertheless, she had to admit that Frederick was right about allowing Claire to spread her wings a little, as the girl had more than pulled her weight. Maybe, Minette thought, she would give that other idea of his – an occasional tea dance at the Saturday Club

49

– her consideration, but only if her daughter merited it.

For her part, Claire was revelling in the attention. Although thrilled to intercept admiring glances from two young British Army officers present, she was careful not to eclipse her mother. Should Minette join a group where she happened to be, Claire would immediately step aside. The respectful gesture won further accolades from Frederick's guests: what a nice child, they said, so thoughtful towards her elders.

When Claire crept into bed later that night, careful not to disturb Christina, she was filled with hope that further enjoyable sorties such as this might come her way again. Arranging the pillow to her satisfaction, she suddenly recalled the *frisson* of alarm she had felt upon noticing the quantities of alcohol James was consuming throughout the evening. The sight of his flushed face had dredged up echoes of misery from the past – echoes she hastily suppressed. Her final thought before falling asleep was to wonder if her mother had also noticed?

Minette had indeed taken note of her eldest son's copious drinking, which had hurled her into a terrible sense of *déjà-vu*. Was he embarking on the same drink-sodden path as his father before him? If so, she knew from many years of unhappy experience that little could be done to prevent it. She would remember to mention it to Frederick, who might be the only one able to influence James to take better care.

The next day, Claire woke earlier than usual, energised by the success of the previous evening. Folding her arms behind her head, she lay in bed for a while to re-live the best parts. What a pleasure it had been to entertain in that sophisticated manner, so different from the dull little dinners her mother gave now and then for her cronies. For once she seemed pleased to have had her assistance, for Claire couldn't remember any other occasion when she had received unstinting praise from her mother.

Now, there was something quite different for her to look forward to. As Frederick's guests, the family had been invited to go for a picnic in the British Army sailing boat the following day. The plan was to set off for an hour or so across the Hoogly, the mouth of the great Ganges River where the city of Calcutta sprawled untidily along its banks.

Claire had been sailing before, and recalled the experience as being far from enjoyable. She had disliked the constant rolling of the yacht, and her face had been lashed by stinging salt water whipped up by the wind. Neither had she appreciated being ordered about by self-important members of the crew from the Calcutta Sailing Club. Thankfully arriving back on dry land, she had sworn never to repeat the horrid experience.

However, tomorrow's sail would be different, for there would be a full-time Indian crew on board to look after guests. Claire had learned from her previous boating experience was that rubber-soled shoes were imperative, and possessed a pair of white tennis shoes that she imagined would do.

The day of the picnic dawned, and Claire got up early to make sure she was impeccably turned out for the occasion. Since her sister was inclined to wear even duller garments than usual, she also intended to keep an eye on Christina's choice of outfit. Her sister's behaviour was definitely odd these days, and Claire intended to get to the bottom of it. But for now, it was important to make a good impression on Frederick's guests.

As always, a giant fly in the ointment for everyone was *Snivelling Sonia*.

Who could be relied upon to draw attention to herself by whining incessantly or creating a horrid scene. The prospect of spending an afternoon as captive audience for Sonia's tantrums was simply unbearable. Tattling was the brat's favourite pastime, her every tale cunningly embellished and accepted by Minette as gospel. Thanks to Sonia's spite, Claire had received many an undeserved clip round the ear from her mother. Today she intended to ensure that she and Christina were seated as far from the little horror as possible, for only then would they be able to relax and enjoy themselves.

"I've already chosen my dress," Christina ventured whilst Claire was buried in the wardrobe, riffling through her dresses. "I thought this fawn one would be all right."

"Let's have a look," Claire popped her head round the wardrobe door. "Oh, for pity's sake – *not* that rag! It makes your hair look positively ginger."

"Would it?" Christina put a hand up to her auburn hair. "But isn't it sort of gingery, anyway?"

"Not *that* sort of ginger." Claire abandoned her own search to go over to her sister's cupboard. "Look," she said after a few minutes' search, "why don't you wear this pale blue one with the white daisies? I've never seen you wearing it."

Christina shook her head. "It's too…too loud. I can't bear people staring."

"Loud? Don't be ridiculous! How can pale blue be loud? Put the thing on and let me see."

Christina meekly obeyed, then waited for her sister's verdict. The garment was too pretty, she thought miserably. Somebody like herself didn't deserve to look pretty.

"Perfect!" Claire made her turn round. "See, I told you it was exactly right for today, and your white tennis shoes won't look too silly with it."

Turning away, she went back to selecting her own clothes, and finally decided upon a demure white crêpe dress, its plainness relieved by a pink scarf wound about her waist.

Over the next half an hour, the O'Hara family gradually assembled downstairs ready for departure. Claire was aware that Charlie had vacillated about going on this boat trip at all, not wanting to spend any length of time with the brother he cordially disliked. But seeing him come down to join them, she was pleased he had decided to go after all.

Minette duly appeared with Sonia looking angelic. The girl was dressed in frilled white cotton *broderie anglaise,* a cornflower blue sash round her waist and a bow of the same hue adorning her flaxen curls. Peering from behind her mother's back, the girl stuck out her tongue at her sisters. Claire opened her mouth to tick her off, but reluctantly shut again. There was no point in starting off the day with a hideous row.

At the quayside, Claire and Christina hurried towards Frederick who was waving to them, both girls anxious to distance themselves from their mother and her irritating acolyte. Once up the narrow gangway to the deck, the girls were offered a glass of chilled champagne. Charlie, meanwhile, remained on shore with his mother until Frederick came to relieve him, and then lost no time in dashing up the gangway to join his sisters.

Sipping her champagne, Claire was secretly thrilled that the two young officers she had met at Frederick's dinner party were present. She discovered their names to be Clive Anderson and Percival Foster-Smythe. Smiling, they raised their glasses to her, and she blushed prettily, thinking how nice it would be if they were seated at the same table for the picnic lunch.

As soon as Frederick and Minette were on board, ropes were cast, and the yacht set off across the Hoogly. Claire relaxed, finding it decidedly more stable than her previous experience. Eventually, the boat glided along the banks of the Ganges to a pre-selected spot in the shade of overhanging trees.

The crew went swiftly ashore to set up two trestle tables that they covered with white linen tablecloths. Each table was laid with silver cutlery, snowy napkins and fine crystal glasses that sparkled in the dappled sunlight. A tiny vase of fresh flowers adorned each table. Claire regarded the scene with immense satisfaction. This was much more how she imagined a day's sailing should be, a far cry from lurching about on slippery decks, nibbling rubbery sandwiches washed down with warm lemonade.

To their relief, the two older girls were placed at a table with Charlie and the two young officers. A short distance away, Frederick and James sat at the other table with Minette and Sonia who had already found a reason to whine. Two pleasant hours over a delicious lunch passed all too quickly, rounded off with coffee and mints.

On local leave for ten days, Percival and Clive told their luncheon partners that their regiment was located near Ootacamund in the Western Ghats. Percy, clearly the joker of the two, amused his audience with droll anecdotes about a pompous senior officer and his extremely un-cooperative horse.

Laughing helplessly, Claire suddenly sensed a presence behind her. Glancing round, she was dismayed to see her youngest sister standing behind her chair. With a sly little smile, Sonia waited until there was a pause in the conversation.

"Claire, what does the word *floozy* mean?" she asked with an innocent air. "Because Maman says you are behaving exactly like one."

The girl abruptly got up from the table, her face flaming, eyes burning with tears of mortification. Whirling, she ran back to the boat followed by a distressed Christina.

Charlie glared at his youngest sister. "What a nasty little toad you are!" he exclaimed in disgust. "Go on, clear off back under whatever slimy stone you crept out from, and I don't care a damn if you tattle to *Maman.*"

Sonia burst into her customary tears. "Oh, I will…oh, I most certainly *will*, you horrid thing! I only asked Claire a question."

Sobbing melodramatically, the girl ran back to her mother and throwing herself on her knees, buried her face in her lap. Minette put comforting arms about her youngest daughter. "There, there, sweetheart, whatever is the matter? Don't cry like that or you'll make yourself sick. You haven't hurt yourself, have you?"

"N…no, it's that horrid Charlie," Sonia hiccoughed, "He called me a n…nasty toad, and told m…me to get back under my slimy st…stone."

Minette glared across at her younger son. "*Charlie!* What a dreadful thing to say to your little sister! Apologise at once."

Her younger son was unrepentant. "Certainly not! She richly deserved it. We were all having a laugh at Percy's story, when along comes Sonia to spoil things as she invariably manages to do."

"I won't have Sonia upset like this, do you hear me?" Minette snapped. "She'll make herself ill. You ought to know that by now."

James had heard enough. "For God's sake, *Maman*," he barked, "don't you know by now what a brat your darling Sonia actually is? Charlie was right to give her a flea in her ear."

Minette stood up and put a protective arm about her favourite child's shoulders, her expression furious. "And *you* can keep your unpleasant opinions to yourself, James O'Hara. I cannot allow Claire to ruin Freddie's lovely lunch party like this." Picking up her skirts, she stalked towards the boat, an avid-eyed Sonia clinging to her arm.

Claire and Christina were sitting on a bench in the stern of the boat. The older girl was still crying, despite Christina's efforts to comfort her. They looked up to see their mother bearing down, Sonia lodged on a hip, the girl smirking in anticipation of a delightful revenge on her eldest sister.

"Claire," Minette coldly demanded, "what is the meaning of this ridiculous hysteria? How *dare* you cast a blight on Freddie's lunch?"

If Claire was rendered speechless by the unfairness of her mother's attack, Christina was not. She looked up, her violet eyes uncharacteristically hard.

"It most certainly *wasn't* Claire who ruined things, *Maman*. We were all laughing at an amusing story when Sonia came sneaking up, and in front of everyone told Claire that you said she was behaving like a floozy. It was fearfully embarrassing, and Claire has every reason to be upset."

"As a matter of fact," she snapped, "I *did* say Claire was behaving like a floozy. I watched her laughing far too loudly, mouth wide open…quite dreadful! Sonia was only speaking the truth, and the poor child doesn't even know what the word means. She probably imagined she was complimenting her big sister." Minette affectionately ruffled Sonia's fair curls.

"*Rubbish!*" Claire jumped to her feet. "Sonia knew exactly what she was saying. But why did you need to make such a remark in the first place? *Why?* I was only laughing at a funny story, and that hardly constitutes behaving like a slut."

"Don't contradict me, you impertinent girl! If only you could have seen yourself shrieking with laughter and lolling about in your chair... such coarse behaviour. It wouldn't surprise me if those young men have been given quite the wrong impression." Turning to go, Minette paused to glare at her two eldest daughters.

"Kindly do something about your red face," she ordered Claire, "and then both of you are to rejoin your table without further drama, if you please."

Bending down, she picked up her youngest, her expression softening as she looked down at the fair head nestling against her bosom. "It wasn't your fault, sweetheart," she murmured. "Claire was being histrionic – as usual."

Sonia gazed up at her mother, her pale blue eyes tragic. As Minette began negotiating a descent down the gangway to shore, she turned her head to deliver a triumphant grin at her infuriated sisters.

Burning with resentment, Claire stared after her mother's retreating back. It was unbelievable how that girl got away with bloody murder so often, but Sonia had taken things too damned far this time. She intended to see to it that she that got her come-uppance...one way or another. Even if it was only putting the biggest dead cockroach she could find in the little monster's bed.

Meanwhile, she knew she had better paste a smile on her face and go back to the table. It would not do to allow her companions to think she was given to the vapours. Perhaps she could claim an unexpected attack of migraine had caused her precipitate departure.

Chapter Four

The morning after the picnic, Claire lay awake in her bed, a secret smile on her lips. Despite the mortifying scene at the lunch table, Percy and Clive had behaved as though nothing untoward had happened. Thankfully, they appeared to have accepted her claim of suffering the onset of a bad headache. The remainder of the afternoon had passed uneventfully, for which Claire was deeply grateful.

Arriving back at the quayside, Percy had stepped forward, ostensibly to give Claire a steadying hand down the gangway to shore. But he had taken the opportunity to whisper his intention of calling on her as soon as possible. Hugging herself with delight at the memory, she planned to question Charlie for more details about this charismatic young man, who was showing such an interest in her.

True to his word, two days later Percival and his friend, Clive, rang the doorbell at Number Two, Camack Street. The young men were shown into Minette's office, whilst an excited Claire waited at the top of the stairs, praying her mother was not putting the kibosh on things.

Ten minutes later, the young men left the house and Claire's spirits sank like a stone. What on earth had been said to them? They hadn't even waited to see her. She would never forgive...

"Claire?" Charlie put his head round the door. "*Maman* wants you in her office."

"What about?" she asked sulkily. "I bet Percy wanted to ask me out, and she's said no, of course."

"No idea, old thing."

Claire made her way to her mother's office, convinced that further humiliation was about to be heaped on her and gloated over by the awful Sonia. Knocking at the door, she went in.

"Ah, Claire," Minette looked up over her glasses. "As I am certain you already know, Percy and Clive were here just now. They came to ask if they might escort you to a tea dance at the Saturday Club this weekend."

Claire stared at the floor, studiously avoiding eye contact with Sonia who was peering from behind her mother's chair. If she was about to receive a wigging, it was the bloody limit the little horror should be allowed to witness it.

"After that disgraceful display at the picnic the other day, you hardly merit any such concession," Minette coldly told her daughter. "However, against my better judgement, I am allowing you to go on the understanding you are home by half-past six. Is that understood?"

"Yes *Maman*." Claire could hardly contain her jubilation.

"On second thoughts," her mother added, "I shall ask Charlie to accompany you. He's a responsible boy, and can be relied upon to keep a level head."

Leaving the office, Claire sought out Christina to tell her the good news that she was going to a tea dance at the popular Saturday Club. What fun! Even if she had been ordered to be home by half-past six. She was also secretly pleased that Charlie would be joining them. She didn't know those two young men very well, and in her brother's company she wouldn't feel entirely on her own.

Upon questioning Charlie, Claire discovered Percival to be an aristocrat. The eldest son of Brigadier, Lord Stanwicke of Louth in Ireland, he was following in the footsteps of his military father and grandfather before him. Despite his lofty ancestry, however, Percy was very approachable and funny, his fair hair flopping over laughing blue eyes. Claire had scarcely been able to take her eyes off him at the picnic.

And now he had actually asked her out dancing, and had gone about it in the correct manner by seeing her mother first. She drew in an ecstatic breath, wondering this might be the beginning of a fabulous romance? Maybe followed by marriage in the fullness of time? The girl hugged herself: Lady Claire Stanwicke…what a fine sounding name! It would also end her secret worry over the hideous label of illegitimacy…

After what seemed an eternity, Saturday finally dawned. Agonising over what she should wear, Claire finally decided upon an azure blue chiffon dress with a matching headband. She had not yet tampered with the neckline, so it was suitably demure and would meet with her mother's approval. Christina's eyes shone in admiration of her sister, and even Charlie told her she looked rather dashing. Reassured, she excitedly looked forward to her first dance.

A carriage duly arrived in front of the house, and the two young officers stepped out. Minette herself opened the front door, her youngest daughter beside her, and Charlie and Claire close behind. Courteously bowing to Minette, Percival then smiled at the young girl he had come to collect, his eyes alight in frank admiration.

"I say, Claire, you look absolutely terrific!" he exclaimed. "I'll be the envy of every other fellow at the Saturday Club."

"Half-past six, remember," Minette's brusque voice brought Claire down to earth. "And not one minute later."

"Yes ma'am!" Clive assured her. "We'll make certain of that."

Before anybody could move towards the waiting carriage, the air was rent by agonised screams coming from the nursing home next door. Further hellish screams rang out before somebody inside hastily closed a window. There could not have been a more graphic demonstration of Marguerite O'Hara's occupation, and Claire wanted to sink through the floor.

Sneaking a glance at Percival, she was relieved to see his impeccable manners concealed the dismay he must surely be feeling. Doubtless, female members of his family kept such matters strictly private to themselves. Unlike here, at Claire's own home, where screeching frequently provided a hideous background to family life.

Suppressing a desire to dissolve into mortified tears, she smiled and accepted Percy's hand to assist her into the carriage, her brother and the two young officers following behind. The incident was not mentioned by anyone.

The Saturday Club tea dance exceeded all expectations, and Claire was glad to have attended those hated dancing lessons over the years. There were several other young people in their party, but she was pleased to note that Percy insisted on dancing exclusively with her. Encircled by the young officer's arms, the afternoon was nothing less than magical!

"You're quite the most ravishing girl I've ever seen," Percival murmured against Claire's hair. "Not just fun to be with, but you dance like an angel. Believe me, young lady, I mean to see more of you before my leave ends."

By the time Claire and Charlie returned home, arrangements had been made to go to the Saturday Club tea dance at the end of the following week, the last day of Clive and Percy's leave. The young girl went to bed that night with stars in her eyes, certain that she and Percy were now quite desperately in love.

The following week dragged by. Claire amused herself by choosing what she would wear for the dance, her final decision being a gown of white muslin peppered by raised white polka dots and its neckline discreetly lowered. Pearls and soft white slippers would complete an ensemble that could almost be bridal, thought the girl dreamily.

During the week, Claire, Christina and Charlie were sitting out on in the cool of the veranda one evening. Minette was next door at the nursing home, attending to a newly arrived woman in labour.

"I hope we aren't about to be subjected to the sort of racket we endured when Clive and Percy came to fetch us the other day," Claire remarked feelingly. "It was dreadfully embarrassing, wasn't it?"

"Um...yes, it was pretty bad, I must admit," Charlie looked up from the racing magazine he was reading. "Clive thought someone was being attacked, and could hardly believe it when I told him it was a female giving birth. He didn't seem to know our mother presided over a nursing home."

"I don't know how you can be so...so *pragmatic* about it. That sordid episode might easily have ruined things between Percy and myself! Luckily, he didn't seem to care."

"Well, we don't have much choice in the matter, do we? In any event, there can't be much to be ruined between you and Percy, surely? You've only seen the fellow twice, and according to Clive he's expected to become engaged to some wench in England."

"What?" Claire's mouth fell open. "Engaged? But he loves *me*...why, he said as much last Saturday."

"Clive did say that Percy is none too keen to get married yet, the reason why he opted for another tour of duty in India. But he's only got another four months to go before he's back in his family's clutches. So don't get your hopes up, old thing."

"I'm sure this other girl couldn't hold a candle to Claire," Christina loyally declared. "Now that Percy has met her, the one in England can't count any more."

"Well, I advise you not to count your chickens," Charlie got to his feet with a yawn. "Defying one's parents is no easy thing...as we should know."

Claire went to bed later that night, her confidence shaken. All of a sudden there was an unknown rival for Percy's affections. She would have to think how to strengthen his feelings about her, in order to ensure his rejection of his parents' choice of bride.

"Claire?" Christina's voice came out of the darkness. "If you marry Percy and go to live in Ireland, what's going to happen to me?"

"You'll come too, of course! I couldn't do without you, Chrissy darling."

Saturday came round at last, and an excited Claire waited with her brother for the carriage bringing her beloved and his friend to collect them. Wearing Christina's cloak firmly fastened, concealing a small adjustment to her neckline from her mother, she felt confident of ensnaring her young man.

Later that afternoon at the club, held closely against Percy's chest whilst dancing to a slow number, Claire was supremely confident of his feelings for her.

"You smell wonderful!" breathed the young man in her ear. "And you look more gorgeous than ever every time I see you. How do you do it, my sweet girl?"

She leaned back to gaze into his eyes. "Oh Percy, I can hardly bear it that you are leaving tomorrow. You won't forget me, will you?"

"Forget you? Don't be silly, darling! We'll write of course, but I hope you won't be tempted to run off with another fellow whilst I'm away."

"Never! I'd wait forever for you, Percy."

"Darling, there is something I have to ask you, but not in here," he shook his head. "Far too public. Is somewhere private where we can go?"

Claire caught her breath. Was he about to declare himself? Glancing over at Charlie, she saw he was absorbed in conversation with Clive.

"There's a small garden just outside the front," she ventured. "It goes round to the back of the building where there's a bench under the trees. Shall I pretend to go to the powder room, and then slip away to meet you there?"

"Excellent! What a clever girl you are," he smiled. "Wait until the music stops, but make sure you don't attract the attention of your watch-dog brother."

Ten minutes later, Claire was sitting on the bench in a secluded area of the clubhouse garden. Her eyes were starry with anticipation as she waited for her young man to appear. Would he propose on one knee in the time-old tradition? Or would he take her in his arms and whisper it? Either way, she would say, "yes, yes, *yes!*"

But Percy did not come.

Fifteen minutes went by, and she frowned in concern. What could have delayed her suitor? There came the sound of footsteps on the pathway, and Claire looked up expectantly. But it was not Percival who came striding across the garden. It was her brother Charlie, his expression thunderous.

"You stupid, *stupid* girl!" he hissed through clenched teeth. "What on earth possessed you to meet that fellow out here? I just happened to overhear the fellow sniggering to Clive that his little popsy was, "ripe for a spot of hanky-panky" behind the clubhouse. Believe me, the only thing on that cad's mind was to seduce you before leaving Calcutta."

"*No!*" Blanching, Claire gazed at her brother. "That can't be true, because he said he loved me and had something very special to ask me."

"And I have an excellent idea of what that might be." Charlie's good-natured face was grim. "I threatened to black the fellow's eye for trying to take advantage of you, and he laughed, saying you had clearly indicated yourself ready and willing."

Claire's eyes swam with tears of shock and humiliation. "I can't go back in there and face everybody. I *can't!* I...I just want to go home. Now!"

"Don't worry," he took his sister by the hand. "I've already said you aren't feeling well. One of my friends has offered his carriage, so we can leave immediately."

Unbeknown to Claire leaving the dance floor, a young Scotsman had been sitting on the balcony of the mezzanine floor, idly watching the dancing below. His eyes rested on a laughing dark-haired girl whose white dress swirled as she danced, allowing the tantalising glimpse of a shapely ankle now and again. Leaning across to the man sitting next to him, he asked if he knew the identity of the vision in white.

"Think that's Claire O'Hara, eldest daughter of the Frenchwoman who runs a nursing home in town," the friend answered. "Why, Jack? Interested? Isn't she rather on the young side...cradle-snatching and all that?"

John Cameron MacLeod smiled, but said nothing more. The girl *was* actually of interest to him, but his companion's remark was also true. She was, indeed, almost painfully young. It was the first time for over a year that he had felt a flicker of interest in a female, his bride of only a few weeks having tragically died of yellow fever on her way out to India. It had not been a love match, but Audrey's death had hit him hard.

Jack first arrived in India when he was twenty-four years old. From the age of twenty, the young Scotsman had worked for Wallis & Fairbairn in South Africa, an old and established diamond and coal mercantile firm. Dedicated to his job, he had swiftly climbed the company ladder.

When it was suggested that he accept a transfer to Calcutta, Jack was reluctant to uproot from a country he had grown to love, and also lose friends and associates. But he had eventually come to realise it would be a superb career move. Calcutta was the capital of all India, and the hub of British Government. He would also be in line to take over the company branch upon the eventual retirement of Edward Woodson, his immediate boss.

Not long after his arrival in Calcutta, Jack discovered a keen interest in local politics that slotted in perfectly with his new position as number two to the branch manager. Once a rugby player of an international level, an injury had put a stop to the sport. Now at the age of twenty-eight, an occasional game of tennis or golf was all that he could manage, and even that was not always easy to fit into his busy schedule.

Aware he was not particularly well endowed with personal charm, he had decided long ago it was hardly a requirement for him to acquire social graces. Intelligent and conscientious, it was business and politics that were of paramount importance to the young Scotsman.

That was perhaps why Edward Woodson had recently made the suggestion he should consider re-marriage in the near future, pointing out that the Calcutta branch was swiftly expanding. He would soon be expected to entertain substantially, and at a rather larger residence than his small flat in Ballygunge. Visiting politicians would also require looking after, and the arrangement of occasional conferences of a political or business nature would be involved. It therefore stood to reason that a wife would be an asset in such circumstances, besides the irrefutable fact that a married man presented an impression of general stability.

Initially outraged that professional advancement should hinge on his acquiring a suitable wife, Jack had reluctantly seen the sense in it. He knew the organisation of even a simple cocktail party might well result in disaster, since he had no idea how to go about it. Of course, most girls would know exactly what to do.

Nevertheless, finding this paragon was easier said than done. In his private opinion, most unattached young women in Calcutta were inclined to be flibbertigibbets, their heads filled with tripe about fashions and a desire to attend as many parties as possible. In choosing a wife, he would expect her to be reasonably intelligent, attractive, and above all – capable. Maybe a few discreet enquiries would not go amiss with regard to the background of this girl, Claire O'Hara.

After returning home early from the tea dance, Claire was unusually subdued during supper. Looking intently at her eldest daughter, Minette demanded to know if she felt ill? Fearful of further interrogation, Claire hurriedly assured her mother she was merely a little tired from dancing all afternoon in the heat.

Once safely back in her bedroom, the devastated girl wept as though her heart would break. It was inconceivable that the handsome young officer had cynically viewed her as nothing but a...a *plaything*, to be eventually cast aside. A fresh storm of tears convulsing her body, she sobbed into the already sodden depths of her pillow.

The following morning, Claire busied herself with a few household tasks she had let slide recently. If Minette was surprised over her eldest daughter's domestic diligence, she made no comment, merely reminding her that a discussion regarding her choice of career was due. Casting her eyes heavenwards behind her mother's back, Claire failed to notice Sonia's pale blue eyes glued to her face.

"Claire, why did you sigh and roll your eyes up to the ceiling while *Maman* was talking to you?" she tittered. "Is there a nasty bug crawling about up there?"

"No, but I can see a poisonous insect attached to her skirts that's badly in need of a good swatting!" snapped her sister, and left the room before Sonia could react.

Making her way down to the stables, she found Charlie attending to one of the carriage horses that had lost a shoe. Looking up at his sister, he grinned. "Glad to see you've recovered after yesterday's fiasco, old thing! Good riddance to bad rubbish, as regards those army idiots."

"Yes." Claire answered shortly. "But I would like to go to next week's Saturday Club tea dance...if you'll take me? Maybe Chrissy will come too as she loves dancing. Thing is, I don't want anyone thinking I'm nursing a broken heart, for God knows what Percival said about me after we left."

"You may be right," Charlie straightened from his task. "I'll see *Maman* about it in a day or two."

The young man gazed thoughtfully after his sister's retreating back as she walked back to the house. He had deliberately omitted details of his conversation with Clive whilst waiting for his sister to fetch her cloak.

The officer had followed Charlie outside, with the intention of explaining his friend's behaviour.

"Charlie," Clive had earnestly begun, "at no time did Percy mean to give your sister the impression that anything other than a bit of fun might be in the offing. Thing is, he's already committed to a girl who comes from the same kind of family as his own. And lovely though Claire is, she does rather lack the necessary background. Her behaviour with him was really quite forward, so Percy assumed she was up for it."

Charlie had felt dizzy with rage. He was astonished the fellow was sufficiently insensitive not to realise his remarks were equally insulting to him, as they were to his sister. Absorbed by his job at the racecourse, it was the first time the unpalatable fact was thrust down his throat that he might be considered not quite the thing by society. Of course, that hellish racket coming from the nursing home hadn't helped matters. Charlie grimaced at the memory. It struck him with a shock that their mother's insistence upon faultless behaviour had considerable substance, after all. Any *faux-pas* on their part, however small, would be judged more severely than the miss-steps of other young people whose parents happened to be at the forefront of society.

The young man's lips twisted wryly. The irony of the piece was that his mother's despised origins were vastly superior to the majority of these judgemental people. How many of them could count ages-old French nobility in their family tree? His expression pensive, Charlie put his tools away, picked up his belongings, and made his way back to the house. He would have a word with his sister about the importance of taking care not to put a foot wrong whilst in the public eye. And why.

To Claire's surprise, her mother did not require urging to allow Christina to go to the next tea dance at the Saturday Club. She remarked that it might do her good, for she seemed to have become far too withdrawn of late. She did, however, renew her efforts to persuade her eldest daughter to reconsider her future career.

"I really believe you are being extremely foolish in refusing to take up nursing," Minette began. "Aside from ensuring an excellent income, just look at these beautiful pearls I was given by that Maharajah whose wife I delivered of a son last year. It came as a gift in addition to my usual fees, you know."

Claire glanced at the triple string of matchless pearls her mother invariably wore round her neck these days. But even the attraction of such gifts was not sufficient to sway the girl from a deep disgust of her mother's field of nursing.

"*Maman*, it's really not something I want to do," she said carefully. "For you it may be a vocation, but not for me."

"Don't be ridiculous!" Minette snapped. "It's a question of governing one's mind towards something worthwhile, instead of the rubbish that fills your head these days. Frankly, I can't see you as a teacher…you're far too selfish and impatient. Now, after a sound training in Scotland with Aunty Jane looking after you—"

"*No!*"

"And why not, pray?"

Cornered, the girl finally exploded. "Nothing on God's earth would persuade me to take up your revolting occupation!" she shouted. "It's always about what *you* think – what *you* want. Nobody else's opinion ever counts, does it, *Maman?*"

"How dare you?" Minette gasped, incandescent with fury. "You bad-mannered, ungrateful piece of work, spoiled rotten, and…" she stopped short.

Claire had gone.

Eventually, it was Frederick who interceded to more or less reconcile mother and daughter. A truculent Claire waited in vain for her mother to forbid further Saturday Club tea dances. Minette waited for further displays of rude defiance from Claire, but that also failed to materialise. Nevertheless, the atmosphere between the two crackled with unresolved tension.

The following week, Minette informed her older girls that they had been enrolled at the Ballygunge Teachers' Training College for the beginning of September. Christina was to specialise in Mathematics. And Claire? That was up to her, for Minette washed her hands of the affair. Her eldest daughter had two months to decide.

At the end of that week, Charlie and his two sisters set off for the Saturday Club tea dance. Claire was determined to be at her scintillating best, and Christina was excitedly looking forward to the dance. She had never danced with a member of the opposite sex, and was feeling a trifle self-conscious at the thought. But, she reassured herself, should she be unable to bear being so close to a man, she could always claim to have twisted her ankle and sit down.

To her surprise, Christina discovered she adored dancing with young men. She knew she danced well, and there was little requirement to make polite conversation. Her cheeks were flushed pink and her smile natural for the first time for months.

Returning from a trip to the ladies' powder room, Claire found her table empty of people. Glad of a respite, she fanned herself with a beer mat and reached for her glass of lemonade. Suddenly becoming aware of a presence beside her, she glanced up to see a man looking down at her, his green eyes enigmatic despite a cordial smile.

"I beg your pardon, but is this Charlie O'Hara's table?" the man enquired with a small bow. "I'm John MacLeod...Jack to my friends."

"I think he must still be on the dance floor, Mr MacLeod," Claire smiled, holding out her hand. "I'm his sister, Claire."

"Delighted to meet you, Miss O'Hara. Charlie rides one of my horses on the track," Jack explained. "I'm a bit of a racing fanatic. Do you also ride?"

"Er...no. I had an accident when I was very young and lost my nerve. But I love horses, and we have my mother's lovely old chap at home, as well as our carriage horses, of course."

"Jack! I didn't expect to see you here," exclaimed Charlie, returning to the table. "I've never thought of you as someone who might like dancing?"

"Only when obliged to, I'm afraid. No, I came looking for you. I wondered if you would consider riding my other horse, *Jamestown Flyer*, next Saturday? His jockey has contracted some kind of fever."

Sitting back in her chair, Claire surreptitiously examined Jack MacLeod over the rim of her glass. Rather older than most other men of her acquaintance, his features were pleasant if not striking. Light brown hair was swept back from his forehead, and she had already noticed his eyes were a rather chilly green. But his appraising glance had made her feel gauche, and she didn't care for that. Her lips tightening, she wished the fellow would clear off back to his own table.

Two months later, at an unusually early hour, Frederick rang the bell at Camack Street. His eyes were red-rimmed, his demeanour sombre, and an apprehensive Claire suspected he had actually been weeping. Watching their uncle go directly to their mother's office, the two older girls hung anxiously over the banister above the hallway, waiting for him to emerge. An hour later, he called the girls to join him downstairs.

"I'm afraid I'm the bearer of terrible news," Frederick told them, tears standing in his eyes. "James," he swallowed convulsively, "James has been killed...stabbed during a brawl over another man's woman, it seems."

Both girls gaped, unable to take it in for a moment. "A *brawl*?" Claire echoed blankly. "Oh God, I just *knew* it! I saw him swilling lots of whiskey at your dinner party, and I thought of how Papa used to be..."

"Your mother is very much in need of your support at this time," Frederick told the two girls. "I beg of you to see that she gets it. I'm going home to obtain further details of what transpired, but I'll be back as soon as I can."

Hand in hand, Claire and Christina ran to their mother's office and went in without knocking. Minette sat stiffly in her chair, staring unseeingly out of the window, her face milk white. Sonia stood behind, fingering a fold of her mother's dress.

"*Maman?*" Claire put her arms about the rigid form. "Can I get you anything? Is there something Chrissy and I can do for you? This is a terrible time for us all..."

"Terrible for me, yes," Minette's voice was level. "But certainly not for you, Claire O'Hara! I remember only too well how you rejoiced to see James leaving home! Oh yes, I know you encouraged him to hate me. Get out, get out of my office...*get out!*"

Blanching in shock, Claire stepped back. Had she heard correctly? Was her mother indirectly blaming her for James's death? Agonised, she glanced over at Christina, whose mouth had fallen open in horror.

"That's a terrible thing to say, *Maman!*" Claire managed at last. "The fact that you and James didn't get on was nothing to do with me."

"*Get out*, I said!" Minette hissed venomously. "I have always known what went on behind my back. Well, he's gone forever now, and I hope your conscience is troubling you. Assuming you have one, of course."

Gasping at the unfairness of her mother's outburst, Claire fled from the room, her sister hard on her heels. Running up to the bedroom, she threw herself on her bed in a storm of weeping.

"Claire?" Christina put a tentative hand on her sister's shoulder. "I'm sure *Maman* didn't really mean those things she said."

"Yes, she did," the girl's voice was muffled. "She always has to blame someone else, and I'm a convenient scapegoat."

"Uncle Freddie will talk sense into her, I'm certain," Christina tried to speak reassuringly. "That's if she says something horrid to him about you."

Claire sat up and looked at her sister from reddened eyes. "I've never hated *Maman* before, but I *really* hate her now. The sooner I can leave this blasted house of hers, the better. As a qualified teacher, I should be able to get a good job somewhere other than Calcutta.

"And me?" Christina whispered. "What about me?"

"Chrissy darling, I've told you lots of times that wherever I go, you will always be welcome to come with me."

Chapter Five

Relations between Minette and her eldest daughter continued to be strained, despite Frederick's efforts towards yet another reconciliation. Neither did Charlie's indifference to his eldest brother's death go unnoticed by his mother, who tightened her lips, but refrained from comment. The atmosphere remained uncomfortably tense.

A week later, Claire and Christina began their respective courses at teacher training college, setting off each day with bulging bags of books. After a lengthy discussion with her sister, Claire had decided to take up infant school training. It offered a shorter course, if potentially tedious from the point of view of being obliged to deal with brats like Sonia. But then, anything was better than becoming her mother's slave at the nursing home.

One Sunday morning, Minette sent an *ayah* to summon Claire to her office. Now what? Her dark brows drew together in a frown. Her mother must have dug up yet another issue to attack her about. Sullenly, she made her way to her mother's office, knocked on the door and entered.

"Ah, Claire, I have received an excellent proposition for you to consider," Minette's tone was deliberately neutral. "One that you would be extremely foolish to turn down."

"Not the nursing business again, I hope?" came the uncompromising reply. "I thought I had made it clear…"

"For once in your life, be quiet and let me speak." snapped Minette, containing her rising temper with difficulty. "This has nothing to do with nursing."

"What then? What is this marvellous opportunity that I cannot possibly miss?"

"Two days ago, I was called upon by a gentleman by the name of John Cameron MacLeod," Minette replied. "I believe you made his acquaintance at the Saturday Club some time ago? It seems you impressed him sufficiently to wish to see more of you."

"*What*?" Claire laughed out loud. "Isn't he that Scottish fellow whose horses Charlie rides? What on earth could I possibly have in common with such an old man?"

"John...or Jack as he prefers to be called, is only twenty-eight years old and hardly qualifies as Methuselah," Minette remarked acidly. "Personally, I can't imagine what a man like that might find attractive in such an abrasive girl as you."

"Well, there's no accounting for taste, is there?" Claire countered. "And seeing as his requirements in a female are so refined, what else do you know about the fellow?"

Minette sat back in her chair, breathing deeply. Claire had always been inclined to impertinence, but her tone was now openly disrespectful. One way or another, she would have to go. Her home was no longer the comfortable haven it once had been, thanks to the hostile atmosphere generated by this damned girl.

Which was why she was viewing Jack MacLeod's approach as positive, for it was entirely possible he might take Claire off her hands. The man was obviously genuine, so any pricking of conscience was unnecessary over the departure of her eldest daughter. As Jack's wife, she would lack for nothing, besides finding herself in the upper echelons of Calcutta society. That aspect should certainly appeal.

Minette pulled herself up short, suddenly aware of her daughter's scrutiny. Realising she was in danger of putting the cart before the horse, her mouth stretched in an involuntary smile. Claire had yet to accept Jack MacLeod as a possible suitor.

"Why are you smirking like that, *Maman*? Are you secretly rejoicing at the thought of marrying me off to that fellow?" Claire enquired with unusual perceptiveness.

"Don't be ridiculous," she replied, flustered to be caught out. "The man has merely approached me with a view to taking you out to dinner. Should anything else transpire later on, that would be another matter for your consideration."

"So, tell me about the man. Does he live permanently in Calcutta, or does he waft back and forth from Scotland?" Claire casually examined her fingernails.

"Well, he would hardly be keeping racehorses in Calcutta if that was the case. Use your brain, for goodness sake."

"I asked a perfectly reasonable question, *Maman*, but if you want to make an unpleasant issue of it, I'm off." Claire turned towards the door.

"Jack occupies a senior position with Wallis & Fairbairn, an old and respected South African firm," Minette continued, as if the girl had not spoken. "The branch in Calcutta possesses sizeable offices and holdings. As I understand it, he will soon need help with increased business entertaining and occasional conferences."

She took a deep breath. "Jack intimated he wishes to know you better with a view to eventual marriage," she finished in a rush, annoyed to have somehow mishandled her approach to the affair.

"I see," Claire's lips twisted scornfully. "So, I'm to be a personal secretary-cum-geisha girl for the most boring man on earth? For your information, *Maman*, if I decide to marry, my future husband will have to adore me. Oh yes, he must also be filthy rich."

"What a naïve little girl you can be at times, your head full of rubbishy dreams that have nothing to do with reality. Can't you understand that Jack MacLeod can offer you a good deal of what you seek?"

Flustered, the girl jumped to her feet and paced to the window. "But I'm still only eighteen. Suppose I meet a rich aristocrat desperate to marry me? Why should I consider someone so ordinary, who speaks with an almost unintelligible accent?"

"It's highly unlikely an aristocrat would consider you as a bride, my dear girl," Minette's reply was dry. "Like tends to marry like, you know."

"What?" Claire stared at her mother in astonishment. "Have you forgotten who your father is, and your grandparents for that matter? If they aren't noble, then—"

"I've forgotten nothing." Minette answered tightly. "It's time you understood that we are not recognised by my family, for reasons that don't concern you. Any airy-fairy aspirations you might be nurturing about being a member of the French aristocracy could result in embarrassment to you. I cannot advise you strongly enough to set your sights lower down the social scale."

Claire opened her mouth for a heated retort, but then closed it again. She had been about to inform her mother she knew precisely why their family went unrecognised by her French grandparents. But she remembered how emphatic Uncle Emile had been that the visit to her childhood home should be kept quiet. She would not betray that, but nevertheless felt confused and angry.

"In any event, Jack is coming for dinner with us this evening, so please make sure the table is correctly laid with the appropriate silver and glassware," she heard her mother say. "It would also be nice if you remembered your manners, and treated us to a pleasant demeanour."

Minette returned to the papers on her desk, indicating to the glowering girl with a wave of her hand that the discussion was at an end. It was to be hoped she would eventually see sense, but keeping a civil tongue in her head would do for the moment.

Claire bounded up the stairs in search of her sister, who she discovered weeding pot plants on the balcony. "Chrissy, do you remember that peculiar Scots fellow who was chatting to Charlie for ages at the tea dance a few weeks ago?"

Straightening, Christina planted her trowel in the earth. "Jack Mac-something-or-other? A rather nice man, I thought."

"Jack MacLeod. Well, he's been to see *Maman* with a proposition. It seems he's in need of a capable wife to cope with entertaining and such, and indicated he wanted to see more of me with marriage in mind."

"Why, that's wonderful Claire." Christina smiled in genuine pleasure. "Imagine, my sister might become a *burrah-memsahib*! Does Charlie know yet?"

"No." Claire answered shortly. "And I see no reason for jubilation. The man's a crashing bore, and I frankly can't imagine spending the rest of my life with him."

Christina stared silently at her sister, unable to comprehend her attitude. She had thought her brother's friend rather personable as well as nice looking.

"Why aren't you girls laying the table for lunch?" Charlie popped his head round the girls' bedroom door. "I'm absolutely starving."

"You're always starving," Claire told him grumpily. "For someone who happens to be a jockey, you put away incredible quantities of food."

"Why the glum face? Fallen out with *Maman* again, hmm?"

"Not exactly. But she's trying to fob me off on your friend, Jack MacLeod."

Charlie gaped. "What do you mean…fob you off? Jack's a really nice chap, and I happen to know he moves in elevated social circles. Frankly, I can't imagine why he would want to chase after the likes of you," he finished with brotherly candour.

"Thanks for nothing, Charles O'Hara! As a matter of fact, he's doing exactly that, but for such dull reasons. He has to entertain, and apparently needs to acquire a wife he can order about to organise parties and other functions."

"You have such a way with words, Claire," remarked her brother. "I would have thought you'd be cock-a-hoop to have snared a man like Jack MacLeod. Most girls in Calcutta would give their eye-teeth for such an eligible bachelor."

"I absolutely agree with you," Christina nodded. "Come on, give the poor fellow a chance. You're forever grumbling about your course at college, and the prospect of having to deal with little monsters every day. Wouldn't being Jack's wife be preferable to that?"

"Since you think he's so wonderful, marry him yourself," Claire muttered. "I'm sure I can do better than marry a boring old businessman. With our family origins, I should be considered a suitable wife for—"

"*For God's sake!*" Charlie exploded. "Have you already forgotten the business over that scoundrel, Percival what-is-name? Clive told me in no uncertain terms that his pal's objective was to have fun with a girl of little account...and that meant *you!* He went on to say that Percival couldn't possibly marry a girl from Claire O'Hara's background, pretty though she might be."

Seeing the shock on his sister's face, Charlie softened his tone. "Perhaps I should have told you this before, but I wanted to spare you. What you have to understand is that the same thing applies to all four of us. As far as the world is concerned, we are the offspring of the local midwife who runs a nursing home. In other words, we are tainted by the dreaded label of *trade*."

White-faced, Claire stared at her brother, her self-confidence shaken to the core. Aside from the revelation of the full extent of Percival's disgusting perfidy, she was forced to appreciate the truth of what Charlie was saying. All of them were indeed viewed by many as springing from a decidedly dubious background.

"You never know, this thing with Jack MacLeod might turn into a marvellously romantic affair," Christina exclaimed, her eyes shining with enthusiasm.

"Exactly," Charlie nodded. "Now, for heaven's sake, let's have lunch before my stomach thinks my throat's been cut."

Lying on her bed under a gently turning fan, Claire had a great deal to think about during that hot and airless afternoon. Christina lay next to her, absorbed in a book.

"Chrissy, do you ever think about marriage and all that sort of thing?" she asked curiously. "In light of *Maman's* transparent haste to be rid of me, has it occurred to you that it might be your turn in a couple of years?"

"No, I shall never marry," Christina's answer was definite. "I am happy to dance with a chap, or even to have one as a friend, but no more than that. Added to which, I could not bear the humiliation of admitting to an officiating priest that my parents were not properly married."

"For heaven's sake, you aren't still worrying yourself to death over that rubbish?' Claire propped herself up on an elbow. "It would have no significance whatsoever to a man who adored you."

"Hmm! I can just imagine fellows falling over themselves to marry a dull thing like me," was the younger girl's cynical rejoinder. "No, I don't want to go through all that, thanks. But I shall enjoy watching your romance blossom."

Later that evening, Claire went about her toilette in preparation for the evening ahead. She wore a mauve georgette layered dress with a dropped waistband, her hips cinched by a plaited sash of the same material threaded through with gold braid. A narrow gilt headband held back her mass of dark hair. Smudged, misty blue eye shadow enhanced the vivid eyes, her lips tinted rose. A dab of perfume, and she was ready to face the evening.

After much soul-searching, she had decided not to make up her mind about Jack MacLeod for the moment. There was no hurry, surely? Even if her mother had clearly indicated she was anxious to see the back of her. Perhaps she had been too hasty in dismissing the suggestion as being preposterous.

Charlie's lecture that morning had made a deep impression. It did not sit well that she and her family were considered by Calcutta society as being beyond the pale. Here was an opportunity to become a *burrah-memsahib*, and think how that would confound the lot of them – the girl reflected with cynical amusement. Yes, she would carefully watch the fellow during the evening, and try to imagine what it would be like to spend the rest of her life with him.

Jack MacLeod arrived on time, and the family and Frederick gathered for cocktails in the cool of the veranda. Charlie was clearly delighted to see his friend, and the two immediately began a conversation about horses and racing. Frederick and Minette were laughing about something, and Christina was busy in the kitchen helping the *ayahs* with preparations for a late dinner.

Claire stood to one side, a glass of her brother's latest attempt at an innovative cocktail in her hand, the acrid taste of which she didn't care for in the least. Casually wandering towards a large pot plant, she surreptitiously tipped the viscous liquid into the earth. Turning back to the group, she was horrified to see Sonia's eyes fixed on her.

"Claire, you shouldn't pour your drink into *Maman's* favourite plant," giggled the little horror. "It might poison it, and think how upset she would be then."

"*What?*" Minette whipped round, glaring at her eldest daughter who flushed to the roots of her hair. "Did you…?"

Claire exhaled in relief to see Frederick's hand touch her mother's wrist in gentle warning. Now was not the time for a domestic row, he seemed to be saying. With a sigh of annoyance, she relaxed, and the awkward moment passed.

The dinner was excellent, served by the two *ayahs* as deftly as any pompous *bearer* might have done. Overcoming the earlier moment of embarrassment, Claire talked animatedly about their recent trip to France, whilst carefully watching Jack's attitude towards her. The decision to go further must be hers to avoid any possibility of rejection. That would be unbearable after the *fiasco* with Percival.

To Claire's chagrin, Jack smiled politely, but then turned away to chat with others at the table. Piqued, she wondered why the fellow seemed impervious to her sparkling conversation? Uncle Freddie's guests had responded satisfactorily, hadn't they? Even Christina merited more attention, the girl thought grumpily.

Jack hid a smile, noticing his ruse was meeting with success. Claire was accustomed to being the centre of attention, and she was transparently irked to be set aside. He felt certain she would now leave no stone unturned to gain his attention. Good!

Continuing a covert appraisal of the family in general, he noted the two older girls were well brought up and highly educated. And in light of the unexpected elegance of tonight's dinner party, it stood to reason that they would also have been properly schooled in the art of entertaining by their mother.

He also admired Claire's almost gypsy-like appearance, her vivacity and attractive smile. Watching her in the light of flickering candles, it struck Jack that he would like to see her gracing his own dining table at some future point in time.

Later that night Claire lay in bed, ruminating over the events of the evening. Jack had thanked Minette for her hospitality, courteously kissing her hand. Claire and Christina merited a small bow in their direction, and Charlie had then escorted Jack to the front door, and was heard to bid him goodnight.

No mention had been made of further visits, or of a personal invitation to Claire.

The evening had been frustrating, thought the girl glumly, since there had been no sign of Jack MacLeod's particular interest in her. Maybe he had already written her off, having seen her humiliated by that repulsive Sonia? Foolish to have been weighing up the possibility of marriage to the fellow, when it seemed unlikely she would be given the choice. Closing her eyes tightly, Claire tried to sleep.

Two days later, a written invitation from Jack was delivered to Camack Street. The O'Hara family was cordially invited to attend Opening Day at the Calcutta Racecourse the following Saturday. They would also join him for a Champagne Luncheon in the Members' Tent before afternoon racing resumed.

The Calcutta Turf Club Members' Tent.

Claire could scarcely believe she was to join the exalted ranks of wealthy racehorse owners, and other important personages in Calcutta for the day! She intended to be up early on Saturday morning to make sure her appearance was perfect for the special occasion. And Christina's choice of outfit would undoubtedly require close supervision.

Saturday dawned, and Claire was up early to ensure nothing was left to chance as regards her outfit and that of her sister. She had chosen a dress of cool pale pink muslin, and bullied Christina out of a shapeless brown garment, and into a blue lawn frock that enhanced the colour of her eyes. Both girls went downstairs, and were soon joined by Minette and Sonia. Charlie had left early for the racecourse since he was riding two of Jack's horses.

At eleven years old, Sonia was still dressed in frills like a child of three – Claire thought disgustedly. One could only hope the little toad would be kept under firm control, to avoid a repetition of those humiliating remarks of hers.

Elegant in a well-cut dark suit, Jack arrived on time to collect his guests and ushered them into the comfortable interior of his new car, a highly polished Daimler. Upon arrival at the crowded racecourse, Claire revelled in the frenetic atmosphere generated by bookies shouting the odds to one another, smartly dressed people milled about, placing their bets and studying race cards for the day's meeting. Jack appeared to know everybody of note who greeted him with evident pleasure. With impeccable manners, he went out of his way to introduce Minette and her daughters to his friends and many acquaintances. One particular couple, familiar to Claire through her earlier friendship with their two daughters, greeted her effusively and with apparent affection. Having previously been treated by the couple as something of a 'hanger-on', she realised the change in attitude was due to Jack MacLeod's presence at her side.

Nodding coolly to the obsequious couple, Claire turned her back and moved on to make animated conversation elsewhere. The two glared after her in outrage, realising they had been snubbed by a chit of a girl. Glancing nervously at her host to see if he had noticed her impolite behaviour, she grinned to see Jack's eye close in a wink.

Before luncheon was served in the Members' Tent, several smartly uniformed *bearers* wended their way through the guests offering glasses of chilled champagne. Others followed in their wake, bearing silver salvers heaped with hot and cold canapés. The atmosphere was buzzing, the conversation largely to do with racing later in the afternoon. One of Jack's horses had already won a race, and the other placed – both ridden by her brother, Claire realised with sisterly pride.

As it turned out, Minette was unable to join them for lunch, thanks to Sonia noisily kicking up a fuss about remaining outside for a picnic lunch with Christina. No longer inhibited by her mother's eagle-eyed presence, Claire was thrilled that Sonia's tantrums had served a useful purpose – for once.

By the end of the afternoon, Claire made the discovery that being Jack's partner for the day was a thoroughly enjoyable experience. One that she fervently hoped would soon be repeated. After the final race had ended, Jack suggested they should leave for home immediately, to avoid being caught in a traffic crush at the gates. Deposited back at their house, Minette and the two older girls thanked their host for a wonderful day.

"A pleasure, ma'am," Jack smiled at the Frenchwoman. "I wonder if I might take Claire out to dinner tomorrow evening? If she is happy to go, of course."

"I'd love to," her eyes shone with pleasure. "What time should I be ready?"

"Seven o'clock? And what time should I bring your daughter home? Is ten o'clock too late?"

"Ten o'clock is exactly right," Minette replied. "We generally close up the house by eleven, except for the nursing home, of course." She glanced down irritably at the girl pulling at her skirt. "Sonia, will you *stop* doing that!"

Claire and Christina looked on in amazement. It was the first time either of them had heard their mother speak sharply to Sonia, whose eyes now brimmed with easy tears.

"*Mam…Maman,*" she stammered brokenly. "I can't b…bear you to be cross with me." With a strangled gasp, the girl collapsed in a heap at her mother's feet.

Agitated and guilt-ridden, Minette began gathering her youngest daughter in her arms. "Claire, come and help me with this poor child, will you?" she ordered. "Don't just stand there gawping!"

Hurrying forward, the older girl saw Sonia cross her eyes and her tongue rudely flick out behind her mother's back. So the little horror was managing to take centre stage after all – she thought savagely – just as she thought to have got away unscathed. What on earth must Jack think of her family?

Apparently unconcerned by the drama, Jack made sure that Minette needed no further assistance with her burden. Inclining his head to both older girls, he climbed back into his car and drove off at speed.

Claire's dinner date the following evening was followed by several more in different restaurants she had not known existed. Jack was thoughtful and pleasant, even amusing at times. Garden parties and lunches at private homes followed, and one evening they attended a rather rowdy beach party. It was a social whirl that Claire thoroughly enjoyed, and found herself fully accepted by Jack's friends and associates.

But not once did Jack kiss Claire goodnight, or even try to hold her hand. Torn between relief and confusion, the girl wondered if this restraint was normal between courting couples. There was nobody whom she could ask – certainly not her mother! Christina suggested it might be because he respected her, but she was unsure. Having indicated eventual marriage, she expected Jack to be rather more romantic.

The weeks flew by, and Jack continued to take Claire out to social functions in addition to intimate dinners at different venues. It was at one such dinner at an exclusive Italian restaurant that Jack reached across the table to take her hand.

"My dear Claire, do you think you could accept me as your husband?"

Jack's eyes ranged over the lovely face across the table from him. "I'm not the most exciting man in the world, but I would do my best to make you happy."

Claire's joy over Jack's proposal was tinged with disappointment. There had been no protestations of love, and he still hadn't kissed her. But did she love him? Perhaps she did, for she looked forward enormously to being in his company. Never mind, those things might come about later on.

"I would very much like to marry you, Jack," she said at last. "But you haven't said anything about, well...whether you care for me?"

"You must know by now that I'm no silver-tongued Prince Charming, but of course I care for you...in my own way."

Mesmerised by the green eyes regarding her, Claire nodded. It rather seemed that this was all she was likely to get by way of romance. Well, she had much to gain in compensation for that, his personal commitment for instance.

Producing a scarlet leather box from a pocket, Jack opened it to reveal a diamond cluster engagement ring. Removing it from its velvet cushion, he slipped it over Claire's finger and briefly carried her hand to his lips.

The young girl gazed, enthralled, at the beauty of the sparkling diamonds. How far she had come since that awful experience with Percival! Now she was engaged to a proper man...not some silly boy with disgraceful things on his mind.

"It's rather unexpected, but I'm obliged to go to South Africa on business next week," Jack told his new fiancée, "but it will only be for two months, a good deal of which will be travelling. I'll write to you as often as I can, but I'm sure you will have plenty to do whilst I'm away. Choosing a wedding dress, for instance."

Back at Camack Street, Claire showed off her gorgeous ring to the family. Charlie, in particular, was delighted by her engagement to a man for whom he had a great deal of respect. Christina smiled joyously, lost in admiration of the diamond ring. Only Sonia sulked, resentful that everyone's attention had been diverted to her eldest sister. Eventually, she could stand it no longer.

"Claire, did you know there was a *huge* blood stain in your bed this morning?" she confided, her pale eyes wide. "Mailie was so cross about having to change the sheet."

Her face flaming in agonised mortification, the girl rushed from the room in tears, her happiness punctured yet again by her youngest sister's spite. Christina and Charlie sat there stupefied, scarcely able to credit the girl's crass remark.

Sonia smiled innocently.

"Sweetie, we don't talk about those things in front of other people," Minette gently explained to her youngest daughter. "They must be private to us ladies."

"I think I had better be on my way," Jack said with great diplomacy. "Please tell Claire I will fetch her for tennis tomorrow at about five o'clock."

"Jack, I'm sorry if you—" Charlie began.

"Don't worry about it, my friend," Jack interrupted. "Goodnight to you all."

Chapter Six

"You bloody, *bloody* little cockroach!" Claire yelled, shaking Sonia by the shoulders until her teeth rattled. "You've embarrassed me for the last time, do you hear? Try anything like that again, and I'll beat the living daylights out of you."

"*Maman*!" screeched the struggling girl. "Claire's killing meeee..."

"Squawk all you want – nobody cares," Christina told her unsympathetically. "And don't bother bawling for your mother, she's out to lunch with Uncle Freddie."

"I hope a notion of ordinary decency has now been shaken into that empty head of yours." Claire shoved the girl into a nearby chair. "And should you be nurturing ideas of being my bridesmaid, you've another think coming."

"I'll tell!" Sonia scrambled to her feet. "I'll tell *Maman* you said 'bloody', and that you tried to kill me! You've been horrible to me too, Christina."

Both older girls left the veranda without bothering to glance at the red-faced, blubbering girl. After enduring years of her unmitigated spite, Sonia richly deserved some kind of punishment, and neither girl regretted dealing with her. Even with the knowledge of certain retribution subsequent to Minette hearing of it.

Enough was enough.

The following afternoon, Claire emerged from the shower to dry herself off, her tennis clothes laid out in readiness on her chair. Christina lay on the other bed, reading under a ceiling fan that squeaked rhythmically as it whirled.

"That's better, it's such a sweaty afternoon, isn't it?" Claire rubbed at her damp hair. "But I'm going to be a lot sweatier after a few games of—"

"Claire!" Minette burst through the door, Sonia trailing eagerly behind her. "What is this I hear about you physically attacking your little sister? Have you gone mad, you dreadful girl? The poor child is already delicate, and you shook..."

"You – *out*!" Grabbing Sonia by the back of her dress, Claire frog-marched her out of the room and slammed the door shut. "I can't bear that brat ear-wigging whilst you scream at me," she told her mother. "Sonia deserved what she got, and it was far from an attack. Now, I must get myself ready if you don't mind."

"Don't you dare to brush me aside, you impertinent girl," Minette's colour was high. "Leaving all those red marks on Sonia's arms..."

"If Sonia has red marks on her arms, she's probably done it to herself, *Maman*." Claire replied shortly. "Chrissy saw the whole thing, so why not ask her?"

"I'm aware that Christina was party to the violence, and I'm surprised at you," Minette glared at the younger girl on the bed. "You should know better than to allow a frail child to be manhandled. As for you, Claire, consider yourself gated for a week."

"Gated?" Claire laughed. "Sorry, *Maman*, but those days are over. Remember I'm engaged to be married, so things have changed." Picking up her racquet, she walked to the door. "And another thing, please don't attempt to force your darling Sonia on me as a bridesmaid – it won't work."

Skipping down the staircase, Claire was conscious of a heady sense of freedom from her mother's dictatorial influence in her life. Outside the gates, Jack had already arrived dressed in tennis whites. With a smile, he helped her into the car and they set off to join a group of other players at the tennis club.

Three days later, Claire and Frederick were at Howrah Railway Station. They were seeing Jack off to Bombay, where he would be boarding a liner the following day bound for Durban in South Africa. To her surprise, Claire was feeling bereft – even tearful. She had been in Jack's company almost every day, and now two months of emptiness stretched before her. Seeing her distress, Jack bent to lightly kiss her.

"How does a wedding in November sound?" he was gruffly affectionate. "I think it would be a rather cooler ordeal for our guests."

"Absolutely wonderful," Claire gulped. "I just wish you didn't have to go at all."

"I'll be back before you know it, you'll see," Jack put an arm about the girl's shoulders and gave her a hug. "Frederick, thanks for coming to see me off, and look after my lovely fiancée for me, won't you?"

"Of course!" the older man grinned. "Now, get yourself into that carriage, or you'll miss your train."

On the way back to Camack Street, Frederick tentatively broached the issue of the hostile atmosphere that persisted between Minette and her eldest daughter.

"*Chèrie*, is there nothing you can do to resolve matters with your mother?" he asked. "I know she is feeling it dreadfully."

"Uncle Freddie, the whole thing is about that awful brat she drags everywhere with her," Claire answered stonily. "For years, Christina and I, sometimes even Charlie, have been at the sharp end of *Maman's* tongue because of her."

"I know," Frederick sighed. "Minette has always had a blind spot where Sonia is concerned. I can only think it is because she was left with the nuns as an infant."

"Humph! Believe me, *Maman* has never suffered blind spots where the rest of us are concerned. And whenever she ticks us off, there is that blasted Sonia, sniggering away behind her chair, loving every second. It isn't fair...*Maman* isn't fair, since she seems unable to see any wrong in the little horror. For God's sake, she still carries her about like a great baby."

"Would you at least allow Sonia to be a flower girl at your wedding, Claire? A small concession, but it would mean a great deal to your mother."

"No." Claire was definite. "There are no guarantees that Sonia won't throw a scene during the marriage ceremony or the reception, for that matter. Cast your mind back, Uncle Freddie. She does it again and again to draw attention to herself."

"Yes." Frederick nodded sadly. "I can't deny that."

For the first month since his departure, Claire received several postcards from Jack, which she constantly read and re-read: in particular, when she needed reassurance that her presence at Camack Street was only of a temporary nature. In only a short while, she would have her own home, probably in Alipore, Jack having instructed her to keep an eye open for a suitable property to purchase.

With Christina's enthusiastic assistance, she had chosen the pattern for her wedding dress. A delicate Brussels lace veil was a generous gift from Frederick. Only the bridesmaids' dresses required finalising, and she still had to decide on the flowers for the bouquet she would carry. With every fitting of the beautiful white taffeta gown, her longed-for wedding drew ever closer.

Minette maintained a frosty attitude that the girl found hard to endure. Whenever she was present in the same room, Sonia would pretend terror, dramatically cringing as if she feared being attacked. Claire thanked God for Charlie, whose cheery presence and infectious grin was uplifting from the gloom that emanated from Minette and her disgruntled acolyte.

Halfway through the second month of Jack MacLeod's absence from Calcutta, the regular postcards suddenly came to a halt. Claire was initially unconcerned, overseas post being notoriously unreliable. But after the sixth week, the girl began to feel anxious. Was Jack ill? Had he been in an accident? There was no way to find out.

She toyed with the possibility of visiting the offices of Wallis and Fairbairn, in case they had news of Jack. Christina thought that a step too far, an opinion that Frederick emphatically endorsed.

"It would not be appreciated," he assured Claire, "because the time lapse cannot yet be considered excessive. You would merely appear hysterical. The man's probably run off his feet during a relatively short business trip."

"But a postcard?" Claire persisted, "How long does it take to write a postcard?"

Frederick shook his head, "Don't worry your head about it, *chèrie*, for Jack may be on his way home already. Then you can give him a good grilling for his lapse."

Suddenly, it was three long months since Jack's last communication, and she wept copious tears in the privacy of her bedroom, re-reading the postcards she had earlier received from him. Her wedding dress and veil were now ready, and the bridesmaids' dresses had already been delivered to the girls concerned. The church had been booked for mid-November, now in only two months time. It was only the damned bridegroom who was missing, thought the depressed girl. What if he never came back? How could she bear the shame of cancelling everything…the utter humiliation of being stood up?

But Jack MacLeod still did not return.

Far away in South Africa, Jack had fallen unexpectedly and violently in love with the wife of a senior director of his own company. Possessed of an abundance of blonde hair, grass-green eyes fringed by dark lashes, Anne Winterton was an attractive woman in her mid-thirties. Her rather older husband was frequently absent from home on business trips, and her two sons ensconced at boarding school in England. Bored, Anne was not averse to amusing herself with an occasional flirtation.

At one of the regular Wallis & Fairbairn cocktail parties, she was introduced to the enigmatic young Scotsman on a visit from India. Intrigued, Anne set out to entice him from his shell, and it wasn't long before chemistry between them flared into life. Her husband being conveniently away, the flirtation swiftly developed into a full-blown affair, its very illicitness lending spice to the liaison.

As often as they could discreetly arrange, the lovers booked themselves into inconspicuous hotels to spend long afternoons making passionate love. A sensual woman, and well versed in the sexual arts, Anne brought Jack to heights of ecstasy he hadn't believed possible. Besotted with the woman who had taken over his waking hours...eighteen-year-old Claire O'Hara seemed a million miles away.

Alasdair Winterton eventually returned home to his wife, and grim reality set in for the lovers. Enjoyable afternoon assignations came to a halt, there being too much at stake for both parties. Anne was not prepared to leave her wealthy husband and be deprived of her luxurious lifestyle. There were also her sons to consider, since a cuckolded husband was unlikely to accord their custody to his wife.

Where Jack was concerned, he supposed he had known from the outset his affair with Anne was doomed. Even had she been willing to abscond with him, such a scandalous act would immediately terminate his career. After years of working his way up the company ladder, it was ludicrous to throw it all away in shame.

The last afternoon with Anne left Jack feeling wrung out and miserable. Booking an immediate passage to Bombay, he packed his suitcase in a daze, desperately missing the woman who had come to mean so much to him. In an effort to distract himself until his departure, he visited old friends he had not yet taken the time to visit. It was only then that he thought about Claire, the girl he had left to stew for months in Calcutta.

It had been neither kind nor gentlemanly on his part, and God alone knew whether she still wanted to marry him. But after knowing a sophisticated woman of the world such as Anne, did he really want to marry this young and inexperienced girl? It was a decision Jack knew he must make during the long sea voyage back to India, and it was with a heavy heart that he boarded the liner four days later.

Upon his arrival back in Calcutta some weeks later, Jack returned to his flat in Ballygunge, somewhat disoriented after so long an absence.

He wandered restlessly from room to room, a glass of over-warm beer in his hand having forgotten to instruct his *bearer* to keep the icebox filled. Finally, in desperation, Jack decided to visit his horses at the yard where they were stabled, and perhaps have a word with the trainer. Now that the weather was noticeably cooler, racing should soon be in full swing.

"Jack?" exclaimed a familiar voice. "Good Lord!" Charlie O'Hara came round the corner of the stable building, a saddle over his arm. "So you are back at last. We were beginning to wonder if you had been swept away by a tidal wave...at the very least."

"Yes, I...er...I wasn't very well for quite a while." Jack cursed himself, it having slipped his mind that Claire's brother might also be at the stables.

"It's not so good at home, you know." Charlie's tone was cool. "It's been months, and apart from a few postcards Claire received at the outset – nothing. Since you happen to be engaged to my sister, why did you suddenly stop writing to her?"

"I believe I told you just now that I've been sick," Jack answered irritably. Not entirely a blatant lie, he reflected. He *had* been sick – sick with love for a married woman. "I daresay I'll be along shortly to make my excuses to Claire."

Striding away, he was uncomfortably aware of the young jockey staring after him in astonishment. Charlie was not accustomed to being given the brush off by his good friend. He would make amends when they next came across each other.

During the long sea journey back to Bombay, he had made the decision to go ahead with his marriage to Claire. His firm expected him to acquire a wife – Anne was unavailable – so it might as well be the O'Hara girl. In the meanwhile, he supposed he should put in an appearance at Camack Street. Heaving a sigh of resignation, Jack imagined the tiresome histrionics and reproaches he would be obliged to endure.

That same evening, Claire was sitting on the veranda, lost in thought and nursing a glass of *nimbu pani*. Christina sat opposite, mending a tear in her blouse.

"Penny for your thoughts, Claire?" she looked up from her task. "Are you still feeling depressed about Jack?"

"Depressed? Why, I just *love* being made a fool of!" replied her sister sarcastically. "He's been away for over five months, four of them without a single word. The latest gossip buzzing round Calcutta is that he's been playing around with some blonde tart."

Christina was silent, having run out of comforting excuses for Jack MacLeod's extraordinary behaviour. Poor Claire. So far, she had dealt with the inevitable whispers over the continuing absence of her fiancée with admirable dignity. But for how much longer could the poor thing pretend to the world that all was well? Really, one expected better from a man of Jack's standing, Christina thought crossly.

"I've been thinking of going back to college," Claire told her sister. "I've only missed a couple of terms, and I can catch up on that easily enough. Anything is better than fiddling about here, watching Sonia gloat over my situation."

"Actually, that might be a good idea…"

"Hello, you two!" Charlie appeared, his red hair still damp after a shower. "Any excitement since I've been out? Where's *Maman*?"

"Next door, dealing with a woman who arrived in a hurry." Claire sounded bored. "Uncle Freddie is coming for dinner, so how about a game of bridge afterwards?"

"Why not?" Charlie bit his lip, wondering whether to tell his sister he had seen Jack that afternoon. The chap had been behaving in the most extraordinary manner. And it now appeared he had not yet bothered to visit Claire. Completely unacceptable!

"Claire, I think you should know Jack is back in Calcutta. I saw him briefly at the stables earlier this afternoon."

Claire blanched, and then flushed with anger. "How nice. He had the time to visit his damned horses, but not the girl he is supposed to be marrying in a few weeks."

"He mentioned he hadn't been well," Charlie offered, "it was apparently the reason for being incommunicado for months."

"Sick, my foot!" she exploded. "A few lines on a blasted postcard would not have exactly sapped his strength. I take it he means to come and see me at some point?"

"Yes, he mentioned a visit…shortly, he said."

But Jack did not appear at Camack Street that evening, or the next day. It was the two days after that when the doorbell rang, and an *ayah* showed him into the sitting room. Informed of his arrival, Claire deliberately took her time to join him. Asking Christina to make sure Sonia was not eavesdropping, she went downstairs to the sitting room, where Jack rose to greet her with a somewhat forced smile.

"How have you been, Claire?" he asked taking the girl's hand, but found it was quickly withdrawn.

"Good evening Jack, good of you to call," her voice was cool. "Charlie did mention he had seen you at the stables a few days ago."

"No sarcasm please, it doesn't suit you," he said quietly. "I imagine he will also have told you that I've been unwell?"

"Yes, he did." Claire's eyes resembled chips of blue ice. "So what terrible disease did you have that precluded you from handling pen and paper for months?"

"One of these…um…obscure tropical infections that make you feel pretty lousy," Jack improvised. "Frankly, I didn't feel like doing more than I absolutely had to. But I realise it was inadmissible on my part not to remain in contact."

"Yes, it certainly was, and the unreasonable length of time you have been away has given rise to unpleasant rumours. It seems you found yourself some blonde in Durban to play with, and couldn't be seen for dust."

Jack stared at the girl in dismay. Was it possible that word about his relationship with Anne had already reached Calcutta? God knows, they had tried to be careful. He suddenly became aware of Claire's vivid eyes scrutinising his face.

"That's nonsense," he said at last. "As you must be aware, European communities thrive on salacious gossip."

"Ah, but sometimes there is no smoke without fire, as the saying goes. With no word from you for months on end, I didn't know what to think."

Waiting for his reply, Claire's expression was composed. Jack had expected fury, tears, hysterical recriminations – certainly not this cool dignity. It took him aback, as it became uncomfortably clear she did not believe a word of the lame excuse he had fabricated for her benefit.

"All I can say is that I'm sorry you had to put up with that sort of thing. But where do we go from here? Do you want to end our engagement?"

"I don't know what I want at this moment in time, Jack. There is also the fact that you have been in Calcutta for several days, but it is only now that you can be bothered to come and see me. How am I supposed to interpret that?"

"Busy. Very. A great deal to catch up on at the office. I do realise that I should have visited you much earlier, but—"

"Yes, you should." Claire interrupted shortly. "Shall we leave it for now, whilst we both give some thought to the possibility of a future together?"

"If that's what you want, Claire. But may I take you out to dinner in a day or two?"

"We'll see...perhaps next week."

As the door closed behind Jack, Claire let out her breath, and sank into a nearby chair. Keeping her composure had been a mighty effort, but on the whole she felt she had acquitted herself well. It was clear he wished to retain the plan to marry her. That gave her an advantage, but she would keep the fellow waiting for an answer.

"Well? How did it go?" Christina peeped round the door. "I take it Jack's gone?"

"Yes, for the time being. He knows I don't believe the rubbish he's spouting about illness, or being over-burdened at the office. But I also know he wants the wedding to go forward. It seems clear that Jack doesn't really care a damn about me, so why does he still want to go ahead with marriage?"

"Think back to the beginning, Claire," Christina said reflectively. "I remember you telling me that *Maman* said he needed a wife to help with entertaining and so on. I imagine that won't have changed."

Claire stared at her sister. Of course! How stupid to have forgotten that salient fact. She had lost sight of it before he left for South Africa, imagining that she and Jack had forged something rather less pragmatic between them. Hot tears pricked Claire's eyes, threatening to undermine her control...and were fiercely suppressed.

"There we are then," she managed to say. "But two can play at that game, I imagine. Marriage to Jack MacLeod is the key to getting the hell out of here – away from that damned nursing home, *Maman's* sour face, and that poisonous brat of hers. As his wife, I will be accepted by Calcutta society, a discovery I made before he cleared off to Durban." Claire smiled humourlessly. "For my part, I shall entertain his dull guests, arrange cocktail parties, and organise boring conferences. A fair swap, I think."

But despite her overt bravado, Claire was crying inside.

"I suppose so," Christina answered uncertainly. "But can you be happy with that, Claire? Something so...so cut and dried?"

The older girl hesitated. "Before Jack left, I was sure he felt something for me – as I did for him. Perhaps there's a chance we can rekindle that, and move on to something even better?"

"It's your whole life, Claire," Christina persisted. "You must be absolutely sure it's what you want."

"After what Charlie said about our family's dubious status here, it has to be better than nothing," she replied dryly. "But in the meantime, it won't kill Jack MacLeod to cool his heels in uncertainty for a while."

Over the next few days, there was general excitement in the house with the novel installation of a telephone. It would largely do away with the sending of messages via a boy on a bicycle or on foot. But the *ayahs* did not care for it at all, and categorically refused to go near it when they heard the bell shrilling. To them there was something unnatural, maybe evil, to hear a disembodied person speaking to one from miles away.

A week after Jack's visit, a large bouquet of flowers arrived for Claire, accompanied by a note. The office boy delivering it was told to wait for a reply. Opening the envelope, she scanned the single line.

"Forgive me please, and may I take you out for dinner next Saturday?"

Claire smiled. It was time to stretch a point, perhaps. Searching out a fountain pen, she helped herself to her mother's lavender notepaper and an envelope.

"I am pleased to accept, and will be ready by seven."

She hesitated, her pen hovering above the sheet of paper, about to sign her name. Since Jack's note could hardly be construed as a love letter, she, too, would leave it unsigned.

That Saturday evening, Claire took more than her usual pains with her appearance. Having resisted the ultra modern shingled hairstyle as not suiting her, her hair curled loosely about her face, swept to one side by a gold clip. Her dress was cool muslin, the identical blue of her eyes, their dark lashes enhanced by a touch of mascara.

Jack arrived on the dot of seven o'clock in the evening, looking debonair and quite handsome, Claire privately thought. She was gratified to notice a spark of interest in his eyes whilst complimenting her on her appearance…an encouraging beginning perhaps? Only time would tell.

Three weeks later, having resumed her position in society as Jack's intended, Claire was nevertheless far from confident regarding her forthcoming marriage. Although he had gone out of his way to atone for his transgression, presenting her with chocolates, perfume, and a gold bracelet laden with charms, the man seemed disassociated from the relationship, leaving Claire confused and unaccountably disturbed.

Minette had renewed her demands that Sonia be confirmed as her sister's flower girl, but Claire remained obdurate – to her mother's vociferous chagrin.

"That you continue to spite your little sister like this, frankly leaves me speechless, Claire O'Hara," Minette said angrily. "It's clear you relish hurting her feelings."

"Better she doesn't come to the wedding at all," declared the bride-to-be, unmoved, "for only then can one be certain of no embarrassing disruption to the proceedings."

Livid with anger and disappointment, Minette turned on her heel and stormed off.

The venue for the honeymoon had also been up for discussion. The final decision was to spend nine days at Puri, a seaside resort not too distant from Calcutta. A booking was subsequently made at a small beach hotel, run by two Dutch ladies whose cuisine was unrivalled by all accounts.

Frederick and Minette interviewed a talented designer from a local flower company for the decoration of the church interior. His suggestion of garlands of white blossoms interwoven with boughs of lush greenery was appealing, as well as large displays in the same colour scheme to be placed on either side of the altar. Music and hymns for the service were selected, and a professional photographer engaged. Everything was in place for the wedding in ten days time.

Claire went for a final fitting to her wedding gown at Hall & Anderson, a recently opened departmental store in central Calcutta. To her consternation, the pearl strewn bodice of the taffeta gown hung loosely on her body, the result of a considerable amount of weight that she had lost. Naomi Bernstein, the head seamstress, clucked crossly about young girls starving themselves to a shadow in the name of fashion. On the verge of tears, Claire assured her she hadn't, but that the last months had been…stressful.

Naomi glanced up sharply, her wise black eyes taking in the mauve shadows under the girl's startlingly blue eyes. Clearly, there was something not quite right here. She had three daughters herself, and was well qualified to recognise signs of inner disquiet.

"What is upsetting you so, little one?" she asked gently. "Don't worry, your wedding gown can easily be taken in. Are you perhaps having second thoughts?"

Caught off balance by Naomi's insight, tears spilled down Claire's cheeks, and she stifled a sob. "No...yes, I'm not sure I'm doing the right thing. On the surface I have everything to gain, but I don't believe my... my fiancée cares a jot for me."

With a gasp, Claire's rigid self-control dissolved, and she burst out crying like a small child. "Mrs B...Bernstein, I feel so terribly, terribly sad!"

Naomi put her arms about the girl's shaking form. "Have you talked to your mother about it?" she asked. "Sometimes mothers are best placed to help with—"

"*My mother?*" Claire laughed through her tears. "I think she would be the very last person whose advice I would seek. This entire marriage boils down to an arrangement between my mother and the man I am to marry. He needs a wife to ease advancement within his firm, and my mother has a daughter she would be happy to be rid of."

"And you? Does this man appeal to you, Claire?"

"Maybe not at first, as he seemed so much older. But we went about together for a few months, had fun, and I thought..." Claire choked, unable to continue.

"What happened to change your mind about him?" Naomi asked. "Obviously, it was something momentous."

"He went on business to South Africa for two months, and was away for five. After the first month, I heard nothing from him. But I did hear gossip about him taking up with some blonde woman. When he eventually came back to Calcutta, he didn't bother to come and see me for days. He's odd, disconnected, not the person I knew before he left. Oh, he still wants to get married...I fit the bill, you see." Claire laughed cynically through her tears.

"Claire, I truly believe everyone in this life deserves a second chance. Whatever happened in South Africa is in the past. The man came back for *you*. You know, there are many marriages where bride and groom are not in the throes of a grand passion." Naomi smiled, seeing she had caught the girl's attention.

"Sadly, that sort of thing can fizzle out in a relatively short time. Relationships based on friendship are the most successful, and love often develops afterwards. Think about that, my dear."

Standing on the pavement outside the store, Claire shook her head in bewilderment. It was not like her to lose control and bawl like a baby in front of an almost perfect stranger. But it had been comforting to be enfolded in Naomi's arms, something she could not recall her mother ever doing. Wonderful to have found someone so kind, so wise, whose sound advice she knew she could depend upon in future.

In general, she had taken in Naomi's views about marriage. Might there really be a chance to find happiness with Jack? She had certainly thought so, prior to his going away. Maybe as time passed, they would resume the comfortable, if unromantic relationship they once had? Perhaps it was worth a gamble after all?

The marriage ceremony was to take place at Calcutta's Saint Paul's Cathedral. After the official photographer had completed his task, the reception would be held at Frederick's home in Alipore. This had been at Claire's impassioned request, pointing out that should the venue be at Camack Street, screams from women in labour at the nursing home next door would hardly lend the desired ambiance. Her eyes hardening, Minette pursed her lips, but didn't argue.

Watching the preparations for his wedding progressing apace, Jack wished he could feel excited over the prospect. His bride was undoubtedly a lovely girl, and his boss, Edward Woodson, had declared her to have the makings of a perfect company wife. She was surprisingly intelligent for her age, and would make a pleasant and interesting companion with whom to share his life.

But she was not Anne.

Chapter Seven

Inside the dim interior of the cathedral, Jack stood beside his best man, awaiting the arrival of his bride. Despite being Calcutta's cold weather season, he felt distinctly over-warm in his morning suit with its high collar and cravat. And there were a good many more hours ahead to endure, he reflected grimly.

Presbyterian by birth, Jack had no interest in religious matters. He was therefore content for the ceremony to take place in this great Catholic cathedral that lent itself well to such an event. The soaring, vaulted roof allowed air to circulate freely, thus giving an impression of coolness to the perspiring wedding guests seated below. Magnificent stained glass windows provided a colourful background to the bishop's elaborate scarlet and gold-encrusted vestments, echoed by the cloths draped over the altar behind him. A tableau of spiritual majesty.

Sitting in flower-decorated central pews, people talked quietly amongst themselves whilst waiting for the bride. Most were Jack's friends and business acquaintances, but guests of the O'Hara family took up only a single pew. Resplendent in beautiful feathered hats and elaborate gowns, ladies were fanning themselves, and gentlemen tried not to appear over-heated in grey morning suits.

Glancing towards the rear of the church, the bridegroom was seized by a fleeting desire to take to his heels and vanish from the scene. Common sense then prevailed, and his panic dissipated as the organ swelled to Elgar's *Pomp and Circumstance*, heralding the arrival of the bride.

An indrawn breath of admiration was clearly audible as Claire advanced slowly down the aisle, her hand resting lightly on her brother's arm. Four bridesmaids followed, holding up a long veil of Brussels lace, and a fine half-veil fell over her face. Despite his reservations, Jack's eyes were riveted on the approaching vision.

The young woman had never looked more beautiful, her dark hair drawn up into a loose knot encircled by strands of jasmine. In her hands, she held a bouquet of the same delicate white blooms encircled by green foliage. The elegant bodice of her soft taffeta gown was scattered with seed pearls that proceeded in swathes over the flowing skirts. Only her hands were seen to tremble…wedding nerves, it was said.

Pausing in front of the bishop, Charlie formally placed his sister's hand into that of her future husband, and stepped to one side. Jack lifted the half-veil covering his bride's face, and was taken aback to see the vivid eyes brimming with tears.

As the service progressed, Claire composed herself and made her responses in a clear voice. She and Jack went to sign the register, and the new Mrs MacLeod walked down the aisle on her husband's arm to *The Trumpet Voluntary*, and then out through the cathedral doors into the sunshine.

The reception at Frederick's home was predictably lavish, a luncheon set out for guests under an enormous marquee on the lawns. Excellent wines flowed, the cake was then cut, after which the best man and Jack gave short speeches. It was clear that festivities were likely to continue late into the evening, long after the bride and groom had departed in a flurry of thrown rice and confetti. They were to spend their first night together as man and wife in a suite at the Grand Hotel – a gift from Frederick – and would leave the following day for their honeymoon at Puri.

Gazing out of the hotel bedroom window, Claire tried not to think about the night ahead. She was glad of these few minutes alone, Jack still being downstairs in reception to check on train timetables. Taking advantage of his absence, she had divested herself of her wedding gown and veil, and meant to take a tepid bath before changing into one of her new outfits for dinner.

The gown she intended to wear that evening hung from a hanger on a corner of the wardrobe – a gorgeous, peach coloured affair. Everything in her aubergine leather suitcase was brand new, and Claire was thrilled with *trousseau*. It was what lay in store when they returned to the bedroom that made her feel vaguely apprehensive.

In theory she knew what to expect from biology lessons at school, when she and her classmates had tittered over their unfortunate mistress's halting explanations. But there had also been wild rumours of blood spatter, pain, and a desperate need for endurance. At the time, Claire had thought the business sounded positively gross! Did it hurt *that* much? Did it last *that* long? How often did it take place? All these were unanswered questions, but Claire supposed she would soon know. Now for that lovely cool bath…

Emerging from the bathroom wrapped in a fluffy towel, Claire was disconcerted to find Jack half-lying across the bed in his dressing gown, reading a newspaper.

"Ah, there you are. I was wondering if you had absconded already," he grinned. "So, tell me, Mrs MacLeod, how does it feel to be a married woman?"

"Er...taking to it like a duck to water," Claire returned with a smile. "Have you been waiting ages for the bathroom? Why don't you have a shower now whilst I dress?"

Putting the newspaper aside, Jack rose and crossed over to the girl, who, clutching her towel about her stared up at him, mesmerised. Kissing her lightly on the lips, he picked her up bodily and carried her over to the bed, then kissed her more deeply with increasing desire. He gently pulled away the towel from her clinging hands, so Claire lay naked before him, apprehensive and deeply self-conscious. Shrugging off his dressing gown, the girl saw Jack was naked and already erect. Positioning himself above his new wife, he began making love to her, and with mounting urgency exploded into violent orgasm.

"*Christ, Anne! How I love you, love you, love you, my darling girl!*"

Stiffening in agonised shock beneath her husband's body, a warm tear trickled down Claire's cheek as her mind took stock of what had just happened. Jack had bellowed out a name whilst making love to her – not hers – but that of another woman.

On their wedding night.

Wriggling out from under Jack's heavy body, Claire seized her *peignoir*, and running into the bathroom, locked the door behind her. Turning on the shower, she stood under the tepid blast, her tears mingling with the water sluicing over her head. Sobbing uncontrollably, she grabbed a nailbrush and scrubbed at her body, desperate to be rid of every vestige of contact with the man now dozing on the bed.

It was past all credibility that her husband of only a few hours had just betrayed her by pretending she was some other woman. This *Anne* must be the blonde tart that the Calcutta gossips had whispered about, whose sexual favours he had clearly enjoyed countless times. The insult was insufferable.

Satisfied at last, Claire emerged from the shower, wet hair dripping down her back. Although she had managed to regain control of herself, an occasional involuntary sob still shuddered through her body. Wrapping herself in a towel, she sat on the bathroom stool and attempted to marshal her scattered thoughts.

Outraged she most certainly was, but she was married to this man so it was no longer a question of going home to confide in Christina. Nevertheless, she would not gloss over what Jack had just done to her. She would confront him, and watch him scuffle to extricate himself from the tricky situation. Should it turn out to be a hideous mistake, he would be appalled to have inadvertently insulted his very new bride. But what if this Anne woman turned out to be the blonde floozy at the heart of those beastly rumours during Jack's visit to Durban? She would just have to play it by ear.

Claire quickly rubbed her hair dry with a towel – thankful it would fall into shape being naturally curly. Slipping on her *peignoir*, she unlocked the door and padded barefoot back into the bedroom. Only lightly dozing, Jack opened his eyes and looked over at his wife. Even with damp hair, the little thing was looking attractive. A virgin she certainly had been, but she really did need to be brought up to scratch in the sexual department! Couldn't expect to just lie there with a scared look on...

"Jack, who exactly is *Anne*?" Claire did not intend to beat about the bush. "You know, that woman you *love, love, love* so desperately?"

Husband and wife stared at each other in shocked silence. "I have no idea what you are talking about," Jack hastened to recover himself. "A figment of your over-active imagination perhaps?"

"Don't treat me like an idiot!" Claire snapped. "I may be young and inexperienced, but I also possess a brain. So don't try to fob me off with patronising rubbish. It has to be every girl's worst nightmare to realise the man making love to her is actually pretending she's somebody else."

"It has nothing to do with you," he answered stiffly. "Anne was someone I was fond of at one time, if you must know."

"And still are, judging by that distasteful display just now," Claire retorted. "So, when did your...er...association with this woman end? Assuming it has, of course?"

"Don't be ridiculous," Jack said tightly. "I married you, didn't I? Drop the subject, if you please."

"May I remind you that it was *you* who brought it up in the first place, bellowing in my ear about how passionately you love this Anne woman!"

"If you were offended, I'm sorry," Jack got off the bed and walked over to the bathroom. "But oblige me by finding something else to talk about."

The bathroom door closed behind her husband, and Claire's face flushed scarlet in thwarted fury. How *dare* the arrogant pig saunter off without bothering to answer? Why, he hadn't even bothered to deny having feelings for that damned woman.

Taking advantage of his absence from the bedroom, she dressed swiftly and made up her face. This was supposed to be their wedding day, she thought fiercely. Maybe Jack would reflect a little whilst in the shower, and realise how badly he had hurt her. Would he not wish a happier way to begin a marriage that was still only a few hours old? She would give him the opportunity to apologise, and then do her best to be an amusing companion this evening. No easy task, but the *Anne* business must be put to one side for the time being.

During dinner, neither mentioned the earlier unpleasant scene in the bedroom. Claire laughed, told anecdotes, and poked gentle fun at the odd pompous guest at the wedding reception. Inside, the girl was begging for an affectionate response from her husband that did not materialise. Jack sat opposite, silent and withdrawn, making little effort to reciprocate her efforts to converse.

Later that night, Jack once again exerted his right of intercourse, silently, and without any attempt to consider the girl he had married. Inordinately upset, Claire acquiesced, hot tears of disappointment trickling down her face and into the pillow. So much for her hopes of a new beginning.

Waiting until he had rolled over and had begun to snore, Claire crept out of bed and into the bathroom. Once again, she scrubbed herself clean of her husband's attentions. She received the impression of being "used" as a convenient receptacle for her husband, anathema to the young girl as she reflected bleakly on the remaining days of her honeymoon.

The following morning, Jack once more availed himself of his wife's body, again without speaking a word. As her husband turned away, Claire was unable to suppress a sob as tears again trickled down her cheeks. Raising himself on an elbow, Jack stared down at her, his eyes cold.

"What are you blubbering about, for God's sake?" he asked irritably. "I hope you aren't trying to infer that I'm hurting you?"

"N...no," the girl choked. "Just a bit...bit tired after yesterday's excitement."

Jack swung his legs out of bed and stood up. "Well, I sincerely hope your exhaustion to be a transient thing. It would be a colossal bore to be treated to waterworks every time I lay a finger on you."

Gasping at the injustice of the remark, Claire turned her back on him. Where had that kind man gone? The one who used to compliment her, look into her eyes...say sweet things? *Vanished.* Gone with the ship that took him away to Durban for months on end, and more so since she confronted him about that woman.

Puri turned out to be delightful, as were the hotel proprietors, who welcomed the couple with great warmth and showed them to a comfortable double bedroom. They discovered the meals had a decidedly Dutch influence, deliciously different from usual hotel fare. Whenever required, the honeymooners were given a substantial picnic lunch to take to the beach, and a moveable striped awning was also lent to provide shade.

Clad in one of her new bathing suits, Claire spent her mornings swimming, dozing, or reading a book under the awning. After a brief swim, Jack occupied himself with office paperwork, or perused out-of-date English newspapers.

In silence.

Back at the hotel, the spinster ladies shook their heads in bewilderment over the bizarre behaviour of this recently married couple. The husband was heard to address his new wife in a coldly courteous manner, and she replied with equally chilly indifference. Evening meals were taken in relative silence...all the more noticeable in contrast with the animated chatter from others in the dining room.

Upon their return to Calcutta, the MacLeods moved into a small rented house in Alipore, the district where they intended to eventually purchase a property. The house was staffed by only two servants, a *bearer* to take care of Jack's clothes, and a washing *ayah* who would also look after Claire's possessions. Frederick lived close by, so it became convenient for the couple to dine with him, until such time as they were settled in a new home. Sunday lunch was to be taken with Claire's family.

That first Sunday lunchtime, Claire and Christina were delighted to see one another and exchanged fierce hugs. Neither had been separated before in their lives, and under the pretext of fetching something from the bedroom they once shared, Claire rushed upstairs, her sister at her heels.

"Is everything all right?" Christina sat down on the bed and patted it by way of invitation. "You look a bit tired…aren't you sleeping properly?"

"Oh Chrissy, sometimes I wish I was back at home," Claire threw herself down beside her sister. "Being married isn't all it's cracked up to be, you know."

"Wasn't the holiday at Puri a success, then?" Christina's forehead wrinkled in concern. "All those days at the seaside sounded heavenly to me."

"To me too…until I discovered my husband happens to be madly in love with some female called Anne!" she burst out. "Oh God, the humiliation is *unbearable*."

"But…but how did you find out about this woman?"

"My darling, brand new husband screeched out her name whilst making love to me, yelling how much he '*love, love, loved* her'. Claire looked across at her sister, her eyes awash with tears. "He then refused to discuss it, or even reassure me the damned woman was firmly in the past. He now barely speaks to me. Insists on his marital rights, though… revolting business, it is too. I can't wait to get under the shower to get rid of the muck and stink." Claire wrinkled her nose in disgust. "I'm quite unable to please Jack these days, so I very much regret having married him."

Putting an arm about her sister's shoulders, Christina gave her a comforting squeeze. Horrified by Jack MacLeod's changed attitude, she could understand her sister's disgust to be viewed as a possession to be used at will. Her mind skating over the more unsavoury details, she could think of nothing helpful to say.

"Perhaps you should stop trying to win Jack's approval," she said at last. "That can only open you up to further hurt. Leave him to his own devices, and think instead of the advantages you will enjoy as his wife."

Seeing she had her sister's attention, Christina warmed to her theme. "Concentrate on the lovely home you will soon be living in, and the fun of buying lots of gorgeous furniture for it. You'll give wonderful parties, and receive lots of invitations to all sorts of things. Leave Jack out of the equation for the time being."

Claire stared in astonishment. Good common sense advice from her little nun-like sister? In her distraught state, and futile efforts to create a lover in a man clearly indifferent to her, she had lost sight of the benefits of her new status.

"Thank you, darling Chrissy," she leaned over and kissed her sister's cheek. "Can't believe the idiot I've been making of myself, probably from reading too many soppy novels. Thanks to you, I'm not feeling quite so depressed about things." Linking arms, the sisters went down to join the others on the veranda for a pre-lunch cocktail.

The following week went by without further unpleasantness or drama. Although he was relieved not to be subjected to further histrionics from Claire, Jack was less than gratified to notice her newly pragmatic attitude. He had been irritated by the girl's obvious desire for affection, but this new indifference felt like a draught of cold air, and he missed her girlish enthusiasm.

The first time they had made love on their wedding day, Jack recalled an eager, if inexperienced cooperation on Claire's part. Now she submitted to his advances without complaint, but lay immobile as a log, eyes tightly closed, her face turned away in apparent disgust. It would not surprise him if she yawned, and asked if he had finished – he thought savagely.

It did not occur to him to analyse why.

Since she was no longer abasing herself by begging for her husband's affection, Claire's flagging self-esteem began to re-establish itself. But despite this, she still secretly worried about the faceless woman lurking in the background. Was it the South African tart? Or was it one closer to home? But anxious to establish an attitude of cool equanimity, she concealed her anxieties from her husband.

The purchase of a beautiful property in Alipore went a long way to distract Claire from obsessing over her husband's attitude. In possession of a graceful colonnaded portico, the house was situated in the centre of magnificent gardens shaded by tall trees. To the rear of the house, a separate building provided stabling for ten horses, with a further annexe for several vehicles. Servants' quarters were discreetly positioned behind high hedges several yards from the main house. The young woman was enchanted with her spacious new home, relishing the absence of appalling screams that so frequently filled the air from her mother's nursing home.

Jack took charge of overseeing the complete redecoration of the exterior of the house. But for the interior, he sought Claire's advice regarding colour and texture in flattering recognition of her impeccable taste. New furniture and carpets arrived, as well as light fittings, and the most modern of overhead fans. Making use of Jack's Daimler motor car and uniformed driver, Claire paid a visit to Hall & Anderson to arrange for curtains throughout the house to be made.

It was also an opportunity to visit Naomi Bernstein, anxious to ask her advice on the difficult situation in which she found herself. Christina's advice had helped, but she needed the older woman's counsel as to how she could best face the loveless future looming ahead of her.

Naomi was delighted to see the young woman again, if privately dismayed to note that mauve shadows under the vivid eyes had returned. Claire had also lost weight – again. Slim she had always been, but the girl was now bordering on being too thin.

Listening to the unhappy tale unfolding, and the effect it was having on the usually vivacious Claire, Naomi shook her head. The lack of imagination, clumsiness, and sheer idiocy of Jack MacLeod's handling of his young wife was past belief. Somehow, she must find a way of helping the poor girl view her marriage in a more positive light.

"Your sister's advice to you is extremely sound, Claire. It would not do to continue battering your head against a brick wall, and you are going to have to be rather grown-up with regard to the obscure woman in your husband's life." Naomi hesitated.

"Have you considered the fact that Jack might want children? Most men do. Having a baby will bind him more closely to you, and perhaps be a new beginning? He will also want to entertain, and, of course you will excel there. Impress the man...be his friend. Make yourself indispensable. But also get on with things that interest you, and make sure you have enough money to do it."

"A baby?" Claire pulled a face. "I don't think I want to tie myself down with that at the moment. But you're right about becoming his friend – no easy thing, since the man barely addresses me."

"All you can do is try, but do take the time to enjoy life, my dear."

Later that afternoon, Claire lay on her bed under a slowly revolving fan, mulling over her conversation with Naomi. Money. She hadn't even thought about that. Jack paid whenever necessary, but Claire had no personal allowance. Nor did she have access to funds. That must change. It would not be an unreasonable request, and Jack could well afford it.

Having discovered the knack of entertaining from the days of Frederick's dinner parties, Claire was filled with new determination to establish the MacLeods in Calcutta society. As for those pretentious persons who once had looked down their nose at her, she would ignore their existence. There were far more worthwhile people around, who would be only too happy to befriend her.

Re-energised by a vision of things to come, Claire rose from her bed, showered, and went to speak to their recently employed *kensama*. He was a prize they had inherited from a recently departed aide to the British Governor. Accustomed to catering for large numbers, he would be unfazed by the MacLeods' lunch and dinner parties.

The weeks went by, and Claire found a certain fulfilment in the elegance of her home, in particular, her gorgeous cream bedroom. Upon moving into the new house, it had been decided that she and Jack would have separate bedrooms. Nevertheless, Claire was informed a double bed was necessary for hers, for those occasions when her husband chose to visit. Secretly delighted to be gaining her privacy for at least some of the time, Claire acquiesced with a smile.

At his wife's request, Jack arranged for her to have a personal bank account, into which he placed a generous sum each month. He also opened a signatory account at Hall & Anderson. Thanking him with grace, Claire rewarded him by going out of her way to be an amusing companion.

Claire's first dinner party for Jack's boss and his wife was a great success. The meal was excellent, the wines well chosen, and the conversation lively and interesting. Presiding at the dinner table, Claire made a point of charming Delia, Edward Woodson's rather staid wife. By the end of the evening, it was clear they were both singularly impressed with Jack's young bride.

Pleasantries between husband and wife, however, did not extend to the bedroom. Jack continued to exert his marital rights several times a week, which Claire found increasingly distasteful as time went on. It crossed the girl's mind to wonder if her husband's sexual demands were because he wished to pretend the body beneath him was his tart? Revulsion flared...and was hastily suppressed, remembering she was obliged to tolerate the insult.

"For Christ's sake, must you squeeze your eyes shut and lie like a bloody log whilst we make love?" Jack ground out during an early morning visit to his wife's bedroom. "It makes me feel as though I'm attempting to reanimate a dead body."

Wriggling out from beneath her husband, Claire slipped on her *peignoir*, and turned to look down at him, her eyes cold. "In the circumstances, I'm amazed you expect me to react in any other way."

"Circumstances? What circumstances?"

"That you continue to pretend I'm someone else does not inspire me with ardour, I can assure you."

"Christ, not *that* again!" Jack irritably rolled over on his back, and laced his hands behind his head. "Why do you always have to regurgitate that rubbish time and again? Don't you have everything you want?"

"We are not speaking of possessions," Claire countered. "I have nothing to complain of there. You have been very generous. But, I, too, have kept my side of the bargain. At our cocktail party the other evening, several people told me they admired your impeccable taste in finding a wife who was such an asset. But you...why, you barely give me the time of day."

"I freely admit you are of great value to me, Claire. However, that hardly extends to your behaviour in the bedroom, does it? It would be nicer if you managed to refrain from expressing your distaste for my attentions quite so openly."

"Whatever I may or may not express is involuntary, believe me. Heavens, I must go for my shower, or I shall be late for an appointment with the Hall & Anderson fellow about garden furniture for the rear lawn. Maybe one day we can think of sinking a swimming pool? There's certainly enough space for one."

Secretly fuming, Claire disappeared into the bathroom. Jack remained on the bed, disgruntled, but dismissive of the effect his attitude was having on his young wife.

Chapter Eight

The first year of her marriage sped past for Claire, fully absorbed as she was in setting up her new home and interviewing servants. Her excellent organising skills were required for receptions following conferences, as well as cocktail parties and a few formal dinners for Jack's political or business associates. Vivacious, and scintillating with delight over her successes, the young woman was in her element.

With Naomi Bernstein's competent assistance, in addition to her own eye for fashion, Claire acquired a distinctive wardrobe and racks of expensive shoes. When fashion dictated a higher hemline, she was delighted to display her dainty ankles without shocking Calcutta society. Amused, Claire noticed other women aping her stylishness with varying degrees of success. For one who was considered a nonentity at one time, she supposed she should be flattered to find herself copied so slavishly.

Not long afterwards, the young woman discovered herself to be pregnant. Jubilantly aware it would spell an end to her husband's visitations to her bed, she lost no time in giving him the good news. She was surprised to see his face light up with genuine pleasure, kiss her, and say how he would hope for a son. Hugging the news of her pregnancy to herself during the rest of that week, Claire made the announcement to her family over lunch on the Sunday.

"How lovely," Christina enthused. "Imagine! Me, an auntie!"

"Jolly good, old girl." Charlie grinned at his sister. "But I forbid you to teach your child to call me *nunky*, or something equally vile."

"And you will be a grandmother!" Claire told her mother with some relish. "You'll have to let me know if you want to be called Gran...or perhaps just Nan?"

"Certainly not Nan, thank you," Minette retorted, aware of her daughter's thinly veiled malice. "Grannie will do nicely. Now, we must have a discussion about..."

"Not now, *Maman*," Claire hurriedly cut short what she knew her mother was about to suggest. "For heaven's sake, I've only just discovered my condition."

Minette shrugged and turned away. Marriage certainly hadn't softened the girl's abrasive stance. Frederick had told her of Claire's social successes, and that the MacLeods were fast becoming sought-after guests at parties. Hard to understand with that attitude of hers – she thought sourly.

"Would you consider Sonia as one of the baby's godmothers, Claire?" she asked, hoping her daughter would find it awkward to refuse. "She would be so thrilled."

"Sorry, but godmothers are already chosen," the mother-to-be gaily fibbed, "and since Chrissy is to be one of them, I can hardly add another sister."

Pursing her mouth, Minette stared coldly at her daughter. Spiteful girl! It was obvious she intended to continue victimising harmless little Sonia. She must remember to ask Jack to intervene on her favourite daughter's behalf, as he might over-ride his wife's slight against the poor child.

After lunch, Christina and Claire walked down to the stables to see Turka. Despite his great age, the little Arab horse was alert and whinnied shrilly as the visitors approached. Rubbing his forehead, Claire smiled affectionately, having always had a soft spot for the old boy since she and Charlie had looked after him in Simla years ago.

"You are going have your baby at *Maman's* nursing home, aren't you?" Christina suddenly asked. "That's what she meant to ask you just now, and I know she'll be dreadfully hurt if you didn't."

"Certainly not! After years of being forced to endure the frightful place, I'm not about to join the ranks of those screeching women. I shall have my baby at home, under the care of Doctor Ross, whom I have already consulted."

"But Claire, how can you?"

"*No*, Chrissy! I couldn't bear to be ordered about, have my baby taken over, and that blasted Sonia foisted on me as a godmother. It's out of the question."

Aware of her sister's obstinacy, Christina sighed and allowed the subject to drop. In any case, she had news of her own to impart.

"I'm going to Simla for six months or so to teach Maths," she told her sister. "For nothing of course, except board and lodging. It will be wonderful to see the nuns again, although dearest Mother Clementine won't be there," Christina looked sad, thinking of the wonderful old lady who had died three years previously.

"But why are you going for so long, Chrissy" Claire asked with a frown. "You'll be back in time for the baby's birth, I hope?"

Christina hesitated. "I...I'm giving myself time to think about becoming a nun," she said at last. "I don't know if I'm worthy of the Calling, so you see—"

"*What?*" Claire interrupted in horror. "For God's sake, Chrissy, you can't be serious? What about all those sins you are forever bewailing? Such as enjoying dancing with men? And that heinous sin of gluttony you claim – should you happen to like what you are eating? Have you thought about those gorgeous, silky under-things in your drawer...to exchange for a flea-ridden hair shirt under smelly black robes? *Do* think everything through properly, Chrissy darling."

Her eyes filling with tears, the younger girl flushed. "But I really do want to."

"Go and see the old bats if you want, but for heaven's sake don't allow yourself to be led by the nose into something you would regret – sooner or later. Besides, I'll need you when the baby comes. We've always done things together, haven't we? I'd feel lost without you!"

Christina was silent, her beautiful dream in tatters. She wasn't angry with Claire, because everything she had said was perfectly true. She supposed she should be grateful to her sister for pointing it out before she made a fool of herself. But the disappointment was still crushing...

"Darling Chrissy, do buck up!" Claire took one of her sister's limp hands. "I want you to come and live with us after the baby is born. I've missed you dreadfully, you know, and we have never really been separated before. You can still go off every day and teach if you want, but you don't have to. Of course, you'll have your own bedroom, and even a little sitting room to be private whenever you feel like it."

"Leave Camack Street?" Christina said blankly. "Goodness, there arc lots of things to consider before I could do such a thing, Claire. I don't know what *Maman* would say. And think of poor Charlie coming home each day with only Sonia to talk to."

"I wouldn't worry too much about him from now on. Our brother is besotted with the new Police Commissioner's daughter – Rose, I think she's called. Jack often sees him in the Saturday Club bar after work, and he told me that wedding bells might even be in the offing."

"Really?" Wiping her eyes, Christina gave a watery smile. "As a matter of fact, a letter was delivered for Charlie the other day. He snatched it up from the hall table, and rushed down to the stables to read it. Bet it was from the girlfriend!"

"There you are, then. And if Charlie gets married and has his own home, it will be *you* coming home to Snivelling Sonia each day. What a nightmare!"

"But Jack? Surely he won't want me intruding in his home? No, Claire, it's not—"

"Jack likes you very much, Chrissy. Besides, he will be relieved not to be expected to coo over the baby every evening when he comes home. Aside from keeping me company, it will also free me to deal with Jack's business entertaining. So, you can see how invaluable your presence would be to both of us."

"I...I'll think about it, Claire. But I shall still go to Simla for a while."

"Suit yourself. But please don't write to tell me you're becoming a nun after all. I can't bear the thought of you doing such an awful thing."

Christina tried to smile, failed, and walked towards the stable doors. "Better go back to the house, or *Maman* will think we're plotting against darling Sonia."

A week later, Claire's joy over having her bed to herself each night was blighted by the torment of morning sickness. Why was it called morning sickness – wondered the afflicted young woman – on her knees in front of the lavatory for the fourth time that day? It left her exhausted, and disinclined to do anything but lie miserably on her bed.

On days when the nausea seemed less violent, she would get up in the evening and sit on the veranda to read. Occasionally, she would play bridge with Jack and a neighbouring couple, David and Felicity Miller, who had a baby a few months old. Felicity was, therefore, in a prime position to pass on information regarding pregnancy and birth, none of which the mother-to-be found in the least way reassuring.

Claire had vaguely assumed she would employ an *ayah* to take care of the baby, but Felicity earnestly assured her that only a proper Nanny would do. In the Millers' case, it was a pretty Anglo-Indian girl clad in a spotless white uniform, who was seen almost every evening pushing a pram on the *maidan*. Although she accepted a nanny was necessary, Claire secretly resolved to ensure her own would not be so pretty. Since his wife held no appeal for him, Jack might find an attractive nanny rather too tempting...

Claire's relationship with her mother remained frosty, a chill that increased when Minette discovered her daughter was refusing to have her baby at the nursing home. Hurtful it undoubtedly was, but she was also infuriated over the inevitable questions it could provoke. What might people think, if Minette's own daughter was delivering her baby elsewhere?

Claire remained determined, however, explaining that she wanted to have her baby at home, and under the care of her own doctor. Finally losing her temper over her mother's ceaseless nagging, she stopped going for Sunday lunch at Camack Street.

Morning sickness miraculously vanished soon after the fourth month, and the young woman bloomed during the remainder of her pregnancy. Convinced the baby would be a boy, she pondered names for the awaited cherub who would possess her dark hair and blue eyes. Both parents-to-be eventually agreed upon the names, William Robert, the latter being the name of Jack's father.

Curious to know more of her husband's family, Claire idly asked if they were aware of their son's marriage? If so, why had they not registered the fact, even by a card?

"Of course they are," came her husband's short reply. "But my parents are rather preoccupied with my younger brother's affairs at the present moment."

Claire drew her own conclusions from that somewhat dry comment. Jack might not be on good terms with his family in Scotland, presumably why there had been no contact. He did not care to enlighten her.

As the months wore on, Claire regarded her swelling stomach with acute dismay. Would her poor body ever regain its original slenderness? In addition, there was the sleeplessness and discomfort caused by the infant kicking and heaving throughout the night. For God's sake, thought the tearful mother-to-be, why did the activity invariably take place at night? She fervently hoped that, after the birth, the baby would understand that nights were for sleeping...

Increasingly uncomfortable, Claire could scarcely wait for the day she would have her body to herself again, and enjoy wearing lovely clothes instead of hideous tents. Disgruntled in the heat, she was sometimes tearful when Jack returned from the office. Taking one look at her glowering face, he would pat her gruffly on the head and retreat to his study with a *chota-peg* of whisky. There, he would remain ensconced, until the *bearer* announced that dinner was served.

On a hot and humid night, Claire was sitting alone in the veranda, unable to sleep. She had been trying to read by the light of a hurricane lamp, but finding she was unable to concentrate, the book lay open on her lap. Shifting her bulk to a more comfortable position, she was suddenly conscious of an odd sensation in her lower stomach, then a warm rush of liquid from her nether regions soaked into the chair cushion beneath her. Fearful that the dreaded birth might be imminent, she stumbled into her husband's bedroom to wake him. Jack hurriedly leaped out of bed and went to telephone the doctor. Susan, the recently employed nanny, was also summoned, and she and the apprehensive young woman retired to a spotless room that was fully equipped for the delivery of the new infant. Squeezing her eyes shut with the onset of another painful contraction, Claire wondered if she would endure what was to come without howling like a banshee...

Diana Elizabeth MacLeod came squalling into the world three hours later, and was placed into her exhausted mother's arms. Bewildered, Claire stared down at the wrinkled little face with its slate-coloured eyes, head topped with tufts of ginger hair. On the verge of hysteria, she wondered what could have happened to her eagerly awaited baby boy? Enduring hours and hours of frightful agony just to produce this wizened, angry little creature?

Her eyes filling with tears, Claire thrust the screaming infant at the hovering nanny, muttering that she needed to rest. Alarmed by the anguished expression on the new mother's face, Nanny Susan carried the infant away to be cleaned in an adjoining room. Madam is probably just very, very tired, she thought.

Later that morning, Jack saw his new daughter for the first time. Although secretly disappointed the baby was not the son he had hoped for, he stood for a few moments beside the crib, watching the infant's tiny mouth vainly grope for a source of food. Unable to find it, the little face crumpled and released a surprisingly loud bellow.

The nanny hurried to pick up the wailing baby, and produced a feeding bottle containing a few ounces of glucose water. Gently moving the rubber teat against the tiny lips, the infant grasped it in her mouth and began to suck greedily. That might do for a short while, but the nanny knew she would soon need her mother's milk.

Seeing her husband enter the bedroom, Claire closely examined his face for signs of disappointment that the baby had turned out to be a girl. She found none.

"I imagine you will have seen your horridly ugly daughter?" she demanded, tears of weakness trickling down her face. "I can't believe I went through that hell, just to produce a scrawny red shrimp!"

"Well, I'm no expert on the appearance of newborn babies," Jack replied, concealing his dismay over Claire's outburst. "But I've heard it said that for a day or two, they can seem flushed and on the skinny side. I'm sure there will be an improvement in a few days' time. Anyway, congratulations on Diana's safe arrival, my dear, and now I'll leave you to rest." He hastily left the room, unwilling to argue with his clearly upset wife.

A tap at the door, and the dumpy figure of Nanny Susan appeared, carrying the baby enfolded in a soft white towel. "May I come in Madam? I have a small person here who is very, very hungry. Does Madam know what needs to be done to prepare your breasts for feeding?"

Not receiving a reply from her mistress, Susan placed a pillow across Claire's knees, on which she gently placed the grizzling infant. She then pointed to a bowl of warm sterile water on the bedside table, and a few balls of cotton wool in a saucer.

"This is to clean your nipples before feeding baby," Nanny Susan explained, and stood back with a smile.

With bad grace, Claire exposed a breast, and wiped the nipple with a ball of wetted cotton wool. "I really don't see why I need to do this right now," she said grumpily. "Can't it have some other milk until I feel stronger?"

"Madam, it is not only milk that baby needs, but colostrums, and only you can give her that. This protects baby from infection and—"

"Oh, carry on then," she heaved a resigned sigh. "Do whatever needs to be done, and then leave me be to get over it all, for heaven's sake."

Nanny Susan gently directed the baby's lips over the nipple, which she immediately seized in her mouth. Blissfully closing her eyes, she began sucking with enthusiasm.

"*Oh, my God!*" Claire gasped, sitting bolt upright. "What's it doing to me? Ow...OW! Susan, get it off me, will you? It's biting my nipple... and my stomach is *killing* me."

"Please Madam, it's perfectly normal..."

"No, the damned thing is *chewing*..."

Panic-stricken, Claire yanked the baby off her breast, and the horrified Nanny only just prevented her from falling to the floor.

Abruptly wrenched away from the food she craved, the infant set up an indignant howl. Bursting into tears, the new mother stared in distaste at the scarlet-faced, screaming baby. For God's sake, the thing wasn't only hideous...it also had the instincts of a cannibal!

"Madam...*please* Madam?" begged the nanny in desperation. "If you feel your stomach tighten, it only means your body is trying to get back to normal."

Claire paused to look at Susan, a flicker of interest in her eyes. Seizing the moment, the Nanny pressed home the point. "Truly, Madam, the baby's sucking shrinks the womb faster, and it will help your body to become nice and slim again."

"Madam, may I put baby back to feed?" Susan ventured timidly, "and then she will stop crying and go to sleep."

Sulkily, Claire allowed the Nanny to put the howling infant back on the breast, who stopped crying to begin a frantic sucking. Teeth clenched against the discomfort, she forced herself to imagine a brand new wardrobe...

During the feed, Susan retreated to a chair on the other side of the room, reluctant to leave the baby alone with this mother. After all, Madam had nearly dropped the child, and one couldn't help noticing how she kept calling her little daughter *it*.

A few weeks ago, Susan had been thrilled to be selected from several other candidates, for employment as the MacLeods' nanny. Now she was not so sure, not having come across this strange attitude in a new mother before. She only hoped there wasn't to be a scene every time her mistress was called upon to feed her child, as she didn't know how best to handle such an awkward situation.

"Susan," Claire's voice broke through her thoughts, "how much longer must I endure this? Apart from being damnably painful, it's making me feel like a bitch feeding a litter of puppies."

"Just a little bit on the other side, Madam," Susan soothed, "and then it's finished for four hours."

"*Four hours?*" Claire gaped in horror. "Do you mean to say I have to go through this disgusting business again in only four hours time?"

"Yes Madam, four feeds a day are necessary for the first weeks of baby's life. After she has put on enough weight, the number of feeds can be reduced." Susan tried to reassure her mistress. "I'm sure you understand the need for frequent feeds right now?"

"I suppose so, but I mean to ask the doctor how soon I can stop this breast-feeding business. I'm sure it can manage perfectly well on cow's milk."

Diana thrived satisfactorily over the next months, despite her mother having abandoned breast-feeding after only three weeks. The wrinkled appearance of her skin vanished, and the tufts of red hair were transformed into a halo of red-gold curls.

An engaging child, she nevertheless failed to enchant her mother who remained distant and largely disinterested. As a result, Diana demonstrated an unfortunate preference for the comfort of her nanny's wide lap. On the rare occasions when Claire picked up her daughter, the child would scream, struggle, and hold chubby arms out to the nanny. Almost flinging the child at Susan, Claire would stalk off in a towering rage.

Jack, on the other hand, clearly adored his little daughter. Calling her by the pet name of Di-Di, he frequently came home early to play with her before bedtime. The baby girl was entirely at ease with her father, and her first word was, predictably, 'Dada'.

Dimly aware of being unreasonable, Claire couldn't help resenting her small daughter's attachment to Jack and the nanny. It was inconceivable to her that her own baby girl preferred plump Susan, and laughed with delight when Jack appeared in the nursery. Caught up in a vortex of illogical jealousy, Claire even considered dismissing the nanny. Common sense prevailed, however, realising such an impulsive gesture would severely curtail her personal freedom. But despite ordering quantities of pretty baby clothes to be made, Claire's sense of isolation persisted...

Emile de Beaurepaire's arrival in town distracted Claire from domestic irritations. She hadn't seen anything of him since the holiday in France, nor had he been able to attend the wedding. He was presently spending a few days with Minette, before his return to France.

A message from Emile arrived at Jack's office. Would he and Claire be free to have lunch with him at the new Indian restaurant on Park Street? Minette and Frederick would also be there, as well as Charlie and his girlfriend, Rose.

Claire was delighted. She looked forward to finally meeting the girl who had managed to ensnare her brother, and whom she had only seen from a distance. Possibly, it was an opportunity to mend bridges with her mother, an icy silence between them having persisted for months. As a result, Minette had seen little of her granddaughter.

Charlie duly arrived…but without his girlfriend. Noticing her brother seemed unusually subdued, Claire assumed it was disappointment because Rose was not present. She meant to discover exactly why at the first opportunity.

Emile's lunch party proved to be tremendous fun. He and Jack clearly enjoyed each other's company, discovering a shared interest in politics and racing. The curries and different rice dishes were deliciously spicy and much enjoyed by everyone…with the exception of Emile's Italian guest.

Vittorio di Rossinanti was on his first trip to India. Noticing the quantity of water he was obliged to consume during the meal, sweat beading his temples, Claire smothered a grin. The Italian *signor* was clearly finding the spiciness difficult to handle!

Despite his burning mouth, Vittorio made no secret of the fact that Jack MacLeod's attractive young wife was very much to his taste. Claire glanced at her husband to see his reaction, but he seemed not to notice, nor to care less. A subtle reminder of the ice water flowing in the man's veins – she thought resentfully.

Warmed by the Italian's attention, the young woman's self-esteem received a welcome boost. Her eyes sparkling with laughter at Vittorio's slightly *risqué* asides, Claire intercepted a glare of disapproval from her mother across the table. In direct consequence, she was provoked into flirting outrageously, encouraging the delighted Italian to utter further fulsome compliments. His dark eyes admiring, he leaned over to tell her she was, *una signora molto bella*.

"You and your husband must visit Tuscany when next you travel to Europe," the man earnestly declared. "It would be my honour to welcome you to my home, and make the visit…memorable."

Aware of the Italian's thinly veiled meaning, Claire smiled dazzlingly. "Why, how very kind, Vittorio! I've no idea if Jack might be planning a trip to Europe, but in the event that he is, I shall insist on a visit to Italy."

"*Eccellente!*" His white teeth flashed. "Of course, you will wish to see a great deal of Emile, so perhaps my villa on the French Côte d'Azur would be more convenient for a visit? It would be more exciting than a stay in the beautiful, but dull countryside in Tuscany. Please come soon… there is much I wish to show you, *mia cara signora!*"

The light flirtation was as stimulating to the young woman as a glass of fizzing champagne. Ignoring her mother's outrage, Claire smiled dazzlingly at the Italian, then glanced quickly away, dark eyelashes sweeping her flushed cheeks.

"And I shall look forward to being shown...everything, *Signor* di Rossignante," she murmured, then turned away to speak to Charlie who was sitting on her other side.

"Charlie, where's Rose?" Claire asked without preamble. "I understood she would be joining us for lunch?"

"I can't for the life of me understand it, Claire," Charlie's usually pleasant countenance darkened. "Rose's father has suddenly started putting all sorts of obstacles in the way of my having anything to do with his daughter."

"Well, what does Rose have to say about it?" Claire demanded with a frown. "When I spotted the two of you at the Saturday Club last week, she was clinging to your arm and gazing up at you in adoration."

"She's...she's upset, of course," Charlie answered, "but I suppose one must understand that she daren't defy her father, who happens to be the new Police Commissioner in Calcutta," he finished glumly.

"What Rose's father is – or isn't – has nothing to do with it, Charlie," Claire's tone was robust. "Is she completely spineless, or what?"

"Don't be so hard on her!" Charlie fired up in defence of his absent love. "It's all very well for you, but Rose is...delicate."

"Poor old Charlie!" Claire looked affectionately at her brother. "You really are smitten, I can see that. Look, has it occurred to you that Rose's father might imagine that you may be nurturing dishonourable intentions towards his darling daughter?"

"What?" Charlie stared at his sister. "I never thought of that. Right, I'll make an appointment as soon as possible and ask his permission to marry Rose. I can also reassure him that I'm earning well enough to keep his daughter in fine style. When I eventually retire from racing, I intend to train with my own yard."

"All I can say is that Rose is damned lucky to have you to as her future husband," Claire leaned over to kiss her brother's cheek. "And I'm sure you will find that her father appreciates your courteous gesture in coming to see him."

"Hope so," he grinned, "as I have the distinct feeling Rose might not appreciate a clandestine elopement on the back of my new Rudge motorcycle."

Two days later, Jack and Claire went to the theatre accompanied by their friends, the Millers. The play was a production of Shakespeare's *Hamlet* by the Calcutta Amateur Dramatic Club, and the final curtain went down to standing applause. Before returning home, the four decided to go for a nightcap at the Saturday Club.

To Claire's amazement, Charlie was already ensconced in the bar, alone, and clearly the worse for wear. Glancing blearily in their direction, he lurched unsteadily to his feet and attempted to force a smile. Horrified that her usually moderate brother had become inebriated to such a degree, Claire hastily helped him back on the bar stool before his legs gave way.

"Charlie, what's the matter?" she asked. "Has *Maman* been bitching at you again?"

"No, not *Maman*, it's...it's—"

Too choked up to speak, the young man laid his forehead on the surface of the bar and weeped helplessly. Alarmed to see his brother-in-law's terrible distress, Jack immediately led the Millers away to a table a discreet distance from the scene. If anyone could get to the bottom of things, Claire would, and rather more easily without an audience.

Shielding her brother from curious stares, Claire tried once again. "Come on, tell me what has upset you so dreadfully?"

Charlie looked up with bloodshot eyes. "Rose. I've lost my darling girl. It's over. Finished...by order of her goddamned snob of a father."

Sitting down on a stool next to him, Claire silently stroked her brother's shaking shoulders. What on earth had been said to induce this devastation? Just a short time ago, Charlie had been planning to ask for Rose's hand in marriage. Obviously, he had been turned down... but why?

"Tell me what happened during your interview with the Police Commissioner," Claire gently probed, "from the beginning."

"I...I made an appointment to see him without difficulty, but when I entered his study, he launched into a tirade, ranting about my 'impertinence' in pestering him at his home. He said he suspected I was nurturing 'unrealistic aspirations' with regard to his daughter."

Charlie swallowed convulsively at the memory. "He informed me that he had forbidden Rose to have anything further to do with me. I asked for his reasons – *Christ*, what a stupid question! Reminding me that my origins were already dubious, he went on to say he had not realised my family background to be highly so undesirable. Not only was my mother running some kind of nursing establishment in the back streets of Calcutta, but it had also come to his ears that the French so-called 'widow' had never been married at all. Her progeny were therefore illegitimate."

The young man's face contracted in pain. "Of course, that meant me. He said that should his daughter be 'shackled' to the likes of myself, she would be precluded from the social *milieu* she had every right to expect for herself. He...he advised me to cast my eyes a great deal lower down the social scale in future."

Claire gazed at her stricken brother, appalled. It was the same old business of their mother's occupation. Would they *never* be free of the taint? Had *Maman* sensibly married Uncle Freddie at the outset, none of this unpleasant rubbish would have ever come about, she thought for the umpteenth time.

Suddenly recalling something else Charlie had said, she suddenly frowned. What was that about being illegitimate? How on earth had *that* vile allegation come to light? Nobody knew of it but themselves...Claire's jaw dropped in horror.

Christina!

She must have bleated to that damned priest, known to be the biggest town crier in Calcutta. She had warned her sister to keep her silly mouth shut, and would certainly have a stern word or two with her when she returned from Simla. But now, she must find a way of comforting her deeply unhappy brother.

"Charlie, I beg you not to take to heart the arrant rubbish that pretentious man was spouting. Everyone knows the Calcutta police force is no great shakes socially, and the fellow's probably incapable of recognising a chap from good a family. Remember you are the grandson of a French..."

"None of that nobility stuff is likely to make an impression, Claire." He took a long swallow of the whisky in front of him. "You've never really understood that, have you? The bottom line is that I'm seen to be socially beyond the pale, and as a result, Rose is lost to me for good. It's...it's hard to come to terms with that."

"So what does Rose have to say about it? Is she so feeble she can't splutter a protest? Fine broken reed she's turning out to be."

"Don't, Claire!" Charlie shook his head violently. "Don't you dare criticise her. Rose is a gentle girl, brought up to respect her father's wishes. I...I admire that in her."

"*Pshaw!*" exploded his sister in disgust. "How can you admire someone who allows her father to treat you so shabbily? It's a damnable disgrace!"

"Claire, will you shut up about Rose," Charlie snarled, signalling to the bar tender to refill his glass. "It's none of your damned business."

"It most certainly is my business when I see my brother mistreated in such a terrible manner!" Claire retorted. "Why don't you spend the night with us? Jack can bring you back here in the morning to pick up your motorcycle. And please don't drink any more...you aren't used to it, you know." Seizing the freshly refilled glass of whisky, she moved it away from her brother's reach

"For Christ's sake, mind your own goddamned business?" Charlie roared in sudden fury. Leaning across his sister, he grabbed back the glass, amber liquid slopping on the bar surface. "Bossy and interfering, you're getting as bad as my mother. Now for pity's sake, Claire – *bugger off!*"

Taking a step back, Claire's eyes glittered with unshed tears. Her brother had never before spoken to her so roughly. Compressing her lips, she made her way back to where her husband was sitting at a table with the Millers. His eyebrows lifted in silent enquiry, but she shook her head despondently.

Jack glanced over at the young man propped up at the bar, his head resting on folded arms on the bar surface. Getting up, he made his way over and placed a sympathetic hand on the thin shoulder that shuddered with irrepressible sobs.

"Come home with us, old chap," he unconsciously echoed Claire's earlier suggestion. "Things will seem better in the morning, and we'll find a way to sort it out. Come on, my friend." Taking his brother-in-law by the elbow, he found himself violently shaken off.

"Leave me alone." Charlie took a swig of his drink. "I'll go home later on, an' face dear ol' *Maman's* harangue." The young man was having noticeable difficulty in enunciating his words. "Fiersh ol' bat she's becoming theesh days."

"Charlie, you can't be serious about going home on the Rudge? Insane in your condition! Come on, old chap, be sensible." Jack attempted once more to engineer the intoxicated young man off the bar stool.

"*Bugger off,* will you?" Charlie snarled, wrenching his arm away and nearly falling off the stool. "I'll g' home when I want, so go back to yer' bossy wife. Dunno how you shtan…stand it," he shoved his empty glass across the counter to be refilled.

With a sigh of resignation, Jack returned to the table where Claire was anxiously waiting with the Millers. Shrugging, he shook his head and sat down to finish his beer. Stubborn little devil, he thought. But he was damned if he was going to leave him to his own devices, as the silly fellow might try riding that machine home.

"Claire, I'll stay on here for a time, and maybe pour your brother into the Daimler after he's entirely incapable of resisting. Go home with Dusty and Felicity, and I'll see you later, hopefully with your brother."

"Thank you, Jack," Claire looked gratefully at her husband. "I've never seen Charlie is such a terrible state before. *Maman* would be horrified, even though his troubles are largely down to her."

"What do you mean?" Jack frowned down at Claire. "How can she have anything to do with the situation?"

"I'll explain later," Claire hurriedly replied, unwilling to go into detail in front of the Millers. "Thank you again, and with any luck you won't have too long to wait."

Two hours later, however, Charlie was still at the bar, unaware of Jack sitting in the shadows a discreet distance away. He alternated between brief dozes with his head on the bar surface, and further demands for whisky. At last, the yawning barman indicated the club was closing down for the night. With a muttered curse, Charlie staggered to his feet and lurched out into the night.

Groping in his pocket for keys to his motorcycle, he became aware of a car drawing up beside him. His brother-in-law got out, and held the car door open for him.

"Come on, be a good lad and get in," Jack caught the young man as he staggered and almost fell. "Tomorrow we'll talk…man to man."

"Whaddaya doin' here?" Charlie muttered. "For Chrissake, will you people jus' *leave me 'lone*?" he suddenly yelled, glaring at Jack in drunken obstinacy. "Get into y' blasted car an' go home."

Before Jack could move, Charlie started the motorcycle, and gunning the engine roared off down the road, tyres squealing in protest. Hurriedly jumping back into his car, Jack followed at a safe distance. The night was hot and humid, a constant drizzle hampering visibility. Peering through the misted up windscreen, he managed to keep the motorcycle in sight as it threaded an erratic path through the evening traffic.

Squinting against the blinding reflection of headlights on a wet road from oncoming vehicles, Jack thanked God it was not as busy as it might have been. The motorcycle suddenly veered left into heavy traffic on Chowringhee, vanishing ahead of cars, vans, rickshaws, and hordes of horse-drawn vehicles.

Jack swore softly, his eyes raking the flow of vehicles for a glimpse of the green Rudge, knowing Charlie was going in the wrong direction. Pulling over to the side of the road, he stopped the car to decide what his next move should be. A throaty roar from behind told Jack his young brother-in-law had realised his mistake. Speeding past the Daimler, the Rudge shot across oncoming traffic towards a tramway, a van driver's mouth falling open in terror as he desperately tried to avoid a collision.

His hands clutching the steering wheel, frozen in helpless horror, Jack saw the motorcycle glance off the van and cartwheel through the air into the path of an oncoming trolleybus. There came the deafening clash of metal grinding on metal, the screech of brakes, and screams of the injured filling the night air, already thick with the overpowering stench of fuel.

Almost falling out of the car, his breathing ragged with dread, Jack ran towards the scene of carnage. Victims of swerving vehicles had been flung across the road, their bodies twisted like rag dolls. The few who had survived the crash squatted numbly by the roadside, or were wandering mindlessly away into the darkness.

Cars were turned upside down, wheels slowly spinning, some with passengers trapped inside. Partially hidden under the trolleybus, a twisted heap of green painted metal was barely recognisable as the Rudge motorcycle. In agonised apprehension, Jack gazed wildly about him, but there was no sign of Charlie.

Frantically searching amongst the mass of injured humanity, Jack suddenly spotted a flash of coppery hair, half-hidden in a gutter on the far side of the road. With an oath, he dashed towards it, dodging people, rickshaws and traumatised onlookers, to kneel in the filthy street, looking down at Charlie's lifeless body sprawled on its back. Dirty gutter water had washed the still face almost clean of blood that had oozed from a hideous gash exposing white bone on his temple. Eyes, startlingly blue under the streetlights, stared sightlessly in apparent surprise.

His own tears mingling with the rain, Jack reached down and gathered up the mangled body of his young brother-in-law. Carrying his tragic burden back to the car, he was struck by the inconsequential thought of how light Charlie was. Gently laying him along the back seat, he edged himself in beside the slight body to wait for the police and ambulances to arrive.

It was almost four o'clock in the morning when Jack finally turned into his own driveway. Having relinquished Charlie's body to an ambulance that would take it to a hospital mortuary, Jack had been obliged to submit a harrowing witness statement at the police station. Ironically, it was the Police Commissioner, himself, who conducted the interview, and Jack savagely noted the imbecile's face was devoid of pity, despite being aware of the European corpse's identity.

With a heavy heart he had driven to Camack Street, knowing it was his duty to inform Minette of her son's untimely demise. Already alarmed by the doorbell ringing insistently in the middle of the night, the Frenchwoman had blanched, a hand pressed against her mouth as if to prevent a scream. Pulling herself together with a visible effort, she muttered thanks to Jack for his consideration, and vanished into her office. As he left, he could hear Minette giving way to overwhelming grief.

Now, it was his dreaded duty to tell Claire of her brother's tragic fate.

Chapter Nine

"*NO!* Oh, Christ...*no!*" Claire screamed in agonised disbelief. "Did you actually see Charlie, Jack? How can you be sure it's him?"

"I held him in my arms," Jack told the distraught girl. "There was nothing anyone could do for him, nor for a great many other people involved in that accident."

"Other people? I don't care about other people when it's my darling brother who..."

"Well, you should care!" Jack snapped. "Especially since the pile-up was the direct result of Charlie's erratic behaviour on that blasted machine of his."

In her extreme grief, Claire was beyond reason. "Couldn't you have forced him to get into the car? He's such a skinny thing, I'm sure you could have managed..."

"Stop it, Claire!" Jack controlled his own anger with difficulty. "You must know I tried my damnedest to persuade the obstinate little devil to come home with me. He saw me off...rather as he did to you, my dear girl. I'm afraid the fault lies entirely at your brother's door."

"What?" Claire wildly shook her head. "Easy to blame him because he's dead...*dead!*" her voice rose hysterically. "That bigoted Police Commissioner and his pathetic daughter can count themselves responsible. As for *Maman*, I'll never forgive her for this, never!"

"Come on, Claire," Jack put his arm about her heaving shoulders. "Drop the recriminations for now. Have a lie down on your bed, and I'll send Susan in with a snifter of brandy to help settle you. Maybe the doctor should come?"

Her body shuddering with uncontrollable sobs, Claire allowed herself to be led into the bedroom. Sitting numbly on her bed, she was seized by a devastating sense of loss that the good-natured brother she had always adored had gone forever.

Over the next three days, Claire remained in her bedroom, inconsolable, and refusing to eat. She vacillated between screaming vengeance against Rose and her father, and sobbing until she was physically sick. Neither would she have anything to do with her baby daughter. Distraught himself by the tragedy, Jack was at his wits' end.

Driven to desperation by his wife's continuing inability to come to terms with her brother's death, he eventually sought Minette's help. Accompanied by a tearful Christina who had returned from Simla only days before, the Frenchwoman entered her daughter's bedroom, Sonia close behind. Claire lay on her bed, facing the wall.

"Whoever that is...leave me alone. Just *go*, will you?" she snapped in a bad-tempered voice. "How many more times do I need to say it?"

"*Chèrie*, I'm told you aren't coping with Charlie's death," Minette approached the figure on the bed. "You must stop this endless grieving, Claire, for it achieves nothing. You have a responsibility towards little Di-Di, as well as your husband."

"*What?*" Claire turned a ravaged face to glare at her mother. "*You* are preaching to *me* of family responsibility?" she yelled. "When you are indirectly responsible for Charlie's death? Look at the result of your so-precious independence, not to mention the fact you didn't bother to get yourself properly married in the first place."

As her daughter's words sank in, Minette took a step backwards, a hand going involuntarily to her throat. Claire looked at her sister who stood as if turned to stone, her eyes puffy with weeping.

"Go on, Christina...tell our mother how you consider yourself illegitimate, just like you told that damned priest who promptly blabbed the juicy titbit all over Calcutta! *That's* the reason why the Police Commissioner had the nerve to fling Charlie's 'dubious origins' and 'highly undesirable background' in his face! Telling our brother that the circumstances of his birth rendered him unsuitable, even as a companion for his spineless daughter."

Colour suffused the younger girl's face, then receded, leaving her white to the lips. "It w...was in *Confession*!" she stammered. "F...Father O'Donnell isn't supposed—"

"How could you be so stupid?" Claire interrupted scornfully. "I told you a million times the blasted man wasn't to be trusted!"

"And if I've told you once, I've told you a thousand times, that your father and I were *legally* married." Minette had recovered herself. "Why do you always have to over-dramatise everything in such a sickening way, Claire?"

"Oh, go back to your precious nursing home that means so much to you, *Maman*," she said tiredly. "A long time ago I badly needed my mother…but you weren't there for me. I don't need you now, so clear off, and take your awful appendage with you."

Her face taut with a mixture of hurt and fury, Minette whirled and left the room, a glowering Sonia trailing in her wake. As she stalked out to the waiting car, a warning from Jane Ogilvy, her closest friend throughout the years, surfaced to the forefront of her mind. Long, long ago, she had begged Minette to sanctify her civil marriage to Patrick O'Hara in the eyes of the Catholic Church. Aside from any religious aspect, Jane had emphasised the impact it would have on the status of her children within the existing codes of society.

But the issue had been set aside, and then it was too late. Patrick was dead. In the years that had followed, it had never entered Minette's mind that it would return to haunt her in such a devastating way. Banishing the image of Jane's reproachful face from her mind, Minette's mouth firmed. That the tragedy of her son's death might be laid at her door simply did not bear thinking about. Even indirectly. No, it was easier to concentrate on Claire, who seemed to be developing into a cold and vicious person.

Minette glanced back at the young girl following in her wake, thanking God she would always have the comfort of her sweet Sonia. Settling herself in the Daimler with her youngest snuggling up close, she instructed the driver to return to Camack Street.

"I'm so terribly, terribly sorry," Christina whispered. "I can hardly believe Father O'Donnell would betray the confidence of the Confessional…"

"Well, he did," answered her sister shortly. "And it's not me to whom you should be apologising, but poor Charlie. Only you can't, because he's dead."

"*Don't!*" Christina burst into noisy tears. "Don't be so cruel! As it is, I can hardly bear it that Charlie has gone…"

Looking at her stricken face, Claire felt a flicker of shame. Of course, the poor thing must be feeling as devastated as herself. It was mean to have rubbed it in as she had. Swinging her legs out of bed, Claire put her arms about her weeping sister. The two young women huddled together, tears mingling, mourning the loss of a brother beloved of them both.

Charlie's funeral took place the next day. During the service, Claire did not bother to even glance in her mother's direction. Neither could she bear to watch the flower-bedecked coffin holding her brother's body being lowered into a freshly dug grave. Catching Frederick's eye, she was aware he was silently begging her to speak to Minette. Her lips compressing, she sought Christina's hand, and the two girls held hands tightly until the end. Leaving the cemetery, she pointedly ignored her mother.

Over the following weeks, the rift between Claire and Minette remained firm, neither of them prepared to try and resolve matters. It troubled Christina, although she understood her older sister's reasoning and, in principle, agreed with her. Their lives would indeed have been transformed had their mother agreed to marry Frederick, that kindly man who, for years, had played an important part in their lives. Fiercely loyal, he adored Marguerite de Merencourt...who casually took him for granted.

For Claire, there was much that acutely reminded her of Charlie's bright presence. She could not bear to go to the racecourse, neither would she tolerate conversations relating to Jack's string of racehorses that her brother used to ride. Even the Saturday Club was off limits, for it brought back memories of how she had failed to bring her brother safely home on that fateful night. Another unexpected blow was that Turka, the old Arab horse that had taught Charlie to ride, died quietly in his loose box two days after her brother's death. She swore it was from grief...

Unable to rescue Claire from the depression swamping her, Jack persuaded Christina to stay for a time, but even her presence did little to lift Claire's leaden spirits. The doctor eventually recommended a trip away from Calcutta, a destination devoid from painful association with her dead brother.

Subsequent to a private consultation with Minette and Frederick, Jack decided he would speak to Edward Woodson about the possibility of combining business with pleasure. He planned to take Claire to Cape Town in South Africa for a few weeks holiday, but he would first be obliged to briefly visit his company's head office in Durban. It was the only way he could take compassionate leave.

Just as soon as business was concluded, he and Claire would take a leisurely train journey to Cape Town. He would rent a villa by a beach, where they could spend three relaxing weeks before sailing back to India.

From all accounts, the accommodation and service was superb on the train, lacking nothing by way of luxury. The railway carriages possessed wide picture windows, through which passengers could view the vivid beauty of the African countryside, maybe spot a few wild animals roaming in the bush. Each carriage possessed a dedicated steward who would attend to every requirement. With a wry grin, Jack felt certain Claire would relish that particular aspect.

His main reservation was a small risk of coming across Anne Winterton during their few days in Durban. He had no wish to re-open old wounds, and neither did he want to run the risk of Claire maybe sensing something amiss. But maybe he was over-dramatising the situation, for there would be a great deal else to distract her.

When told of the South African holiday, Claire merely nodded indifferently. Neither did she seem perturbed at the prospect of her baby daughter staying with her estranged mother during her absence. Jack shook his head. Although he was relieved not to be subjected to infuriated outbursts from Claire, it concerned him that she did not appear to care about leaving her child for such a time.

Listlessly following Jack's suggestion that she organise herself a new wardrobe to take on holiday, Claire visited Hall and Anderson's departmental store. She made her way to the fashion department, seeking out her old friend and mentor, Naomi Bernstein, who had always understood her.

Although delighted to see the young woman, Naomi was concerned to note new shadows under the sapphire eyes. Her general demeanour was lacklustre, and she was thinner – yet again. Watching the girl absently riffling through a catalogue, Naomi casually asked if all was well at home.

Claire's mouth compressed, and involuntary tears sprang into her eyes. "Oh, Naomi, I can't begin to tell you what a nightmare my life has been. Charlie, my darling, darling brother was killed in a terrible car crash. Even now, I dream about it..."

In between sobs, Claire recounted details of the tragedy to the horrified dressmaker, who recalled the young jockey as being a pleasant young chap. Why was it, she wondered savagely to herself, that nice people seem to disappear from the face of the earth, whilst the rascally majority continue to thrive?

Glancing at Claire's grief-stricken face, she could see it was time to put a stop to the excessive and unhealthy grief overwhelming the girl. After all, the poor fellow had been dead for over five months, and it was clear she was hovering on the brink of a nervous breakdown.

"Dearest girl, I understand how sad you feel over the loss of your brother, but it is high time you put your grief to one side. You have a family that depends on you. No, *don't* shake your head at me like that!" Naomi's tone was unusually sharp.

"Do you think Charlie would want you to drift through life like a miserable little ghost? Wallowing in a sea of self-pity? Of course not." Naomi took Claire's hands and looked into her tear-filled eyes. "You know perfectly well he would have hated it."

"Yes, but—"

"And since you are not in the least way responsible for your brother's death, *do* stop behaving as if you were." Naomi continued inexorably. "As a matter of fact, it's your husband who has borne the brunt of this tragedy. Was it not he who retrieved your brother's dead body? I think you should remember that, young lady."

Claire's mouth had fallen open in shock whilst Naomi was talking. Had it been anyone else lecturing her, she would have exploded in rage. As it was, she was startled to be confronted by a vision of herself in a not-so-attractive light. It was shaming, and Claire was brought up short.

It was true she had given little thought to Jack's mental anguish over Charlie's death. He had been very fond of her brother. She also remembered how he had carried Charlie's dead body to the car, waiting there, until police and ambulances arrived. That must have been a terrible experience. Reluctantly, she reflected how patient he had been over her own intransigent behaviour, even to planning an unexpected holiday. Instead of being appreciative, she had remained self-obsessed.

Claire hugged the older woman. "I know you're right, Naomi, and I've been thoughtless where Jack is concerned. I'll try to make up for it during our holiday."

"Good girl!" Naomi smiled, pleased that Claire had not fired up in a fury. "Now, let's look at cocktail dresses, and maybe a long evening gown in this gorgeous material we unpacked only this morning? We should also think about beach outfits."

Half an hour later, Claire left the shop, feeling decidedly happier than when she walked in. Having chosen a good-sized wardrobe to take away on holiday, she was discovering a renewed interest in attractive clothes. Her resolve to be a generally nicer person did not extend to her mother, despite Christina's pleas to patch things up. She refused to even consider it, as Minette was the common denominator of her family being viewed as social pariahs.

The weeks flew past, and the morning of the MacLeods' departure to Bombay finally arrived. Claire was looking forward to the trip, Jack having booked them to stay at the Taj Mahal Hotel for two days. Leaving her to amuse herself, he would be absent in meetings with business associates and government ministers for most of the day. On the third day, they would board a great liner bound for Durban in South Africa.

Jack's driver was already outside the house in the Daimler, ready to drive the MacLeods to the station. His instructions were to return and collect Christina, little Diana and the nanny, and then deliver them to Camack Street. A hired van was parked behind the Daimler, where two house servants were loading it with trunks and leather valises, the car's boot being adequate for overnight luggage and Claire's vanity case.

Jack was outside to oversee the loading of luggage, when an elegantly attired Claire emerged from the bedroom in a cloud of perfume. Christina was still in the nursery, busy with last minute packing of her small niece's possessions. Moments later, Nanny Susan appeared in the hallway, little Diana in her arms.

"Come Baby...give Mummy a big kiss goodbye," Susan encouraged the toddler. "Quickly now, she'll be leaving very soon."

"NO!" Diana leaned away from her mother. "No wanta kiss!" The child stared at Claire with defiant china blue eyes. "*No kiss Mama!*"

"Don't then, you stupid child!" Claire straightened up, annoyed to have bent to receive her daughter's kiss. "And Susan, will you stop calling my daughter, Baby. She has a name, so please use it."

"Yes, Madam," Susan answered in her soft sing-song voice, bewildered by the unexpected attack. She knew better than to argue with her mistress, however.

"And for heaven's sake, will you *do* something about your speech," Claire snapped, still smarting from the child's rejection. "I don't want Diana to start speaking with a *chi-chi* accent, thank you."

"Yes, Madam," Susan muttered, wondering how she could improve her speech to her mistress's satisfaction. Not for the first time, she wondered about the security of her post in the MacLeod household. It was often such an uphill battle to please Madam.

There was, however, little that she could do about Di-Di's hostile reaction to her mother, which was hardly surprising since Madam spent so little time with her child. On the rare occasions she came into the nursery, she seemed only interested in finding fault with unimportant things. It was rare that she bothered to even talk to the little girl.

It had already occurred to Susan that her mistress might be jealous of the attachment her small charge had to herself. But what did she expect? Di-Di was with her all day long, and it was Susan's hand – her hand alone – that attended to the baby girl from the day she was born.

Sensing tension in the atmosphere, Diana leaned her head against the nanny's shoulder and began sucking her thumb. With an irritable exclamation, Claire smacked the child's hand away from her mouth. Wide-eyed with shock, Diana set up a piercing howl that brought Christina running from the nursery.

"Darling, whatever is the matter?" Christina stroked the child's copper curls. "Are you crying because Mummy is going? Don't worry, Auntie Christina will look after you."

"If you must know, she's bawling because I smacked her hand for thumb-sucking," Claire interrupted. "Diana knows perfectly well she's not to do it, but I daresay dear old Susan allows her to suck away to her heart's content behind my back."

"But, she's still only a *baby*!" Christina exclaimed in shocked tones. "You can't expect such a little thing to remember all your rules and regulations."

"Oh, don't start preaching, for pity's sake!" Claire snapped. "I'm Diana's mother, and it's up to me to decide what is best for her, don't you think?"

"What's going on here?" Jack asked, coming up the steps to join the *fracas* in the hall. "Di-Di, come and say goodbye to your daddy!"

Seeing her father, the little girl stopped crying and wriggled down from the nanny's hold. Smiling through her tears, she toddled over to him holding out her arms to be picked up. Laughing, Jack tickled her ribs, making the child squeal delightedly. With a final kiss, he handed his daughter over to Christina. Resting her face against her aunt's shoulder, thumb back in her mouth, she nevertheless kept a wary eye on her mother.

Watching the interaction between Diana and her father, Claire felt herself excluded as if from a magic circle. A wave of anger washed over her, seeing her child happily go to everybody – with the exception of herself. It really was *too* humiliating! Why couldn't she have had a sweet baby boy, who would have adored his mummy? It simply wasn't fair, and she ground her teeth in frustration.

Forcing a smile, Claire kissed her sister, and then swept out of the house to the car. Jack followed, carrying his briefcase and several folded newspapers under his arm. Ready to be the fascinating companion as always – thought Claire nastily, as her husband got into the car beside her.

The two days in Bombay passed in a whirl of pleasant activity. Tired from the train journey, Claire ordered breakfast from room service, and went back to bed for a couple of hours. Later she would join her husband and two business associates for lunch at the Willingdon Cricket Club, a surprisingly green oasis on the edge of central Bombay.

The following afternoon, the MacLeods attended a swimming party given by a wealthy business associate at Juhu Beach. Clad in a new white swimming costume, Claire reclined in a deckchair shaded by a clump of palm trees. She had just refused an invitation to join the group of people who were running down the beach to bathe in the decidedly opaque sea. God alone knew what filthy disease one might catch! Much more amusing to remain here in the shade, holding court to a couple of unattached chaps, neither of whom cared to immerse themselves either.

On their last evening, Jack and Claire attended a formal dinner at the Governor of Bombay's residence on Malabar Hill. It was an opportunity for her to wear one of her beautiful new evening dresses, a navy chiffon creation encrusted with seed pearl flowers dotted here and there. A double string of pearls completed the ensemble. Surreptitiously glancing at her husband, the young woman was elated to have perhaps seen a spark of admiration in his eyes.

Self-confident, sparkling, and witty as she invariably was in the public eye, Claire was complimented by the Governor over her grasp of world affairs. Turning to Jack, he congratulated him for netting such a treasure who was not only attractive, but extremely intelligent. By the end of the stay, her natural insouciance was on the way to recovery.

The MacLeods were, of course, travelling First Class. Claire could not help feeling a thrill when their steward showed them to a magnificent stateroom, every surface bedecked with bouquets of flowers. A bottle of champagne stood cooling in an ice bucket, together with a basket of exotic fruit. Comfortable-looking armchairs were set around a low table, and Claire noticed the cabin's soft furnishings were of superb quality. A narrow door opened into a good-sized, well-equipped shower room.

Resting on the wide double bed, a glass of champagne in her hand, Claire sighed with pleasure. So far, the holiday was great fun, and Jack had not yet attempted to read his newspapers when they were alone. That, in itself, was encouraging.

Perhaps she should seize the advantage to try and enchant her husband during this cruise? After all, he had clearly been pleased over her beguilement of his crabby old business associates the other evening. Would it not be a crowning glory to gain the love of her dour Scotsman at last?

Claire was pleased to note that she and Jack were seated at the Captain's table for dinner. The enormous dining room was complete with crystal chandeliers, its opulence of décor making it seem incredible to be on the high seas. Attentive stewards ensured diners lacked for nothing, and glasses were kept filled with a selection of fine wines.

They were in the company of two middle-aged couples, and two men travelling on their own, apparently of importance in the political world. Wisely, Claire set out to converse almost exclusively with the two matrons at the table, in the certain knowledge it would place her at an advantage for the rest of the voyage. And it did.

Weeks at sea passed in an agreeable haze for her. Mornings were spent lying in a deckchair with a book, tanning her skin to a golden shade enhancing the vividness of her eyes. Jack was generally absent all morning, having received a permanent invitation to visit the Bridge. By the time she joined her husband for lunch, Claire made sure she had showered and changed into a pretty day frock.

Noticing young Mrs MacLeod's deepening colour, compliments flowed from the two unattached men at the table that evening, as well as from the Captain himself. To her secret delight, Claire detected interest in Jack's eyes, confirmed later when he asked her for a dance in between courses at dinner. Nestling against her husband's chest, Claire smiled in anticipation of the night to come.

Jack did, indeed, make love to his wife that night. And for the first time since her wedding night, Claire made an attempt to cooperate, certain to elicit the response she so desperately sought. But it was quickly over, and Jack rolled over to fall asleep at once. Choking back tears of bitter disappointment, she lay awake in the dark, praying she would not fall pregnant from such a lacklustre experience.

Deciding to punish her husband for his indifference of the previous night, over dinner the next evening, she engaged in animated conversation with one of the unattached men at their table. Oblivious of emotional undercurrents, the delighted fellow was only too happy to reciprocate the attractive lady's faintly *risqué* banter.

Unperturbed, Jack puffed at his cigar, and cradled a balloon glass of fine cognac with appreciation, seemingly unaware of his wife's efforts to inspire jealousy. Neither did he appear to notice that she danced several times with her admirer. On the pretext of a headache, Claire angrily flounced back to the cabin at the end of the meal.

She spent the next day brooding, unable to understand why the man first blew hot and then cold, and she was at a loss as to what to do next. Finally, she decided to set it aside, and not allow her husband's unnatural attitude to ruin her holiday.

The ship finally docked in Durban's beautiful harbour. The weather was fine and warm and without any lingering humidity. After disembarking and passing through Customs, the MacLeods took a company car to the hotel where a suite of rooms had been booked for their stay.

Gazing out of the car window during the drive to the hotel, Claire was entranced by the sheer beauty of the countryside. Trees and foliage along the road glistened vibrantly green after a rainstorm the previous day, and she glimpsed impressively large properties along a beach of white sand, shimmering beside an aquamarine sea. How lovely to own such a property, she thought enviously.

The car turned up a gravelled drive, and came to a halt under the colonnaded entrance portico of the Palace Hotel, an imposing building encircled by magnificent gardens. Boughs of purple wisteria wound their way about the supporting columns, and brass carriage lamps were fixed on either side to illuminate the area during hours of darkness. A liveried doorman came to open the car door for the MacLeods to alight.

Two dark-skinned boys in scarlet livery appeared, and in no time trunks and valises were loaded on to a purpose-made trolley. A boy at each end, they wheeled the trolley up a ramp and disappeared into a side door.

After registering at the reception desk, an obsequious under-manager showed Jack and Claire to their suite. Composed of three airy rooms, there were displays of fresh flowers on every surface, and a folded newspaper lay on a low table in front of comfortable armchairs. That should warm the cockles of Jack's heart – thought the young woman sourly – a perfect excuse not to talk.

Sitting down in an armchair, Claire glanced through a train brochure for the journey they were to embark upon to Cape Town in three days time. She had never actually seen a wild animal, except for miserable creatures incarcerated in zoos. But here it might be possible to see elephant, zebra and lion...how marvellous that would be!

"Don't forget we are expected for cocktails with Sir Alan and Lady Braithwaite this evening," Jack spoke from behind the newspaper. "Please make sure you are ready in plenty of time. Remember he's the Managing Director of Wallis & Fairbairn, and it simply won't do for us to turn up late."

"Don't worry, I'll be ready," Claire answered, putting down the brochure. "I suppose I had better have a short snooze before my bath."

Chapter Ten

Jack frowned and looked at his watch for the fourth time. Claire still had not emerged from the bedroom, and the company car had been waiting outside for ten minutes. Five minutes more, and they were going to be late – precisely what he was anxious to avoid. Claire really could be the bloody limit at times! Intending to chivvy her up, Jack strode towards the bedroom.

"Here I am!" the object of Jack's bad-tempered cogitation emerged in a waft of expensive perfume. "And don't accuse me of being late, because I'm not." Claire twirled in front of her husband, the fine straps of the sapphire silk gown she wore in perfect contrast with the golden tan of her shoulders. "So, how do I look?"

"Very nice, but you're cutting things too damned fine as usual," Jack grumpily told her. "The car has been waiting for ages outside the hotel."

"Why, I'm quite blown away by your enthusiasm, Jack," she remarked caustically. "I might as well wear sackcloth and ashes, for all you seem to notice."

"Don't start that rubbish, for God's sake!" Jack turned to leave. "And how like you to pick a fight just as we're about to leave for an important reception."

"Yes, I can see it's too much to ask that my husband gives me a few seconds of his attention," Claire snapped as she stalked to the door. "Don't worry, I shall go out of my way to charm your precious Sir Alan and his wife."

Ten minutes later, the limousine deposited the MacLeods outside the entrance of the Braithwaite residence. Emerging from the car, Claire was impressed by the very size of the house, the columns of its wide portico heavy with purple bougainvillea. Unusually informal, it was Sir Alan, himself, who came out to greet them, followed by his wife. Jack and Claire were ushered into a reception room illuminated by banks of candles, where people were chatting, sipping champagne, and sampling delicacies offered by liveried black servants. A trio of musicians played softly in the background.

"We've been dying to meet Jack's mysterious bride," Helen Braithwaite told her as they entered the room. "Especially when we regularly hear from Calcutta what a terrific asset you are, and how well you organise endless social occasions for the company."

"How kind of you to say so, Lady Braithwaite!" Claire was genuinely pleased. "Actually, I enjoy it for one meets so many interesting people."

"Do call me Helen, my dear," smiled the older woman. "Now, who shall I introduce you to first? Oh yes, come and meet Oliver and Gillian Fermoyne. Jack may remember them from years ago?" Helen started towards to a group, Claire close behind. Glancing over her shoulder to make sure Jack was following, her mouth fell open in amazement. Only a few feet away, her husband was standing as if frozen, staring across the room at someone. Raw longing was etched on his face, and he closed his eyes momentarily as if in acute pain. Light-headed with shock, Claire followed the line of his gaze to a tall blonde woman leaning nonchalantly against a wall, a glass of white wine in her hand. Holding Jack's gaze, the woman's wide mouth quirked, as if the two of them shared a delicious secret.

Black rage rose as a tide in the young woman's throat, threatening to choke her. This must be the woman who had led Jack astray when he was supposedly engaged to her. Whose name had exploded from his lips, whilst making love to his bride of a few miserable hours! Now, he was casually exposing her to the humiliation of seeing him look at another woman with undisguised love. Claire's breath came short and fast. Added to which, it seemed Jack's feelings for his tart remained constant, despite the existence of his wife and a child he claimed to adore.

Despicable cad! Claire gasped, desperately trying to suppress her fury. How dare he treat her in such a cavalier manner? This cruel revelation for Jack's indifference was a devastating slap in the face. As for her earlier naïve efforts to gain his affection – she now cringed with mortification! Especially since the bloody man must have been aware of it, secretly laughing to see her making an utter fool of herself.

"Claire, are you feeling all right?" Helen was looking at her in concern. "Would you like to sit down for a moment?"

"No...no thank you Helen," the girl pulled herself together and forced a laugh. "I felt a little giddy for a moment, probably due to weeks on a rolling ship."

"Yes, I remember how odd it felt to be once more on dry land," Helen replied. "It should have disappeared by tomorrow. Let me introduce you to Oliver and Gillian."

The remainder of the evening seemed interminable. Fighting an overwhelming desire to claw the blonde woman's smug face, Claire smiled, laughed and chatted vivaciously, the effort costing her every ounce of self-control. And despite herself, she was drawn to surreptitiously watch the sickening interaction between her husband and the blonde woman. The battle to control her turbulent emotions was exhausting, and Claire longed to return to the hotel. Then, at long last, it seemed reasonable to plead tiredness. Her expression carefully blank, she signalled to her husband that she wished to leave. Locating Sir Alan and Helen, Claire thanked them for their kind hospitality, and complimented them on their beautiful home. Helen smiled with pleasure, and took the girl's hands in both of her own.

"My dear, I know Jack will be busy at the office for the whole of tomorrow morning, so how would you like to do some shopping? Anne here, has offered to take you round the best of our shops, then the two of you can join Jack and Alasdair for lunch at our local Club."

Anne? Claire felt sick.

"That sounds like fun," she answered, smiling at her blonde adversary who had come over to join them. "How kind of you to give up your morning to me."

"Good." Anne nodded. "I'll call for you around ten o'clock, shall I? We'll do the shops first, and then have a cup of coffee before joining the men for lunch."

"Lovely!" she agreed, noting the expression of horror on her husband's face with immense satisfaction. "I shall be ready promptly at ten."

A profound silence existed in the car on the way back to the hotel. Glancing sideways at her husband's grim profile, Claire grinned maliciously into the darkness. *Excellent!* Let the bloody man spend his morning worried to death, wondering what juicy details might be divulged to his darling wife!

Gazing unseeingly out of the window, Claire reflected on how uncharacteristically stupid it was to have brought her to Durban. It beggared belief that Jack had taken the risk of disturbing the proverbial hornets' nest! Perhaps he was sufficiently arrogant to imagine she lacked the perception to notice what was under her very nose? He was about to discover the error of his ways.

Having observed the undeniable chemistry between her husband and the Winterton woman throughout the evening, Claire was convinced that given the opportunity, Jack would commit adultery without a second thought. She would make certain of putting the kibosh on *that* – she thought grimly.

That night, Jack insisted on making love to his obviously reluctant wife with unusual intensity, unaware – or uncaring – that she lay stiff and immobile beneath him, her eyes squeezed shut in angered disgust. For Claire, it was the ultimate insult to be pretending to have sex with that hag, at whom he had been making sheep's eyes all evening.

As soon as she was able, Claire slid out of bed and crept into the bathroom. Turning on the shower, she let the water run until it was as hot as she could bear. Scalding tears of humiliation running down her cheeks, she scrubbed at her body in an effort to wash away every vestige of her husband's attentions. Satisfied at last, she dried herself off and returned to bed. Staring into the inky darkness, Claire resolved to return the insult one day – and in spades!

The following morning, Claire was still asleep when Jack left the hotel for the office. Waking an hour later to find the room empty, she ordered a pot of coffee from room service, and propped up on her pillows, began planning on how she should handle her husband's tart later that morning.

Rather than pretend ignorance of their grubby hole-and-corner affair, she decided to allow the woman to think Jack had confessed the liaison to his wife. It would be interesting to see her reaction to that. She would also put a spoke in the hag's wheel, should she be contemplating a renewal of delightful assignations with her husband.

Promptly at ten o'clock that morning, the Wintertons' car drew up outside the hotel entrance. Impeccably turned out, Claire was waiting in the foyer, her dark hair casually brushed into a curling halo. Seeing the limousine arrive, she skipped down the front steps, and waited for the driver to open the rear door. From the back seat, Anne Winterton watched the girl approaching with a thoughtful expression.

"Good morning Mrs Winterton, I do hope I haven't kept you waiting?" Claire said breathlessly, climbing into the car. "I've been so looking forward to this expedition."

"I've only just arrived, so you are bang on time," Anne assured her. "And do please call me Anne. Mrs Winterton makes me feel positively ancient!"

"Thank you, I shall! As for being ancient, why, that's ridiculous!" she declared. "I only hope I look as good when I'm your age."

The older woman glanced sharply at the girl, wondering if she detected a touch of cattiness? Apparently not, for Claire MacLeod was smiling ingenuously. Nevertheless, the allusion to Anne's superior age stung, and her lips tightened. Maybe this jaunt was not such a good idea after all?

Leaning back against the seat, she mused over why she had impulsively offered to escort Jack's little wife on a shopping expedition. She supposed it was curiosity, maybe to look over the girl he had married and gain some insight into their personal life. She also needed to make up her mind whether this girl was a threat with regard to Jack's devotion. She was attractive enough, and Anne felt more than a twinge of jealousy.

Lovers had come and gone over the years, but Jack MacLeod had remained special to her. When she heard he had married some girl in Calcutta, she had wept and thrown tantrums with jealousy for days, much to her husband's mystification. Fortunately, Alasdair had put it down to 'that time of the month'.

Now, amazingly, Jack had returned to Durban, albeit with the inconvenience of a wife. It crossed Anne's mind, however, that she and Jack might arrange a private moment or two together. Alasdair was leaving the following day on a business trip, so the coast there would be clear. Obviously, something had to be arranged to distract the silly little thing sitting next to her...

The next two hours passed pleasurably enough for Claire, the shops displaying fashions rather more up-to-date than in Calcutta. Loaded with parcels, she followed Anne into a café where they were escorted to a table. Sinking into a chair, she reflected aloud that an extra *valise* might have to be bought for her lovely new purchases.

A pot of coffee and a cake stand duly arrived, but Anne shook her head and carefully fitted a cigarette into a long jade cigarette holder. A waiter immediately appeared, ready to strike a match. Drawing in the smoke with evident pleasure, Anne allowed it to escape through her nostrils. Enjoying a large slice of Victoria sponge cake, Claire couldn't help being fascinated by the elegance and beauty of the jade cigarette holder. She could just imagine the air of sophistication it would inspire in Calcutta, and resolved to buy an identical one at the first opportunity.

Taking a sip of her coffee, Anne regarded Claire over the rim of her cup. "Aren't you afraid of putting on weight by eating all that cake?" she enquired. "Personally, I wouldn't dare to run the risk of looking chubby in my clothes."

"I don't think I need to worry just yet, Anne," Claire answered, mopping crumbs from her mouth. "My mother says that one must take care of what one eats only after the age of forty…and I'm still a long way from that."

Yet another oblique reference to her age! Anne raised pencilled eyebrows, but did not reply. Was this girl so damned obtuse that she was unable to realise her stupid remarks were offensive?

"It's marvellous to see Jack again after so long," she casually changed the subject. "We saw a great deal of him during his last visit to Durban."

"Yes," Claire answered coolly. "I know. After all, he over-stayed his trip by several months due to your…er…*liaison*, did he not? Of course, Jack and I were not married at that time, but your husband can't have been too thrilled! Or did he not know of it?"

Taken completely off-guard, the older woman flushed a dull red. "My dear girl, I can't imagine what you hope to gain by such a tasteless insinuation. I really think—"

"Oh, come off it, Anne!" Claire grinned. "No point in denying it, as Jack and I have no secrets between us. Don't worry, I can be the soul of discretion. Of course, things must be different now," she continued conversationally. "We both place great value on our marriage, and have the added bond of a baby girl whom Jack simply adores. I know he would never risk jeopardising that. Goodness, isn't this coffee delicious? I must remember to buy a couple of tins to take home to Calcutta."

Stunned beyond her wildest imaginings, Anne stared into her coffee cup as if to seek answers in the dregs. For God's sake, had Jack really regaled his wife with details of their affair? Aside from being hurtful, it was insane for he must know how important it was for secrecy to be maintained. Alasdair must *never* find out. Her husband had forgiven an earlier discretion, but should he discover this infidelity, Anne knew he would rid himself of her without hesitation. She certainly did not want that.

She cast a furtive glance at the girl whom she had badly underestimated, and her mouth firmed. It was imperative to silence the creature.

"I have no idea what you are talking about, my dear Claire," Anne stated coldly. "Figments of a jealous little girl's imagination perhaps? Neither will I listen to slanderous allegations against the fine man you married, and should you aspire to become a senior company wife, I advise you to consider your words well before opening your mouth in this disgraceful—"

"Say whatever you please, Anne," Claire interrupted, her tone equally icy, "but you and I both know the truth of the matter. Perhaps I should make it clear that I will not tolerate a revival of your hole-and-corner affair with my husband? In such an instance, I would be obliged to seek Helen Braithwaite's advice."

Visibly shaking with fury, Anne abruptly leapt to her feet, the chair legs scraping on the floor. Placing her hands flat on the table, she leaned towards the girl sitting calmly opposite, rouged lips drawn back over her teeth.

"Don't think to threaten me, you little vixen!" she snarled. "Jack would be simply appalled to know of your disgraceful attempts to sully our names. Personally, I've had more than enough of you, so kindly return to the hotel at once. My driver will take you. I leave it to you to explain why you were unable to join us for lunch at the club."

Unruffled by the threat, Claire grinned at the infuriated older woman. "Oh, I daresay he and I will have a laugh about it later on. About lunch today, I forgot to mention I had accepted an invitation elsewhere. Sorry about that – remiss of me! Thank you for your time this morning, dear lady, it has been positively...*illuminating*."

Back in the hotel bedroom, Claire dumped her parcels on the floor and kicked off her shoes. Well, Jack's tart had been seen off, she was sure of that. Without a shadow of doubt, the woman would now be tattling about her to Jack. So what? Claire mentally shrugged. Her dear husband hadn't a leg to stand on. And should he be unwise enough to lecture her, she would remind him of that. Meanwhile, she would order a sandwich from room service, her claim of a lunch date having been a fib.

Three hours later, Claire was dozing on her bed when Jack burst unceremoniously into the bedroom. His expression thunderous, he strode over to confront his wife.

"What the *hell* do you mean by that insulting attack on Anne Winterton this morning?" he bellowed. "Inferring she was promiscuous, of all things? The poor woman was stunned to hear a stream of sordid language coming from my wife! How dare you behave in such a disgraceful way with a company director's wife?"

"Stop right there, you damned hypocrite!" Claire sprang from the bed to face her husband, a long pent-up fury spilling over. "Don't you accuse me of sordidness, when you and that woman were once gaily indulging in tawdry shenanigans behind her unfortunate husband's back! At a time when you happened to be engaged to *me*!"

"How did—"

"You've got a nerve, Jack MacLeod! When I think of how I was forced to put up with you bawling another woman's name in my ear on our wedding night!" Claire spat. "How I am regularly obliged to endure the insult of you pretending I'm that woman every time we make love! How sleazy is that, might I ask? Having put up with your wishy-washy attitude towards me for years, I'm damned if I'll allow you to take up cudgels on that bloody tart's behalf."

Speechless, Jack stared at his wife, amazed by the violence of her reaction, and appalled his affair seemed to be common knowledge. Anne had not specified that during her tearful complaints about Claire. Who else knew of it? Christ Almighty, hadn't they gone out of their way to be discreet at the time? Although in the past, a scandal of this enormity could terminate his career, and would certainly spell ruination of Anne's reputation as well as her marriage to Alasdair Winterton.

Watching her husband's set face, Claire laughed without humour. "Yes, I can see how horrified you are to discover your grubby little liaison is out in the open. Well, I've had enough, Jack. I've tried hard to please you – with scant success – and I'm tired of being treated as an item you have paid for, entitling you to disregard my feelings. In the existing circumstances, I'm sure Sir Alan will not hesitate to arrange a passage for me to return to India at once."

With a final disdainful glance at the stupefied man, Claire snatched up her bag, slipped on her shoes, and stormed to the door. Dark curls wild about her face, cheeks flushed with anger, she turned to launch a parting shot across her husband's bows.

"By the way, in the event of a divorce you can forget all about keeping Diana. She's only little, and so she will remain with me."

Closing the door quietly behind her, Claire left the suite and clattered down the stairs, uncaring that her agitated appearance might be noticed. Her fury had surprised her by its intensity, and she really needed to calm down. Fresh air and a walk in the gardens might help to disperse the seediness of Jack's affair from her mind.

Alone in the bedroom, Jack stared unseeingly out of the window, at last realising what a mess he had made of his marriage. He had known from the outset that Claire was young and romantically inclined, and he had set out to make her fall in love with him. Over the following weeks, however, he had been surprised over how much he enjoyed Claire's sparkling personality and her undoubted intelligence. In fact, he had looked forward to their time together.

Until he met Anne.

In a rare flash of self-recognition, Jack supposed he had more or less disregarded the girl he had gone on to marry, on the assumption that the freedom of spending money on whatever she wished would satisfy her. A mistake. He had been unprepared for the fury and bitterness she had unleashed just now. His mind went back to the lunch he had shared with Anne and her husband earlier that afternoon.

Due to Claire's oddly unexplained absence, an awkward atmosphere had prevailed at the lunch table. Alasdair finally went to sign the lunch chit, and taking advantage of her husband's absence, Anne had told him of Claire's lewd insinuations against her whilst seated in a popular café in town. Embarrassingly, Claire's vulgar language had begun to attract the attention of other people – she said tearfully – and unable to bear it any longer, her driver had returned the girl to the hotel. Perfectly understandable – Jack had thought in shamefaced fury.

He now knew Claire's insinuations related directly to his affair with Anne. But how the hell did she find out? And how was he to proceed, having just had the threat of divorce hurled at his head? Knowing his wife, he realised she meant what she said and Sir Alan could well be made aware of the sorry business.

It suddenly occurred to Jack that he did not want a divorce. If not in love with Claire, he was comfortable with his marriage. He even took a quiet pride in the many accolades his wife regularly received from peers and business associates. She possessed the amazing ability to mix at any social level, and her efficiency in organising conventions and formal entertaining would prove an inestimable loss. And of course, there was little Di-Di...

Jack distractedly ran his fingers through his hair. It was imperative to think of a way to prop up his tottering marriage. He cursed his own rank stupidity in bringing Claire to Durban in the first place, imagining nothing could go wrong in a matter of three days. And he had underestimated his wife's perspicacity.

Sitting on a bench in the gardens, Claire observed her husband leave the hotel in a company car. Good! She could now return to the bedroom and lie down for a while. Her rage had cooled, and she needed to think carefully about her next step.

Lying on her bed, Claire clasped her hands behind her head. Incandescent with fury, she had flung the possibility of divorce at her husband. But she was also pragmatic enough to realise that might not be to her advantage. In the event of carrying out such a threat, she stood to lose a great deal, possibly even her lovely home.

Nevertheless, the thought of continuing with the present arrangement – laughingly called marriage – was deeply abhorrent. In point of fact, it was to her advantage that she was young enough to begin again, albeit with the added baggage of a small child. But a competent lawyer would see to it that they were financially secure. Maybe that would be the best way forward after all…

There came a knock at the door.

Claire opened her eyes, and then sat up abruptly. Good Lord, had she dozed off? Swinging her feet to the floor, she padded barefoot to the door and opened it. A young black boy in hotel uniform stood there, clutching an enormous bouquet of flowers.

"*Jambo*, Mem," he exclaimed, teeth flashing white in a huge smile. "See, much lovely flowers for de ladee!"

"Thank you," Claire returned the flunkey's smile, and groped in a saucer of coins for tipping purposes. His smile widening further to receive such a handsome tip, the boy saluted, and then vanished.

The flowers were indeed beautiful, and Claire took them into the bathroom where she discovered two glass vases on a shelf. Choosing the larger of the two, Claire filled it with water, and began to arrange the blooms. She noticed a small envelope attached to a stem which she carefully detached, and extracted a note.

My dearest Claire,
I find myself to be a complete idiot not to have better appreciated
the outstanding wife you have always been. Can you forgive me?
Jack

No words of love, Claire noticed dryly, but it was clear he was extending an olive branch. And to avert the possibility of being shamed in the eyes of his boss, no doubt. Provided she could barter an improved attitude towards herself, the conciliatory gesture might be worth considering.

Reading the note once more, Claire's expression hardened. It did not require much imagination to know exactly why Jack wished to retain her as his wife. The adored one was unavailable, so she was the next best thing. After all, Sir Alan Braithwaite and his wife had extolled her virtues as a valuable asset to her husband.

She recalled how Jack had once referred to their marriage as a 'bargain' between them. Well, it was precisely what he was going to get in future. She would fulfil the duties expected of her as his wife, but henceforth she would live her own life as she wished. As for her husband, he could continue pining for his blonde tart, or console himself with other more readily available ones in Calcutta.

Claire no longer cared.

Dressing with her usual care, she made her way downstairs, certain her husband would be licking his wounds in the bar. Male heads turned to watch the attractive young woman, chin in the air, walking briskly through the busy hotel foyer. As she expected, Jack was indeed sitting in the bar, a glass of cold beer in front of him. Seeing Claire approach, he rose to his feet and scanned her face in the hope his flowers had wrought their usual magic. Disconcertingly, he noticed his wife's eyes resembled chips of blue ice. Edging herself on to a bar stool next to him, Claire did not beat about the bush, but came straight to the point.

"Thank you for the flowers, Jack. They were lovely. Now, I've been giving our present situation a good deal of thought, and have reached certain conclusions. I believe it would be best if we remember our marriage was one of convenience for both parties. A 'bargain', was how you once referred to it, remember? If we agree to fulfil our designated parts of the 'bargain' free from emotional entanglement our life together should proceed satisfactorily. Therefore, you are at liberty to live your life exactly as you wish and without reference to me...as I shall expect to live mine."

Claire smiled grimly at the stupefied expression on her husband's face. "Naturally, discretion must be the watchword," she continued conversationally. "Neither of us should embarrass the other through foolish lapses of discretion. We must present a united front to society, vital in relation to your firm as well as within government circles. So, Jack, are we agreed?"

Jack MacLeod stared at the composed young woman. Claire had set out conditions regarding their marriage in a cool and business-like manner

– a far cry from her usual warmth and vivacity. A distinctly cold draught had replaced that, which Jack hoped would prove to be temporary.

"Why don't we take this one step at a time," he prevaricated. "Remember we still have our holiday in Cape Town to look forward to."

"I haven't forgotten. So, are we agreed on the new arrangement between us, Jack?" Claire stared at her husband, her eyes still glacial. "I must insist on an answer before we go any further."

"In principle, I suppose so," Jack took his wife's hand, shaking his head in bewilderment, "but this cut and dried attitude isn't like the Claire that I know."

"Oh, this is very definitely me…a brand *new* me!" Claire removed her hand from her husband's clasp. "You should be pleased, even relieved, not to feel burdened by pretending affection for me. Now you have complete freedom to day-dream…of old times perhaps?"

Jack's mouth tightened at the jibe. "Nevertheless, I hope you will keep an open mind about everything, Claire."

"My mind is open to fresh and enjoyable opportunities, Jack, not necessarily of a sexual nature, might I add," Claire smiled without humour. "Now, would you order me a whisky and soda please?"

Chapter Eleven

Upon her return to Calcutta, Claire was feeling refreshed and revitalised. Brisk and smiling, she was up and about early each morning, briefly visiting the nursery to select her small daughter's clothes for the day.

There had, however, been a serious setback to Claire's improved outlook on life: Diana appeared to have forgotten her mother. Should she attempt to pick up the child, she clung to her nanny, yelling and kicking. Humiliated, Claire muttered darkly about Diana having been spoiled rotten by a doting grandmother.

Alarmed by the tense atmosphere, Jack asked Christina to return to the house, thinking the presence of her sister would please his wife. Diana was thrilled to have her auntie at home once more, but her delight merely emphasised the child's hostile attitude towards her mother. Secretly sick at heart, Claire began to ignore her small daughter.

The cold weather season in full flow, cocktail parties followed formal dinners, and as always, Claire's conversation sparkled, enchanting the stuffiest of her husband's business associates. She threw sumptuous cocktail parties at her own home, and frequently entertained members of parliament on a visit to Calcutta from London. It soon became noticeable that young Mrs MacLeod was becoming a distinctive hostess in India's capital city.

Thrilled by her achievements, she shamelessly adopted Anne Winterton's habit of a jade cigarette holder, the better to enhance her image of sophistication. She also took to arriving at a venue a few minutes late, and paused on the threshold with a lighted cigarette in a long jade holder held in one manicured hand. Advancing into the room with a brilliant smile, she was aware of having made a sensational impact. Smiling grimly to herself, she wondered what her dear husband might be making of it all...

The Calcutta Polo Club prevailed upon Claire to host a dinner party for a visiting team from the Punjab for the forthcoming tournament. The Maharajah and *Maharani* of Godrapur proved to be welcome additions to the dinner table, both of them English educated and appreciative of

British humour. Claire found their easy charm immensely refreshing, and resolved to ensure she and Jack saw more of them.

Affectionately referred to as *Godri* by his lively young wife, the Maharajah was a bluff, bearded individual, given to roaring with laughter at his own jokes. Sunita, his *Maharani*, effortlessly and with impeccable taste, managed to combine European elegance with the grace of a priceless silk sari, its edges heavily encrusted with gold thread. Expensive Italian leather slippers peeped from beneath her skirts. Recognising a potential close friend in Sunita, Claire encouraged Jack to cultivate the Maharajah as much as possible. Both were avid bridge players, as well as being passionately fond of horse racing. It was therefore an easy task, and her circle of personal friends would benefit from the addition of the attractive, emancipated young *Maharani* of Godrapur.

Soon after returning to Calcutta, Claire developed a passion for the Pekinese, a small Chinese dog, possessed of large eyes and a *retroussé* nose that tended to make them snuffle. Anxious to please his still-distant wife, Jack presented her with two puppies. Thrilled with her gift, Claire personally attended to their every need, and insisted their baskets should be placed in her bedroom at night.

Several times a day the puppies were taken out to play in the gardens, frequently accompanied by their devoted mistress. And in the relative cool of evening, the sweeper was detailed to take them out on leads for a short walk on the *maidan*, amusing passers-by to see the pups trotting along on their comical, bowed little legs.

Now firmly on her feet, Diana once tried to play with the puppies whilst they were in the garden. Minutes later, she had been banished howling to the nursery. Chasing one terrified puppy and then and the other, the child had inadvertently trodden on a puppy's foot. Squealing shrilly, the little animal ran to its mistress, tail tucked between its legs, holding up the injured paw. Infuriated, Claire delivered a sharp slap to her daughter, telling her to take better care where she put her clumsy feet. The incident did nothing to improve matters between mother and child.

Subsequent to much persuasion from Claire, a swimming pool and tennis court were in the process of creation in the rear gardens of the house. The young woman was delighted, for it would undoubtedly make their private entertaining more varied and enjoyable. She would give tennis parties, followed by an English-style tea. Evening swimming parties would also be on the agenda, an alfresco supper to be provided

147

afterwards. How people would fight to be invited, she thought with satisfaction, and probably even more so than to her cocktail parties.

After much nagging from Christina, Claire grudgingly agreed to have lunch at her mother's house one Sunday. Since their return from South Africa, Jack had regularly lunched with Minette and Frederick, but Claire still refused to go, preferring to remain aloof and unforgiving towards her mother.

There must surely be a reconciliation between them now, Christina thought with relief, knowing Minette had felt hurt by the exclusion from the life of her eldest daughter, of whom she was secretly proud. Christina intended to make certain Claire was given no excuse to change her mind.

Frederick arrived at the house to collect his two "daughters" in his beautiful new Rolls Royce car. Diana was also to go, and this time without the nanny. Jack had left earlier to go to the racing stables for a chat with his trainer, but he would be joining them later. Frederick was privately pleased the nanny wasn't to be dragged along. The poor woman probably needed a few hours to herself, Christina having confided that Susan was only able to take time off when she was able to relieve her.

As Frederick drew up under the entrance portico, Christina was already in the hallway, Diana comfortably lodged on a hip, and a bag filled with the child's toys looped over her arm. Nanny Susan was also present to watch the departure.

"So, how's my favourite little girl?" Frederick tickled Diana under her chin, making the child giggle. "Would you like a ride on your old uncle's shoulders?"

Beaming, Diana held out her arms and Frederick hefted her on to his shoulders, two little hands gripping each side of his head. "No hair-pulling now, *ma chèrie*!" he begged the grinning child.

"Uncle Freddie!" Claire emerged in a waft of perfume, and offered him a cool cheek to kiss. "Sweet of you to come and pick us up. Oh, for goodness sake, Diana, you're dribbling all over poor Freddie's head! Susan, come and take her will you?"

The nanny lifted the child from Frederick's shoulders, but finding herself unseated from her perch, Diana threw herself on the floor, shrieking. Flustered, the nanny tried to pick up the child, but with little success.

"Stop that noise at once!" Claire strode forward and stood over her yelling daughter. "Diana, if you don't shut up, you'll get a jolly good spanking!"

"Come on, sweetie, get up now!" Christina sought to evade further confrontation. "Be a good girl for Auntie Christina."

Ignoring her aunt's cajoling words, the scarlet-faced child continued her tantrum, bawling and drumming her heels on the floor. But upon seeing her mother advance – hand upraised – she scrambled to her feet and ran to her aunt, burying her face in her skirts. "Don' like Mama!" Diana threw over her shoulder.

"And nobody likes *you* when you behave like a horrid brat," Claire cheerfully told her daughter. "The threat of a good slap often solves the problem better than useless entreaties to be good," she added with a meaningful glance at her sister.

"Shall we go?" Frederick suggested, keen to avoid the possibility of a domestic row. "I believe Minette is waiting to have a glass of champagne with us."

Walking into her old home, Claire saw her youngest sister lurking in her favoured position behind Minette's chair, twiddling a fold of her mother's skirts in her fingers. Some things never change, she thought acidly, but with luck and a following wind, Sonia might keep her mouth shut whilst she was there.

"Nice to see you after so long, *Maman*," Claire murmured, depositing a perfunctory kiss on her mother's cheek. "Thing is, I've been terribly busy with business entertaining since we arrived back from South Africa."

"Well, Jack managed to find time to come and see me," Minette retorted without thinking. Seeing her daughter's face freeze, she wished she could withdraw the words. "Of course, I'm delighted you could come for lunch today."

"*Da-da*!" Diana spotted her father entering the veranda. Rushing towards him, she stretched up her arms. "Di-Di up! Pick Di-Di up, Dada!"

His face softening at the sight of his little daughter, Jack lifted Diana to sit on his folded arm. "Hello my darling, and have we been a good girl today?"

"No, she certainly hasn't!" Claire snapped, irritated as always by the child's attachment to her father. "As a matter of fact, she's been a revolting brat. Ask Uncle Freddie, if you don't believe me."

Feeling herself in danger of being undermined in her father's eyes, Diana turned to fix him with a bright blue stare. "Love Da-da, but don't like Mama!" she told him in a hoarse whisper. "Nasty Mama!"

"Well, I'm off to drink my champagne somewhere else," Claire declared, controlling her temper with difficulty, "so that Jack can continue drooling over his darling daughter without interruption."

Standing by the French windows in the sitting room, Claire lit a cigarette and puffed furiously. It never failed to upset her when the unpalatable fact that her own daughter didn't appear to like her became obvious to others. And now the damned child was actually tattling to her father!

"Claire?" Christina spoke from behind her. "Did you have to be so beastly to Jack? He didn't deserve that parting shot, you know."

"I suppose not," Claire answered grudgingly. "But I'm fed up being continually humiliated by that damned child."

"How can you say that about your own daughter?" Christina was shocked. "If she seems odd with you, it's because you don't bother with her. Nanny Susan says—"

"I'm not interested in what that stupid woman has to say," Claire interrupted. "Diana occasionally needs discipline which she only has from me, since you and Susan allow her to get away with murder."

Christina sighed. Claire seemed to have developed such a complex personality these days. For instance, she didn't understand her sister's distant attitude towards Jack, who appeared solicitous of her requirements and comfort. And what about Di-Di, her little daughter, from whom she expected a high standard of behaviour, but seemed incapable of offering her affection to offset these demands.

It made Christina sad to watch her prickly sister unconsciously falling into the same trap as Minette, especially since Claire never ceased to reproach her mother for her earlier neglect. But mentioning such a sensitive issue to her sister was more than she dared do.

"Still standing on your dignity, I see, whilst *Maman* and Jack are cooing over your noisy child?" Sonia had sidled in, ready to taunt her hateful eldest sister. "I'm certain Diana thinks the nanny is her mother – and you, of course, are the wicked witch."

"Still the sweet creature I remember, caustic acid dripping from every word!" Clare glared at her youngest sister. "Bugger off if you can't find anything nice to say."

"How dare you swear at me like that?" Sonia spat. "You may be sure I will..."

"...tell *Maman* on you!" Claire finished scornfully. "Aren't you rather on the old side to resort to that boring mantra of yours? But then, why am I surprised? You *are* still wearing a small child's frilly little frock. Bit on the slow side, our Sonia!"

"I really *hate* you, Claire!" the younger girl hissed through clenched teeth. "You've always gone out of your way to make me miserable, my whole life. You are mean and nasty, and don't deserve your wonderful husband and child. Even *Maman* thinks that, because I heard her saying so to Uncle Freddie the other day."

"Is that so?" Claire turned pale with fury. "And who is she to set herself up in judgement of me? Especially if one considers how she's managed to blight all of our lives by not getting married properly, that very thing which caused Charlie's death."

"Stop it!" Christina shouted, almost in tears. "Stop saying all these dreadful things to each other! You should both be ashamed."

"Clear off back to your darling mother, you snivelling little wretch," Claire snarled, ignoring Christina's plea. "And you can tell her I won't be staying for lunch after all, as the vicious tongues in this house are too much for me to stomach."

Whirling, Claire stormed out of the house, leaving a distraught Christina staring after her. Calling to Jack's astounded driver who had been enjoying a quiet doze, she instructed him to return home to Alipore. He could return later for *Sahib*. She should never have agreed to go to her treacherous mother's house in the first place, Claire seethed. But, by God, it was for the very last time.

Later that afternoon, Jack returned to the house with Diana. Christina had decided to remain at Camack Street, Minette having been inordinately upset by Claire's precipitate departure. Neither Christina nor Sonia sought to discuss the reason why.

Before dinner that evening, Jack and Claire were having a pre-dinner drink out on the veranda. Jack had his usual *chota peg* on the table in front of him, whilst Claire sipped her whisky-flavoured soda water in a tall glass.

Lighting a cigar, Jack glanced over at his wife, thinking how attractive she was looking in a mauve and white pinstripe gown. Her hair was brushed back into a shining mass, moving gently about her face in the breeze from an overhead fan. Dark lashes fanned her cheeks, and she was smoking a cigarette. The only jarring aspect was that Claire's mouth was set in an ominously straight line.

"Did you imagine your unpleasant exchange with Sonia could not be overheard on the veranda?" Jack decided to take the initiative. "Including, of course, those hurtful comments regarding your mother?"

Inhaling smoke from her cigarette, Claire considered her reply. She had been so infuriated with her youngest sister, she hadn't thought about being overheard.

"I had every reason to lose my temper, Jack," she said at last. "Did you not hear what Sonia said to me...or was your hearing selective?"

"You never tire of accusing your mother of being responsible for Charlie's demise, do you, Claire?" Jack chose to ignore Claire's tart enquiry. "Has it never occurred to you that she suffers terrible grief over the untimely death of both her sons? I believe it to be unnecessarily cruel to rub salt in the wound."

Her expression mutinous, Claire stared wordlessly across the darkened garden. It hadn't been her intention to hurt her mother unnecessarily, but now it was too late. The damage had been done: anyway, what she had said was perfectly true.

"Another thing I would like to know, is why you resent the affection I feel for our daughter?" Jack demanded, annoyed by his wife's studied silence. "I happen to love Di-Di, and if you don't like it, too bad! But should you wonder why the child feels distanced from you, I suggest you examine your own attitude. For Christ's sake, you lavish more love on those damned dogs than your own baby girl."

"My dogs reciprocate affection," Claire returned sharply. "Which is more than one can say for that bloody-minded brat who can do no wrong in your eyes."

"I'll thank you not to use language like that to me...it's singularly unattractive. And you might remember the 'brat' also happens to be your daughter."

Claire abruptly stood up, her eyes glittering with angry tears. "I'll use whatever language I want, thank you, Jack. And you can have dinner on your own, for I find my appetite has vanished." With an irritable swish of her skirts, she stormed off to her bedroom and slammed the door behind her.

The following morning, Claire decided to pay a visit to her friend and mentor, Naomi Bernstein. Striding agitatedly up and down Naomi's private fitting room, Claire recounted the miserable events of the previous day.

"Claire, might it not be a wise move to visit your mother, and finally

152

clear the air between you?" Naomi tentatively suggested. "You've often told me your youngest sister is an appalling liar, so the remarks she attributed to your mother could be her own invention, born of malice."

"No." Claire's reply was short. "In this instance I believe Sonia, since it's typical of something *Maman* would say about me. I've never been able to do anything right in her eyes, but this time I shall never forgive her."

Shaking her head sadly, Naomi sighed. The spiteful outburst by this girl's sister had gone deep, effectively sealing the fate of possible reconciliation. Naomi nevertheless wondered if Claire was aware she was in danger of echoing Madame Marguerite's often overly critical attitude? It was maybe not the right moment to mention such a thing, however.

"Claire, why not go off on a holiday on your own?" Naomi suggested at last. "Stay with that nice French uncle of yours, perhaps? The hot weather is almost upon us, and I'm sure it would be more fun than joining other wives at some hill station."

"Brilliant idea!" Claire brightened. "I'll write to Uncle Emile at once, and ask if he can have me to stay for a couple of months."

Returning home in the car, Claire grinned, anticipating a wonderful holiday in France. In the unlikely event that Jack decided to accompany her, his time away would necessarily be brief, having to return to work and the British India Office would undoubtedly require his presence.

Sadly for Claire, the pleasant contemplation of a few months away in southern France crumbled into dust the following week. Reluctant at first to recognise signs, she was eventually forced to accept the unwelcome fact she was pregnant again, even bursting into tears at the doctor's surgery.

The thought of her body swelling to grotesque proportions was dismal enough, but she knew Jack would not allow her to travel in her condition. Not even by rail to a hill station. She would be obliged to remain in Calcutta throughout the hot weather season, and the young woman viewed the months ahead with dismay.

Jack was delighted by the news of another child, and hoped his wife would provide a little brother for Diana. Claire spent much of each day in her bedroom under the fan, dwelling morosely on her rotten luck. Despite Christina returning to stay, she was unable to revive her leaden spirits. The younger girl was relieved when term began at college, an excellent excuse to be away from her sister's depressing company.

The following months dragged by for Claire, assailed once again by bouts of violent morning sickness. Prickly heat rashes appeared in the creases of her increasingly bulky body that added to her misery as the pregnancy progressed. Her temper sharpened, and Christina deemed it wise to keep Di-Di well out of her mother's way. She prayed that the arrival of a new baby might ignite maternal feelings in her sister that so far, seemed to have remained dormant.

Diana was quickly growing into an attractive child, her mop of bouncing coppery curls framing a mischievous little face. Intelligent and outgoing, she was given to arguing tirelessly about anything she did not understand, or an order deemed unreasonable. Teasing her mother's dogs to yapping hysteria was a favourite occupation, and she would run away laughing, followed by Claire's enraged invective. The nanny was summoned to catch her, and yelling defiance, the child would be dragged away.

The little girl was, however, intrigued by the news that there was to be a new baby in the nursery. Of course, the newcomer was coming especially to play with her – a notion nobody attempted to correct. Such an idea might deflect possible jealousy, and allow her to look forward to the infant's arrival.

The hot summer months dragged by interminably, and then on a sweltering night Claire's baby was finally born. Sweat-sodden and exhausted, the new mother raised herself on an elbow to examine the new arrival. Oh God…*not another girl*? Agonised, she looked at the wizened little face with its thatch of gingery hair, horridly reminiscent of Diana as an infant. Yet again, she was deprived of her longed-for baby boy.

Turning her face into the pillows, Claire howled like a wounded animal. Somewhat taken aback by this display of misery, Jack bent to kiss his wife, taking care to hide his own disappointment the baby was not a boy. From an inside pocket he drew out a navy leather case containing a diamond bracelet, ordered months ago from Cartier in Paris.

"Claire, I'd like to give you this small gift to celebrate the safe arrival of our beautiful baby girl."

The new mother rolled over to look up at him, her eyes red with crying. "How can you say that, Jack? You must know it's hideous. Why, oh *why* is this happening to me? I so badly wanted my little boy!"

"For heaven's sake, Claire, calm down!" Jack exclaimed in alarm. It dawned on him that that his wife's reaction was how she had viewed Diana as a newborn, almost as if her own child disgusted her. Shaking his head in bewilderment, he handed his gift to Claire by way of a distraction.

Despite her overwhelming disappointment, Claire gasped with pleasure at the beauty of fine interwoven silver cords interspersed with diamonds fashioned as stars. She noticed it was expandable, worn on the wrist or on the upper arm as a 'slave' bangle. Looking up at her husband from slightly puffy eyes, she smiled. "Thank you, Jack, it's simply beautiful."

Later that afternoon, Christina brought a thrilled Diana to see her new baby sister. Holding the side of the cot with both hands, the child stood on tiptoe to peer down at the sleeping infant. A moment later, she glanced up at her aunt, clearly perplexed.

"Monkey? Why that monkey in *baba's* bed, Auntie?" she asked. "Where's Di-Di's new sister?"

"Christ Almighty!" screamed her mother in outrage. "Take that child out of here if she's going to make damned silly remarks."

"Come Di-Di," Christina hustled the startled child out of the room. "No, sweetie, Mummy isn't angry with you, she's just a little tired right now," Christina was aware she was gabbling. "I'll bring you back a little later to see your baby sister."

"Not in my bedroom, she won't!" Claire snapped. "Oh, *no*, it's starting to yowl again…Chrissy, call Susan to take the baby away and give it a bottle. I'm not going to start that revolting business of breastfeeding again so soon. I'm too tired and fed up to cope at the moment."

Despite her somewhat inauspicious entry into the world, Daphne, the new baby, grew into a pretty little girl. Wavy hair, the same coppery colour as her sister's, framed a pixie-like face, and she possessed a rather more amenable personality than Diana.

For her acquiescence alone Claire took to the younger child, a preference she made little effort to conceal. After all, hadn't Diana always resisted her mother's efforts to draw closer to her? Too bad if she didn't like it – Claire informed Christina – who unwisely dared to mention the fact. In any case, Diana continued to enjoy adulation from her besotted father.

Inevitably, Diana began to display signs of jealousy towards her younger sister. Whenever she imagined nobody was looking, she would pinch a plump arm, or make a deliberate attempt to trip up the toddler. Nervous of her older sister, Daphne would stagger as fast as her small legs would carry her to the security of her mother's arms. Despite Claire's vigilance, mysterious red or mauve bruises still manifested themselves on the younger child's limbs. Furious, Claire delivered a few good spankings to the offender, who dashed off howling, to tattle to her father about her mother's unfairness.

Eventually, it became noticeable to Jack that Diana's simmering resentment was due to Claire's marked preference for her small sister. In his view, it was not a matter to be pushed aside as of no consequence. Determined to broach the subject with his wife, he engineered a discussion about it one evening.

"I think we had better discuss the rather nasty atmosphere developing between our two little girls," Jack began. "I believe the whole thing boils down to Di-Di seeing you constantly cuddle Daffy but never her. What I would suggest is—"

"For God's sake, Jack, I can't credit you are—"

"Allow me to speak, if you please," Jack snapped, annoyed. "It's important we resolve this issue as soon as possible for the sake of both children."

Claire had jumped up angrily, but now sank back into the chair. "Fine, but don't try to create a victim of Diana, I beg you. You must have seen the evidence of all those vicious pinch-marks and bruises on Daffy's arms and legs?"

"Yes, I know about that, but I don't think the answer is to continually wallop Di-Di. If you gave her a cuddle and a few minutes of your time, I'm sure there would be a significant improvement in the child."

"I imagine you are pulling my leg, Jack?" Claire stared frostily at her husband. "Why, I can't even kiss that child goodnight without a fuss of some kind. She doesn't want affection from me...but her sister mustn't have it either. It's a case of 'dog in the manger' where that child is concerned. Sorry, but I will not allow Diana to continue tormenting her little sister, and if she isn't careful, she's going to earn herself more than an occasional smack."

"Claire, don't take that belligerent tone with me," Jack took a deep breath, keeping a tight rein on his temper. "I'm trying to have a reasonable talk with you, so stop flying off the handle."

Claire stood up, her face closed. "This is how I see things: Daphne recognises me as her mother, but Diana does not. Frankly, I'm not prepared to continue battering my head against a brick wall where that child is concerned. You're her darling Daddy, so just carry on giving her

156

sneaky treats in compensation for her sister's existence, won't you?" she finished nastily.

"You...you really are so bloody unnatural!" Jack finally exploded. "I understood a mother's love for her child was unselfish and fiercely protective. Trust you to be an exception to the rule."

"Think whatever you please," Claire's disdainful glance flicked over her husband's person, "as it's of no consequence to me."

The following months passed swiftly enough for Claire, re-absorbed in perfecting her position in society as one of Calcutta's leading hostesses. Invitations to Tea and Tennis afternoons were popular with the younger set, and evening pool parties were also sought-after. Occasional elegant picnics on the banks of Diamond Harbour were attributable to Claire's organisational skills.

A golden couple, Jack and Claire were on a pinnacle of social success.

But on a personal level, the relationship between the two remained strained, at times degenerating into full-scale hostility. Although he was pleased over the popularity of his attractive and vivacious young wife, Jack remained indifferent to her on a personal level. His resolve to review his attitude to their marriage seemed to be forgotten, and neither did he think to conceal from his wife that, for him, the act of making love was merely a sexual release.

Claire was disappointed – bitterly so. She kicked herself for imagining that subsequent to the horrendous row in Durban, some semblance of intimacy and warmth might be re-kindled between them. What a joke! Taking a cue from her husband, Claire abandoned all pretence that her husband's touch afforded her pleasure. She would lie immobile in passive resistance, her eyes tightly closed in clear disgust during his assault on her body.

If Jack noticed the degeneration of his wife's attitude, he gave no indication of it.

Chapter Twelve

Summer months were once more fast approaching, and the oppressive heat caused much of the social life in Calcutta to grind to a halt. Anxious not to remain in the steamy city, Claire decided to take the children and their nanny up-country for two of the worst months. She decided on Ranchi, an attractive hill station on the lower reaches of the Himalayas, which did not involve an over-long train journey. Jack was required to remain at the office for the time being, but declared an intention to rejoin his family for the final two weeks of their stay.

The journey was nevertheless tedious, and unused to confinement for hours inside a railway carriage the children were fractious and demanding. Then as the little mountain train drew into the station at Ranchi, the cool freshness of the air and lushness of the countryside went some way to improving Claire's faltering good humour.

The hotel where they were booked to stay proved simple but comfortable, and Claire enjoyed her first complete night's sleep for a long time. What a welcome revelation it was to cuddle under warm, fluffy blankets during a chilly night...after the oppressive heat of Calcutta! Even the simple act of dressing without bursting into a sweat seemed divine, and make-up stayed fresh throughout the day.

The two little girls were also benefiting from the cool mountain air. Cheeks became rosy, and their appetites improved significantly. An outgoing child, Diana lost no time in going outside to play with other children staying at the hotel. Daphne, however, clung to her mother, whining, or crying should Claire briefly disappear from view. Despite her pleasure over Daffy's attachment, the child's clinging was becoming unpleasantly reminiscent of Sonia.

Common practice at most hill stations, enthusiasts took it upon themselves to organise family fun and games every afternoon. No effort was too great in order to inveigle others at the hotel into participating, the prospect filling Claire with horror and dread. Necessarily, she put in an appearance with her two little girls, but making sure it was as brief as she could diplomatically manage. Having done her duty, the children were sent off with the nanny for a walk. Claire was then free to read or doze on her bed, there being little else of interest to do.

After three weeks of jolly family afternoons, Claire's patience was wearing thin. She longed to return to the vibrancy of Calcutta despite the sweltering heat, even that being preferable to dying of boredom in the mountains. To make matters worse, there was the dismal prospect of sickening jollification for weeks ahead.

One morning, Claire was having a late breakfast in the hotel dining room, the book she was reading propped against the teapot. Suddenly there were guffaws of male laughter coming from the hallway, and four young cavalry officers clattered into the dining room. Making their way over to a free table, they noticed the attractive, dark-haired young woman reading at nearby table.

One of them walked over to Claire, bowed, and with an engaging smile introduced himself as Robin Frencham from Wiltshire. Would she care to join them for a cup of coffee? Claire smiled but shook her head, restraining a desire to accept with an effort.

After a few minutes of persuasion, however, she allowed herself to be escorted to his table. The other young men rose courteously to their feet, all three of them smiling in obvious pleasure. Pulling out a chair for her, pots of coffee and tea were ordered from a hovering *bearer.*

At last, Claire was in her element exchanging banter with the young officers, who clearly found her wicked wit highly amusing. When she left the dining room, it really did seem that life was looking up at last! She had taken care to make her new friends aware she was married, and had two children. Nevertheless, they had invited her to accompany them on afternoon sightseeing trips they were organising.

A few days later, Claire noticed significant glances being exchanged between families staying at the hotel. Gossip about her activities with the young officers was rife, and further perpetuated by private Ranchi residents who gathered at the hotel bar for a drink every evening. Annoyed, Claire haughtily ignored the unspoken inference she flouted convention, for she was never alone with any one of the officers.

The young woman's halcyon days came to an abrupt halt, for Jack suddenly arrived to rejoin his family. Extremely tired, all he wanted to do was relax in a deckchair on the hotel lawn, read newspapers, or sleep. Conversing with his wife was not on the agenda.

Her new friends having departed back to their regiment, a disgruntled

Claire had no option but to take up the boredom of family activities with the children once more. To her discomfiture, however, snide muttering continued. Deeply resentful to be judged by these tedious provincial types, Claire looked forward to a return to civilisation.

Diana was thrilled to see her father, and Jack spent an hour every afternoon playing with his daughters. Small hill ponies were brought up to the hotel by a local *syce*, hoping to entice a few children to ride. Diana begged her father to allow her to sit on a pony, and it soon became apparent that the child possessed a natural ability. She sat astride the scrawny animal, fearless, exhorting the *syce* leading it to walk a bit faster.

Daffy began whining that she also wanted a ride. Removing a reluctant Diana from the pony's back, Jack lifted the younger child into the saddle. No sooner had the animal taken a step, Daffy began screaming that it was going too fast. Startled, the pony shied, and Jack only just managed to grab the child before she fell off.

Alerted by her younger daughter's screams, Claire hurried over and gathered the howling child in her arms. "For heaven's sake, what's wrong, my precious? Did Diana do something to you?"

"Nobody has done anything to her," Jack told his wife. "Daffy whined about wanting to ride, but when I lifted her on to the pony's back, she began screeching and gave the poor animal a fright. Don't worry, she's not hurt."

"No, but she's jolly funky!" Diana giggled. "Look at her bawling, just like a baby."

"And you are so brave, I suppose? Little Daffy isn't a clumsy great creature like you. She's dainty and—"

"*Claire!*" Jack interrupted his wife. "Remember what I told you about setting one child against the other. It's not fair."

But Diana had shrugged off her mother's remark, and was once more on the pony's back. "Let go, *syce*," she told the owner, "I want to ride by myself."

Picking Daphne up, Claire flounced back to the hotel, the child continuing to bleat in her ear. Irritated, she detached herself from the child's clinging hands, handed her over to the nanny, ignored the high-pitched wails, and returned to the hotel.

Ordering herself a tray of tea and buttered scones, Claire retired to the sitting room with a book. She would enjoy hour or so on her own, until the children's suppertime. Half an hour later, however, Claire's peace was shattered by her husband storming into the sitting room. Seeing his wife sitting in a corner, he marched over to confront her, his face tight with anger.

"There are a few things I wish to make clear," Jack stated coldly, "and this has nothing to do with Daphne before you leap to her defence. Frankly, I would have thought you would be aware that inappropriate behaviour gives rise to salacious gossip. I am therefore less than impressed to have my attention drawn by others to my wife's repeated indiscretions with unattached men."

Slamming down the book she was reading, Claire's expression darkened with growing anger. "What the hell are you talking about? What indiscretions? I can hardly get up to much, stuck here with—"

"Be quiet, Claire! I won't allow you to shout me down this time."

The young woman clamped her mouth shut and subsided in her chair. What the hell was the man carrying on about? One might imagine she had…

"I'm speaking about my wife rattling about the countryside in the company of four young military men. I'm reliably informed that you abandoned your children to the nanny in order to clear off with these fellows, so it's hardly surprising you provoked talk. Have you *no* common sense at all, you stupid girl?"

"How dare you speak to me like that?" Claire spat. "If you choose to believe a gaggle of scandal-mongers then more fool you, Jack MacLeod! I did occasionally go for a drive with four well-mannered young men, but I made no attempt to conceal the fact that I was married and had two children. The whole thing was above-board, and in full view of everyone here."

Claire drew a breath, ragged with rage. "I have nothing, *nothing* to feel ashamed about. Believe me, those fellows were a damned sight better company than the purse-mouthed prudes who have enjoyed regaling you with ridiculous tales about me."

"Be that as it may, I'm frankly amazed at your stupidity in casting convention to the four winds and—"

"I hardly think you are well-placed to preach about conventional behaviour to me," Claire glassily stared her husband in the eye. "Perhaps we should drop the subject?"

White with rage that his long-ago indiscretion was once again flung in his face, Jack took a deep breath.

"In future, you will observe the niceties of conventional behaviour, and conduct yourself in a proper manner whilst in the public eye. Do I make myself clear?"

Turning on his heel, he strode away, Claire glaring after him but for once at a loss, wondering how she would face those smug imbeciles out to make trouble for her with their well-embellished exaggerations. How they would rejoice to see her discomfiture! Oh God, let the time pass quickly so she could take up the threads of her life in Calcutta again. Holidays at a hill station would not be on her agenda for the foreseeable future – if ever.

Two months after a return to Calcutta, Claire was still seething with resentment over what she perceived as Jack's unmerited attack in Ranchi. For God's sake, it was as though she had been caught in *flagrante delicto*! As things stood, she could scarcely bear to look at him, never mind submit to his sexual requirements. Lying unmoving during nocturnal visits, she would try to detach her mind from what was happening to her unwilling body, and think of something rather more pleasant...

Company entertaining had increased significantly, as well as that for the government since Jack's appointment to the staff of 1st Marquess of Willingdon, the new Viceroy of all India. Juggling his time at the office with his new duties, he was obliged to regularly spend a few days away in the new capital city of Delhi. Claire looked forward to these brief absences, but when Jack was in Calcutta, she went about her duties of organising dinners, cocktail parties and conventions with her usual efficiency and flair.

Despite her involvement in the social arena, she found the continuing strain of her unsatisfactory marital situation depressing. So it was with joy that Claire welcomed the arrival in Calcutta of her friend, Sunita, *Maharani* of Godrapur. The two young women arranged to meet for *tiffin* at Firpo's, the ever-popular restaurant whose Italian proprietor liked to boast his ice creams were made in heaven.

Delighted to see her friend, Claire regaled her with all the latest gossip around town, and described the daunting amount of entertaining in which she was currently involved.

"One advantage of having a bossy mother-in-law, is that she takes care of all that sort of thing," Sunita laughed. "All I have to do is look decorative, and produce a baby from time to time."

"But anyone can see your husband loves you to bits, Sunita," Claire remarked, with more than a touch of envy. "Unfortunately, the same cannot be said of mine."

"But you're such an attractive girl, and Godri said you are well-known as a leading light on the social scene here. Your husband must surely appreciate that?"

"Humph!" Clare snorted derisively. "If only you knew. He's happy enough with my efforts, I suppose, but Jack is in love with a woman he met years ago in South Africa. I'm only second best."

"Oh, you poor thing," Sunita exclaimed sympathetically. "But he must still make love to you, Claire? You do have two little girls after all."

"Oh, Jack does his stuff, but he only manages to do it by pretending I'm his tart."

Sunita sat back in her seat, shocked by the revelation. It seemed inconceivable that the suave Scotsman should privately treat his wife with such disrespect. It was clear that Claire was unhappy, but what an awful conundrum it was.

Gazing affectionately at her attractive Indian friend, Claire recounted the series of events during the weeks at Ranchi, resulting in a hellish row with her husband. Since then, their already difficult relationship had worsened, almost to open hostility.

"And I hadn't even done anything scandalous with those fellows, Sunita! But after the busybodies had regaled Jack with God knows what tales, he was prepared to believe the worst."

"Claire, do forgive me, but I believe you are managing this business in entirely the wrong way." Sunita leaned across the table to place a hand over Claire's. "If you continually lock horns with your husband, it can only aggravate matters. In future you must handle him rather more cleverly, and above all – *be discreet*. Men are proud, but much can be overlooked, provided it is hidden from the public eye," she winked meaningfully. "But as the saying goes – sauce for the gander can never be sauce for the goose, unfortunately."

"Don't fling Jack's affair in his face again, for it will only infuriate him," she continued, seeing she had Claire's undivided attention, "and please, no more bull-in-the-china-shop impersonations as it won't serve your purpose. Let it all go…wipe the slate clean. On the other hand, the hot weather is almost upon us again, so my advice is to clear off to Europe and have the most marvellous time. Do what you want, whenever you want, and with whom you want…but remember to be the soul of discretion."

Claire stared at her friend. Why, everything Sunita had said made perfect sense. That trip to France she had been obliged to forgo due to being pregnant? She would write to Emile at once.

"Sunni, you're a genius!" she exclaimed. "The idea of clearing off somewhere, preferably nice and far away from Jack, really appeals to me."

"Well, you're lucky to have that lovely uncle in France...have you thought of staying with him?"

"Do you know Emile?" Claire enquired, surprised. "And yes, I was thinking of asking him if I might come on an extended visit."

"Emile is an old friend of my father's," Sunita explained. "Whenever he visits India, he stays with him for a few days, and the two old boys go off on tiger shoots with Godri and my brothers. In any event, I'm certain he will know lots of interesting people."

"Heavens, it really is a small world," Claire grinned, "and I know Emile to be a perfect host from the last time I was in France."

"My friend, you will find it much easier to toe the dutiful line after a couple of exciting months away. Who knows, you might find your husband has missed you."

"I doubt that, but I don't really care what he thinks these days. As far as I'm concerned, Jack can do as he pleases...as I have every intention of doing."

After lunching with Sunita, Claire went home in a decidedly more light-hearted frame of mind. She even sought out her two little girls who were happily playing with a ball in the back garden. Unseen, she stood for a moment, watching the two children enjoying each other's company for once. Daffy was laughing, and even Diana's face lacked its habitual scowl. How sweet they can be at times, Claire thought.

The ball suddenly bounced near her feet, the girls spotted their mother, and the spell was broken. Diana stood by stiffly, her expression neutral, whilst the younger child's face creased into a discontented grimace.

"Mama...Daffy wanta to stay with Mama!" she whined. "Don't wanta play with Di-Di! Wanta—"

"Stop that silly noise, Daffy," Claire said sharply to the younger child. "You were playing together very nicely just now."

"No, Mama, I wanta—"

"*Daffy*! If you don't stop whining, you can go back to the nursery. Why can't you speak in a normal voice?"

Daphne stopped, her mouth falling open to hear the stern tone in her mother's voice. Even Diana looked up with interest at this unusual turn of events.

"That's better. Now, would you like to come and sit with me whilst I have my whisky and soda? Diana, would you like to come too? Susan, please ask the *bearer* to bring two small glasses of *nimbu pani* for the *babas* to the veranda."

Taking Daphne by the hand, Claire walked towards the house, Diana trailing in her wake, her hands behind her back in case her mother tried to hold her hand.

The tray of drinks arrived, and just as Claire lifted her glass, Daphne tried to clamber on her lap, knocking her elbow so whisky soda spilled down her elegant ensemble. Determined to achieve her purpose, Daphne's grimy little hands clutched at her mother's skirts, renewing their grip as soon as Claire managed to detach her clothing. In moments the expensive silk material had been reduced to a soiled rag, creased beyond hope.

"*For Christ's sake!*" Claire shouted, looking down at herself. "Just look at what you've done to my lovely new dress, you naughty girl. You deserve a good smack!"

Turning to the nanny hovering in the background, Claire continued the tirade. "Why are these children so filthy, Susan? You aren't paid to allow them to get into this disgusting state."

"They were playing ball, Madam," Susan strove to keep her tone conciliatory. "It's not easy to keep the girls clean in the garden, especially after it has rained." Inwardly raging over her mistress's injustice, the nanny herded her charges away to the nursery, both children going quietly for once.

Since the holiday in Ranchi, Susan's life had been made a misery by Daphne's unhappy wailing for her frequently absent mother. It was also a strain having to be constantly on the alert to prevent the older child from teasing her sister, or inflicting nasty pinches. She was extremely fond of these children whom she had raised from birth, or she would be seeking an alternative situation – the nanny thought resentfully. Madam's moods were hard to predict, and her temper impossible. At least Mr MacLeod was easier to get on with, and he was good with the little girls.

It therefore came as a pleasant surprise when her mistress entered the nursery the following day with a sunny smile. Neither did she do her usual inspection of the room, poking about as if searching for something to criticise. Susan wondered what the reason could be for such a miraculous change? She hoped it would last longer than a day...

Chapter Thirteen

To Jack's bemusement, Claire's demeanour towards him underwent a radical change. Her good humour seemed unassailable, and she carried out her various duties with a smiling countenance. No longer did he receive the impression his wife was delighted to see the back of him, should he be obliged to travel to Delhi or Bombay on business. A pleasant change indeed!

For her part, Claire went about with a song in her heart. Emile had replied to her letter, expressing immense pleasure to be welcoming his niece's eldest daughter once again to his home. He understood her desire to absent herself from that dreadful Calcutta summer climate, and she should stay for at least two months, if not three.

Choosing her moment with care, she broached the proposed trip to France to her husband. Replete after an excellent dinner, a balloon glass of fine cognac in his hand, Jack saw no reason why she should not accept Emile's kind invitation.

The young woman joyfully prepared for her holiday, which included several smart additions to her already extensive wardrobe. The girls would remain in Calcutta, as Claire earnestly assured her husband she needed time to herself after the extensive cold weather entertaining she had undertaken. The children would go next time, but for now she needed a complete rest.

A tiresome difficulty arose, however, subsequent to Jack's recent visit to Camack Street. He regularly took his daughters to see their grandmother, Claire having refused to set foot in her mother's home. It therefore fell to him to ensure Minette occasionally saw the grandchildren she loved, a gesture for which she was profoundly grateful.

Over a cup of tea that afternoon, she and Jack were watching the two little girls throwing a ball for her new puppy to chase on the lawn. Jack casually mentioned Claire's intended holiday in France, staying with Emile de Beaurepaire.

"But are you not going as well?" Minette asked in surprise. "A change of scene would do you good, I'm sure."

"Unfortunately, I can't," he answered ruefully. "I've recently become a member of the Legislative Council, so together with all my other commitments, it would be quite impossible to leave India at this time."

"Well, I suppose the little girls will enjoy it," Minette mused. "I imagine the nanny will also be taken, as I cannot imagine Claire managing the children on her own."

"Well, no." Jack hesitated. "She feels in need of a proper rest, having been heavily involved with functions and business entertaining over the winter season. She says she wants to go by herself to restore her *esprit*."

"Humph!" Minette snorted derisively. "For one who constantly harps on my lack of maternal obligation, she's not doing any better with this ridiculous plan to leave her small children for weeks on end. That girl spends her entire life resting, if you ask me. How you put up with that rubbish, Jack, is frankly beyond me."

"Actually, I've been thinking about organising a family holiday at the seaside when Claire returns from Europe. Life for me should be less hectic in early September, and the girls will see something of their mother before she's back on the social treadmill."

"In that case, do make certain this holiday is not open-ended. You must tell that young madam exactly when you expect her back in Calcutta. Otherwise, the excitement of the French social scene may stifle any concern that might trouble her over the date of her return."

"You are right, of course.' Jack nodded. "I'll tell Claire to be back by the end of August. I know she's planning to leave at the end of May, so ten weeks in France should be plenty of time to recover her spirits."

Minette looked askance at her son-in-law. "Prepare yourself for battle, dear chap, for my dear daughter is unlikely to take kindly to being given orders."

"*What?*" As her mother had correctly predicted, Claire was infuriated by her husband's demand that she return to Calcutta by the end of August. "For God's sake, it will still be dreadfully hot! I was planning on being back around the end of September."

"No, Claire, I want you here by the end of August," Jack's tone was adamant. "It would not be good for the girls for their mother to be away longer than necessary. Even three months must be a long time in their young lives, don't you think?"

"No, I don't, as it's perfectly ridiculous! Have you considered the fact that half my time away will be spent on board ship?

"I have given the matter of your holiday a great deal of thought," Jack answered evenly. "Which is why I am arranging a ten day holiday at the seaside for us upon your return to Calcutta. It will give you and the girls valuable time together."

Preparing to argue the toss with her husband, Sunita's advice came to mind. *Lose a battle to win a war* – she had said. And she supposed this must be classified as a "battle." Privately raging, Claire managed to paste on a brilliant smile.

"You're absolutely right, three months away from my family is more than enough," she said brightly. "And your idea of a seaside holiday sounds great fun. Don't worry, I'll certainly be back in time for that."

Surprised, if faintly suspicious by his wife's unusual tractability, Jack nodded, and deposited a peck on her cheek. Gathering up his belongings, he left the house for the office…failing to see his wife childishly stick out her tongue at his retreating back.

The passage to France passed quickly, modern ships possessing a turn of speed hitherto unknown to Claire. She then took the train to Bordeaux where Emile met her, a huge smile on his face. Enveloping her in a bear hug, he proudly led the way to his latest purchase, a dark grey Rolls Royce motor car, and drove it expertly back to his home on the Beaurepaire estate.

Passing through the village of Saint Emilion, Claire thought of those grandparents who lived close by. Was the old man still alive, she wondered? But the vitriol flowing in that grandmother's veins should keep the vile woman going forever! She had no desire to renew the acquaintance of her mother's family.

That evening, Emile and Claire attended a dinner party given by Emile's older brother and his wife at the Château de Beaurepaire. Max and Amélie greeted Claire warmly, asking after Minette and other members of the family. Claire was obliged to tell them of her brother's untimely death, as it became obvious the news had not reached them. Genuinely upset, the Beaurepaires hastily changed the subject, seeing Claire become a trifle tearful. They recalled Charlie as a pleasant young man.

Half an hour later, another guest arrived, and Vittorio di Rossignanti was ushered into the salon. Brightening visibly to see Claire, the Italian bent over her hand, his lips warm on her skin. Blushing like a girl, Claire was glad she had made the effort to look her best in hyacinth crêpe with matching slippers.

Throughout the evening, Vittorio missed no opportunity to let Claire know how attractive he still found her. Dark eyes caressing, he whispered how he hoped to see more of her during her stay in France. Starved of affection from her husband, the young woman bloomed in the warmth of his attention. The personal attention she had more or less received from Jack in the early days of their relationship.

Before he became caught up with the Winterton hag.

Claire's expression hardened. Jack might not care a hoot for her, but this man clearly thought differently, and his open admiration made her feel alive...desirable! On that first occasion when they had met during Emile's lunch in Calcutta a few years ago, the Italian had openly flirted with her. Claire recalled how Jack had been insultingly indifferent. She wondered if she should allow a flirtation with this extremely good-looking and charming man to develop further...

The following weeks passed in a delightful blur for the young woman, filled with picnics, dances, and best of all a trip to Paris, where Claire was taken to the theatre, to the ballet and opera in that beautiful city. Shopping along elegant tree-lined boulevards, she purchased an evening dress from the salon of a world-famous *couturier* – perfect for the Christmas Ball at Calcutta's Government House, she thought happily.

Declining a ride on horseback, Claire went for a walk with Emile each morning in the surprisingly verdant Bois de Boulogne. Elegantly dressed people were also out and about to enjoy the morning air, some with well-coiffed little dogs trotting alongside on bejewelled leads. The casual sophistication of the Parisian scene was breathtaking to the young woman, and the heat and filth of Calcutta seemed a million miles away.

Next was a visit to Deauville in time for a much-vaunted Race Day, and Emile booked them into a rather grand hotel in the centre of town. Amazingly, it happened to be the very hotel chosen by Vittorio di Rossignanti for his stay. Meeting them in the hotel foyer, he expressed astonishment over the coincidence. Claire, however, had her own ideas about that...

Subsequently, the three of them went about together over the following days, much to Claire's private pleasure. Better still, Vittorio's residence was apparently not far from the Beaurepaire family villa at Saint Jean de Luz. Emile had been talking about spending a few days at the seaside, once the racing was at an end. It stood to reason they would be seeing a good deal of the Italian.

The crowning event of Claire's visit to the resort was a summer ball, given by a local dignitary at his family château nestling between hills behind Saint Jean. It was an ideal opportunity to wear her expensive new evening gown that would blend in satisfactorily with other guests, who were undoubtedly the cream of French society. It was a memorable evening for the young woman, and she resolved to investigate the social scene on the Côte d'Azur, reputed to be even more exclusive than Saint Jean.

Preferably, without her dreary husband.

The next weeks flew past in a whirl of delightful activities. Suddenly – depressingly – Emile reminded Claire it was time to book her passage back to India. Back to a 'holiday' Jack was arranging at some bug-infested beach along the coast from Calcutta. Where her husband was likely to be buried inside newspapers or paperwork of some kind – as entertaining as always. She would be left to cope with children peevish in the sweltering heat, or whining to be taken down the beach to swim in a sea opaque with pollution. A delightful prospect!

It was ridiculous to return to Calcutta whilst it was still so hot! It would make better sense if she could think up a credible pretext to remain in France for a further few weeks, should it be convenient to Emile, of course. Claire approached her host over breakfast the following morning.

"Emile, I wondered if I could stay on a little longer with you? It's still dreadfully hot in Calcutta, and I've been feeling so much better lately. If I left in early September, I would be home in plenty of time to start organising Jack's business entertaining."

"Of course, *ma chèrie*, I'm more than happy for you to remain for as long as you wish. But would Jack not be upset over your delayed arrival? And your small children might be missing their mother? Perhaps it's not such a good idea."

"Jack? Oh, no, he's bound to be fully occupied with the Legislative Council, in addition to his other commitments to the Viceroy," Claire cut in quickly. "As for the girls, they are in the care of my mother who spoils them dreadfully. I doubt they have even noticed my absence."

"In that case, *chèrie*, it will be my pleasure to have your company for a while longer," Emile murmured, if somewhat doubtfully. "Provided you can assure me your so-nice husband will not be annoyed. I would not care for that at all, Claire."

"Jack will be pleased I'm having such a wonderful time, Emile. He was very concerned over my state of health before I left, you know."

"*Bon*! In that case, we will leave the booking of your passage until September. By the way, we are expected for dinner at the Martinets' home in Périgueux this evening, luckily not too far away." Emile suddenly frowned. "*Chérie*, I have to go away for a few days on business around the twenty-fourth of August. Will you be nervous staying here on your own? Amélie would put you up at the château, if you prefer?"

"No, no...please don't bother her," she hastened to assure him. "After all these parties, I shall probably need a restful few days. I can always go for walks in the fresh air, much as my sister and I did the last time we were here."

Back in her bedroom, Claire breathed a sigh of relief, guiltily aware of having trodden a fine line between evasion of the truth...and an outright lie. Well, she was committed now, so she would thrust uncomfortable thoughts aside and enjoy the weeks ahead. She wondered if the Italian would be a guest at the Martinets that evening? It might be of interest to him that she would be on her own for a time...

Vittorio was indeed present that evening. Delighted to see Claire again, he managed to manipulate his hostess's place settings to ensure he was seated next to the young woman at dinner. Openly admiring, he seized an opportunity to whisper how gorgeous she was looking in cream lace, a fresh camellia nestling against her dark hair. The Italian also couldn't believe his luck to learn that Claire would soon be spending a few days alone. How fortunate it was that his wife, Sophia, had returned to Tuscany with their four children some weeks before.

Vittorio knew he must tread carefully, however. Claire was Emile's great-niece, whom he guarded closely in the absence of her husband. Apparently, Jack MacLeod was of political significance in India, and it would not do to create the slightest whiff of scandal. Nevertheless, he sensed Claire was not averse to his overture, so there was every chance it could lead to a delightful liaison – however brief. In Vittorio's experience, the very brevity of an affair left one with the best of memories...

Five days later, Emile set off from his home, trying to suppress a feeling of unease over leaving his young relative by herself, albeit with a household of servants. There was more than a touch of Minette's headstrong tendencies in her daughter, for him to leave with a quiet mind. In any event, there was nothing to be done about it now.

Hearing Emile's car depart, Claire was excited, certain her Italian admirer would soon be in contact. It would be wonderful to spend time with a man who not only thought her attractive, but also clearly enjoyed her company. Unlike her husband who barely registered her existence in his life. For God's sake, it was like living with a stranger except when he chose to exercise his marital rights. *Ugh!* She preferred not to think about that. Nor would she allow herself to brood over the rights and wrongs of things, which could ruin these few days alone with the handsome Italian.

The following morning, Claire was having her breakfast outside on the terrace when she heard the low growl of Vittorio's white roadster entering the gates. Smiling, she replaced her cup on its saucer, and went to greet her admirer.

"I see you haven't wasted any time in coming to see me," she remarked teasingly, "as Emile only left late yesterday afternoon."

"*Cara*, I have been counting the hours," assured the Italian, his teeth flashing in an answering grin. "May I have the pleasure of taking you out for lunch at a restaurant where the food is known to be excellent?"

"That sounds wonderful! But in the meanwhile, come and join me for a cup of coffee."

"*Un momento, per favore*," Vittorio reached inside the car and drew out a shawl of the softest cream wool. "A small gift against the chill of evening."

"Oh, it's absolutely heavenly," breathed the young woman, never having been given a present by any man, except her husband or Frederick. "So soft and cuddly." She held the garment against her cheek. "Thank you so much."

"The pleasure is all mine," the man told her. "Now, where do we go for that cup of coffee you promised me?"

Later that morning, Claire was sitting opposite the Italian in a restaurant deep in the centre of a forest. The narrow lane leading to it had been rutted and lumpy, causing her to wonder what kind of establishment would be hidden away like this? However, the restaurant had already been full of diners...a sure sign of good food. And the meal had certainly fulfilled all expectations, in particular the dessert of *vacherin aux fraises* that Vittorio had ordered for them both.

A tiny cup of coffee in front of her, Claire fitted a lighted cigarette into her jade holder. Silently contemplating the young woman, the Italian wondered if she was aware of her own sensuality. Vivacious as well as intelligent, she was a refreshing change from his usual *piccole amiche*, and he didn't want to frighten her by rushing matters. Claire should set the pace as to how their relationship developed – or not, as the case might turn out. For now, he would drive her back to the Dower House, and perhaps leave her with something to think about.

Parking the car outside the house, Vittorio turned to the young woman sitting beside him. "*Cara mia*, would you care to dine with me at my home tomorrow evening?"

"Oh...er...yes, I'd like to see your house," Claire stammered, caught off-guard. "Is it to be just...ourselves?"

"Yes, unless you wish a chaperone to join us? Unnecessary, I assure you."

"No, of course not," she replied quickly, having regained her equilibrium. "That would be ridiculous, since I'm hardly a blushing schoolgirl! I would love to dine at your home, Vittorio."

"Good girl." Leaning over, he kissed Claire lingeringly on the mouth, and then got out to open the car door. "Thank you for a delightful afternoon, *cara*."

Later that evening, she lay in a warm bath, mulling over the events of the day. There was no doubt as to the Italian's intentions – strictly dishonourable – but oh, how attractive he was with those liquid dark eyes of his!

Vaguely aware of a need for compensation over her loveless marriage, that had consolidated over the years into a burning desire to be avenged on Jack MacLeod, the man who made such casual use of her body. Unconsciously clenching the sponge in her hand, she smiled grimly. Oh, yes...the charming Vittorio was definitely the answer!

Despite her bravado, during the course of the following day Claire found she had to mentally block reservations over her decision to commit adultery, chastising herself for pathetic cowardice. Would Jack hesitate if his tart made herself available? Of course not! He wouldn't give a damn about the girl who just happened to be his wife.

Beautiful in cornflower blue, her dark hair held back by a headband of pearls, Claire waited for the Italian to arrive, nervous anticipation lending an extra sparkle to her eyes. Was this wise? Would she live to regret having dinner alone with this attractive man? Worse still, would she be able to conceal her revulsion of sexual activity from Vittorio? Maybe she should back away now whilst there was still time...

When he arrived to collect her that evening, the frank admiration reflected in the Italian's black eyes went a long way to dissipating Claire's earlier doubts. Walking over to where she was sitting, he reached for her hand and turning it over, pressed an intimate kiss on the inside of her wrist. "*Carissima mia*, how very beautiful you look."

Settling the bedazzled young woman in the car, Vittorio tucked his gift of the soft shawl about her knees and drove the short distance back to his home. Getting out of the car, Claire caught her breath at the sheer beauty of the villa, situated high up in the hills. Leaning against the stone balustrade enclosing a wide terracotta terrace, she could see tiny figures of farm workers far below, slowly trudging towards their homes. A kidney-shaped swimming pool lay just below the terrace, its azure waters reflecting the last golden rays of the summer sun.

Servants were conspicuous by their absence, presumably having been sent off duty for the evening. It crossed Claire's mind to wonder if any of them might report their master's extra-marital activities to his wife? No, Vittorio would never take such an insane risk. He clearly valued his family, despite rarely talking about them.

"What is that saying you English have...a *pound for your thinking*?" The Italian came up behind Claire, and bent to kiss a bare shoulder.

"Almost right," she laughed, feeling her skin prick pleasantly at the touch of the man's lips. "The expression is, *a penny for your thoughts.*"

"But, that is what I said, no?" Pretending bewilderment, he gently turned the girl to gaze into her eyes. "Claire, why do you seem...anxious?"

"I'm not, of course I'm not. I was merely admiring your home and the magnificent view from here. Is all this land yours?"

"Yes, the villa is in the centre of its own pastureland, and beyond there are fields of crops which also form part of the estate."

"Complete privacy...how lovely! Tell me, do you sometimes swim naked in your pool?" Claire enquired, surprised by her own daring.

"Often, *cara mia*," Vittorio handed Claire a glass of chilled champagne, "but it is too cool to do so this evening. Sit down a moment, and tell me about your exciting life in Calcutta. And how you stand that terrible heat? Me, I would *die!*"

Three glasses of champagne later, followed by a delicious meal of fat prawns in a creamy garlic sauce, the plate mopped clean with chunks of fresh brown bread, Claire was feeling relaxed. Two further glasses of red wine added to her euphoric state, and she now savoured the aromatic flavour of Grand Marnier, a *digestif* liqueur. The night air was noticeably cooler, and Claire gave an involuntary shiver.

"*Cara*, are you feeling cold?" Vittorio asked in concern. "Shall we go inside now?"

Entering his salon, Claire was ushered over to a thickly cushioned couch. Sitting next to her, the man leaned forward to kiss her gently on the mouth.

"I have been wanting to do that all evening, *cara mia*," he whispered. "You are very beautiful, you know, very seductive, and your husband is a lucky man."

"I doubt he would agree with that," Claire answered shortly, "Jack is a rather cold individual, and not in the least way romantically inclined."

"*Impossibile*! With a woman such as yourself, making love should be a highlight of his days," Vittorio's warm lips traced a line from the young woman's neck down over her shoulder. "So exciting…so sensual."

Claire trembled, an unknown excitement flooding her body, and unaccountably breathless, her mouth opened in unconscious invitation. Rising to his feet, the Italian wordlessly picked Claire up as though she were a featherweight, and carried her through to his bedroom.

"*La bella donna*, I want to make love to you…as you ought to be loved," he whispered against Claire's hair, "and from the very first moment that I saw you."

Her senses tingling, Claire was dimly aware of the softness of fur as she was placed on a wide bed. Kicking off her high-heeled shoes, she stretched out her arms to the man, who bent to thoroughly kiss her, then divested himself of his clothes.

Vittorio kissed every exposed part of her body whilst deftly removing her clothing, until she lay naked without shame…to her own utter incredulity. Sinking to his knees, he parted her thighs and his tongue flicked out, exploring the darkness of the most secret parts of her body. Claire gasped, her eyes snapping open in shock and began to resist: then seized by a rush of unfamiliar pleasure, her body seemed to have a mind of its own. With a moan of ecstasy she grasped the man's thick hair with both hands, her thighs unconsciously falling apart to receive her lover.

Two hours later, Claire awoke, guessing she must have dozed off subsequent to an hour of intense lovemaking. Vittorio had taken his time, caressing her body in erotic places she hadn't known existed. And just as she thought the pleasure was past bearing he plunged into her body, bringing her to heights of unbridled passion she hadn't believed possible. The experience had left her gasping and satisfied.

Languorously stretching out her arms, she was conscious of a sense of fulfilment such as she had never known. During all those years as Jack MacLeod's wife, all she had ever felt was revulsion for the sexual act that seemed to increase as the years went by. A legacy of her wedding night, perhaps, when her new husband had carelessly, shockingly ruined a young girl's romantic expectations.

Suddenly aware of being watched, Claire turned her head to look into the amused black eyes of her lover. God, just looking at him made her feel breathless and sexy. Far from her usual desperation to rush away and shower herself clean, she was conscious of an overwhelming desire for her lover to take her again, which Vittorio promptly did, and with great expertise.

Initially, the Italian had been astonished by Claire's sexual inexperience...bordering on innocence. *Dio*, it seemed as if he was attempting to deflower a virgin! Yet she had been married for some years, and even had two children. He shook his head in disbelief. *Signor* MacLeod must be the clumsiest of idiots to take his own pleasure without thought for his wife's feelings.

Vergogna su lui!

But how different Claire had quickly become! His earlier suspicion that depths to her sexuality existed not far below the surface had proved correct. The Italian smiled, his eyes sparkling with pleasure, knowing he was responsible for the transformation to wild abandonment and a willingness to explore the unknown. It was also true that she triggered a fresh response in himself, a man of experience, if not entirely a *roué*!

"I think you had better run me home soon." Claire reluctantly swung her legs over the side of the bed. "It wouldn't do to give Emile's servants something to gossip about, but I'd like to shower first, if you don't mind."

Ten minutes later, Claire emerged from the house. Fresh and unruffled, she skipped down to where the Italian was waiting in the car, its engine already running. Her first sally into the world of adultery had gone marvellously, and no longer would she jump through hoops to entice her charmless husband to make love in a credible manner. Now that she knew what it was to reach heights of unbridled passion – frankly, Jack MacLeod could take a running jump.

The days flew past, and it was finally time for Claire take passage back to India. Reluctant to abandon a lifestyle that eminently suited her, she fiercely hugged her uncle, thanking him for putting up with her for such an age. Boarding the ship, she stood at the railing in the stern, sadly watching the French coast dwindle to a dark smudge on the horizon.

Chapter Fourteen

Even in mid-September, the heat and intense humidity in Bombay was suffocating, blasting Claire full in the face so that she gasped upon emerging on deck. Wrinkling her nose at the familiar pungency of the dark green waters lapping about the ship, she went over to side overlooking the quayside where people stood in groups, waiting to greet disembarking passengers. In order to leave the port, they would be obliged to wend their way through a mass of fruit and vegetable stands, feeling stifled by the heat and heaviness of the air, not improved by smoke from *beedies* infiltrating the atmosphere.

Shading her eyes, Claire scanned the crowds, searching for a familiar face. Emile had sent a telegram with her passage details to Jack, so surely there would be someone here to meet her? For God's sake, the ship had dropped anchor an hour ago, she thought irritably. After the mildness of climate and civilisation of life in Europe, Claire was finding a return to the reality of life in India to be something of a shock.

A white handkerchief wildly flapping attracted her attention. Squinting against the glare of the sun, she recognised Christina and Frederick standing in the shade of a nearby building. Waving in acknowledgement, Claire returned inside to collect a small suitcase she had left at the Purser's Office. Her cabin trunk would be off-loaded later on, an exercise that would undoubtedly take some time. Taking the transport ferry to shore, she clambered up a set of slimy stone steps to the cobbled quayside where her sister and Frederick were waiting to greet her.

Beaming in genuine pleasure, Claire ran forward to hug her sister, noticing with a prickle of apprehension from the corner of her eye that Frederick was looking unusually grim. Nevertheless, he kissed her soundly on both cheeks, before departing to identify Claire's trunk from a swiftly growing pile of luggage on the wharf.

"Chrissy?" Claire asked, glancing at Frederick's retreating back. "Is there something the matter with Uncle Freddie? He's not sick is he?"

"No," Christina shook her head. "He's just not very pleased with you right now. I imagine you will know why."

"As a matter of fact, I don't, but I'm sure you are about to enlighten me?"

"Claire, you are *three whole weeks* late," exclaimed the younger girl heatedly. "Talk about overstepping the mark! Didn't you think about your two little girls, waiting, and waiting for you to come home? Jack is absolutely livid, especially since he was obliged to take the children to Gopalpore on his own. He said you knew perfectly well he was planning a family beach holiday at the beginning of September."

"*Oh, for God's sake!*" Claire exploded. "So what if Jack went to the beach on his own? All he ever does on holiday is read his blasted newspapers and give me the silent treatment. I assume Susan went with him? Yes? In that case, I fail to see the problem. Anyway, I'm here now, aren't I? Ready to do my stuff for his bloody entertaining."

"Must you swear like that, Claire?" Christina looked upset. "You know very well you're in the wrong, regardless of what you may say."

"She's right, you know," Frederick had rejoined the girls, a *coolie* close behind, bearing Claire's trunk on his back. "Those months you had in France, weren't they enough for you? It hadn't crossed my mind that you could be so damnably self-centred, Claire, capable of not thinking twice about disappointing your two little girls."

Her brittle bravado rapidly eroding, Claire was upset that Frederick should speak so sharply to her. Bolstering a wilting morale, she fiercely blinked back the treacherous tears threatening to undermine her composure. After all, those extra weeks were worth every ticking off that might come her way! Jack MacLeod could rant to his heart's content, but she now had a marvellous secret. Her sense of self-worth was restored, and the door to future delightful liaisons now lay wide open...

The three undertook the lengthy train journey to Calcutta in relatively cool silence. Claire pretended to sleep, unwilling to discuss her absence in any detail. Christina either slept or read a book, whilst Frederick concentrated on official-looking papers from his briefcase. The chilliness of the atmosphere grated on Claire's nerves to the point where she was heartily relieved when the train finally pulled into Howrah Station. Of course, she still had Jack to face, and should he imagine she would be grovelling for his forgiveness...he had another think coming.

Jack MacLeod was irritably waiting on the other side of the barrier, having been obliged to take time out of his busy day to collect his wife. Watching Claire approach, he noticed how fresh and rested she seemed,

178

despite the rigours of a long train journey. But not in the least way, regretful – he thought savagely. Thanking Frederick and Christina for undertaking the task of meeting Claire, he placed a perfunctory kiss on his wife's cheek.

Silence prevailed in the car as the driver made his way to Camack Street to drop off Frederick and Christina. Stealing a glance at her husband's profile, Claire saw nothing remotely reassuring in his expression. The silence was equally profound during the subsequent drive back to the house in Alipore.

As the car drew up under the entrance portico, Jack finally addressed his wife. "When you have seen your daughters, Claire, I would like a word with you in my study as soon as possible, if you please."

"Very well." Claire shrugged indifferently, anxious to conceal the apprehension she was unable to prevent. "In half an hour or so, I imagine."

The front door opened and Nanny Susan appeared, a little girl on either side of her. Daphne leaned shyly against the nanny's starched skirts, but Diana had seen her father and ran forward with a shout of joy.

"Daddy," Diana held up her arms, "can you give me a ride on your shoulders?"

"In a moment, poppet," Jack indicated Claire who was just emerging from the Daimler, "after you have said hello to Mummy."

"Hello," Diana threw a cursory glance towards her mother. "Pick me up, Daddy."

"Aren't you going to give me a kiss, darling?" Claire ground her teeth with repressed irritation. "I haven't seen you and Daffy for such a long time."

"No! Kiss Daffy instead," the child replied, not even glancing at Claire, "'cos she's the one you like best."

Breathing deeply, Claire approached her younger daughter who still clung to the nanny. "Come and see the lovely present Mummy has for you, darling."

Daphne looked up, intrigued by the mention of a present. Releasing the nanny's skirt, she hesitantly walked over to her mother who bent to kiss her.

"What about me?" Diana suddenly demanded, "don't I get a present too?"

"I don't give presents to rude children," Claire told her eldest daughter.

"Daddy?" Diana looked at her father. "It's not fair if Mummy gives Daffy a present but not me."

"Do as you mother asks, Di-Di," Jack frowned, "and I'm sure she will also have something for you."

Walking over to Claire, Diana deposited a barely discernible kiss on her mother's cheek. "Now can I have my present?"

"What about the 'magic' word?"

"Please, please, please!" the older child glared angrily. "Is that enough for you?"

Her patience snapping, Claire straightened. Taking Daphne's hand, she stalked up the steps and into the house. "When you decide to stop being an unpleasant little girl," she threw over her shoulder, "we'll see about a present for you, and not before."

Daphne was delighted with the Breton doll her mother gave her, and cuddling it to her chest, allowed Susan to lead her away to the nursery. Glowering blackly, Diana remained with her father.

Mindful of Jack's demand for her presence in his study, Claire nevertheless took the opportunity to have a cool shower and change into fresh clothes. An hour and a half later, she tapped on the study door and entered. Her husband was seated at his desk, looking over papers but upon seeing Claire, he rose to his feet. Meeting his chilly green gaze without flinching, the young woman settled herself in a nearby chair without waiting for an invitation. She fitted a lighted cigarette into her jade holder, and casually exhaled a stream of blue smoke in her husband's direction.

"Would you care to explain why you chose to ignore my specific wish that you return to Calcutta by the end of August?" Jack concealed his annoyance to have smoke blown in his face. "You knew I was arranging a family holiday at the beach."

"Oh, for God's sake, Jack, *must* you make a huge drama over trivia?" Claire drawled with a long-suffering sigh. "I was benefiting so much from the cooler climate, that it seemed ridiculous to return to the stinking August heat."

"Don't take me for a fool, Claire!" Jack snapped, his Scot's accent becoming more pronounced as his anger mounted. "You have always enjoyed rude health, despite the heat, and your everlasting complaints of exhaustion. So what – or who – was the reason for your extended stay in France?"

"What can you mean, Jack?" Claire's vivid blue eyes opened wide, and then she laughed out loud. "Please don't tell me you're jealous, because I won't believe that for a second. More 'dog-in-the-manger', I suspect. As for the beach holiday, I'm amazed you think the prospect was sufficiently attractive to bring me racing back to Calcutta! Whenever I've been on holiday in your scintillating company, all I have ever known is the occasional bad-tempered grunt from behind a newspaper."

Jack's lips tightened angrily. "I don't care for your frivolous stance, Claire. Believe me, I won't tolerate idle gossip about my wife's behaviour, either here or in France."

"Don't you dare take the moral high ground with me, Jack MacLeod," came the hot interruption. "You are hardly in a position to do so, remember."

"I want you to understand once and for all," Jack fought to control his temper, "that I will not allow this disgraceful neglect of your children in future. As regards the way you choose to lead your life, I sincerely hope your general behaviour befits my position here in Calcutta. Unblemished."

"Then you had better listen to me now, dear chap!" Claire's eyes sparked fire. "I accept that I should have come home earlier, if only for the girls' benefit. But I have every intention of returning to Europe during the hot weather, and nothing will prevent me. Next time, however, I shall take the children with me."

Silence followed Claire's angry statement. Jack stared at his wife, suddenly aware of her undeniable beauty when roused. It crossed his mind to wonder anew if Claire's protracted holiday in France was due to some bloody fellow sniffing after her? Had she…could she have actually taken a lover? His jaw tightened. By God, if that proved to be the case, he would take steps to see the bugger off.

Correctly reading the changing expressions on her husband's face, Claire smiled grimly. "My dear Jack, do please remember the 'bargain' we agreed upon in South Africa. I would fulfil my duties as your wife, entertain your guests, and attend to general social requirements. I also agreed to bear your children, something I have already carried out. In return, I should have everything I wished within reason. And in light of no real intimacy existing between us, we must surely allow each other freedom of choice relating to sexual partners."

"What rubbish is this?"

"The only rule being utter discretion," Claire continued inexorably "that we may present a united front to the world. Personally, I have done nothing I am ashamed of, neither have I broken any part of our 'bargain'.

I can't help but wonder if the same can be said of you, my dear chap?"

Flushing a dull red, Jack stormed out of the room and a moment later, she heard the car drive off. Taking a shaky drag from her cigarette, Claire's mouth relaxed into a pleased smile. With luck and a following wind, her husband might be put off visiting her bedroom – for tonight, at least.

After a game of tennis that evening, a thoughtful Claire sat on the edge of the new swimming pool in the back garden, sipping a weak whisky and soda and dangling her over-heated feet in the cool water. The accusation of neglecting the children had struck home, despite her outwardly defiant stance. It wasn't only Jack who had flung that at her, but Frederick and her sister had also voiced their dismay.

Had she really been guilty of neglecting her girls? The idea had been sufficiently disturbing for her to visit to the nursery before going outside. Both children were fast asleep, a dimmed light in an adjoining room indicating Nanny Susan's vigilance.

Under a mosquito net, Diana lay on her back, her short vest rucked up to her armpits. Red-gold curls lay in damp whorls on her forehead, despite a gentle breeze from the ceiling fan whirling overhead. In sleep, the child's face had relaxed its hostile expression, the unusual vulnerability provoking an unexpected rush of affection in Claire for her first-born daughter.

Next to her older sister, Daphne lay curled up on her side, ardently sucking her thumb whilst fast asleep. Her wavy hair, much the same colour as Diana's, clung to the sides of her perspiring face. But what a pretty little thing she was, Claire reflected as she gently tried to remove the child's thumb from her mouth. At once the small face screwed up ready to wail, so she hurriedly allowed the thumb to remain *in situ*.

Before leaving the nursery, Claire placed a light kiss on her daughters' cheeks, rosy with heat and sleep. With a sigh, she wondered why they became so irritating when awake, each in her own way. Had this not been the case, her relationship with both girls would be vastly improved. Nevertheless, it was important to bridge the yawning gap between herself and her children.

Taking a sip of her drink, Claire wriggled her toes in the cool water, her gloomy mood lightening. She was not the dreadful mother everyone seemed determined to portray. At the same time, why must her life continually revolve around two small children? A nanny attended to them on a daily basis, and if Christina wished to martyr herself – that was her choice. Surely, it was a question of keeping a proper perspective on one's day-to-day life in general? One thing was certain, however, she would be spending future summers in Europe – with the children, if needs be.

To Claire's utter dismay, Jack availed himself of her body that same night, despite the earlier unpleasant scene. As always, the act took place in silence until Jack rolled away to begin snoring. Slipping out of bed, the young woman lost no time in hurrying to the bathroom, standing under the shower, scrubbing and sluicing her body clean. She then crept back to bed, disgust keeping her awake long into the night.

How different it had been with Vittorio! Although she was not in love with the Italian, he had taught her what she had the right to expect from the sexual act. And Jack? Claire's mouth assumed a straight line with resentment. For him she was merely a convenience, a fact he did not bother to conceal. She could only hope he would be too tired to visit her room again for some time.

Days turned into weeks, and weeks into months, as Claire immersed herself in a whirl of social activity during the cold weather season. Increasing involvement with the government translated into an increased number of cocktail parties and formal dinners at the MacLeod's home. Claire's excellence in organisation and manner in which she made her guests feel welcome, invariably elicited a wave of complimentary remarks from visiting government dignitaries and her husband's business associates. She revelled in such accolades, and even Jack was moved to appreciation.

"Colonel Atkinson rang me this morning to say how much he and his wife enjoyed yesterday evening at our home. They thought you had put on a truly marvellous show, the dinner was superb and the guests interesting. The Colonel asked how you organised all of that, and still managed to look ravishing into the bargain?"

"How sweet!" Claire's face broke into a smile of genuine pleasure, "I thought they were lovely people, and I wish all our guests were as easy to please."

"I'm very grateful," Jack told his wife. "An excellent opinion from important people such as these enhances my position within government circles."

"Good," she replied airily. "I'm glad you are happy with my efforts, Jack."

"Er...is there anything that you would like? Some jewellery perhaps?"

"Thank you, but no," Claire shook her head. "But I would like to learn how to drive a trap, if you can find someone who would teach me? I've always loved horses, but I can't bring myself to ride, having lost my nerve as a child. Driving will allow me contact with a horse, but in a different way. Besides, it looks tremendous fun!"

"I'll make a few enquiries." Jack nodded, surprised by the request. "Frederick might know of an army fellow interested in making a bit of extra cash on the side. As regards a suitable horse, I remember there was a nice little mare retired from the polo field last season, that seemed quiet enough."

Thanks to Hugh Amesley, the young army officer who had undertaken to teach Claire, in a matter of a few weeks she was becoming a competent carriage driver. Sophie, the ex-polo pony, possessed of a sweet and gentle nature, took to her new task of drawing a buggy without missing a beat. Practice sessions took place around the perimeter of the racecourse, during the early morning whilst it was relatively cool and few people were about. Claire was thrilled with her new skill, and could scarcely wait for a suitable opportunity to show it off. How unique it would be for a woman to be seen to be driving a buggy by herself! And as time passed, so her confidence grew.

An international polo tournament due to take place the following month presented itself as being ideal. Being a popular sport with Indian and European communities alike, it generated enthusiastic crowds of spectators lining the pitch at every game. They would arrive in droves, fully equipped for the occasion with picnic hampers, folding tables, stools and sometimes even their dogs.

Teams from princely states all over India would soon be arriving to compete at this much-vaunted occasion, and Claire knew a team had recently arrived from England. She was particularly excited because Sunita would undoubtedly be accompanying her husband, as the Maharajah of Godrapur captained a visiting team.

"Hugh, what do you think of letting me drive Sophie over to the polo ground at the start of the tournament...by myself?" Claire casually asked her instructor on the way home from driving practice one morning. "Brilliant idea, wouldn't you say?"

Hugh turned to stare at her, his mouth falling open in consternation. Was this a joke? Claire MacLeod did rather enjoy a giggle at his expense on occasion. Maybe not, for the blue gaze he encountered was clearly in earnest. *Christ*! What was he to say to her? More to the point, what would Jack MacLeod have to say if his wife took part in such a jape? Quite a lot – thought Hugh, with feeling.

"Er...bit on the daring side, don't you think?" the officer muttered uncomfortably. "Not sure your husband would like it, ma'am."

"Rubbish!" Claire declared forcefully. "Jack has no say in what I choose to do. Do stop being so frightfully stuffy," she added, expertly guiding Sophie up the rear driveway to the stables. "I thought you said I was now a competent carriage driver?"

"Yes, yes, of course you are...but don't you think it too much of a risk? Think of the noise, lots of people and loud music blaring? The mare might not—"

"For heaven's sake, Sophie must be used to that sort of thing after her years as a polo pony." Claire pulled up, and a *syce* came running over to take the sweating horse for a cooling shower. Climbing down from the buggy, she glanced at her instructor with a charming smile. "Do think about it, Hugh, and we can discuss it again next week?"

The officer gazed unhappily after Claire's retreating back. He had come to know the young lady rather well, and in fact he admired her determination to excel in what she had set out to do. But this madcap scheme of hers would test his resolve to assist the lady in her quest for excellence to the very limit! Maybe he should try a diplomatic approach, and point out the possible impropriety of her suggestion?

Hugh Amesley failed to convince Claire that her daring idea was not the thing to do. The young woman relentlessly out-argued the unfortunate young man, who finally relapsed into reluctant silence. The racecourse entrance was not at all far away, Claire reminded him. If he was so worried, Hugh could borrow the *syce's* bicycle and ride behind the buggy at a discreet distance. And he should remember her sweet Sophie had never put a foot wrong...

"But it must be our secret," Claire was emphatic, "so no running off to tell Jack who is even stuffier than you are. Oh, what fun it will be to give those *burrah-memsahibs* something other than each other to gossip about," she said with a giggle.

"I'll try." Hugh smiled weakly, conceding defeat despite his reservations. "But promise me you won't try anything faster than a trot, and remember I'll be on the bike behind you to check."

"Trot it will be, I swear!" Claire grinned triumphantly. "Now, I must plan what Sophie and I are to wear for the occasion."

Saturday, the day of the polo tournament, dawned fine and cool to everyone's relief. Claire visited the stables early, anxious to ensure her horse and equipment met with her approval. Wearing a dress of pink voile that she knew suited her well, a straw hat hung down her back by ribbons of the same hue. Pretty bows of the identical pink decorated each side of Sophie's bridle and the driving whip. Satisfied, Claire returned to the house to have breakfast with her husband.

"Please don't be late at the polo field, Claire," Jack looked up from cracking the shell of his boiled egg. "I have important guests joining our party, and I will need your help with the picnic lunch. Did you remember to ask *kensama* to include *alu-chops* and chutney?"

"Yes, and he looked astonished. How on earth can we expect people to eat bread-crumbed balls of mashed potato and mince with their fingers, Jack? So messy!"

"Then tell the *bearer* to add knives and forks to the picnic basket." Jack returned to his egg. "And plenty of beer for us fellows," he added.

"Doesn't that rather defeat the idea of a picnic?" Claire compressed her lips with irritation. Sipping her coffee, she distracted herself by thinking of the impression she would soon be making later that morning. If only Jack would hurry up and go.

At last, her husband's car disappeared down the drive, and she hurried down to the stables where Hugh was already waiting. In minutes, Sophie was harnessed to the buggy, and taking up the reins, Claire settled herself on the seat. With a final grin at her instructor astride the *syce's* bicycle, she clicked her tongue, and the horse set off at a brisk walk towards the rear gates.

The narrow roads to the racecourse were familiar, and Claire negotiated them without mishap. Nevertheless, Hugh breathed a sigh of relief as the young woman turned into the rear entrance, and made her way towards the polo pitch where spectators were already gathering. He saw Claire pause and allow the horse to graze for a few minutes, presumably to time her arrival at the scene for maximum impact.

Five minutes later, Claire took up the reins and set off towards the pitch at a spanking trot, Hugh pedalling furiously in pursuit. It must be admitted, thought the young officer, the sight of Claire flying along in her buggy was certainly impressive, pink ribbons streaming behind!

If she wanted to make a grand entrance, she had certainly achieved it for everyone was looking away from the polo game, to watch the young woman driving a buggy alone in fascination.

Recognising her husband's Daimler, Claire drew Sophie to a halt behind it, and requested a passing *syce* to find a bucket of water for the mare. It was only then that she noticed Jack bearing down on her, his face tight with anger.

"Why, in God's name, are you making a ridiculous spectacle of yourself, Claire?"

"Spectacle? Oh yes, I'm hoping to impress those ladies whose sole interests appear to be boring coffee mornings, bridge and interminable mahjong games!" Claire smiled sweetly at her husband. "And I wanted you to see the marvellous progress I've made with my driving, after all those lessons you paid for."

Lugging the bicycle across the turf, a heavily sweating Hugh came puffing up to them. Catching Jack MacLeod's infuriated eye, he lifted a shoulder in eloquent and silent apology. Claire meanwhile had spotted her *Maharani* friend, Sunita, leaning from the car window and laughing with delight. Raising her driving whip in salute, she gathered up her reins preparatory to a return home. It had never been her intention to stay long, knowing the increasing heat would be unfair on the mare.

At that moment, play resumed, and the spectators returned their attention to the galloping horses on the playing field. Suddenly Sophie tensed, stirred by a not-so-dim memory from her past. One of the players lofted the ball back up the pitch, and with a joyful squeal, she took off after it at a gallop, seemingly oblivious of the buggy bumping about unsteadily behind her. Caught by surprise, Claire was almost unseated, and clutched desperately at the sides of the wildly lurching vehicle. Regaining her balance, feet braced against the footboard, she hauled on the reins to try and turn the mare away from the chukka in progress.

But Sophie was enjoying herself far too much! Flattening her ears, she saw off a player who came galloping too close with the intention of grasping her bridle. Defeated, all Claire could do was hang on to the reins in terror that they might entangle with the excited mare's legs. Moments later, the mortified young woman endured the ignominy of a team member bringing her horse to a halt, sarcastically enquiring as to what position did the lady imagine herself to be playing?

"Frightfully sorry, but my horse was bitten by an insect," she muttered, scarlet with embarrassment. "Thank you for giving me a hand, but I can manage now. Let go...will you please *let go* of my horse's bridle?"

A flustered Hugh came panting up to the stationary vehicle, and climbed up into it. Satisfied that someone competent was now in control, the player holding the horse released his grip on the bridle. Seeing the young woman beside him was on the verge of tears, Hugh directed a clearly reluctant Sophie through a gap in the spectators towards the rear entrance.

Looking straight ahead, Claire avoided glancing in the direction of her glowering husband who was standing by the car, hands on his hips. She was painfully aware she would have to face him later, but for now all she wanted was to go home.

As they turned in through the rear gates to the stables, delayed reaction set in and Claire dissolved into hiccupping tears. Quickly handing over the mare to a hovering *syce*, Hugh led the distressed young woman away from curious eyes.

"Oh Hugh, I n...never imagined Sophie could do something like that," she wept. "Her mouth was like iron, and she didn't seem to c...care how hard I pulled on the reins! I c...can't understand it, as she's always been s...so easy to manage."

"Poor thing, you must have had a bad fright," the young officer consoled her, stifling a laugh. "But Sophie clearly thought what fun it would be to join in the chukka."

"I'll n...never live it d...down, you know," Claire sniffled. "I saw lots of people k...killing themselves laughing, some shouted rude things. I b...bet you anything that hilarious stories about me will be circulating for months."

"Of course there will be talk about you," Hugh now laughed outright. "*My deah*, did you see the way young Mrs MacLeod controlled that dreadful runaway horse? Jolly brave of her, what? Oh yes, ma'am, you will be remembered for a very long time."

Claire managed a watery grin. It was probably true the incident would be a talking point for months on end...but maybe not in the way she would wish. Doubtless, her loving husband would delight in rubbing in that particular aspect!

Chapter Fifteen

The remainder of the cold weather season dragged past for Claire, forced to endure sniggered asides and amused whispers when she entered a room, even outright laughter on occasion. She overheard someone declare that polo would never be the same again after the *ad lib* entertainment during the last tournament! Humiliated beyond her worst imaginings, the young woman still held her head up high.

In defiance of advice to the contrary, Claire continued driving lessons until Hugh was despatched to another unit in northern India. Silas Ingram, another army officer with a significant sense of humour failure, had been delegated to take Hugh's place. Claire could not bear the man's sour face, and it soon came to her ears he was complaining over his task of playing 'nursemaid' to someone's flighty wife. Furious, she immediately dispensed with Ingram's services.

The heat of the summer months was now well on the way, and most families began making preparations to leave the city for the cool of hill stations. Claire was encouraged to accompany her friend, Felicity Miller and her children to Mussorie, an invitation Claire found easy to refuse, never having forgotten her experiences of Ranchi. Never again would she associate with the likes of those sanctimonious people who took it upon themselves to dictate what she could, or couldn't do.

In any event, Claire had her own ideas about how to avoid the stifling Calcutta heat. She would spend five months in France, despite what Jack might have to say about it. Should old grievances be raked up, she would inform him the children would be going with her – and the nanny, of course.

Claire grimaced, thinking of being obliged to put up with Nanny Susan's obvious, if silent disapproval of her mistress. But neither could she bear the idea of being chained to her daughters' activities for the duration of the holiday. But perhaps Chrissy might like to go? She adored the little girls, and would readily help with their care.

To Claire's relief, Christina declared herself delighted by the prospect of a few months away from the heat. She was recovering from a bout of bronchitis caught from a pupil at the college where she taught, but an irritating cough seemed to drag on forever. A trip to Europe would make a wonderful change.

During dinner with Jack one evening, Claire presented her plans to spend the summer at a resort along the Côte d'Azur. She was astonished to see a wide smile appear on his face.

"South of France?" Jack wiped his mouth with a napkin, his expression quizzical. "Now, there's a coincidence. For once my affairs will allow me to take my family away for a month or so. Nice, on the southern coast seemed a good choice, so I've booked a suite for us at the Negresco Hotel for the end of this month. If you wish Christina to come with us, booking another room is unlikely to present a problem, I feel sure."

"Oh…I see!" Claire tried to conceal her dismay. "How odd that we should have chosen the same area in France. Well, that's settled, then."

"We sail in only ten days time, so I'll get on with booking a passage for Christina as well as another suite at the Negresco. I imagine you intend the girls to sleep in a room adjoining Christina's, so we'll need something with two bedrooms. Shall we have our coffee out on the veranda? *Bearer*, put my cigars and *memsahib's* cigarettes on the coffee tray, please."

Noticing his wife's discomfited expression, Jack rose from the table, pleased to have outwitted her for once. It was clear she had not counted on having her wings clipped, so to speak, but he was damned if he would condone the high-jinks he strongly suspected she had indulged in during that last trip to France.

Claire sat smoking a cigarette, resentfully contemplating those delightful summer months now effectively sabotaged by her husband's announcement. Trust Jack to be casting a blight over everything. He was bound to stop her from visiting casinos, and neither would he allow her to place her own bets on a horse on the grounds it was unsuitable behaviour for a lady. Such rot! What was there now to look forward to?

Claire sat up, struck by a thought. Since his presence seemed to be required almost continually by this or that, it would be unlikely that Jack could stay away for longer than a few weeks. Decidedly more cheerful, Claire sat back in her chair and sipped her coffee. She would put up with his dreary presence with grace, and then kick up her heels when he left!

Diana was delighted her father would be going on holiday with them. She had previously thrown a tantrum, declaring in a horrifying *chi-chi* accent that she would not leave her Daddy or Nanny Susan. Exasperated,

Claire placated the older child by telling her Auntie Christina would be accompanying them to France. Diana calmed down, but Daphne continued to whine about parting from her nanny for such a long, long time...

Fed up, Claire decided both girls had become indulged little brats, and that it was high time they learned to toe the line. Furthermore, they were beginning to adopt that vile accent of Susan's, so the first step would be to get rid of the nanny. The woman was lazy and far too permissive, and the girls happily ran rings around her. Besides which, that reproachful face of hers was intensely irritating. She must go.

A new nanny would be employed upon their return to Calcutta, and they were easy enough to come by. Someone more dynamic, who would ensure the girls behaved correctly at all times and improved their manners in general. A good speaking voice would also be an advantage. It did not occur to Claire, that deprived of the nanny who had looked after them from birth could have an adverse effect on the children. Neither did she think of Susan's possible emotional upset, wrongly assuming it was a job to the nanny that had run its course. Armed with a good reference from the MacLeods, she should easily find another position.

Informed that her job was to be terminated, the nanny was also warned that she must not tell the girls under any circumstances. Upset and weepy, Susan knew the remaining days with her small charges would require supreme self-control on her part. Madam had made it clear that unless she kept silent, she would forgo a generous bonus by way of compensation, and she could not afford that.

The day of departure dawned, and there was a flurry in the household, ensuring all arrangements for management of the property were in place. The luggage was loaded, and the two children waved goodbye to a tearful Susan standing on the steps of the house, watching the car depart down the drive.

A few minutes earlier, Daphne had burst into tears and flown to the nanny, her clinging hands forcibly detached by her annoyed mother from the distraught woman's skirts. Sobbing, she sat beside her sister in the car, begging to be allowed to stay behind with her nanny.

"For heaven's sake, *stop* that silly noise, Daffy!" Claire snapped. "One might imagine you are being punished, instead of going on a lovely holiday."

"But...but I want Nanny Susan to come too," choked the little girl, "I want my nanny! Why can't she come with us?"

191

"Another word, and you'll get a good slap!" Claire was close to losing her temper. Diana looked disdainful over her sister's hysterical display, neither child suspecting their beloved nanny would not be waiting when they returned home.

The passage to France proved to be enjoyable for both Claire and Jack, largely thanks to Christina, who shared the children's cabin and looked after them for most of the day. When Daphne was struck down by a bout of seasickness, it was Christina who mopped up, and spoon-fed sieved vegetables to her once the afflicted child felt well enough to eat.

"Thank you so much for looking after Daffy," Claire gratefully told her sister. "I know it's ridiculous, but the odour of sick makes me want to vomit so I would have been completely useless. When she's recovered, I'll take over the girls."

Christina looked at her sister askance, but said nothing. Claire might mean that now, but she doubted it would come about since she wasn't good at managing her children. She sighed resignedly. Life would be easier for all concerned if she continued looking after them, and besides, she dearly loved the two little girls.

Jack, however, was conscious of Christina looking after his daughters, perceiving it as Claire taking rank advantage of her sister. He voiced his concern over lunch one day, that being the only meal Christina was able to share with them.

"Christina, I'm very aware that you are taking charge of Di-Di and Daffy all day long, and it can't leave much time for you to enjoy yourself, I imagine?"

"Oh, Jack, I really don't mind..." she began.

"Perhaps, but let's be fair about it, shall we? I've decided to pay you a weekly salary for your help with the girls, and we'll have *no* arguments, please!"

Claire smiled with pleasure. She had been feeling guilty over having effectively abandoned care of her children to her sister, so it was only right that she received financial compensation. Darling Chrissy! Life wouldn't be the same without her quiet presence at her side.

The liner duly docked at Cherbourg, and after disembarking, Jack and his extended family travelled to Paris by train. Then came a taxi ride from the station to the Hotel de Crillon on the Place de la Concorde, where they were booked in to spend two nights. The taxi driver chattily informed his passengers that France's King Louis XVI and his Queen

Marie Antoinette were guillotined close to the very hotel where they were to stay. Shuddering, Claire translated for Jack and Christina, imagining how petrified the Austrian princess must have been, surrounded by a rabble baying for her blood.

The Crillon was certainly as luxurious as it's reputation, and the MacLeods' large suites were much to Claire's taste. Both possessed en suite bathrooms, equipped with a quantity of fluffy white towels and a selection of bath crystals.

Christina was unpacking the girls' nightclothes and toiletries when she overheard hysterical giggling coming from the bathroom. Glancing round the door, she only just managed to prevent Diana from popping a 'pink sweetie' from a jar into her sister's willing mouth. Placing the bath salts on a shelf out the children's reach, she was thankful that Claire had returned to her own suite, or Diana would have had a good spanking for such a silly prank.

Over dinner that evening, Claire stared blankly at the back of the impressively large menu in her husband's hands. For God's sake, he'd been perusing the damned thing for ages, and they were all starving! A waiter had come and gone twice for his order, but Jack was still undecided over his choice. A simple meal had already been served to the little girls, and Christina seemed unconcerned by the delay.

Across the table, Claire couldn't help being irritated by her sister's willingness to accommodate Jack's ridiculous foibles. It was hardly an exciting prospect to be landed for weeks with peevish children and a husband who was a crashing bore, she thought gloomily, his presence being the equivalent of an invisible chain around her ankle.

Five minutes later, Jack decided upon roast chicken and potatoes – his usual choice of meal. Suppressing her annoyance, Claire took the menu and ordered for herself and her sister. Aside from the children's chatter, the meal progressed in silence, after which the family retired to their respective rooms for the night.

The following day, Claire took Christina shopping for clothes, having been appalled by the washed-out rag her sister had worn for dinner the previous evening. Despite Christina's protestations, attractive ensembles were duly purchased, and the two young women arrived back at the hotel loaded with parcels. Sulky and bored after hours of shopping, Claire guiltily resolved to make it up to the children. At her enquiry, the receptionist produced a brochure announcing a circus was not far from the hotel.

The children were excited and jumped up and down, despite a circus being an unknown concept to them. Poring over the brochure, Diana was entranced by images of girls doing acrobatics on the backs of galloping horses.

The Big Top was full that afternoon, mostly families with hordes of excited children. Diana sat on the edge of her seat, riveted by the performance, a forgotten bag of peanuts in her hand. Turning to her parents with shining eyes, she declared she had decided to be a bareback rider when she grew up.

Daphne was less enthusiastic, cringing when lions were performing with their trainer, despite Christina's reassurance that she was perfectly safe. Even whilst watching a trapeze artiste's graceful flight through the air, she clutched at her aunt's arm. When several clowns burst through the curtains into the arena, some of them climbed up into the stands and delighted youthful spectators. He eyes widening with fright, Daphne began screaming at the top of her voice.

Aware of the audience's disapproval of the child's hysterics, Christina jumped to her feet and hustled the bawling child outside. Jack was infuriated that his wife appeared unperturbed by Daphne's behaviour, and ordered his family back to the hotel. In his view, it was grossly unfair that Christina should be left to cope with that ridiculous child. Bursting into tears of disbelief, Diana had to be dragged away, swearing vengeance against her sister for spoiling everything.

For once, Claire sympathised with her eldest daughter. Diana had been watching the various acts with open-mouthed delight, and Jack's insistence that they leave the circus because of her sister's histrionics seemed grossly unfair.

On the way out of the tent, she led the crying child to a nearby stand selling toys purporting to be replicas of circus animals. Clutching a black pony adorned in glittering regalia, a mollified Diana followed her parents outside to where Christina was waiting. Daphne had stopped yelling, and now cast envious eyes at her sister's new toy.

"I want one, Mummy," she whined plaintively, "it's not fair if Di-Di has—"

"Fair? Do you imagine that screeching the place down because you saw a clown is fair, you silly little girl?" Claire snapped. "And if you don't stop that horrid noise at once, I'll give you something to really wail about!"

Daphne sulkily hid her face in Christina's skirts, unused to hearing her mother speak to her in that tone. That was usually reserved for her sister.

The next day was spent within the confines of the hotel, nobody being willing to risk further embarrassing episodes in public. Jack disappeared briefly to buy pipe tobacco, a newspaper and magazines. Claire was bored stiff.

The family finally set off on their journey by train to the seaside town of Nice, a popular town on the southern coast of France. Praise God for that, thought Claire savagely, as another day cooped up with the children would have driven her demented.

Armed with a bag filled with comics, games, picture books and puzzles to occupy her daughters, Claire intended to sleep away the hours during the journey south. Her sister could have the dubious pleasure of diverting the two demanding little horrors, because she had had more than enough of them. Wreathed in a cloud of pipe smoke, Jack retired behind a newspaper.

Hours later the train reached its destination, and the MacLeod party exited the railway carriage on to a crowded platform. Feeling tired and grubby from the journey, they were pleased to find the Côte d'Azur rather warmer than in Paris.

Glancing about her, Claire noticed the station was alive with people, many of whom were sporting a healthy tan, and dressed with a casual elegance in keeping with the holiday atmosphere. This was more like it, thought the young woman with satisfaction. Paris had been dull, largely due to the presence of her exasperating children.

Arriving at the Hotel Negresco, Claire and Christina emerged from the taxi into brilliant sunshine, gazing up at the building in awe. Architecturally beautiful, the vast hotel closely resembled a royal palace from a bygone era. An unusual pink dome graced the rooftop over a front entrance shaded by thickets of tropical palms. The famed *Promenade des Anglais* stretched along the other side of the road, and a pebbled beach dotted about with bathing cabins lay just below an esplanade.

The hotel foyer was cool and airy, its opulent cream and gilt *décor* exuding an unmistakable air of luxury and wealth. Hotel receptionists in smart hotel livery stood behind the reception desk, dealing with bookings and queries from hotel residents.

Wheeling a trolley heaped with their luggage, a youthful page escorted

Jack and his family into a lift. The elderly lift operator pushed a handle to the *up* position, machinery whirred, and the lift slowly ascended to the appropriate floor. Jack generously tipped the page, and closing the door behind him, declared he now needed a snooze. Deciding to shower later, Claire unpacked her toiletries and leaving her husband already snoring on his bed, joined Christina and the girls in their suite.

"We had better make a plan for the following day, before Jack makes his usual suggestion of a boring sightseeing expedition," she told her sister as the two young women lay on their stomachs on the bed, riffling through a magazine. The little girls were already in the bathtub, splashing, laughing, doubtless making a fine mess, and Claire was relieved they were not in her bathroom.

It was finally decided that a morning on the beach would benefit both themselves and the children, but Jack would probably give the beach a miss, having an aversion to exposing his body to the sun. They could suggest meeting him for lunch in one of the restaurants by the beach. A *sieste* on their beds would take care of the hottest part of the afternoon, after which there were so many fabulous shops to explore.

The following morning, Claire and Christina left for the beach soon after breakfast. Pausing to buy buckets and spades for the two excited children, they stumbled over an expanse of warm pebbles in search of a less uncomfortable spot. A short distance away, Diana and Daphne immediately set about digging in a small patch of sand they had discovered under some seaweed, their aunt sitting close by on her towel.

Having demanded a deckchair to no avail, Claire regarded the pebbles with distaste and gingerly lowered herself to lie on her towel. Divesting herself of her tunic, she rolled it up to make a pillow for her head. Turning over to lie on her stomach, the sun's warmth blissful on her bare limbs, she drifted into a light doze.

"*Christ!*" Claire ejaculated as icy cold water sprayed over her warm body. "Diana, if this is your idea of a joke..."

"Er...frightfully sorry, dear lady," Squinting against the glare of the sun, Claire looked up into a man's laughing brown eyes. "I'm afraid it was this rascal's fault."

His pink tongue lolling, a honey coloured dog panted beside her, his short tail wagging engagingly as he shook further sprays of seawater from his coat.

"I say, hope you aren't too soaked, ma'am?"

196

Finally able to focus on the individual, Claire saw the brown eyes belonged to a dark haired, deeply tanned man whose white teeth now flashed in an unabashed grin. A scarlet dog lead dangled from brown fingers.

"I'll live," Claire's tone was dry. "What's this chap's name?"

"Toffee."

"Well, Toffee, I can see you have been for a lovely swim in the sea, and how sweet to share the experience with me."

"As a matter of fact, I've been training him to provide me with excuses to introduce myself to attractive ladies, and today he has excelled himself! Charles Rattigan at your service, ma'am."

"Claire MacLeod. Despite having had an unexpected shower, I'm happy to meet you Mr Rattigan."

"Ratty. My friends call me Ratty."

"Charles…that was the name of my brother."

"Was?"

"He's dead," Claire answered shortly. "Car accident."

"Sorry to hear that. May I sit down for a moment?" Ratty sat down without waiting for an answer. "I take it you are on holiday in this neck of the woods? Beaches are always crowded at this time of year, unfortunately. Often hard to find a decent spot."

"Doesn't worry me. So…er…Ratty, where in England do you hail from?"

"The old voice lets one down every time, what?" Ratty tried unsuccessfully to look upset. "How I long to be mistaken for a disgracefully charming Frenchman!"

Claire giggled, her eyes travelling over the man's baggy shorts, rumpled hair and sandy legs. "I think you'll have to change your antiquated style of swimming costume for a start," she remarked. "From where I am sitting, the average Frenchman wears something rather more colourful, and a lot less tatty."

"Ah, fancy coming across an expert on masculine attire! Dear lady, you simply must advise me as to how to change my wardrobe. This being my best beachwear, I fear you would be horrified if you saw the rest of it."

Her cheeks colouring, Claire about to answer him with an amusing riposte, when she became aware of a presence beside her.

"Mummy, who are you talking to?" Diana stared up at the person who was making her mother laugh. "Daffy and I have been swimming with Auntie Christina, and we need our towels now. You haven't made them all sandy, have you?"

"This is my eldest daughter, Diana," Claire suppressed her dismay that the pleasant interlude had been so rudely interrupted. "Christina is my sister, and that's Daphne, my younger daughter with her."

Squatting down on his haunches, Ratty solemnly extended a hand to Diana. "Delighted to make your acquaintance Miss Diana," he said to the astonished child who held out a sandy hand to the stranger. Nobody had wanted to shake her hand before!

Turning to Daphne, who became shy and tried to hide her face against Christina's damp legs, he smiled down at her. "I'm happy to meet you too, Miss Daphne."

"Chrissy, come and meet Charles Rattigan, an Englishman on holiday here like ourselves. By the way, he prefers to be called Ratty."

"Delighted!" Ratty gallantly bent over Christina's hand. "But I'm obliged to correct that last statement, as I actually live here all the year round. A small cottage just down the road in Juan les Pins."

"Oh, how lucky you are!" Claire said enviously. "We live in India, where it's far too hot to enjoy sunbathing like this."

"How long are you staying in Nice?" Ratty casually enquired. "I'm having a few friends round for lunch next Sunday, and I would be delighted if you and your sister would join us?"

"Oh, I really don't think so," Christina replied, before Claire could open her mouth. "We have the children you know, and Claire's husband may be planning something."

"Of course, your husband would also be most welcome," the man replied smoothly. "I have a daily maid who comes to clean the house, and I'm certain she would stay on to give a hand with the children."

Christina was shaking her head, even before the man had stopped speaking. "Oh no, we couldn't put you to all that trouble."

"We would love to come if it's possible," Claire swiftly interrupted her sister with a frown. "Of course, we'll have to check with Jack, but how may we let you know?"

"I walk Toffee every morning on the beach, so are you likely to be here again?"

"Claire, we have to meet Jack for lunch, remember," Christina put in. It's after one already, and he won't be too pleased if—"

"Oh, *do* stop fussing," Claire impatiently exclaimed, nevertheless rising to her feet and dusting herself down. "The lunch place where we're to meet is only yards away, and we don't even need to change, for heaven's sake. "Thank you for the kind invitation, Ratty, and we'll let you know tomorrow what the situation is."

"Excellent. I'll see you ladies here about the same time? Come on Toffee!" With a wave of his hand, the young man sauntered off down the beach.

Unreasonably annoyed, Claire bent to collect up her possessions. It was the first interesting conversation since leaving Calcutta, and trust Diana to race up and ruin it. Not to mention Christina, who seemed determined to discourage the unfortunate chap by carrying on like a blasted *duenna*, so God knows what the man thought.

"Really Claire, I can hardly believe that you picked up that fellow who was lurking about the beach in a most peculiar way," said Christina abruptly, as they trudged over the pebbles towards the line of small restaurants along the esplanade. "He might be a down-at-heel thief, or even a con-man after your money."

"What? Oh, don't be ridiculous, Chrissy!" Claire retorted crossly. "Didn't you hear the man speak? Down-at-heel thieves don't generally speak with an upper-class accent for a start. Secondly, he would scarcely have asked us to lunch at his home, if he spent his days wandering along beaches in the hope of pinching somebody's wallet."

"I still think you should check your purse, "Christina muttered darkly. "He looked jolly disreputable to me."

"I most certainly won't!" Claire retorted. "And furthermore, if Jack hasn't arranged anything, we will go for lunch with him on Sunday – like it or not."

"I'm sure Jack will have no interest in visiting that man's house," Christina unwisely persisted. "Especially when he knows how you picked him up."

"Oh? Since when were you elected Jack MacLeod's mouthpiece?" Claire paused to stare fiercely at her sister. "Don't you *dare* start telling him that kind of rubbish. Allow *me* to handle Jack."

Jack, however, proved unimpressed by the invitation to lunch the following Sunday. "Extraordinary to issue invitations to people one comes across on the beach, don't you think? Personally, I intend to have Sunday lunch at the hotel, and then a nice long snooze on my bed afterwards."

"Goodness, that's *such* an exciting prospect, I can scarcely bear it!'

Claire observed acidly. "I intend to take up Charles Rattigan's invitation, and Chrissy and the girls will come with me. It will be interesting to meet people who live here permanently."

"Suit yourself," Jack replied indifferently, prodding at the food in front of him with a fork. "For God's sake, is this seafood supposed to be a main dish? A few shrimps and all this lettuce seems more like rabbit food, if you ask me. I should have ordered my usual chicken and potatoes, as that at least constitutes a proper meal."

After lunch, Jack and his family returned to the hotel and retired to their respective rooms. Intending to have a stern word with her, Claire followed Christina to her suite.

"Why the gloomy face when I told Jack we would be going to have lunch with Ratty? What on earth can be wrong now?" she demanded. "Even Jack wasn't concerned that his wife might be in danger of being abducted for the white slave trade!"

"I noticed that you took my acceptance for granted," Christina answered grumpily. "I don't think it right to visit that man's house without your husband."

"Why? Do you imagine he intends to ravish my body on the lunch table, maybe in full view of the other guests?" Claire asked sarcastically. "Or is it that you prefer to spend yet another afternoon listening to the girls squabbling?"

"I...I...can't stand it when you are so crude."

"Then stop being holier-than-thou! We are going to have lunch with a few nice people, that's all."

"I suppose so," Christina gave in somewhat ungraciously. "But remember the girls have their bath at six, so we can't stay for long."

"It won't be the end of the world if they have their bath at seven, will it? Try not to be so hard and fast about things. Why, at times you're worse than the nuns."

Claire left the room and shut the door quietly behind her, pretending not to notice her sister's furious expression. Relieved though she was to have Christina's help with the children, sometimes it was like wading through glue when her sister was in one of her obstinate moods. If she began bleating to go back to the hotel after swallowing her last mouthful, it would be too boring for words.

Chapter Sixteen

The next morning, Claire, Christina and the two children were on the beach by ten o'clock. Hiding behind her sunglasses, Claire was in a state of high anxiety in case Charles Rattigan did not materialise. Aside from her own admitted disappointment, his absence would lend credence to her sister's low opinion of him. She was therefore conscious of a surge of ridiculous delight when Toffee came bounding up, barking shrilly with excitement. Ruffling the silky head, she shaded her eyes to watch his owner strolling up in the dog's wake.

"Good morning, ladies!" Ratty grinned, his attire equally as disreputable as the day before. "Do you have good news for me about Sunday lunch?"

"As a matter of fact, we do," answered Claire as casually as she could manage, wondering why she was placing such importance on finding out more about this man. "Unfortunately, Jack has other plans, but we two will be coming with the girls."

"Wonderful! You'll meet around dozen of us layabouts who live here, and I think you will find them great fun."

"If you'll excuse me, I think I'll take the girls for a swim," Christina broke in stiffly. "Would you please pass me their towels?"

"Have an impression your sister doesn't approve of me," Ratty remarked, watching Christina walk down the beach with the two children.

"Chrissy's views on propriety are a bit old-fashioned, I'm afraid," Claire hastily explained. "She's more concerned about me being led astray, than my husband."

"Now, that really does surprise me, Claire MacLeod! If you were my wife, I wouldn't care for some blighter such as myself to be sniffing around."

"Oh, Jack is far too preoccupied with his own affairs to worry about who I might be talking to. Unsurprising perhaps, since we had an arranged marriage." Claire stopped, aware she was divulging intimate details of her personal life to a relative stranger. But for some reason, it seemed important that Ratty should know this about her.

The man blinked, temporarily at a loss over the unexpected revelation. "Good Lord, I thought that sort of thing went out with the Ark," he said at last, thoughtfully regarding Claire. For Christ's sake, the girl was gorgeous and scarcely a likely candidate to become an old maid her parents were desperate to get rid of!

"How did such a thing come about?" he asked gently. "I'm certain zillions of chaps must have been in hot pursuit of you."

She shrugged a lightly tanned shoulder. "Jack needed a wife for business reasons, and my mother wanted to be rid of me. We...didn't get on, you see."

"Are you happy, or is that an impertinent question?"

"I don't really know the answer to that. Jack is good husband in a great many ways, but he didn't love me when we got married. He still doesn't."

"Maybe he didn't at the outset, but he must have come to see what a gorgeous and intelligent girl you are. A treasure. I cannot credit that he still does not care for you?"

Unexpected tears sprang into Claire's eyes, that she angrily blinked back. "Jack doesn't love me because...because he's in love with someone else's wife."

"Good God! How do you live with such an insult?" Ratty was genuinely taken aback. "Most girls I know would want to kill him, and as painfully as possible."

She looked away, dribbling warm sand through her fingers. "The children, of course..." she mumbled vaguely.

"Mummy, aren't you coming for a swim with us?" Daphne laid a damp hand on her mother's arm. "I want you to come *now*."

"Well, I'll trot off now and give old Toffee his walk," Charles got to his feet. "See you tomorrow at more or less the same time, I hope?"

Unused to sympathy, besides being embarrassed to have been so forthcoming, Claire's face was burning as she followed her small daughter down to the water's edge. She had always consoled herself that social position and material benefits outweighed the absence of affection from her husband. But she could hardly admit such a thing to that chap, especially when his opinion of her must already be rock bottom!

Walking swiftly along the beach, Charles Rattigan's mind was occupied by what he had just been told by the most attractive girl he had ever come across. What a bloody waste, and the indifferent husband frankly needed his head examined. Idly, he wondered why he should feel such concern for Claire MacLeod, who was a married woman, after all? How she chose to live her life was her own business, and none of his.

Extracting a rubber ring from a pocket, he threw it as far as he could for Toffee who raced after it yelping with delight. Charles walked along the shallows, the incoming tide washing over his bare feet. For Christ's sake, he had enough problems doing battle with his stiff-necked family in England, without concerning himself about a girl he had only just met on a beach.

Henry, Duke of Hartington and his elegant Duchess disapproved heavily of their younger son's 'rackety' lifestyle as an artist. Furthermore, a few years ago Charles had blotted his copybook by attempting to seduce his stuffy elder brother's fiancée, and that had been the final straw. Subsequently, the offender had been banished from the family home and was paid to stay away, preferably in a foreign country.

The quarterly stipend he had received from his father was not over generous, but sufficient to allow a reasonable standard of living. And he could paint to his heart's content. But it seemed the old man was now in a bad way with serious cardiac problems, and Charles prayed he wasn't about to peg it. His eldest brother would succeed to the title and then? God help the would-be seducer of his lady wife! Charles was in no doubt he would attempt to cut his brother off without a penny. But perhaps his mother might intervene on his behalf? She had always been a softer touch.

The following days passed in a haze of pleasure for Claire who looked forward to the few minutes daily interlude on the beach with Charles Rattigan. Not since her brief encounter with the Italian had she seen undisguised admiration in a man's eyes, and his sense of the ridiculous was vastly entertaining. In addition, he was turning out to be a well-read, interesting and extremely intelligent man.

Although he seemed reticent about his own family, Claire managed to elicit the information that he was the younger of his father's two sons. He also admitted to having been cast as the black sheep of the family, having refused to conform to his parents' ideas of a suitable occupation, which did not include the pursuit of art. A parting of the ways had become inevitable, hence Charles's presence in France.

It seemed that the father was now seriously ill. In the event he expired, the new duke would undoubtedly continue to view his brother's 'bohemian' lifestyle with disfavour, and adjust his monetary allowance accordingly.

"God forbid," Ratty had exclaimed with a comical grimace, "I might even be forced to *work*!"

Claire laughed, seeing through the cavalier attitude to the sensitive man beneath. Oh, why didn't she have a husband like this sweet, sweet man? Life was often so unfair.

On the Saturday before the lunch party at her new friend's home, Claire decided she must take Christina to task over her belligerent attitude towards the man. It simply did not bear thinking about that her sister might display bad manners in front of his friends. The *shame* of it! An opportunity presented itself, subsequent to Ratty continuing his walk along the beach with his dog.

"Chrissy, what on earth is the matter with you?" Claire blazed, smarting over the recent incident of her sister's hostility. She had rudely ignored Ratty's outstretched hand to help her up from the sand. "I've never known you be so...so damned rude to anybody before, and God knows what Ratty must think of you."

"I couldn't care less what that fellow thinks of me," Christina muttered sullenly. "He has no right to bother us like this every single day!"

"*Right*? Does he need a 'right' to pass the time of day with people? As a matter of fact, I happen to enjoy the few minutes he spends in our company, even if you don't. I hope you aren't going to embarrass me tomorrow by being horribly rude."

"I don't think I shall go to that lunch after all," Christina stared frostily at her sister. "Poor Jack, all alone in the hotel whilst you and that fellow are laughing and flirting outrageously. No, I shall stay and keep him company."

Her anger rising, Claire glared at her sister. In the event Christina did not attend the lunch party, she knew it would be impossible to go on her own as Jack would certainly put a stop to it. Making sure the girls were absorbed with their sandcastles some distance away, Claire unleashed her temper.

"For Christ's sake, Christina, *must* you be so bloody pious? One might be forgiven for imagining you are forced on a daily basis to watch Ratty and myself rolling around in the sand together...naked and unashamed!"

"Stop it, Claire! Why do you have to be so horridly vulgar?"

"Why do *you* have to be so damned judgemental? 'Poor Jack'

indeed! There is nothing pathetic about the man, take it from me."

"Sometimes I don't understand you," Christina was now close to tears. "Do you not have everything you want? A kind husband who showers you with jewellery and gifts, a beautiful home, friends and acquaintances fighting to be invited to your home. Not to mention your lovely children. What interest can you possibly have in that rag-taggle beachcomber?"

"I'll tell you what, Christina, he is interested in me as…as a *person*!" Claire ground out. "He *talks* to me, and *listens* to what I have to say. Which is a lot more than Jack MacLeod ever does. For God's sake, even when he is making love it's in utter silence before rolling over to snore!" she drew in a ragged breath. "But there is a reason for that, Chrissy – one, that only I know about."

The younger girl's face was burning with shame whilst her sister was talking. Her sister was clearly miserable, and she hadn't noticed it. Reluctantly, she recalled her dearest Mother Clementine's observation that wealth did not always denote happiness. This was a case in point. But what was that about a secret?

"I'm sorry…I didn't realise. But what reason can there possibly be for Jack's attitude? I always see him as thoughtful and caring about you and the girls."

"Oh yes, he loves his children, no doubt about that. Sadly he doesn't love me, and never has," Claire said bitterly, angry tears trickling down here face. "Jack's still in love with that woman he met in South Africa before our marriage. I only found it out on our wedding night."

Christina's mouth dropped open in shock. Never in her wildest dreams had she imagined anything such as this. Married to a man who did not love you – how terrible! No wonder Claire had always seemed so…so unsettled. Contrite, she touched her sister's face.

"Of course I'll come to the lunch tomorrow. I'll take care of the children, so that you can enjoy yourself with Ratty man and his guests."

Smiling through her tears, Claire hugged Christina, wishing she had confided in her sister a long time ago. "Thank you. Incidentally, the 'rag-taggle beachcomber' happens to be the son of a duke."

The following morning, Claire, Christina and the two children set off in a taxi for Charles Rattigan's house in Juan les Pins. At the end of a winding and somewhat rutted country lane, Charles's home turned out to be a beautifully converted farmhouse in the centre of flowering pink oleander bushes riotously growing around pale stucco walls. A vine, heavy with black grapes, gave the property a *provençale* flavour.

Hearing the taxi arrive, an impeccably dressed Charles Rattigan emerged from the house, smiling with pleasure to see the two young women descend from the vehicle. Placing a light kiss on Claire's hand, he turned to give the taxi driver instructions. But Claire was already asking the astounded driver in perfect French if he would return at six o'clock to collect them. Nodding, the man reversed, and then bumped his way back down the lane.

"Good Lord!" Ratty exclaimed in surprise. "Sounded like a blooming French person issuing those instructions! Even the taxi fellow didn't quite know what to make of it, since most English on holiday here can barely string two words together."

"Ah, that's what comes of having a French mother," Claire laughed "Do you speak French, Ratty?"

"Probably not as well as you, but I get by."

On the back patio, a trestle table had been set out shaded by navy parasols set into holes drilled through the table. With faint surprise, Claire noticed cutlery was laid on the bare wood, a sparkling wine glass, a small water tumbler and a neatly folded checked napkin beside each place setting. Decanters of red wine stood on a side table, next to ceramic dishes filled with green and black olives. Ice buckets containing frosted bottles of champagne were also to hand. Alfresco and sophistication perfectly blended – Claire thought with surprise. So much for Chrissy's 'beachcomber' idea.

Shortly after their arrival, five other guests arrived in quick succession and were introduced to Claire. Looking round for her sister, Claire noticed she had vanished elsewhere with the two children…probably thankfully. Remembering how much her shy sibling hated talking to new people, she smiled in relief, for it absolved her from guilt over leaving Christina to cope. When lunch was announced, she was sure her sister would choose to have her meal with the girls.

Ratty's friends were delightful people, intensely interested in day-to-day life in faraway India. Although she enjoyed chatting to others over lunch, Claire remained acutely aware of her host sitting next to her. Worse still, she knew she was blushing when his hand inadvertently brushed her own.

What was *wrong* with her, that she should start behaving like a silly schoolgirl? The taxi should soon be arriving, perhaps just as well in light of her inexplicable response to Ratty. God, she would die of embarrassment if he noticed her ridiculous behaviour…

"Claire?" asked a soft voice beside her. Glancing up, she looked into her host's brown eyes that reflected a similar excitement to her own. "What are you doing to me, you terrible girl?" he whispered, "Why do I feel such an affinity with you – a married woman – whom I've only met a short time ago?"

Claire's breath caught in her throat as she struggled to answer. For God's sake, now she wanted to fling herself into the man's arms! Then a warm hand imprisoned her own under the table, causing a shiver of excitement to course through her body. Glancing nervously round the table, she was thankful that others seemed oblivious to the static in the atmosphere.

"I think the taxi has come for us," Christina was at her elbow, dispelling the tension. "The girls have started to grizzle, so we had better be getting back."

"Of course, and sweet of you to have seen to them all afternoon, Chrissy." Claire rose from the table and turned to her host. "Thank you so much for a wonderful afternoon, and perhaps we'll see you on the beach tomorrow? Goodbye everybody, it's been lovely meeting all of you," she smiled round at the other guests.

"The pleasure is mine," Ratty murmured, escorting the two young women out to the waiting taxi. "And yes, Toffee and I will definitely see you on the beach."

"Are you feeling sick or something?" Christina glanced at her eldest sister's flushed face with concern. "Is it something you've eaten, do you think?"

'No…no, I feel absolutely fine," she muttered. "Just a bit hot, I suppose. Wasn't it a lovely lunch that Ratty provided? Did the girls eat properly?"

"Not really. Di-Di refused to eat a thing except chips and bread, and Daffy would only eat the ice cream. Then Di-Di started to tease her sister because she was bored, and I had a job stopping Daffy running off to find you so that she could tattle on her."

"Why did you let them get away with it?" Claire was glad of a distraction. "Both of those naughty girls take such advantage of you, Chrissy."

"Hmm, had I insisted they eat properly there would have been ructions from both," Christina tartly retorted. "And had you been obliged to leave the lunch table to sort out your daughters' tantrums, I can just imagine your reaction."

Claire nodded absently, her mind once again preoccupied with Charles Rattigan. Catching herself with a fatuous grin, she hastily pulled herself together. Jack was hardly the most intuitive of people, but it would not do for him to sense anything odd.

That same evening, Jack thoughtfully regarded his wife from across the dinner table. It was amazing how the sea air had wrought a miraculous change in her, he reflected. The exhaustion she continually claimed to suffer seemed to have vanished, her vivid blue eyes were sparkling and there was a hint of colour in her cheeks. Always slender as a reed, her exposed shoulders were tanned to an attractive honey.

"I'm glad to see you looking so well," he commented. "Better make the most of the sun and beach before we have to leave for home.

"No chance of that yet, surely?" Claire looked startled. "Heavens, we've only just arrived."

'We've been in France for almost two weeks already," Jack replied evenly. "I can't be away for too long as you must realise. Don't worry, we still have another week to enjoy before we sail. By the way, is Christina not joining us for dinner this evening?"

"Er...no, she had a bad headache and wanted to rest in a darkened room," Claire answered distractedly, trying to suppress her rising panic. A *week*? One measly week before she left? Just as she thought to have found the soul-mate she had unconsciously been searching for all her life?

"Surely the rest of us don't have to go back to India just yet? I...I'm feeling so much better in this lovely climate," Claire was at her most beguiling. "Can't Chrissy and I stay on with the girls for another month or two? Our little daughters are really benefiting, haven't you noticed the healthy roses in their cheeks?"

"*What?*" Jack gave a snort of derision. "Two more months of staying here, paying the Negresco's exorbitant prices? I imagine you must be joking?"

"No, it would be ridiculous to remain here for such a long period," Claire agreed without hesitation. "But what if I located a small cottage to rent in the area? Please, Jack, I beg you to consider it as a possibility."

Jack stared at the tablecloth, deep in thought. It was true the children were looking better and brimming with energy. And, at least Claire hadn't

208

argued over staying at the hotel where the cost of everything was sheer daylight robbery! If he insisted that the entire family return with him, it would still be unbearably hot in Calcutta. Claire would either relapse into her habitual tiredness, or race off with the girls to a hill station and the house would still be empty. He made up his mind.

"Very well. If you can find an inexpensive rental property suitable for the four of you before I leave, you can stay on here until the beginning of September. That will give you a further six weeks holiday."

"Jack, thank you so much!" Claire was jubilant. "I'll make sure we are back in Calcutta in plenty of time for the cold weather season, I promise."

"I hope so, Claire, otherwise I shall be damned angry," Jack replied dryly. "No repeat performances of your last visit to France, please."

Claire bit her tongue, preventing herself from retaliation over being spoken to as if to a recalcitrant child. Had she not achieved her own way over staying on? Now, she could look forward to weeks of seeing Ratty without worrying about Jack finding out...she was brought up short. Find out about what? Nothing had happened – might never happen. But at least she would have the opportunity of following this attraction to its conclusion, before taking up the persona of Mrs Jack MacLeod once more.

Leaving her husband to have a nightcap in the hotel bar, Claire went upstairs to check on her ailing sister. Before she had even opened the door, Diana's raised voice could be heard, followed by Daphne's distinctive whine. Both children turned to stare at their furious mother standing in the doorway, the toy they had been fighting about lying forgotten on the floor. In the adjoining bedroom, Christina was still on her bed, a damp towel covering her eyes.

"What is the meaning of this, might I ask?" Claire grasped Diana by the back of her pyjama jacket and frog-marched her to her bed, then unceremoniously hustled Daphne into hers.

"Didn't I ask you to be good girls whilst Mummy was at dinner? You both know Auntie Christina isn't feeling well, don't you? And what do I find? Both of you still awake, fighting, and making a hellish racket!"

"Auntie Christina only has a headache because you were nasty to her yesterday!" Diana muttered sulkily. "Daffy and I heard you shouting at her, and she cried a lot afterwards. And why did we have to stay at that man's house, where there was nothing to eat? Then we were bored waiting for you to stop talking so we could go."

"Don't be impertinent, Diana, or you'll get a jolly good slap!" Claire glared down at her seven-year-old daughter. "And don't make out you were starving this afternoon, because I know all about the trouble you two gave your poor aunt over lunch."

"It was horrid...Daffy thought so too," the older child retorted defiantly. "And don't be so mean to Auntie Christina and make her cry, 'cos we love her."

"That's quite enough, thank you! Your aunt was crying because she had a bad pain in her head."

"No, she wasn't! She told you she wanted to stay here with Daddy instead of going to that horrid house, but you wouldn't let her."

Claire went cold, wondering what else this little devil had picked up from the row between herself and Christina. Her ears must have been well and truly flapping!

"Any more rubbish out of you, and there will be no beach tomorrow," Claire told her glowering daughter. "You can stay all day in your room and then you'll really know what it is to be bored, you spoilt little girl!"

"Don't care about the beach! All you ever do there is talk to that man instead of playing with us. I only like his dog."

"But I want to go!" Daphne piped up before an infuriated Claire could think of an answer. "I want to play ball with Toffee, and go swimming."

"Go to sleep now, darling, and you shall. As she doesn't care about the beach, Diana can stay here tomorrow all by herself with a hotel maid to look after her."

"No! You can't leave me here," Diana's blue eyes welled with tears. "I'll tell Daddy if you leave me behind!"

"Oh? And what will you tell Daddy, might I ask?"

"That you love Daffy best, and you're always mean to me."

"Go ahead, you nasty little girl, and your father can take you back to Calcutta with him when he leaves next week." Claire felt weak with relief that nothing more significant seemed to have been overheard.

"Auntie Christina, Daffy and I are going to stay longer in France, but not in this hotel. We are going to move to a little house near the beach with a garden to play in."

"But I don't want to go back to Calcutta," Diana burst into noisy tears. "Why can't Daddy stay here with us?"

"Because he has to go back to the office. I've told you that before.

Now, if you want me to change my mind, we'll have no more clever-dick remarks if you don't mind. Settle down, and go to sleep."

Back in her own suite, Claire sat down abruptly on her bed. She really must take more care not to talk in front of that sly little creature in future. She could easily have alerted Jack and ruined everything.

Her heart sank to see Jack was still awake and reading a magazine. She took her time undressing in the bathroom, hoping to find her husband asleep when she finally emerged. If Jack decided to exert his marital rights, she didn't know how she would be able to bear it.

Unfortunately for Claire, her vivacity during dinner that evening had had an effect on her husband. Jack's magazine was set aside, and he had an unmistakable glint in his eyes as Claire came out of the bathroom.

"You were looking very attractive tonight, my dear," he murmured, beginning to peel off his wife's nightgown. "And so full of beans! Refreshing after those extended periods of terminal exhaustion from which you appear to suffer so frequently."

"Please, Jack! I...I'm really not in the mood tonight."

"Well, I am," he pulled the nightgown over Claire's head, "and since you are never in the mood, it makes no odds, does it?"

With gritted teeth, Claire resigned herself to the inevitable. Positioning himself above his wife, Jack happened to glance down at her eyes tightly shut in an averted face. His anger building over the silent rejection, he went about the sexual act rather more violently than usual, and then rolled over to fall asleep.

Disgusted and sore, Claire got out of bed and went into the bathroom to begin the ritual of washing herself clean. Tears of fury trickling down her cheeks, she savagely thanked God the bloody man would soon be leaving. Until then, she would go to any lengths to avoid a repetition of the repulsive business.

The following week flew by, and Jack's family accompanied him to the railway station to see him off to Paris on the first leg of his journey back to India. Claire was secretly jubilant, having managed to avoid her husband's sexual advances by declaring a very painful menstrual condition. And now, she would soon be free...*free*!

"Daddy, don't go!" blubbered Diana, hanging on to her father's jacket. "I want you to stay here with us, *pleeese*!"

"It won't be long before you come home," Jack reassured his tearful

211

daughter. "You know Daddy has to go back to work."

"Come Diana," Claire tried to take her eldest daughter's hand, but found it snatched from her grasp. "Let your father go *at once*, or it will be the worse for you," she hissed in her ear. "Disgraceful behaviour, and in full view of everyone."

Sobbing, Diana reluctantly complied. Nevertheless, she chose to hold her aunt's hand, whilst bestowing a black look at her mother. Ignoring the sulky child, Claire took Daphne's hand, whilst her husband climbed into the carriage and slammed the door.

With a shrill blast of his whistle, the guard waved a green flag to the engine driver leaning out from his cab. Amid billowing clouds of steam and metallic clanking, the train shuddered and moved slowly down the tracks. A handkerchief fluttered in Claire's hand as she waved goodbye... with joy in her heart.

Chapter Seventeen

On the edge of a pine forest along the water's edge, Claire and Christina were delighted to discover a secluded little beach. Within easy walking distance from their rented cottage, it became a habit each morning to take the two little girls to play in the sunshine. The weather was fine, and Claire would sit on the warm sand, watching the girls fill buckets with seawater to pour into moats around the sandcastles they made. Christina lay on her stomach close by, invariably buried in a book.

Subsequent to the move into the cottage, as each day went by, Claire noticed her sister becoming increasingly tight-lipped with apparent disapproval. She supposed it must be because of the hour or so that she spent with Ratty every afternoon. He would arrive in his rusted old car to pick her up, and drive to the seafront where they would sit on the wall and chat. But she resisted bringing him to this beach, where the two children were likely be present. She recalled Diana's uncomfortably acute observations, and did not want to risk her tongue running loose upon their return to Calcutta.

"Chrissy, just by way of a nice change, can't you make a teensy effort to appear as if you are enjoying your holiday?" Claire demanded one morning, fed up with the tense atmosphere. "Must you look so grim all the time?"

Christina glanced up, her mouth pursing with annoyance. "Frankly, I'm fed up to the back teeth of being party to your trysts with that Ratty man," she snapped. "Lunching at his house was just the tip of the iceberg, as you now tear off to see him every day."

"And what do you suppose I can get up to in the space of a measly hour?" Claire flared. "Or is your smutty little mind working overtime?"

The younger girl's face flushed scarlet with a combination of anger and resentment. "That's right, point the finger of blame at me...you always do! What do you suppose Jack would think about his wife careering off every day to meet another man? *Maman* brought us up to respect—"

"To hell with Jack!" she exploded, driven to indiscretion. "And I don't advise you to fling *Maman* at me as a model of morality. How many times do I have to explain myself to you, for God's sake?"

"Well, I see things differently," Christina truculently retorted. "I see a girl who has everything she has ever wanted, but the grass *has* to be greener on the other side of the fen—"

"I'm sick and tired of your mealy-mouthed posturing, Christina O'Hara!" Claire scrambled to her feet, and grabbed up her possessions. "I've done nothing to be ashamed of, since my friendship with Ratty is as pure as the driven snow. I can see I've been wasting my breath trying to make you understand that, so I'm off."

In a fury, Claire strode back up the beach, aware of the two girls staring curiously after her. Too late, she wondered how much Diana had picked up from the angry exchange between herself and Christina? Shrugging, she thrust it from her mind for the moment, for there was only one person she desperately wanted to see...

That same morning, Charles Rattigan was sitting in his studio, absently staring at a blank canvas on the easel in front of him. Charcoal sketches of a wealthy American woman's face were scattered on a nearby table...a commissioned portrait he had yet to begin. Brushes and tubes of paint lay ready for him to pick up.

Sighing, Ratty distractedly ran his hands through his hair. It was no good. The only face he saw in his mind's eye – wished to see – was that of a very lovely woman, her vivid blue eyes sparkling in a heart-shaped face. Married to another man. For Christ's sake, he had no business to even think about Claire MacLeod! He should just enjoy the brief hour they spent together each day, and try to keep his hands to himself until she vanished from his life. Back to that strange husband of hers.

Meanwhile, it was essential to somehow take his mind off things he could do nothing about. A cup of strong coffee, a croissant and a look through the newspaper should help, after which he would sternly apply himself to that portrait. After all, no work...no money!

A steaming mug of coffee in one hand, a newspaper in the other and a croissant clenched between his teeth, Charles kicked open the mesh kitchen door and went outside on the back terrace to sit at a trestle table. Dumping the mug down, he shook out the newspaper with an impatient rustle.

Absorbed in an article about the cost of property in France, Charles suddenly became aware of a presence accompanied by a whiff of familiar perfume. Glancing up, he squinted at a figure looming darkly against the brightness of the sun. As his eyes focused, he gaped to see an apparition of the woman who was haunting his thoughts to the exclusion of all else.

"Claire?" he whispered, "or am I now hallucinating, for God's sake?"

"Of course it's me, you chump!" Claire laughed delightedly at the dazed expression on Charles's face. "Any chance of a cup of coffee?"

"Absolutely, I've just made a fresh pot," Charles rose distractedly, the newspaper falling unnoticed to the ground. "I...I was just thinking about you."

"Nice thoughts, I hope? I managed to sneak away from Christina and the children, and thought I'd walk over to see you."

"Brilliant idea! As for my thoughts, that would depend what you would term 'nice'. Charles grinned as he disappeared into the kitchen, returning a moment later with another mug of coffee. "What was I saying? Yes, I confess my mind has been filled with thoughts that could be considered disgracefully inappropriate in the existing circumstances. What are you *doing* to me, you naughty little witch?"

"Much the same as you do to me, I imagine," Claire replied seriously. "Whenever we spend that miserable hour together, I have this burning need to fling myself into your arms. Very disconcerting, as I'm not given to that sort of thing."

Putting a gentle finger under her chin, Charles tipped Claire's face towards him and gazed into the blue depths of her eyes. Bending his head, he dropped a light kiss on her parted lips. Startled by the strength of feeling between them, the two stared at each other. Unable to prevent himself, Charles took the girl in his arms and with a muttered exclamation kissed her rather more thoroughly, his tongue seeking hers.

"Christ, you cannot know how much I have longed to do that," Charles whispered. "You're in my thoughts, wherever I go, whatever I do, every moment of every single day. For God's sake, I can't even paint!"

The coffee forgotten, Claire cupped his face between her hands, her eyes dark with desire. "Then don't waste time, Charles Rattigan...take me inside and show me exactly what you mean."

His breathing ragged, Charles picked up the girl in his arms and carried her through the house to his bedroom. Oblivious of anything but themselves, they struggled out of their clothes and fell on the bed, gripped by raw emotion that could no longer be denied. Claire gladly gave herself to him, body and mind, the urgency of their mutual need stoking a fire that culminated in an almost unbearably sweet climax.

Rolling over on her stomach to look at her lover, Claire reflected how his rumpled hair and slow smile gave him a boyishly appealing air. Seeing him naked for the first time, it had come as a surprise how absurdly beautiful his body was, muscular and tanned golden by the sun. Her next thought was surprise that the obscure loneliness that had plagued her for so many years was absent…

"My darling," Charles kissed her shoulder, "I want you to know that I've never experienced anything like this in my life! You're so very special to me."

"Tell me, Ratty," Claire's eyes danced mischievously. "Tell me again exactly how you feel, and what you intend to do about it?"

"I think I'm in love with you, Claire." Charles's warm brown eyes were serious. "I know I have no right to say such a thing, but that's how it is."

The girl's face was bright with joy and she cupped his face with a gentle hand. "No man has ever told me that he loves me, and I love you too, my darling…so very much."

His teeth flashed in an answering smile. "As for what we should now do about it? I imagine the obvious thing is to consummate our love again in the age-old manner, don't you think?" Leaning forward, he gently kissed Claire's lips, then again as desire between them blazed once more into life.

Urgently, desperately, they made love in the truest sense of the word, hands sliding over skin, licking, kissing, exploring the secret and erotic places of each other's bodies and igniting a flame that heated their blood to mindless passion.

Gone were Claire's remaining inhibitions, her fear of rejection, and her deep distaste of physical intimacy. Tears of joy sparkling on her lashes, she gave herself in complete abandonment to this incredible man, the two of them ascending a pinnacle of ecstasy towards explosive release. Exhausted, they fell into a light doze, arms about each other.

"What are we going to do about us?" Charles lit two cigarettes, and gave one to Claire. "I imagine you don't intend to remain in a loveless marriage forever?"

Drawing on her cigarette, she turned over to lie on her back, thoughtfully blowing a stream of blue smoke towards the ceiling. Revelling in a wonderful new contentment, the last thing she wanted to think about was her marriage. There were far too many elements to consider, not least of which were her children.

"Not now, my darling, but we'll make a plan later on."

Glancing at her watch, reality sank in, and Claire sat up abruptly. "God, I must go – right now! If Christina suspects anything, she will become extremely uncooperative as regards looking after the girls, and that will make it impossible to spend time with you. Can you give me a lift back to the top of the lane? I'll walk the rest of the way home so she doesn't spot you with me."

A few minutes later, Claire walked down the lane towards the cottage. The sun was low in the sky, and Claire mentally braced herself for another row with her sister over her lengthy absence. She was right. Christina was incandescent with rage, and declared herself ready to depart back to India at once.

"Don't be silly, Chrissy darling!" Claire cajoled, putting an arm about her sister's rigid shoulders. "You can't sail off into the sunset...just like that. Passages have to be booked and so on. Look, I'm terribly sorry to have been nasty to you this morning. Can you forgive me?"

"I do hope you aren't about to pretend you went for a walk and got lost," the younger girl's tone remained frosty. "I'm quite certain you went off to see that Ratty man, so don't insult my intelligence by pretending otherwise."

"Yes, I did see 'that Ratty man' as you choose to call him." Claire's gaze was ingenuous. "We spent a couple of hours discussing history of art amongst other things, and then went for a walk on the beach."

"Humph! I can just imagine it," Christina huffed disbelievingly. "Do you realise I had to *lie* to the girls about where you were all day? Lying is a sin, and you should know that."

"Must you be so bloody sanctimonious, Christina?" Claire lost patience. "I had better tell you here and now that I intend to continue seeing 'that man' for the remainder of our time in the south of France. I shall see as much as I can of Charles Rattigan, before I'm forced to return to life with a cold fish for a husband."

Christina stared at her hands, her expression morose, and her mind in a whirl. It wasn't that she minded being left on her own with Di-Di and Daffy – they were sweet children. It was the feeling that she was party to a betrayal of Jack, who had always been kind to her. What was she to say should he question her about Claire's activities? What if Di-Di said something to arouse Jack's suspicions? As it was, Claire had just sent her off with a flea in her ear for unashamedly eavesdropping! She hated being

217

at odds with the sister she adored, but there didn't seem to be a middle ground.

"Actually, I did take it in about your miserable marriage," Christina said at last. "And I can see you are happy in Ratty-man's company. But have you thought about how you will cope when you go back to Calcutta?"

"I don't want to think about that at the moment," Claire grimaced. "I shall have to deal with it when the time comes, I suppose. Please, please, won't you let me spend these last weeks as happily as I can?"

"I suppose so," the younger girl sighed in resignation. "But please don't put me in a position where I have to fib to the girls about where you have gone."

"Darling Chrissy!" Claire flung her arms about her sister. "I depend so much on you, and you won't be sorry, I promise! Don't worry, I'll take care to be discreet."

The remaining few weeks before Claire's return to India passed with bittersweet swiftness. To appease Christina and divert her eldest daughter's suspicions, she only left the house at night, once the children were safely in bed. Ratty would wait for her at the top of the lane and then drop her home before sunrise.

More deeply in love than ever, Claire could scarcely bear the thought of not seeing her Ratty each day. Just being close to him made her shiver in excited expectation of what was to come. Their time together was precious, and both desperately wanted it to go on forever. Charles Rattigan, however, was anxious to discuss their future.

"Darling, we have to decide how we intend to go on from here," he smoothed damp hair back from her forehead. It was the night before her much-dreaded departure to Paris, and they had just made love with searing intensity, all the more poignant in the knowledge of their parting the next day.

"You know I want to marry you, don't you, Claire? Not that I have much to offer except myself, and my modest home. You are also aware that my means won't allow an extravagant lifestyle, nothing like that to which you are accustomed. My dear Papa is not known for his generosity, and should he die my elder brother is likely to be worse."

Tears welled in Claire's eyes and spilled down her cheeks. "Ratty, how am I to manage without you? There's nothing I want more from life than to be free to marry you. But what about my girls? If I leave Jack, he would never allow me to take them. Why, I don't even know if *you* would want to accept someone's else's children?"

"Sweetie, there is no question as to that," Charles reassured her. "I love children, and would welcome your little girls with open arms. Who knows, we might eventually have one or two of our own."

Claire attempted a watery smile. "Give me time, darling! It's impossible to make life-changing decisions before I've gone back to India. Once I'm there, it will be easier to decide on the best course towards my eventual divorce. You must also remember that Christina is with me here, and she would see our true relationship as a betrayal of Jack, whom she likes immensely. As things stand, she believes we go for nice long walks along the beaches and talk."

"I understand, but I beg of you not to delay over this, Claire. I shall live for the day when you return to me...a free woman."

An hour later later, Charles stopped the car a safe distance from the darkened house to avoid waking anyone. Turning to him for the last time, Claire noticed the glitter of tears in his eyes and her own control dissolved.

"Come back to me, my darling," Charles whispered to the weeping girl, his voice hoarse with emotion "Life without you would be unendurable."

"I will...oh, I *will*!" Claire choked, fumbling blindly for the car door handle. "As soon as I can, I promise I'll come to you."

Her emotions threatening to veer out of control, Claire jumped out of the car and ran down to the house and through the unlocked front door without glancing back.

Depressed to be losing the woman he had come to adore, Charles stared bleakly into the darkness for a few moments, before starting the car and driving slowly home.

Closing the door quietly behind her, Claire rushed into her bedroom and threw herself on the bed. Burying her face in the pillow, she gave way to overwhelming heartbreak. How...*how* in God's name was she to carry out her promise to return as a free woman? But the idea of a future without her darling man was unendurable.

Later that morning, the subdued young woman packed up her remaining possessions and helped Christina with clearing up the cottage. The rental agent would soon be at the door to check the inventory and collect the keys, and at ten o'clock the taxi would arrive to take them to the station. She was almost grateful to be obliged to deal with these mundane details, distracting her from dwelling miserably on the parting from Charles Rattigan...the love of her life.

Chapter Eighteen

The voyage back to India seemed interminable to both Christina and Claire. The children were impossible, abruptly uprooted from a lifestyle they enjoyed. As the days passed, they became increasingly resentful of their confinement to the ship. Despite being taken for walks round the deck each morning by their aunt, Daphne resumed her irritating whine, whilst Diana amused herself by incessant teasing of her sister leading to tantrums, howling, and constant tale-bearing. Even Christina's patience was sorely tried, and was once driven to smacking Diana for deliberately upsetting her sister's much-relished chocolate pudding on the floor.

"For heaven's sake, Diana, leave your sister alone!" Claire barked at her eldest daughter over lunch one day. "When you behave like this, I could give the pair of you away to the first passer-by!"

Diana stared balefully at her mother. "I'll tell Daddy you said that! He loves me, and he'll never forgive you if you try to give me away."

"Tell him whatever you like, you unpleasant little girl," Claire snapped. "Believe me, your darling father wouldn't care for this frightful behaviour either!"

"I hate this boat, Mummy...when can we get off?" Daphne grizzled. "Why are you always angry with us? Di-Di says you don't like us any more, and that you only laugh with that man on the beach."

"What man on the beach?" Claire managed to keep her tone neutral. "I can't imagine who you mean, since there were lots of men on the beach."

"I mean the man who had Toffee," Diana chimed in. "He used to come and talk to you every day until we went to the new house, and *he* made you laugh a lot!"

"After spending time with you two little horrors, anyone would be able to make me laugh," Claire told her daughter. "Now, are you going to eat your lunch or not? And Daphne, no pudding for you if half of what's on your plate doesn't disappear."

Everyone's misery was increased by the weather becoming stormy. The great ship lurched and rolled, most passengers hurriedly retiring to their cabins until the worst was over. Both children were seasick, requiring constant attention that they only had from their aunt, for Claire was prostrate on her bunk.

The weather improved, and the seas calmed as the ship ploughed her way towards the Far East. The climate gradually changed, and the increasing heat and humidity began taking its toll on those unaccustomed to it. Still miserable and off-colour after the storms, Claire found her daughters' continuing shenanigans impossible and frequently lost her temper. Luckily for the girls, Christina came to the rescue, and enabled her sister to rest in her cabin.

When a faint blue shadow was detected on the horizon, indicating the still distant shores of the Indian continent, every passenger felt awash with relief their ordeal would soon be over. Within the hour, the ship steamed into Bombay's busy harbour, and an all-pervading stench of the dark green waters afflicted passengers who emerged on deck to watch the liner's slow advance. Most of them hastily retreated indoors.

Dropping anchor some distance from the quayside, the ship was approached by ferries transporting passengers across the harbour to the cobbled wharf where rickety food stands shouldered one another. Sun-blackened vendors squatted in groups, many of them smoking *beedies*, or merely passing the time of day. Cobbles shimmered in the intense heat making it impossible to walk over without sandals, even by feet calloused by a lifetime of walking barefoot.

A loudhailer barked, requesting passengers to prepare for disembarkation. It startled Claire who had been dozing on her bunk, hoping to overcome the nausea convulsing her despite the calm seas. Swinging her feet to the floor, she was seized by sudden dizziness and clutched a nearby table for support. Relieved that it swiftly passed, Claire glanced in the dressing table mirror to check her still flawless make-up, and tuck a few damp strands of hair back into place.

A minion from her husband's office should shortly be arriving, to escort them back to Calcutta. It was important that she pulled herself together, and put a good face on things to avoid any kind of gossip. Through the cabin wall she could hear the children's excited chatter, thrilled to be leaving the ship they considered little better than a prison. Minutes later, Claire, her sister and the two little girls joined the queue on deck waiting for transportation to the jetty.

Having forgotten her hat, the burning heat of the midday sun beat down on Claire's unprotected head and she was affected once again by a wave of dizziness. Hurriedly moving into shade provided by a canvas awning, she stretched out a hand to a nearby railing to steady herself. To her relief, the dizzy spell again passed as swiftly as it had come. Maybe she was sickening for something? Or was it just a sudden bout of heatstroke? In any event, at last it was their turn to embark on the ferry bobbing unsteadily beside the ship.

Clambering up slimy stone steps to the cobbled quayside, Claire breathed deeply to dispel waves of nausea she had suffered during the short trip from the liner to shore. The din seemed horrendous, hawkers touting their wares, scrawny *rickshaw-wallahs* arguing and competing with one another to offer transport to the newly arrived passengers. Everything around her seemed noisier, filthier, and much hotter than she remembered. A moment later, she heard Diana's delighted scream.

"*Daddy*! We're here...*over here*!"

Looking up, Claire saw her husband approaching, looking cool and unruffled. Good God, he had come to meet her himself! Forcing a smile, she offered her husband a cheek to kiss. With a quizzical glance at his wife, Jack turned to hug his daughters whilst Christina waited shyly to greet the brother-in-law of whom she was so fond.

"So, how were the last three months in your little French house?" Jack asked on the way to the railway station. "Far from looking rested after such a lengthy time away, you seem somewhat fatigued."

"I do feel rather tired," Claire admitted, "I only hope I'm not sickening for some horrid bug or other."

"Well, try not to be sick before we get home, my dear," Jack advised his wife unsympathetically, "as that would be most inconvenient."

"Oh, I'll try hard not to be a nuisance, Jack," Claire snapped crossly. "That's last thing I would want, you having come here especially to meet us."

"Yes, your arrival in Bombay dove-tailed nicely with two important meetings I had with government people. But there is also an issue I wish to discuss with you later."

"An issue?" Claire echoed, suddenly nervous that gossip about Charles and herself might already have preceded her arrival. "How very mysterious!"

The company car halted outside the station, and as Claire got out, she sneaked an apprehensive glance at her husband, but his expression was unreadable. Well, she would soon be taken to task, she thought with resignation, for judging by his tone the 'issue' was something adverse.

During the journey back to Calcutta, Christina and both children slept a good deal of the way, made sleepy by the heat and rhythmic rocking of the train as it clattered along the tracks. Claire leaned her head against the plush backing of the banquette in vain simulation of sleep, but acutely aware of Jack thoughtfully watching her. It was also noticeable that he had not yet taken out a newspaper from his briefcase.

"Claire, why did you see fit to dismiss Susan before leaving Calcutta?" Jack asked quietly. "Neither your mother nor I can understand your motives in doing such a thing, particularly when you know how attached the girls are to their nanny."

"What?" Claire opened her eyes, relief washing through her that the 'issue' was something so mundane. "Oh, Susan...well, I've always disliked the woman. She was lazy and incompetent, and allowed the children to run wild and develop disgusting table manners. Have you forgotten the dramas we were forced to endure in France?"

"I don't think you can lay the blame for that entirely at Susan's door," Jack coldly replied. "Had you made yourself rather more available to oversee the upbringing of your daughters, I doubt they—"

"Of course, you are entitled to your point of view, Jack," Claire interrupted angrily, "but don't accuse me of neglecting my children, because I won't have it!"

"I believe Susan's dismissal was an extremely unkind thing to do," Jack continued, unperturbed by his wife's temper. "She brought those little girls up from birth, and I am certain they are going to be very, very upset not to find her at home. Not to mention the poor woman's own grief. I understand you forbade her to say a word to the children about her dismissal, on pain of losing bonus money she would need until her next job."

"For *God's sake!*" Claire exploded. "Surely we are not having an argument over a bloody Anglo-Indian nanny? A replacement can soon be found, with better speech and rather more energy. Hadn't you noticed the girls were beginning to speak with a *chi-chi* accent? No? Well, they were, but these last few months in France have gone some way to clearing that up. Now, can we drop the subject, if you please?"

Disturbed by the raised voices, Christina opened an eye. Seeing her sister's flushed countenance and Jack's glacial expression, she hurriedly

223

closed it again. Unbelievably, the two of them were already arguing! And the glow of happiness she had seen in her sister's face over the last months in France had vanished as though it had never been...

Jack's driver was already outside Howrah Station, waiting for the family to emerge. Christina was dropped off at Camack Street, upset that Claire refused to pop in briefly to see her mother. She had been hoping the months away from Calcutta might have softened her sister's attitude towards Minette. Apparently not.

As Jack had predicted, Diana and Daphne were distraught to discover their beloved nanny was not waiting for them at home. Bursting into loud wails, Daphne looked round for her aunt for comfort, forgetting she was no longer there. Running to her mother, she threw her arms around Claire's legs. With an irritable exclamation, she brushed the child unceremoniously to one side, telling her to stop whining or she would be given something to bleat about. Tears glittering in her eyes, Diana's mouth trembled as she glared at her mother.

"Where's Nanny Susan, Mummy?" she demanded in cold fury. "The *ayahs* say you sacked her before we went on holiday. Why did you make her leave us all alone?"

"I don't believe I need to explain myself to you, Diana," Claire told her daughter, "and kindly don't use that tone to me. Susan has gone, and that is that."

"We want Susan!" Diana began to cry in earnest. "I want her to come back."

"Stop that silly howling at once, Diana. You didn't have your wonderful nanny for all those months we spent in France, remember."

"No, but we had Auntie Christina, and she looked after us," sobbed the child. "Now she's gone home and we're all alone. I hate you, Mummy...I really, really *hate* you!"

Claire had turned to leave the room, but whipped round to deliver a stinging slap across her eldest daughter's face. "Don't you dare speak to me like that, you rude little girl," she snapped. "Hate me if you wish, Diana MacLeod, but respect me you will or you'll earn yourself a walloping! Not another word about that stupid nanny from either of you, do you hear? Now go and wash your hands and faces before supper, and one of the *ayahs* will help you find some pyjamas."

Daphne had stopped wailing to watch the confrontation between her sister and their mother. Seeing Diana stagger backwards, a hand to her smarting cheek, the younger girl scrambled to follow her shocked sister into the bathroom. She had just learned a valuable lesson: never, *ever* argue with Mummy.

Standing under the shower a few minutes later, Claire brooded about the unpleasant scene with Diana. She had meant to broach the subject of Susan's absence to the girls, but for one reason or another it had escaped her mind. Nevertheless, she would not tolerate impertinence from that dratted girl, and maybe she would think twice before opening her mouth in future.

Claire wrapped herself in a towel and sat down on the cork bathroom stool to cool off. What a homecoming this was turning out to be: a boring lecture from Jack, reproachful looks from Christina, swiftly followed by tantrums from her daughters. How she longed to be back in France! Nevertheless, there were domestic matters that needed attending to, such as the employment of a new nanny.

Anyone sent by her mother would not be considered, for a spy in the camp would be intolerable. The successful candidate must be Claire's personal choice. Meanwhile, one of the *ayahs* could be delegated to look after the girls. Leaving the bathroom, she went over to her wardrobe to select something cool to change into before dinner, doubling over as an unexpected wave of nausea seized her. What the hell was wrong with her? It was now unlikely that food had anything to do with these horrid attacks, so a bug of some kind was more probable. Should there be no improvement in her general health, she would see the doctor and get it cleared up once and for all.

An unexpected blow for Claire was that her old friend and mentor, Naomi Bernstein, had left Calcutta. She had set up her own establishment in Bombay, selling exclusive clothing for women and quality cashmere shawls. However, Naomi agreed to become the go-between for letters to and from Charles Rattigan – albeit reluctantly. She also selected a new nanny for the MacLeod girls, Claire having tired of interviewing a procession of useless applicants. Sadie was a pleasant, middle-aged Anglo-Indian woman, convent-educated, and whose speech was excellent.

At first, Diana and Daphne were sulkily resentful towards their new nanny, but made an early discovery that Nanny Sadie brooked no nonsense, answering back, bad table manners or disobedience. However, the girls also found Sadie a wonderful storyteller, as well as a fount of information over games and handicrafts on rainy days.

In a relatively short time, the girls forgot their hostility towards Susan's replacement, and there was a noticeable improvement in their general behaviour and table manners. Delighted by this clear vindication of the step she had taken, Claire cemented Sadie's personal loyalty by a generous raise in salary.

As the days went by, the attacks of nausea increased, and a rather lack-lustre Claire visited her doctor. After a brief examination, Dr Ross burst out laughing.

"My dear Claire, it's not a tonic you require but my congratulations! You are approximately three months pregnant! Had you not suspected that?"

Claire stared speechlessly at the doctor. It simply had not occurred to her that a coming baby might be responsible for her ambiguous ailments. As to who the infant's father might be…that raised a definite question mark.

"Surely it can't be that much of a surprise?" the doctor enquired jovially. "Who knows, the new-comer might be the lad you hoped for the last time."

"Yes, it's something of a sho…er…surprise," Claire answered faintly. "Daphne is now five, so the symptoms of pregnancy have somewhat faded."

"Off you go then, my dear, and give Jack the good news! Remember to make monthly appointments with my nurse before leaving the surgery."

Claire went home, her mind whirling. What might her sweet man say if she told him of her pregnancy? In the circumstances, it might be better to keep it a secret from him until she could ascertain who the father was – if possible.

The following weeks turned out to be busy for Claire, involving a spate of dinner parties at her home for visiting diplomats and Jack's business associates, in addition to organising company cocktail parties, and an elaborate picnic for friends during a polo match. Much to her relief, the embarrassing *faux-pas* she had committed during the previous year's polo tournament seemed to have been forgotten. Run off her feet on a social level, it distracted her from brooding over her condition.

Claire decided to keep quiet about her pregnancy to Jack, wanting to hug the possibility of Ratty's baby to herself until she had thought things out. Her mind shied away from the inescapable fact that Jack would never allow her to take her girls from him. Neither would he release the coming baby, believing he was the father.

226

In the event of leaving her husband, Claire knew she would be labelled as a scandalous woman who had abandoned her children. Could she tolerate such a damning stigma? Never to see her children again, their young minds poisoned against their mother? On the other hand, she would be with her darling Ratty, a decidedly bohemian young man, penniless perhaps, but who adored her simply for herself. Claire's gloomy reflections came to an abrupt halt at this point...

The weeks passed, and Claire realised it would soon no longer be possible to conceal her pregnancy from Jack. Whatever the baby's parentage, it would be foolish to arouse his suspicions unnecessarily. An added advantage was that it also provided her with an excellent reason to withdraw from hateful sexual encounters. She chose an evening when they were sitting out on the veranda, waiting for the *bearer* to announce dinner.

"Jack, I have some news for you," Claire began, staring at the back of her husband's newspaper. "I...we are expecting another baby in a few months time."

The newspaper rustled as Jack lowered it to look at his wife. "What? A baby? Are you sure?"

"Yes, I'm quite sure," she answered evenly. "I didn't realise at first, but when I began feeling sick the doctor confirmed my suspicions."

"When is the baby due?"

"In about four months time." Claire forced a smile. "Remember you had sex with me in Nice, not long before you left for India."

"This, presumably, is the reason for the terminal exhaustion since your return?"

"I expect so. Doctor Ross says that after all the travelling, I must take things easy, and no...er...visitations to my bed, of course."

Jack smiled without humour. "Really? You surprise me. From what I remember, it would be perfectly safe for another couple of months at least."

"*No!*" Claire retorted sharply. "I am not going to endanger my baby, so that's that, I'm afraid."

"Humph!" Jack returned to his newspaper. "As you wish, my dear. By the way, has Edward Woodson contacted you about the Ball he plans to have at the Saturday Club next month?"

"No, not yet. But why does he want to get in touch with me?"

"The Ball is intended to mark his retirement from India, and I believe he intends to ask you to organise it for him. As you may know, his wife is …er…not well, and can't cope with that sort of thing, whereas you have it off to a fine art."

"I see," Claire grinned inwardly, amused by Jack's delicate way of describing the state of Delia Woodson's health. He must be aware it was common knowledge that the lady's interests lay within a bottle of sherry? "Tell him I would be delighted."

The Woodsons' Ball at the Saturday Club was the last social event that Claire agreed to undertake, her pregnancy not yet visible to the casual eye. In impeccable taste, the ballroom was decorated with bowers of mauve and white flowers that perfumed the air beneath slowly whirling ceiling fans. Individual tables around the dance floor bore candles enclosed in circlets of flowers in the same mauve and white theme. Looking about her, the young woman felt she could justifiably be proud of her achievement.

Watching Edward and Delia Woodson greeting their guests, Claire stood to one side, dazzling in a gown of mauve silk moiré. Diamonds encircled her neck and hung in clusters from her ears, the gems sparkling in the soft light of candles. As guests passed by their hosts, standing close by Claire smiled and nodded to them in greeting – the smile becoming fixed with shock to see two unexpected guests in the doorway.

Anne Winterton…accompanied by her husband.

Amused by Claire's obvious discomfiture, Anne's lips twitched…a smirk that did not go unnoticed by the young woman. Pulling herself together with an effort, Claire smiled brilliantly, greeting the couple with commendable grace. Privately, she was seething that her husband had not bothered to inform her of his tart's presence in Calcutta. On an invented pretext, she engineered Jack outside the ballroom.

"Could you not have had the courtesy to let me know of your…er… *friend's* presence at the ball this evening?" Claire spat, incandescent with fury. "The Wintertons' name did not exist on the guest list Edward Woodson gave me."

"A last minute addition," Jack replied stiffly, conscious of the derogatory term Claire pretended to avoid using to describe Anne. "Sorry, it slipped my mind."

"Really? I find that difficult to believe, "Claire retorted. "It amazes me that you should be happy for me to be confronted by that awful woman without warning."

"Perhaps you should remember it was *you* who instigated that unpleasantness in Durban, through your insulting behaviour towards—"

"How *dare* you blame for that incident?" Claire spat. "Still rushing to your tart's defence, I see! You might at least have warned me she was in Calcutta: but no, it was evidently easier to allow me to be humiliated."

"Don't talk nonsense!" Pale with anger, Jack's reply was frigid. "Now, you listen to me carefully, Claire. I absolutely forbid you to instigate any kind of scene with regard to Anne Winterton. But should this modicum of self-control be beyond you, I suggest you leave the Saturday Club and go home. Do you understand?"

Incredulous, Claire gaped at her husband. The last time he had used that hectoring tone to her was in South Africa…in heated defence of his bloody tart. Things did not change it might appear.

"I intend to leave the Saturday Club this very minute," she hissed, her eyes glittering with fury. "Not because I lack self-control as you so charmingly put it, but I don't wish to be present when people notice my husband making sheep's eyes at the divine Mrs Winterton. May I remind you, Jack, there is a baby on the way and according to doctor's orders, I must lead an untroubled existence. In the present circumstances, that's laughable."

Claire smiled humourlessly to see the expression of shock on Jack's face. It was obvious he had not expected her to retaliate so violently, nor that she would actually leave the Ball and go home. "How you choose to explain my abrupt departure to the Woodsons is up to you," she added coldly, "but rest assured that I shall not forget this gross insensitivity on your part in a hurry."

Claire swept away, ignoring curious stares from people standing close by, and instructed a passing *bearer* to inform her driver she wished to return home at once.

Once back in her bedroom, Claire changed from her ball gown into a loose cotton housecoat. Knowing the servants had all gone to bed, she went into the kitchen to mix a cool drink for herself that she took out to the veranda. Sitting down in a rattan armchair, she lit a cigarette, wondering why she had reacted so angrily to another demonstration of her husband's indifference to her feelings? It was nothing new, after all.

Claire smiled grimly. Of course, it was Jack's disregard for her personal dignity in full view of Calcutta society, knowing that gossip had once been rife about his affair with a mysterious blonde in South Africa. Anyone observing Jack and that woman exchanging meaningful glances would not require very much intelligence, in order to put two and two together.

In addition, she had worked hard to organise the event without leaving the smallest detail to chance, including a magnificent buffet dinner. Edward and Delia Woodson had been delighted with her efforts, and what should have been a memorable evening was now effectively ruined...thanks to Jack's cavalier attitude.

Unforgivable.

Chapter Nineteen

The remaining months of Claire's pregnancy dragged on. An increasing girth made her unwieldy and uncomfortable, particularly during the early hours of the morning when the infant was most active. Following the doctor's advice, she swam every day in the pool, and occasionally went for short walks on the racecourse perimeter in the company of Sadie and the two children. Recalling the dismaying weight gain of her last pregnancy, Claire forswore all things fattening in her determination to quickly regain her figure after the birth. The nausea and dizziness had thankfully vanished, so she was able to enjoy a relatively normal lifestyle.

A frosty atmosphere persisted between Claire and Jack, to which the young woman was supremely indifferent. Gone were the days when she was desperate to please her husband...only to receive a metaphoric kick in the teeth for her trouble. Nothing he did could affect her, now that she had her darling Ratty who loved her unconditionally.

The two little girls were fascinated by the idea of a baby growing in their mother's tummy, and argued endlessly about whether it should be a girl or boy. Daphne was quite clear about not wanting a sister who might steal the limelight. As boys were rude and dirty, Mummy might not love him very much. Diana asserted she didn't care what it was, because Daddy would always love her best.

Frequent letters from Ratty continued to arrive through Naomi – loving letters, if touched by puzzlement over the delay in setting a divorce in motion. He was lonely without her, and wanted his beautiful girl back in his arms where she belonged. Claire wept bitter tears, paralysed by the dilemma of the unexpected pregnancy.

Her own letters to Ratty were necessarily filled with vague platitudes, despite her entire being crying out for the man she loved to distraction. Conscious of causing pain to him, Claire was anxious to evade the issue, at least until the baby was born. She would then go forward with her decision to ask for a divorce.

She had seen nothing of Christina since their return from France, her sister having gone up country to Simla. Persistent quizzing by her mother over Claire's reasons for extending her summer holiday had stretched the younger girl's desire for truthfulness to the very limit. Stammering over an extravagant lie to protect her sister, coupled with Sonia's unwholesome delight in scenting a possible scandal, Christina had fled the very next day. She left behind a frustrated Minette...and a sorely disappointed Sonia.

Claire had received a brief letter explaining her sudden departure to Simla for an undecided period. And why. Folding the flimsy notepaper, Claire's expression was grim. *Sonia*! That spiteful little baggage clearly hadn't improved with time. Not to mention *Maman*, who – as usual – stuck her nose in where it had no business to be.

Claire hadn't seen her mother for almost four years, but it was apparent that nothing had changed regarding Minette's low opinion of her. So be it then. An added advantage was that she would be spared the tired old argument about delivering the baby at that damned nursing home of hers.

Months later, just as Claire was fulminating that the baby had passed its due date by a full week...labour began. After an easy three hours, Claire gave birth to a son. With a sigh of relief, she sat up to inspect the infant proffered by the maternity nurse.

The baby was a good weight at eight pounds, bawling loudly to be plunged into a chilly unknown world. Tendrils of dark hair clung to the scarlet little face, eyes tightly screwed up in distress. Thanks to his late arrival, the baby's skin was pale and unwrinkled – quite different from how the girls had been at birth.

Enchanted, Claire held out her arms for her new son.

Half an hour later, the door opened to admit Jack, whose generally impassive face was alight with joy. Walking over to his wife, he kissed her forehead, and bent over the crib to gaze at the infant, cleaned and wrapped in a white cotton shawl.

"Claire, thank you for giving me my boy," Jack's voice shook with emotion. "I have such plans for him...nothing but the best for our son! Tell me what you would like as a present, and you shall have it."

"I don't want anything, but thank you," Claire answered faintly. "I didn't know you wanted a boy this badly. You must have been frightfully disappointed when the girls were born."

"A little perhaps, but you must know that I love my little girls to bits."

"Especially Diana." Claire commented dryly. "Give me five minutes to myself, Jack, and then you can bring the girls in to see their baby brother."

Half an hour later, Diana and Daphne stood beside the baby's crib. Clinging to her father's hand, Diana stared at the sleeping infant with studied indifference. She opened her mouth to pass a remark, but noticing a glint in her mother's eye, she quickly shut it.

"Isn't he sweet?" Daphne breathed, hanging over the crib and stroking the baby's cheek with a slightly grubby finger. "How long before he can play with us, Mummy?"

"Not for a long time, I'm afraid," Claire only just managed to prevent herself from batting the child's hand away from her baby son's face. Indicating to the nanny that the children were to leave her bedroom, she forced a smile at her daughters.

"Go with Sadie now, girls, and you can come to see the baby again tomorrow. Poor Mummy is feeling very tired."

As soon as the door closed, Claire lay back against the pillows with a sigh. She had found her husband's undisguised joy in the new infant disturbing, and likely to cause immense complications in the event of divorce. But this was not the time to think about all that. All Claire wanted to do now was admire her beautiful baby boy.

Six weeks later, Claire walked into the nursery where her son was lying awake in his cot. Named William John, the baby's eyes had remained the slate colour of a newborn, but today a remarkable change had taken place. Looking down adoringly at her baby boy, Claire found herself gazing into a pair of warm brown eyes, identical to those belonging to Charles Rattigan. So William really *was* his son! Her face broke into a delighted smile, fading somewhat as she remembered who had already claimed him as his own.

It was a stark realisation for the young woman that no possibility existed that Jack would ever agree to relinquish the child, categorically refuting any suggestion that the baby was not his. The radical difference in colouring from that of the two girls could be put down as not dissimilar to her own. How the hell was she to extricate herself from this terrible, terrible situation? She would have think of something, but for the moment, she would just enjoy her darling little boy.

Disbelievingly, Diana watched her father bursting with pride over his new son, and spending rather less time with her as a result. Efforts to attract his attention – even adversely – were met with admonishments to behave properly or leave the room. The bewildered girl was forced to accept she had lost her supreme position in her father's affections...

to a horrid, mewling, demanding baby. Burning with resentment, Diana retreated into glowering silence.

Six-year-old Daphne was also feeling left out, puzzled by her mother's obsession with the new baby, the slightest wail causing her to hurry into the nursery. Should she come upon Daphne hanging over the cot, the child was sent off with a flea in her ear. Under no circumstances must baby William be subjected to his siblings' dirt or germs.

Diana had already received a slap for sniggering that her brother should have been christened *Silly-Willy*, and Daphne had also been smacked for purloining William's fluffy blue rabbit. The undisguised favouritism for the newcomer from both parents resulted in bringing the girls closer to each other, both of them holding him responsible for their change in fortune.

It was therefore with great joy that Diana and Daphne welcomed their Auntie Christina who came to tea, both children begging her to stay with them in Alipore. It was an invitation – gladly endorsed by Claire – that Christina happily accepted, having returned to a frigid atmosphere at Camack Street.

Smirking, Sonia had been only too pleased to relate that *Maman* had concluded that some 'skulduggery' of Claire's had been conveniently swept under the carpet. Furious, Christina left for her sister's home that very afternoon. Walking into the nursery to meet her new nephew for the first time, the young woman gasped in shock. The baby gazing up at her was a miniature version of the despised 'Ratty man' in Claire's life.

So much for Claire's claim of an innocent relationship! And how fortuitous that Jack MacLeod had never met Charles Rattigan...for then the fat really would be in the fire! Christina wondered if her sister had told the man he had fathered a son?

"So now you know." Claire spoke from behind, making her jump. "And in case you are wondering, Ratty doesn't know about William – yet."

"Yet?" Christina frowned. "Surely you don't mean to tell him at all, Claire? What about Jack? I imagine he thinks the baby is his?"

"Oh, he absolutely adores William," Claire replied carelessly, "which will make things all the more difficult, should I decide to leave him."

"Leave Jack?" Christina gaped. "You cannot be serious, Claire? Why, you have only known that Ratty man for four months or so. How can you make such a life-changing decision on such a short acquaintance? Have you thought about the girls?"

"I've thought about little else," Claire assured her sister. "But you cannot imagine how wonderful it would be to live with a man who cares about me...*adores* me! In any event, I told you before how things stood between myself and Jack."

Christina glanced away for a moment, but then turned to look her sister squarely in the eye. "As I see it, Claire, there is only one choice you need make. Should you leave him, I think it's certain that Jack will never allow you to take the children. Would you be prepared to abandon your little girls, as well as this baby boy? It seems to me that either you go to your boyfriend alone...or you stay here with your family."

Speechless, Claire's face gradually lost colour. Christina had just dragged out into the open that very thing she had carefully avoided thinking about: the real possibility of losing all three of her children.

"Am I to sacrifice the rest of my life to Jack MacLeod? There *must* be a way of persuading Jack to let the children go. Maybe if he kept Diana..."

"*What?*" Christina was genuinely shocked. "You can't mean that, Claire! Di-Di is your first-born child, and she would be distraught to lose her family forever. One more thing, I don't believe you would leave this luxurious life of yours, to go and live with a fellow who is almost a scrounger on his own family. After all, it's not as though he's the eldest son standing to inherit considerable wealth upon his father's death. No, you told me his family literally pay him to stay away, and they continue to frown on his lackadaisical lifestyle. Why, the fellow's very existence is dependent on his father's bounty and the occasional sale of a painting."

"Money isn't everything," Claire muttered, her mouth trembling. "Charles loves me, and we would have a wonderful life together, of that I'm certain."

"And *I'm* certain you would soon become fed up with living like the proverbial church mouse," Christina replied dryly. "Remember that I know you, Claire, and have you thought how your children would be educated?"

"Don't worry, Chrissy, I'm not about to make snap decisions about anything," Claire prevaricated. "I do realise every aspect has to be carefully considered."

"I'm happy to hear it." Christina relaxed with a grin. "Think how darling Sonia would love to get her sharp little teeth into a snippet like this, and as for *Maman* she'd pass out cold!"

The tone of Ratty's recent letter to Claire seemed depressed. He was missing her terribly, and very much hoped she was planning a return to France. A further blow to his morale had been the death of his father two weeks ago, and his elder brother was the new Duke of Hartington. That fact did not bode well, as he would now depend on his brother's largesse. Edward was known to be a tight-wad, and especially so where his disgraceful younger brother was concerned.

Tucking the letter into its hiding place, Claire was reluctantly forced to realise that Ratty's situation endorsed her sister's prediction of an impecunious lifestyle. Could she do without luxuries she largely took for granted? Not to mention accounts in shops where she merely signed for whatever she wished to purchase?

What about the children's schooling –William's in particular? It was unlikely that the stingy elder brother would fork out for his brother's love-child! Claire shook her head as if to clear it. No, it was all too complicated to think about now.

As the months went by, William developed into a handsome little boy, his velvety brown eyes a constant reminder of her lover to his besotted mother. If Jack perceived anything odd in the child's appearance, he made no mention of it. Coming back early from the office, he would sit out on the veranda, fondly allowing the toddler to play with his gold fob watch, or playing 'ride-a-cock-horse' with William on his knee. Claire would smile over her son's sweet antics, whilst Diana and Daphne lurked in the background – jealously watching – aware of how futile it would be to compete for their parents' attention.

After school, Diana took to spending time down at the stables behind the house. It was a lot better than watching her parents drooling over William – thought the girl savagely. In the cool of the evening, a *syce* would lead Diana on her pony through the back roads to the racecourse where she could ride in perfect safety. Too afraid to ride, Daphne walked behind with Nanny Sadie to watch Diana cantering around the outside perimeter of the racetrack.

For the second time, Claire had guiltily fabricated the excuse of illness to Charles Rattigan, explaining why she was unable to spend the summer months in France that year. Reading Ratty's recent letter that begged again for her return to him, she was overwhelmed with longing to feel his arms about her. Hurrying to the nursery where the three children were having supper under Sadie's supervision, Claire seized her son from his highchair and hugged him convulsively. William was so like her darling Ratty, and this was the nearest she could get to him as things presently stood.

Stopping eating to watch this demonstration of affection for her despised brother, Diana's eyes were glacial, whilst Daphne stared resentfully at her plate. Unable to prevent herself, Diana leaned towards her sister.

"What do you think Silly-Willy does to make Mummy and Daddy love him better than us?" she asked in a theatrical whisper. "Do you think he has a magic secret?"

"*Diana*!" Claire barked, flushing with annoyance. "I've told you time and again not to call your brother stupid things. Once more, and I'll stop your riding."

"Why are you so angry, Mummy?" Conscious she was treading on thin ice, the girl's frustration outweighed discretion. "Auntie Christina told us you used to call Aunt Sonia by a silly name when you were all little."

"You're taking a big risk with these impertinent remarks," her mother's tone was dangerous. "Your little brother is never horrible about you, nor does he create tiresome scenes."

"That's because he can't speak properly yet," Diana replied. "And if he could, I bet he'd tell you how much he hates having his face covered with sloppy kisses in the middle of his supper."

Daphne tittered, and losing her temper Claire almost threw a startled William at the nanny to then frog-march Diana out of the nursery. Slamming the door closed, she swung the girl round to face her.

"I've had enough of your clever-dick comments, Diana MacLeod! You're a nasty jealous piece of work, and I shall tell your father how you continually victimise your poor little brother."

Defiant, Diana wrenched her arm from her mother's grasp. "Tell him what you like, Mummy – I don't care! And I can't think why you adore William so much, since he doesn't even look like anyone in our family. Maybe he's really someone else's baby, and got swapped over when he was born."

Blanching, Claire took a step back with shock. The last thing she wanted was this damned child pointing out differences in William's appearance. Loose talk like this must be nipped in the bud before Jack's attention was drawn to it.

"What an extraordinary remark to make," she said in a calmer tone. "Children don't always look like their parents, you know. You had better not let Daddy hear you say something so unkind about William. Look, if you promise to try and be kinder to your brother, I'll forget about your earlier cheek."

Diana stared at her mother for a long moment, before nodding her assent. Walking back to the nursery, she reflected how strange it was that her remark about Willie's different appearance had made Mummy calm down. She would talk about it later to Daffy, as such a thing might be useful at some other time.

A few minutes later, Claire was standing at her bedroom window, agitatedly smoking a cigarette. The disquieting exchange with her eldest daughter really had ruffled her feathers. At ten years old, Diana was too damned sharp for her own good, and there had been a calculating glint in her eyes. It might be a good thing to try and avoid confrontation, just in case she was tempted to try out the brand new weapon she imagined to have discovered...

In the months that followed, Diana was astonished to find herself the subject of her mother's attention, and blossomed in the warmth of Claire's interest in her daily activities. She found herself actually wanting to please her mother, and the sulky droop to her mouth was noticeably less conspicuous, and the incident relating to her brother's different appearance was all but forgotten.

Daphne, on the other hand, still jealously resented the intrusion of her brother into her mother's affections, and she now perceived Diana's new status as a further threat. She made concentrated efforts to incite her sister to mischief, in order to have the opportunity of virtuously tattling to their mother.

Occasionally she was successful, and finding herself inexplicably in trouble, Diana would discover her younger sister to be smugly responsible. Not daring to retaliate as for fear of upsetting her mother, the older girl satisfied herself by encouraging friends to tease her sister to tears. Rivalry escalated, and a yawning chasm was created between the two girls that would continue to exist over the years to come.

Pampered, cosseted, and spoiled, William grew into a solitary and discontented little boy. Avoided by his sisters, he was rarely allowed to play with other children in case he picked up their germs. After his third birthday, however, it was decided that time was right for William to attend kindergarten. Claire's final choice was an establishment run by a motherly lady by the name of Mrs MacGregor, and it was arranged that William would attend kindergarten three times a week.

Claire accompanied her son to the school to begin his first day. Upon the startled realisation that his mother did not intend to remain with him, William began to howl and clutch at Claire's skirts. Horrified to see her little son so distressed, Claire was persuaded to take Mrs MacGregor's advice, and detaching the clinging hands she hurried outside to the waiting car.

Controlling her own tears with difficulty, Claire did appreciate that this was an important hurdle that William must learn to overcome. Furthermore, Mrs MacGregor had assured her that William's tears would dry up, once his mother was out of sight and he was fully occupied with other children in the group.

Two hours later, Claire returned to the school to collect her little schoolboy. Getting out the car, she heard high-pitched screaming coming from within the school. Heart thudding, she rushed inside convinced her little son had hurt himself. The door to the classroom opened, and a harassed-looking Mrs MacGregor appeared, trying to maintain a grip of the struggling child's hand. William's face was scarlet with rage, snot running from his nose as he tried to bite the hand imprisoning his own.

Appalled, Claire rushed to take back her son from Mrs MacGregor, who was only too pleased to relinquish the yelling child. Enveloping William in her arms, Claire glanced up at the lady with a suspicious frown. For God's sake, William had never behaved like this before! He usually brimmed with self-confidence, even with their friends. Why, she was frequently complimented on how forward he was for his age. Something must be badly wrong with this school, and she fully intended take the incident further...

"Mrs MacLeod, I'm afraid I cannot accept William here as a pupil," Mrs MacGregor told Claire before she could open her mouth. "He refuses to do anything we ask of him, screams and kicks out at other children when they come near him, and he's been trying to bite me for the last few minutes. It simply won't do."

"I...I can't imagine why he should do such a thing," Claire stuttered, taken-aback. "My William is usually a sunny little chap, so maybe one of the other children did something nasty to him?"

"To the contrary, it was your son who was trying to attack other children in the most aggressive manner," Mrs MacGregor contradicted sharply. "It's as though William is completely unused to integrating with other children."

"So what do you suggest if you won't have him here?" Claire asked, deflated. "It was for the very reason of mingling with other children that I wished him to attend kindergarten."

"Perhaps if you begin by asking friends with small children for tea?" Mrs MacGregor said more gently. "But you must watch that he doesn't lose that temper of his."

By the time the car had reached home, Claire had half-convinced herself that the unfortunate incident at the school had not been the still-sniffling William's fault. But she would take the woman's advice and hold little tea parties for his benefit. It would then be plain to see that the problem lay with that horrid little school.

Chapter Twenty

Claire immediately arranged a tea party with her neighbour, Felicity Miller, who agreed to bring Adam, her own little boy. Only a week apart in age, the two children had spent little time with each other, Sadie having been forbidden to take William on the *maidan* to play with Adam and other children.

Whilst Claire and Felicity were chatting over tea on the veranda, Sadie and Adam's nanny escorted the two boys to the nursery. Minutes later, William returned, bawling, and ran to his mother to hide his face in her lap.

"Darling, whatever is the matter?" Claire smoothed her son's dark hair back from his face. "Have you hurt yourself, my poor love?"

"Ad...Ad...Adam took my best-est car, Mummy!" the boy hiccoughed. "He w...won't g...give it back."

"Madam, William won't let his friend touch any of his toys," Sadie said quietly from the doorway. "Perhaps if Madam would come to the nursery and see?"

Glancing at Felicity, whose eyebrows were raised in astonishment, Claire took William by the hand and followed the nanny back to the nursery. If this nonsense was about William's favourite toy, surely something else could have been found for Adam to play with, for heaven's sake?

Adam was sitting cross-legged on the floor, absorbed in running William's blue car up and down accompanied by his idea of engine noise. When Claire asked him for the car, the little boy handed it to her at once. Thanking him, Claire picked up a nearby red fire engine and gave it to him in exchange.

Grabbing the blue car from his mother, William's eyes then fixed upon the toy in Adam's hands. Dropping the blue car on the floor, his face creased discontentedly and he set up a whine for the fire engine. When Claire told him no, as Adam was now playing with it, the whine became screams of rage.

"*Want it!*" William yelled, tap-dancing with fury. "Give it to me *now!*"

Horrified, Claire suddenly realised everything Mrs MacGregor had said about William was probably true. Her precious son was somehow evolving into a selfish and unpleasant child. How *could* this have happened? Whose fault was it...surely not her own? Reluctantly, she recognised that she and Jack were directly responsible for spoiling the boy, and this was the result. Something must be done, of course. Meanwhile, William had to be distracted from further embarrassing displays. The paddling pool – that's it! The little boys would play nicely there together.

Clad in swimsuits, the two boys set off down the garden, followed by their nannies carrying towels and toy sailing boats. Mortified over her son's behaviour and apologising profusely, Claire rejoined her friend on the veranda.

"I don't know what to do about William's new behaviour," she confided. "He was a sweet little chap until I took him to that kindergarten you suggested."

"Claire, you cannot blame the school," Felicity said firmly. "William was only there for a couple of hours, and Mrs MacGregor is a hundred per cent reliable."

"But how has he suddenly become so...so selfish, and rather nasty with it?" Claire muttered, hating to admit something unpleasant about her son. "We've always been proud of how polite and self-possessed he is with our friends."

"Claire, don't you realise William has never really mixed with other children? You won't allow your nanny to take him out on the *maidan* after tea, which is when all the nannies congregate there with their charges. That's what he really needs."

"What? Expose him to God knows what dreadful disease? Do remember William has two sisters at home to keep him company."

"I know, but they...er...don't have much to do with him, do they?" Felicity strained to be diplomatic, recalling Diana had confided to her eldest son that she avoided her brother like the plague. "And there is quite a disparity in age."

If Claire needed further confirmation that William's behaviour should be taken in hand...she was about to receive it. Walking down to the pool area with Felicity, Sadie could be heard remonstrating with a glowering William who stood in the paddling pool, a toy sailing boat in each hand. Adam stood to one side, waiting quietly for William to relinquish the boat he had just snatched.

Without hesitation, Claire strode forward and took one of the boats from her son, who gaped in amazement. Handing it to Adam, she told him he could take it home with him, because William had two. Thwarted, William threw himself down on the grass, bellowing with impotent rage. Now completely mortified, Claire watched Felicity leave with her son and his nanny. By the set expression on her friend's face, it was unlikely that she would reciprocate the invitation to tea.

Before dinner that evening, Claire was sitting out on the veranda in her husband's company, smoking furiously. Although it went against the grain, she felt obliged to ask Jack's opinion as to what should be done about the unpleasant side of William she had seen that afternoon. As usual, she found herself gazing at the back of a newspaper.

"I'm worried to death about William's attitude towards other children," Claire began, suppressing an urge to snatch the offending newspaper from her husband's grasp. "He refuses to play or share his toys, even with a child whom he knows."

"Humph!" Jack grunted from behind his newspaper. "He's a delightful little chap in my opinion, and most of our friends would agree with that."

"That's just the point." Claire frustration began to build. "I agree that William is charm personified with adults, but he becomes very nasty with other children."

"Nothing to worry about, I'm sure."

"*Jack!*" Claire almost shouted. "Will you please put that bloody newspaper down and listen to what I am trying to tell you?"

With an exaggerated sigh of resignation, Jack carefully folded the newspaper and put it down on the table. Filling his pipe with tobacco and then tamping it down, he glanced up at his wife. "Since a child's tantrum is assuming immense dimensions in your mind, presumably there is little else to occupy you at the moment," he remarked. "William is entitled to show occasional displeasure like anyone else, I imagine? Sounds like a lot of rot to me."

"Pity you didn't see him in action this afternoon," Claire blazed. "And in front of Felicity Miller, whose little Adam provided a well-mannered foil to our son's horrid, *horrid* behaviour. The only thing Felicity can suggest is to send William out on the *maidan* with Sadie so that he learns to mix with other children."

"Sounds like a sensible idea, and I can't imagine why you haven't allowed it before, Claire. After all, the girls went out to play with their friends on the *maidan* before William was born. Then it stopped, since Sadie couldn't be in two places at once."

"*Disease*...that's why!" Claire snapped. "Children who have coughs and colds or worse are still taken out there, not to mention filthy pie-dogs running around. God alone knows what germs they carry."

"Nonsense, all of that is sheer nonsense!" Jack picked up his paper. "In my experience, children have played on *maidans* without mishap for umpteen years. Felicity is right in what she suggests, but if you are determined that William might be exposed to some vile disease, then you must resolve the problem some other way."

It was eventually Sadie who provided a possible solution. "Has Madam considered adopting a small boy from the orphanage in Kalimpong? I know it well, and the people who run it are very reliable."

"Oh Sadie, I don't think I could take on an Indian child," Claire said at once. "The culture is different and so is their upbringing, I imagine."

"Madam, there are also European children there," Sadie persisted. "Some half-half, but others are babies born to young English girls who are...er...not married, I believe," she finished awkwardly.

"Really? Then that's certainly worth thinking about. I'll mention it to my husband and see what he has to say."

As the day wore on, Claire became convinced that adopting a little boy was the answer to her son's refusal to associate with another child. Like it or not, William would have no choice but to accept the presence of a new 'brother'. Should she decide to leave Jack, of course she would include the adoptee with her own children, all supposing he would agree to release them.

That same evening, Claire and Jack were sitting together beside the pool, having just cooled off with a swim. It seemed an ideal moment to gain her husband's full attention, there being no newspaper or magazine in sight. Watching him fill his pipe, she rehearsed her approach and then waited until it was alight.

"I've been giving a great deal of thought to William's disgraceful behaviour," Claire began, ignoring Jack's immediate frown. "Although you and Felicity Miller apparently see no problem with it, I'm not prepared to expose my son to disease on that filthy *maidan*. Instead, I'm exploring the possibility of adopting an orphan boy, a white child, born out of wedlock and abandoned to an orphanage. William would then be obliged to share his with a new 'brother'."

"Good God!" Jack exploded incredulously. "Have you taken leave of your senses entirely, Claire? Bringing a child of dubious origin into our home, as a sort of *plaything* for William? I can scarcely credit the suggestion as being worthy of consideration."

"Try not to be so damned obtuse, Jack!" Claire snapped. "The existing situation is that our son is labelled as a social leper by other mothers. Unsurprising since William behaves so disgracefully. Frankly, I'm deadly ashamed."

"In my view, a great deal of hoo-hah is being made over nothing. I imagine all children must go through phases at one time or another, without their parents taking draconian measures like the one you suggest. Send the boy out on the *maidan* with his nanny like every other child in Calcutta! He'll soon learn how to fit in, and it would be much simpler in the long run."

"I thought I had made it clear that I'm not prepared to risk William's health in that way. Can't you see how lovely it would be for him to have a playmate at home?"

"No, I can't." Jack's tone was dismissive. "He already has two sisters to contend with, and I doubt he would care for a strange boy muscling in on his life."

"Well, unless you can come up with a better idea, I shall do whatever's best for William, like it or not."

Jack stared at his wife's closed face for a moment before answering. "In that case, Claire, you would do well to consider a few salient points before committing yourself to any foolish arrangement. First, I will never be willing to pay for two sets of boarding school fees. Secondly, you won't succeed in dragooning me to adopt someone else's illegitimate brat. You can depend on that."

"How unpleasant you can be and with so little effort, Jack MacLeod!" Claire blazed, wrapping a towel about her body and getting to her feet. "What would the cost be in subsidising a little boy? Give him a decent chance in life? Very little, relative to what is spent in this house on booze and entertaining. Have you no altruistic feelings? Imagine talking about boarding school when William is only three years old...how ridiculous!"

Snatching up her cigarette case and holder, Claire walked back to the house to change for dinner, before she lost her temper entirely.

"You had better think things through, Claire!" Jack called after the retreating figure of his wife. "I am not...I repeat *not* prepared to accept

245

responsibility for a strange child brought into my home. Is that clear?"

Without answering, Claire went into the house and slammed the door behind her. Despite Jack's ominous prognostications, she intended to go ahead with her plans. In time, even he would appreciate the improvement in William's behaviour, and notice the bond that would inevitably form between the two children. He would then be obliged to re-think his mean-minded refusal to take on responsibility for the poor orphan child.

The next day, Claire contacted the orphanage, informed them of her requirements and set about making travel arrangements. Kalimpong was reportedly a charming hill station in the foothills of the Himalayas, and Claire welcomed the prospect of experiencing the freshness of mountain air again. It stood to reason that she could not make the journey alone, so she decided to solicit the company of her long-suffering younger sister.

Mulling it over, she decided she must persuade Christina face to face, rather than by telephone, which made it easier for her to think up an excuse. Unfortunately, it would also mean a visit to her mother's home. Claire had not seen Minette since the blazing row between them some years ago, and neither had they spoken to each other. The situation would be undoubtedly awkward. But she need not stay longer than was necessary in order to sweet-talk Christina into submission.

Late the following morning, Claire was driven over to her mother's home, and Minette herself opened the door. Astounded to see her elder daughter standing on the doorstep, her face broke into an involuntary smile, thinking Claire had finally come to heal the breach in their relationship. Bestowing a perfunctory kiss on her mother's cheek, Claire enquired if Christina was at home. She was, and pushed past a curious Sonia who was peering over her mother's shoulder.

"Come in, come in, *chèrie*," Minette stood back to allow Claire to enter the hallway. "How well you are looking these days. Frederick is here for lunch, so please do join us, or at least have an *aperitif*. Lovely to be *en famille* again, Claire."

Minette led the way to the sitting room where Frederick sat smoking in an armchair. His eyes lighting up to see Claire, Frederick rose to his feet, an arthritic condition clear in the awkward movements. Walking forward, she affectionately kissed the kindly man who should have been her father.

"Claire, my dear girl," Frederick hugged her emotionally. "This is a day that I have been longing for, as you must know."

Guiltily aware that the reason for her visit was not for the purpose of mending bridges with her mother, Claire hugged him back. "Darling Uncle Freddie, it's lovely to see you after such an age. Goodness, I suppose you haven't even met my little boy yet, have you?"

"No, we haven't had the pleasure of that yet," Frederick replied dryly, "but Christina fills us in now and again."

Not *too* much, one trusts, Claire thought with private amusement. "Well, I shall bring him for tea one of these days. William is rather a lonely little chap, as the girls don't bother much with him, but we've come up with an excellent solution to that."

Realising she intended to lead her mother and Frederick to believe that she and Jack were in agreement over the proposal, Claire deliberately closed her mind to the fact. She was not about to allow her plans to be ruined by her skinflint husband's dogmatic attitude. She would try not to tell a blatant lie...but just allow the assumption she had Jack's wholehearted agreement. Pasting a brilliant smile on her face, Claire outlined her plan to adopt a small boy from the orphanage in Kalimpong.

"So you see how wonderful it would be for William to have a brother to play with, as well as giving some poor little chap the chance of a better future."

Sitting back in her chair, Claire sipped her drink, surreptitiously watching the reaction of her audience from beneath her eyelashes. Minette was looking quizzically at her elder daughter, and Sonia had open disbelief written all over her face. Frederick stared into his glass as if to consider the matter with care, and Christina's eyes shone in admiration of her sister's selflessness.

"Anyway, I intend to get on with making arrangements to travel as soon as possible." Claire suppressed a further guilty qualm. "Of course, the child will be European, but born to a young girl in...er...unfortunate circumstances."

"Claire, *ma chèrie*, you cannot conceivably mean to go all that way on your own?" Frederick exclaimed. "It simply would not do."

"No, no!" Claire told him hastily. "I was going to ask Chrissy if she would like to keep me company."

"I'd love to," Christina assured her. "How long a trip are you planning, Claire? I've never been to Kalimpong, but the nuns say it has a lovely climate."

"I suppose we'll be away for five days or so, inclusive of travel and so on," Claire replied, "and it will also depend on how much paperwork needs attending to with regard to the adoption process."

"What about if I came too?" Frederick suddenly broke in. "Makes the trip rather more proper, and I can perhaps help with the business side of things."

"Uncle Freddie, I should love that!" Claire's vivid eyes sparkled with enthusiasm. "Can we leave the day after tomorrow to avoid the weekend rush at the station? In the meanwhile, I'll telephone the orphanage and confirm our request to adopt a little boy."

"Claire, if you don't mind my saying so, it all sounds most commendable and Christian, but I can't help feeling there is more to this than meets the eye." Minette finally spoke. "Philanthropy has never been your strong point, *ma chèrie*."

"Absolutely right!" Sonia butted in. "When have you ever been anything else but self-serving, Claire? The new Lady Bountiful? Rubbish… we know you far too well!"

"Why don't you shut that mouth of yours that keeps flapping out of control?" Claire rounded on her youngest sister. "Venomous insect that you still are, Sonia O'Hara!"

"*Maman*? Claire shouldn't talk to me like that," Sonia looked at her mother, her face a picture of fury. "She's always so vile to me."

"Your own fault, Sonia," Frederick told the glowering girl. "You had no business to pass unpleasant remarks like that. Just be quiet now, will you?"

"Oh Freddie, that's a bit hard don't you think?" Minette broke in. "I'm sure Sonia meant no harm, in fact—"

"My God, nothing changes, does it *Maman*?" Claire said wonderingly as she stood up to leave. "Always the same old excuses for that nasty piece of work you adore."

"Now, that's completely unnecessary!" Minette exclaimed, "Claire, I think you should apologise to your…" her voice trailed to a halt. Her daughter had already gone.

Back in the sanctuary of the car, Claire let out her breath in a long sigh of relief. The last half an hour at her mother's home had been trying, thanks to that spiteful little baggage, but at least she had not entirely lost her temper.

Guilt began seeping into her consciousness, having allowed Christina and Frederick to believe she had Jack's permission to go ahead. Well, it was done now, and the whole thing was for the benefit of her William, after all. Nevertheless, she must hope and pray that neither Christina nor Frederick had occasion to speak to Jack before departure.

Claire's luck was in, and there were no untoward dramas before the three of them set off on their long train journey up-country towards the Himalayan Range. The journey would take several hours, so a sleeper was booked to enable them to relax in peace and quiet. Having told Jack she was going to spend a few days with friends at a hill station, she felt weak with relief to have left without him discovering her real intention. Rocked by the rhythmic motion of the train, she slept away the hours.

Descending from the train in Kalimpong, Claire became aware of the delightful scent of wild flowers carpeting the banks on either side of the little station. The air was fresh, oddly reminiscent of the months she had spent with Ratty on the Côte d'Azur, now more than three years ago. Her eyes pricking with unexpected tears, she hurriedly blinked them away. This was no time to indulge in futile emotional regression.

Minutes later, the three travellers were seated somewhat uncomfortably in the back of an aged taxi, uncertainly bumping its way along a narrow rutted road. It was only a short distance to the orphanage, but they were thankful when the vehicle turned into a courtyard and shuddered to a halt in front of a row of whitewashed buildings. Stiff from recent confinement in the railway carriage, Frederick slowly got out of the taxi and arranged with the *taxi-wallah* to wait. The promise of doubling his usual fare ensured the fellow's delighted cooperation.

Following an arrow directing them to the most imposing of the buildings, Claire led the way up some steps to the front door where a brass ship's bell hung against the wall, presumably to announce the arrival of visitors. Claire had only rung the bell once, when the door opened to reveal a well-corseted European lady of indeterminate age.

"Mrs MacLeod?" she asked, smiling pleasantly. "I'm Alice Rayner, one of the principals here. "Delighted to meet you, and I trust your journey wasn't too tiring?"

"No, it wasn't too bad at all," Claire shook the lady's hand, before turning to her companions. "This is my stepfather, Frederick Le Barre, and my sister, Christina, both of whom have been kind enough to accompany me."

"Please come in," Alice ushered the visitors into a sitting room, and indicated a few rather aged armchairs arranged around a low table, on which stood a vase of pink roses.

"Would you care for some tea? I'll run along and warn Matron that you have arrived, and would like to meet the children in a few minutes time. I'm afraid there are only two little boys who meet your criteria, Mrs MacLeod. Most children available for adoption are either babies in arms or rather older than four."

"Oh?" Claire looked taken aback. "I understood there to be quite a wide choice?"

"There is indeed, but only if you would be prepared to accept a half-caste child? I understood you only wished to see European children."

"Absolutely!" Claire hastily replied. "I believe a white child would encounter fewer social problems in Calcutta, and would fit in with my family rather better."

Alice nodded. "I see. Please excuse me for a moment or two, and I'll have tea sent in to you presently."

Several cups of tea later, there came a knock at the door. A stout woman dressed as a nurse came in, holding the hands of two small children on either side of her. At a quiet instruction from her, the older of the two boys came forward.

"My name is Roy," the boy told Claire, "And I am veree happee to be meeting with you, madim."

The child's sing-song accent immediately set Claire's teeth on edge, being horridly reminiscent of the departed Susan. Nevertheless, she smiled to set him at ease. The way he spoke wasn't the poor boy's fault.

"And how old are you, Roy?" Claire enquired, glancing at the other child who seemed little more than a toddler, his chubby face capped by a thatch of red hair.

"I jus' four years, madim," the boy answered, "and Timmy, he onlee two an' bit."

The nurse advanced into the room, and gently pushed the redheaded boy forward. A pair of china blue eyes examined Claire minutely. Then popping his thumb into his mouth, he leaned shyly against the nurse's starched apron.

Alice nodded to the nurse, who departed with the two children. It was to be hoped the elegant Mrs MacLeod would decide to accept one of the boys. A magnificent placement for any child, and from what the lady had said there were three other children in the house. She could foresee no impediment to an adoption.

"Well?" Claire glanced round at Frederick and Christina. "Personally, I think the younger boy to be more suited to be William's companion.

What do you think? The trouble with the older one is that he speaks with a frightful *chi-chi* accent, and I simply cannot have William adopting speech like that."

"I thought him very sweet," Christina ventured. "But of course, you will know best which child suits you."

"Do you really think Roy's accent to be something that cannot be eradicated with time, Claire?" Frederick asked. "He seemed very personable for a child of his age."

Claire shook her head. "*Chi-chi* tends to stick, I'm afraid."

And so it was decided. Little Timothy was to become William's new brother. As soon as the lengthy formalities were completed, including a medical certificate giving the boy a clean bill of health, the nurse reappeared with him.

Bewildered, Timothy looked up at the nurse then across at Claire, his eyes widening as he sensed a monumental change was about to take place. His lower lip trembling, the little boy could not understand he was about to lose everyone and everything he had known in his short life. Seeing the child's sudden apprehension, Christina dropped to her knees and took him in her arms, whispering how happy he was going to be with his new family. Reassured by Christina's gentle voice, he clung to her for security as they made their way outside to where the taxi was waiting.

The journey back to Calcutta was uneventful, a somewhat tearful Timmy sleeping much of the way. As the train meandered down to the lower plains, the child's red hair darkened with perspiration from the increasing temperature. Gently wiping the little face with its sprinkling of freckles across a snub nose, Christina hoped Timothy would not suffer the misery of prickly heat ravaging his delicate skin.

Thankful that Christina was coping so well with Timothy, Claire asked her to spend a few nights in Alipore to help him settle down in his new home. Enchanted by the sleeping child, Christina gladly agreed.

It was six o'clock in the evening when Claire arrived home with Christina and Timothy, Frederick having been dropped off at his own house in Alipore. She led the way to the nursery where she knew William would be having his supper. Christina followed close behind, Timothy in her arms. Seeing his mother, William squeaked with excitement and scrambled down from his chair, holding out his arms to be picked up.

"Why did you go away?" he demanded plaintively. "I missed you lots and lots!"

"Did you darling? Well I'm home now, and I've brought you a lovely present."

"Present?" William asked gleefully. "Can I have it now?"

Putting William down, Claire moved aside so that he could see Christina with Timothy in her arms. A puzzled expression settled on William's features, and he looked up at his mother with a frown.

"Where's my present, Mummy? And who is that *baba*?"

"His name is Timothy, and he is your brand new brother, darling," Claire told her son. "You can call him Timmy, and he has come to live with us. What fun! Think of all the lovely games you and he will have together."

Both little boys silently surveyed each other. Then Timothy's face broke into a delighted grin. "*Baba!*" he exclaimed, pointing at William. "I like *babas*!"

It was the first time Timothy had spoken since leaving the orphanage, and Christina hugged him to her. "I'm sure William will like you too, Timmy."

"*No!*" William's eyes glistened with tears. "Don't want that horrid boy here!"

"William, don't be silly," Claire only just managed to stop her son from launching himself with clenched fists at the child in Christina's arms. "Now sit down and finish your supper, please."

Forcing the struggling boy back into his chair, Claire turned to the nanny. "Sadie, please would you ask *kensama* for a plate of food for the new *baba*, I'm sure he must be hungry. William, will you stop this nonsense at once!"

"What on earth is going on here?" Jack stood in the doorway. "Why is William screeching like a banshee?"

Claire swung round to face her husband, having forgotten he was due to return from the office at any moment. Her face crimsoning, she also recalled a certain economy of truth regarding his agreement to the adoption. Avoiding Christina's eyes, she turned to him with a brilliant smile.

"Jack, come and meet Timothy...the newest member of our family," she exclaimed brightly, "a little brother for William."

Indicating to his wife that he wished her to join him outside the nursery, Jack grimly turned to his wife. "I thought I'd made myself clear that I was against your hare-brained scheme to bring a strange child into the household? How dare you disregard my wishes in such an underhanded way? Who helped you with this ridiculous project of yours, and where has that brat come from, might I ask?"

"As a matter of fact, Timothy has been raised by a perfectly respectable orphanage in Kalimpong. Frederick and Chrissy came with me since I could not make the journey by myself. They cannot be blamed in any way, Jack, as I imagine they thought you were aware of the adoption plan."

"God Almighty!" Jack's eyes were as cold as green glass. "Is there no end to your deceit, Claire? So you duped Frederick and your sister into this ridiculous escapade? *Unbelievable!*"

"I...I'm truly sorry, Jack," Christina spoke up, having joined them in time to hear Jack's explosive remark. "Claire should not have gone against your wishes, but Timmy is here now, so what is to be done? I cannot imagine you mean to send the poor child back to the orphanage?"

"Frankly, I don't care." Jack replied shortly. "It might be better in the long run if the boy *was* sent back. Your sister is fully aware of my views on the matter, insomuch that I'm not prepared to accept responsibility for somebody else's illegitimate offspring. Neither will I finance boarding school fees for him, when William goes off to school."

"You can't mean that Jack!" Claire blazed. "You have contributed nothing to resolve the problem of William's nastiness to other children, but you are quick to criticise my own effort at a solution."

"Don't beat about the bush! There is nothing whatsoever wrong with our son...he's a delightful child. As usual, you blow everything out of all proportion."

"Speaking of boarding school, how do you imagine William will be received if he is unable to integrate properly with other children?" Claire hissed. "Your darling son will be chucked out on his ear, that's what. Now put *that* in your bloody pipe and smoke it!"

"I'll thank you to stop being so damned offensive, Claire," Jack's own temper began to fray. "Whatever you decide to do, just remember what I have told you. And in the event you suffer memory failure, I'm sure Christina here will fill in the gaps." Stiff with anger, Jack strode away, calling to the *bearer* for his *chota-peg*.

"What an arrogant bloody—"

"Shut up, Claire!" Christina snapped unexpectedly. "Just because I tried to help out just now, doesn't mean I'm not aware of how deceitful you have been. Uncle Freddie would be mortified to learn he had been party to something so…so underhand!"

"Can't any of you understand that it's for William's benefit?" Claire flung up her arms in frustration. "Timothy will help him to associate with other children, and then they can go to kindergarten together. My project will be a wild success, you'll see."

"Claire, will you listen to yourself?" Christina was almost wringing her hands. "The way you talk, one might imagine you are providing William with an elaborate piece of equipment…not a living, breathing child! Timothy is entitled to his own life…not just as second-class citizen to your son."

"If that's what you think, then why don't you clear off home, Christina O'Hara?" Claire flared. "You're not indispensable, you know."

"Oh, I shall. But only after I have settled that poor little boy, who has been wrenched away from all that he knows…and for what? I won't be at your beck and call after this shady business, believe me!"

"Suit yourself."

Claire stalked back to the nursery where Nanny Sadie was spoon-feeding Timothy his supper on her lap, watched by a glowering William. Ruffling the child's red hair as she passed, she deposited a kiss on her son's cheek.

Chapter Twenty-One

As the days went by, Timothy turned out to be an easy child to care for, and soon captured Nanny Sadie's heart. Despite his young age, he quickly learned to avoid unpleasant confrontation by giving in to William over everything the older boy demanded. Nanny Sadie was uneasy about this state of affairs, but acknowledged it kept the peace.

Nevertheless, William remained resentful of Timothy's presence, and never lost an opportunity to make the child's life a misery. Diana and Daphne went out of their way to protect the little newcomer from William and his bullying, that far too often led to pinching, hitting, stamping or kicking. Outraged, Diana was sufficiently ill-advised to complain to Claire about her brother's nastiness towards Timothy.

"Mummy, I think you should know that William is being jolly beastly to that poor little boy! Timmy has lots of awful purple and blue pinch-marks on his arms and legs, you know. I think you should do something to stop it."

"I suggest you mind your own business, Miss!" Claire snapped. "I've never noticed these dreadful injuries...doubtless one of your flights of fancy. Remember that Timothy is a hundred times better off as your brother's companion, than he would be had he stayed in that orphanage."

"That's a matter of opinion," Diana muttered under her breath. "I can't see how Timmy can be happy being bullied to death...and nobody bothering to stop it."

"For God's sake, Diana..." Claire's voice trailed to a halt, recalling the reason why she wanted William to have a companion in the first place. It was to help him learn to associate with other children in a civilised manner. And pinching Timothy so that he bruised badly was not acceptable. After all, it might have been Adam, or a child belonging to another of her friends. It must stop immediately.

"Thank you for letting me know, Diana. William cannot be allowed to hurt Timothy, and I'll have a word with Sadie about it."

"Sadie can't do anything, Mummy," Daphne supplied, having come to join her sister. "You're the only one William listens to, well...he does sometimes."

As if on cue, there came a scream followed by howling. Claire jumped to her feet and hurried through to the nursery, where Sadie was crouched on the floor, her arm about the younger boy's shaking little body. A pouting William stood nearby, clutching two toy cars behind his back.

"What's going on here?" Claire demanded, glaring at her son. "William, what have you done to Timothy?"

"*This*, Madam," the nanny lifted up Timothy's shirt to reveal a rapidly purpling bruise on his ribcage. "And these are from many, many other occasions." Sadie showed Claire several bruises on the child's body, some still livid, some fading. Gently parting the red hair on Timothy's head, the nanny revealed a cut crusted over with dried blood.

Claire stared, horrified. She had thought Diana to be exaggerating the case, but it was now clear that she hadn't. Seizing her son, she unceremoniously yanked down his pants, and bending the yelling boy over a knee, administered a walloping on his bare bottom for the first time in his life. Not bothering to pull up his pants, Claire grabbed the bawling child by the arms.

"You do anything like that again, you horrid little boy, and I'll give you another good beating." Claire shook the boy until his teeth rattled. "*Do you understand?*"

"Y...yes," he whimpered, shocked that his mother had raised a hand to him.

"Good! And you'd better remember what I said, William, because I meant it."

Claire stalked from the nursery and banged the door closed. Standing unnoticed behind the door, Diana and Daphne had thoroughly enjoyed the unusual spectacle of their revolting brother being chastised.

"About time too!" Diana chortled, earning herself a surly glare from a sobbing William. "That'll teach you not to hurt poor Timmy again, you horrid boy."

"I hope your bottom *really* hurts!" Daphne supplied gleefully. "And if you're mean to Timmy again, I'll tell Mummy and you'll get another great big walloping."

As the months passed, William had clearly taken his mother's threat to heart, as the physical attacks on Timothy mostly stopped. Burning with resentment, he made no secret of the fact that he disliked the younger boy. He discovered an unexpected ally in his father, who noticeably ignored the other child's very existence. Climbing into Jack's lap, William would tearfully confide how much he hated the redheaded boy.

Timothy, on the other hand, avoided the surly older boy as much as possible. He looked forward to the girls' return from school each day, and began calling Claire 'Mummy' in imitation of the other children. For Claire, it was a clear sign the child had settled well into his new home. She now wondered if she might make another attempt to send William to kindergarten...accompanied by Timothy.

Mrs MacGregor was finally persuaded that William's attitude was much improved, and the two little boys began morning school. Naturally gregarious, Timothy loved the company of other children, a sulky William following behind him, this time without howling for his mother. A new problem arose, however: William resented Timothy's friendship with other children, and would cry with jealous rage if the little boy went to play with another child. Nevertheless, he refrained from launching a physical attack – to Mrs MacGregor's heartfelt relief.

As time went by, four-year-old William showed a marked aptitude for his lessons, learning to read and write with ease. Delighted by accolades for his surging ability, William was distracted from obsessing about who might be associating with Timothy. He became a happier child, and looked forward to going to school each day.

Claire had been extremely disturbed by the tone of Charles Rattigan's last letter, indicating he expected her to join him without delay. How was she to explain a further hiatus in asking Jack for a divorce? She could hardly claim illness again. Should she let Ratty know of the existence of his son? What if he sought possession of William? The last thing she wanted to happen was to lose the soul mate she had unconsciously been seeking for years, for that was where her personal happiness lay. The conundrum left Claire sleepless for many a night, but no ready solution sprang to mind.

Bearing in mind Jack's attachment to the boy he imagined to be his own son, she knew he would leave no stone unturned to retain possession of him. Her adultery would be exposed, and the Calcutta gossips would have a field day ripping Claire MacLeod's reputation to shreds. How... *how* in God's name could she survive the shame of that?

Then there was the eternal question of leaving her children behind, who would grow to hate their mother for her abandonment of them. In exchange for what? Living a life of penury, dependent on the begrudging charity of Charles's elder brother...how long would their love survive that? Claire shook her head in confusion. No, she couldn't arbitrarily make such a monumental decision at this time.

In one of her now rather dog-eared magazines, she remembered seeing an advertisement from a farming family in Cornwall. They offered quality holidays for boarding school children unable to travel back to their families in the Far East. The extreme heat of the summer months was now well on the way, so why didn't she take all four children to England? Christina would undoubtedly still be in a sulk, and not wish to accompany her on a trip to Europe. Instead, she could leave the children at that Cornish farm for a few months, and they would have the time of their lives.

Freedom – at last – to join her darling Ratty in France.

Claire's spirits were buoyant, having found a temporary reprieve to the awful decision she would ultimately be forced to make. Her blue eyes ingenuously wide, she told her husband of her intention to possibly rent a cottage on the coast and spend the summer in England. Jack gazed at her speculatively, wondering what Claire might up to on this occasion? He had grown to distrust a studied approach by his wife, suspecting an ulterior motive behind it. On the face of things, it seemed innocent enough. Pity he would be unable to accompany his family at this time, but his presence was required for two months in Delhi on government business.

Claire immediately contacted the farming people, and was gratified to learn they would be delighted to accommodate the four children. Did any of the children ride? They had ponies and horses on the farm, as well as two dogs. Claire was satisfied the children would love their holiday home – Diana in particular. She also wrote to Charles Rattigan, letting him know of her eventual arrival in France.

Ten days later, Claire and the four children sailed for Southampton. The journey was relatively swift, the liner on which they were travelling being one of the most modern of the P&O Line. A particular advantage was that the vessel possessed a well-equipped nursery area, taking charge of children up the age of thirteen. Games and handiwork were on offer, as well as a gymnasium for more active children.

Diana surprised her mother by consistently helping out with the two younger children. On their first morning on board, William began whining to stay with his mother instead of spending the day with other children in the ship's nursery. Without bothering to argue the toss, Diana hauled her loudly protesting brother down the corridor and almost threw him at two surprised nursery assistants. Timothy and Daphne followed close behind, neither concerned about being left for the day.

On arrival in England, Claire and her family travelled by train to Truro in Cornwall, the station nearest to the home of the farming family. Mr Trevellian was at the station with his car, a genial ruddy-faced man, whom Diana and Daphne took to at once.

"Glad to see you all arrived safely," he exclaimed, ruffling William's dark hair. "And are you the new wee lad to join the family then?"

"Er...no, that is my own son," Claire told him, avoiding her elder daughter's penetrating gaze. "Timothy, here, is our newest addition to the family."

"Sorry about the mistake," Mr Trevellian was clearly disconcerted. "It was just that your two girls and Timothy have such similar colouring... um...I'll just load the suitcases into the back of the car."

Tucked away beside two hills, the farm was surrounded by several fenced paddocks where horses and ponies of varying sizes were grazing. Orchards of apple trees in full blossom stretched into the distance, and two enormous greenhouses overlooked a well-stocked vegetable garden. The sun was high in a cloudless sky, and through the car's open window Claire was aware of the scent of newly mown grass.

As the car drew to a halt in front of the house, two black and white shepherd dogs came rushing out, barking excitedly. Getting out of the car, Diana ran to greet the gambolling animals, that recognising a friend, jumped up to ecstatically lick the girl's face. Daphne stepped back nervously, in case she was the next candidate for their affection. Afraid of the exuberant dogs, William refused to get out of the car, howling when his eldest sister grabbed him by the arm and pulled him out.

"This is a lovely place to stay, and I'm not about to let you ruin it for us, pathetic wet blanket that you are!" Diana hissed in his ear. "Now, behave properly or I'll have to ask Mummy to wallop you."

William sulkily subsided, but cringed away when a dog walked over to curiously sniff him. Daphne overcame her nervousness to stroke the dogs' heads, but Timothy flung his arms about the dogs, giggling with delight to have his face washed.

The front door opened, and Mrs Trevellian emerged to greet her guests. A rosy-cheeked woman, her generous waistline was intersected by a checked apron, on which she was wiping her hands. Noticing the dark-haired boy's fright over the lively dogs, she called them over and put them behind a picket gate.

"Sorry about Rip and Runner...they love visitors, but they can be a little over-enthusiastic at times."

"Oh, don't lock them up on our behalf," Claire quickly told the lady. "I have two Pekinese at home so the children are well used to dogs even if yours are a bit larger. William, *stop* that silly noise this minute!"

Mrs Trevellian ushered Claire and the children upstairs to see the bedrooms they would be using. There were comfortable twin beds separated by a bedside table in the girls' room, separated from the boys by an adjoining bathroom they would share. About to make her way downstairs, Diana suddenly paused.

"But where's your bedroom, Mummy? I'd like to see where you are sleeping."

"Darling, I meant to tell you before, but I have to go back to London to attend to some business for Daddy." Claire smiled ingratiatingly at the children, who turned to stare at her, open-mouthed with shock. "You won't even notice I've gone, because you'll be so busy helping with all the animals."

"*Mummy!*" William wailed piteously. "Take me with you, Mummy... don't leave me here all alone!"

"Don't be silly," Claire told her son briskly. "You'll stay here with everyone else and have a lovely time, you lucky boy."

Daphne's face crumpled as if to burst into tears. "How long will you be away, Mummy?" she asked plaintively. "Will you bring back a present for me?"

"A present?" William perked up. "Are you bringing presents back for us?"

"I'll see." Claire was willing to promise them anything in order to get away without a scene. "It will depend on your behaviour whilst I'm away."

Glancing over at Diana, she surprised a look of assessment on the girl's face before quickly looking away. Her eldest daughter was too astute for comfort, and Claire hoped to God she wasn't putting two and two together...

"Don't worry yourself, Mrs MacLeod, your children are in safe hands here," Mrs Trevellian spoke up. "Now, which of you would like to ride a pony?"

Three hours later, Claire was on the train to London. The children had been dealt with satisfactorily, and she could now allow herself to feel excited by the knowledge she would soon be in her darling's arms. And for three whole months...what bliss!

She could soon discard her mantle of company wife and mother of three...to become the attractive, sensual girl Ratty had once fallen in love with. Clothes more suited to life in London or Paris would be left at a left-luggage station, and she would buy a few pretty outfits in appealing colours and a pair of open sandals.

Three days later, Claire stepped down from the train at Nice on the Côte d'Azur. Accosting a porter to carry her suitcase, she made her way through crowds of bronzed holidaymakers towards the station exit. Breathless with excited expectation, she was glancing about when a pair of sun-browned arms seized her from behind. With a surprised squeal, she twisted to look into Charles Rattigan's eyes – identical to those of her son – now alight with undisguised joy.

Uncaring of curious stares, Ratty bent his head to thoroughly kiss the love of his life, and arms about each other, the two walked outside into the warm sunshine. Ratty told Claire about his 'new' car, the old one having given up the ghost a year ago. Claire giggled to see a dilapidated red Ford parked nearby, identified by its owner as being the vehicle in question. She marvelled over the fact that a ride in Ratty's ramshackle car somehow seemed preferable to Jack's Daimler that purred along, its bodywork polished to a high shine by the driver.

Driving down the familiar bumpy lane to the little farmhouse, Claire was seized by the sensation of coming back to where she truly belonged. Whilst Ratty was in the kitchen opening a bottle of celebratory red wine, Claire unpacked her possessions and put them away in a chest of drawers that had been cleared for her benefit. Candles stood on every surface in the bedroom, and rose petals were scattered over the bed.

Entering the bedroom, Ratty placed two glasses of red Bordeaux on a nearby dresser, and lit the candles to offset the early evening dusk. Coming up behind Claire, he pushed aside the mane of dark hair to kiss the back of her neck, the warmth of his lips making her shiver with pleasure. He took her face between his hands, kissing her more and more deeply, murmuring how desperately he needed her, missed her, and that she must stay with him forever.

Breathless and trembling, they stripped off until naked. Picking Claire up in his arms, Ratty placed her on the big double bed, where she was dimly aware of pleading for him to take her now – *now*! With a muttered exclamation, he plunged into the girl gasping and bucking ecstatically beneath him, their mutual desire igniting a flame that blazed towards eventual release.

An hour later Claire lay on her stomach, satisfied and smoking a cigarette. Propped up on an elbow, Ratty's fingers idly caressed the silky skin from shoulder down the length of her slender body.

"What happened here?" he tickled a puckered scar on Claire's right buttock. "Looks like a burn of some sort."

"It was," she replied shortly, reluctant to explain it was the result of her father's drunken fury. "An altercation I had as a five-year-old with a pot-bellied stove."

Half an hour later the two made love once more, this time less hurriedly, taking time to rediscover the secret places of each others' bodies to generate maximum pleasure. Damp with perspiration and shivering in anticipation of mutual fulfilment, Claire gazed up into her beloved's face, her own love for him clear in her eyes.

Later that night, Ratty cooked steaks on a grille set over glowing coals in a metal bin. Knives, forks, napkins, and a bowl of crisp green lettuce anointed with vinaigrette dressing stood on the bare wood of a trestle table. Claire sat on the long bench, elbows on the table, contentedly smoking a cigarette. Jack MacLeod, Calcutta and even her children seemed a long, long way away. The here and now was the existence she had craved for so long, and she was anxious to make the most of every second.

The future? Well, that must take care of itself for the time being.

The following ten weeks passed in a haze of happiness for the lovers. They laughed, picnicked, drove along the coastline in Ratty's wheezy old car to Monaco's casino, sunbathed, made love passionately, and fell ever deeper in love with each other. Neither spoke of what the future might hold, until Ratty finally brought it up two days before Claire's return to England. Distraught at the prospect of leaving him again for the best part of a year, she began to weep.

"M...my children, how can I abandon them when they are so young?" Claire sobbed. "Can't we carry on like this for a couple more years until they are older?"

"Darling, you've been saying that for the last four," Ratty replied tiredly. "How, in God's name, am I to cope without you all over again? It was a miserable enough existence, but I consoled myself the situation was being resolved – which it wasn't."

"Only a little while longer, darling Ratty!" Claire choked. "I'll c... come to you every summer, I promise, and we'll have the time of our lives again."

"I have so little to offer you, I realise that," Ratty said sadly. "Unlike myself, your husband is in the happy position of being able to give you everything you want. I can understand how difficult it would be to give all that up."

"No!" Claire exclaimed vehemently, denying the concerns over which she had been guiltily brooding, making her appear unattractively mercenary – even in her own eyes. "Surely you know by now how desperately I love you, Ratty? I would leave Jack tomorrow, if only he would agree to release the children to me."

For a tense moment, Claire was tempted to tell Ratty of the existence of his son. But caution won the day and she remained silent. As things stood, it would cause chaos if he decided to claim William. Tell him she would, but all in good time.

"Darling?" Claire pleaded. "Will you wait for me? Give me this time now, and we will have the rest of our lives together."

"How am I to refuse you, my own love?" he muttered in dull resignation. "I need you so much, and these last years have been hell, you know."

"I know...I've felt it too." Claire gazed into her lover's eyes. "Have faith in me, darling, and everything will work out," she said with confidence she did not feel.

Washed-out with grief to be leaving Ratty, Claire returned to England and took the train down to the farm in Truro to retrieve her children. All four were looking tanned from activities out in the fresh air, their cheeks rosy with health. Clapping eyes on his mother, William began howling and attempted to bury his face in her skirt.

"For heaven's sake, *do* stop being such a cry baby!" she snapped, vainly trying to protect her smart outfit from William's very grubby hands.

"Mu...mummy!" he sobbed plaintively. "You l...left me for a l...long, long time, and Di-Di was n...nasty to me every day!"

"No I wasn't!" Diana snapped. "All I did was make him wash behind his ears and clean those slimy green teeth of his, the filthy little pig."

"You're a horrid beast, and I hate you! I'm going to tell."

"That's enough, William," Claire hastily intervened. "Diana was quite right to make you wash, you know."

"But she was so mean!" William snuffled. "She dragged me—"

"Well you look just fine to me, William. In fact you've put on a bit of weight."

"Di-Di made me eat lots of horrid things I didn't like," William persisted, glaring balefully at his sister. "Like that icky pink pudding."

"No, she didn't!" Daphne cut in. "Mummy, William kept telling the lady her food was horrible when it wasn't. Di-Di told him to shut up and eat what was in front of him, or he could go hungry."

"I love it here, Mummy," piped up a little voice. "I love the doggies, and I rode a pony evwy day!"

Claire glanced down at Timothy, noticing how he, too, had filled out. "That's good, Timmy. Maybe we will all come back next year. Would you like that?"

"Oh, yes!" breathed the little boy. "I'd love to come back here vewey soon."

"Well, I *don't*," William gave him a black look. "Don't you dare tell Mummy to send us back here…'specially with horrid Di-Di!"

Holding her temper in check, Claire went to settle the account with Mrs Trevellian that proved astonishingly reasonable. Thanking the lady for taking such good care of her children, she booked the same period for the following year.

It soon became clear on the way to the station that three of the children thought the prospect of summering at the farm an excellent idea. Diana chattered animatedly about the horses she had been riding, and how she and Daphne had helped bring in the hay. They had bathed in the stream running through a meadow, and picked wild strawberries for supper. On hot days, Mr Trevellian had taken them to the beach where they swam in a jolly freezing sea, Daphne supplied with a shudder. Then they cooked sausages over a small fire, and made them into sandwiches with freshly baked bread.

"Mummy, I want to tell you what Di-Di did to me on the beach!" William bleated. "She made me sit down on the sand, and she put a ring of horrible dead crabs all round me so I couldn't move…then they left me there!"

"Yes I did," Diana admitted with a mischievous grin. "It certainly kept him in one spot, so we could enjoy rock climbing without listening to his everlasting tantrums."

"Yes, it was a jolly good idea," Daphne supplied, unconscious of her mother's ominously darkening expression. "But Mr Trevellian heard him yelling and took the crabs away, but William kept on bawling until we came back."

Claire stared grimly at her elder daughter, the familiar feeling of irritation sweeping over her. Poor little fellow must have been frightened to death by those crabs. Trust Diana to think up something so cruel, and now she was enlisting her sister's connivance to torture their little brother. It wouldn't do…it simply would *not* do!

On the train to London, Claire ostentatiously presented William with a scarlet sailing boat that she had bought in France, and then gave Timothy a smaller version painted blue. Nothing was produced for either of her daughters. His boat clutched against his body, William immediately eyed the one in Timothy's hands, his mouth turning down discontentedly.

"He's got a blue boat, and I like blue best!" he whined. "I don't like red."

"Darling, yours is much bigger than Timothy's."

"No, I want the *blue* one!" William's face crumpled, and he threw the red boat down on the carriage floor. "Give that to me!" he pointed at the boat Timothy was holding.

"Oh, for heaven's sake," Claire took the blue boat from the bewildered boy, and handed it to William. "There, are you satisfied now? Timmy, you have the red one."

"But that's *mine*!" William squealed. "Timmy can't have my big red boat…I want it for when we get home."

Claire rummaged in her suitcase and produced a toy car. "Here you are, Timmy. You have this lovely yellow car, and let William have the boats."

Both Diana and Daphne had silently watched the unfolding scene with incredulous eyes. Unbelievably, their mother was giving in to the selfish little pest already! No wonder their brother was as ghastly as he was, because Daddy did it as well. Unable to bear it any longer, Diana spoke up.

"Mummy, why do you let William have his own way over *everything*? He's so horribly spoiled that everyone must find his behaviour positively sickening."

Gasping with fury, Claire delivered a resounding slap across Diana's face. "How dare you criticise me, Diana MacLeod! And I have by no means forgotten how cruel you were in my absence towards a helpless little boy."

"I don't care what you say...William is still a repulsive specimen." Holding a hand against her stinging cheek, the older girl's eyes were awash with tears. "Look at him, will you? *Smirking*. Amazing how his crocodile tears have dried up with the joy of seeing you hit me."

"You really are an unpleasantly jealous girl, I'll—"

"Go ahead, Mummy, carry on ruining your darling son, and you'll see how he turns out," Diana ducked to avoid another hefty slap. "I wish Auntie Christina was our mother...at least *she's* fair! But she doesn't come to see us any more, because you were so horrible to her when you first brought Timmy home."

Trembling with suppressed rage, Claire sat back, opened a magazine and pretended to read. The friction with Christina still niggled at the back of her mind, and trust that bloody girl to put her finger on a lingering sore. Belatedly, she wished she had not lost her temper with Diana, because she had taken care of the others in her own way. Maybe her temper was short because she was missing Ratty so dreadfully, and the wonderful, carefree life the two of them had led for those halcyon weeks...

Claire cast a covert glance at her elder daughter, who stared fixedly out of the carriage window, hands clasped together in her lap. Daphne was leafing through comic cuts, Timothy leaning against her. William sat on the edge of the seat, clutching both sailing boats, his expression still discontented. Probably wondering how he can winkle that car out of Timothy, Claire glumly reflected with a rare flash of honesty.

"Diana, I've changed my mind, and you may have the gift I bought for you in France," she said on impulse, producing a small box containing a gold chain and tiny crucifix. "I don't care for the way you treated your little brother, but I suppose you meant well."

"Give it to William, why don't you?" Diana didn't bother to glance away from the window. "He'll start whimpering for whatever it is...and will probably get it. After all, you seem to think he deserves to be given everybody else's possessions."

"Suit yourself." Feeling foolish, Claire flushed angrily and turned to her younger daughter. "Daffy, would you like to open your present now?"

Glancing at her sister, Daphne silently shook her head and returned her gaze to the comic. Not usually given to supporting her older sister, Daphne thought their mother to be grossly unfair on this occasion. William was selfish, badly behaved and had dreadful tantrums. Even that nice Mrs Trevellian thought so. It was only thanks to Diana that the entire holiday hadn't been ruined by their brother's frightful behaviour.

Tightening her lips over her daughters' ingratitude, Claire pretended to read her magazine. In an effort to calm her irritation, she allowed her thoughts to settle on the man she adored – now so far away – whom she would not see for months to come...

Chapter Twenty-Two

Shortly after arriving back in Calcutta, Claire made an attempt to heal the breach between herself and Christina. It involved a visit to her mother's home, and Claire realised her mistake upon unexpectedly meeting her mother face to face in the hall.

"*Mon Dieu*, but you've got a nerve to come here after all this time," Minette told her angrily. "Lying to us over the supposed adoption of that poor little boy, whose life is made a misery by that disgracefully undisciplined son of yours."

"Don't believe everything Diana is telling you," Claire blustered, "that damned girl wouldn't know truth if it hit her in the face."

"You are a fine one to talk about truthfulness," Minette retorted, with a cold glance at her daughter's flushed face. "In my opinion, *Perfidy* should be your middle name. Furthermore, I gather you fobbed off your children to complete strangers, whilst you waltzed off elsewhere for weeks. Does Jack know about that? Don't bother to lie!"

"I…I needed time to myself, if you must know. Whether Jack knows or not is of no interest to me. As for complete strangers, those children had the time of their lives with a delightful farming family in Cornwall."

"Hmm, so I believe," Minette grunted, "which is more than can be said for those unfortunate people trying cope with William's disgraceful behaviour. You simply *must* do something about him."

"But he's doing well at school, *Maman*," Claire said defensively. "His teacher says his progress is outstanding.

"I'm pleased to hear it, but that's not all that matters," Minette said crisply. "The boy must learn to behave in an acceptable manner. I'm astonished you didn't die of shame when you retrieved your family from those people."

"For pity's sake, *Maman*," Claire lost patience, "why do you think I went to the trouble of arranging for Timothy to join my bloody family? So that William has a companion and learns to interact properly with another child – that's why!"

"Kindly don't swear in that vulgar manner," Minette snapped. "From what I hear, the only thing you achieved is that William goes to school without howling for his mother. And don't deny it, you constantly give in to that child's demands – even to your other children's detriment. And that was quite a slap you gave poor Di-Di for daring to criticise your darling son. Not at all nice of you, Claire O'Hara."

"Right, I'm off." Claire stalked towards the front door. "I'm not prepared to listen to any more rubbish about William, who happens to be your *only* grandson!"

"Yes, the grandson whom I have yet to meet," Minette retorted acidly. "But before you go, I want your assurance that there is a plan in place for Timothy when your son goes to boarding school in a few years time. Jack is adamant he will not—"

"I know...I *know*! He says he won't pay school fees for Timothy, the stingy fellow. I suppose Chrissy blabbed a colourful account of that ridiculous row."

"Indeed, she did not. It was Jack who told me of your latest *bêtise*. He is concerned that you have taken over responsibility for that little boy's life, but with no proper substance behind it with regard to his future."

"Oh, for God's sake, *Maman*, Jack may be squawking about things now, but when the time comes, he's bound to change his mind about sending William all by himself to a strange boarding school."

"I sincerely hope so, Claire...if only for little Timothy's sake."

During the drive back to the house, Claire furiously smoked a cigarette, flicking the ash out of the window. Jack's stinginess was the ruddy limit sometimes! And she was sick to death of listening to vicious comments about her boy – *Charles Rattigan's son*. When William looked at her with those warm brown eyes...why, it was the nearest thing to a photograph of her own dear love, that was something she dared not keep.

How she was to cope with the intervening months before it was time to leave once again for Europe, God alone knew. As for Jack's sexual requirements? God, the very *thought* was disgusting, and she would move heaven and earth to avoid the nightmare. If he found himself a convenient tart...well, so much the better.

Meanwhile, she would carry out her social duties, a brilliant smile pasted on her face. And over the following months, she would find a way of ending the travesty of her marriage. Her future was with Ratty, that gentle wonderful man, who already was in possession of her heart.

✻

One evening two years later, Jack MacLeod sat out on the veranda, cradling a *chota-peg* and thoughtfully smoking his pipe. In only a few weeks, the hot weather would kick in and his wife would be making her usual arrangements to travel back to Europe for the duration of the summer. The children would doubtless be deposited at the Cornish farm, and Claire would then vanish to...God knows where? His daughters had told him that each summer there had been no sign of their mother for three months.

Over the past couple of years, prior to her departure to England he had noticed how Claire came alive with energy and vitality. Upon her return, however, she had been lackadaisical and given to bursts of ill temper over the slightest incident. It was clear to him that there was someone whom Claire was anxious to see...and didn't want to leave. Jack's expression was pensive, recalling his wife's 'bargain' of long ago, that they should both feel free to pursue other attractions. Be that as it may, it was abhorrent that his wife might be enjoying sexual pleasure outside her marriage, whilst treating him with ill-concealed disdain.

Jack grinned humourlessly to himself. It would be interesting to note Claire's reaction when he informed her that he intended to accompany his family on this coming leave...for the entire period. He bent to fondle the silky ears of one of the Pekinese dogs that wandered on to the veranda. The children would be pleased about it, in any event.

He gathered it was largely Diana and that orphan boy who enjoyed their time at the farm, both of them revelling amongst the animals. William hated it with a passion, and Daphne grumbled about preparing smelly meat for the dogs, and resented tidying the bedroom she shared with her sister.

A waft of perfume heralded Claire's arrival on the veranda, a cigarette already in her long jade holder. Disdaining the fashion of a shingled haircut, her dark hair curled in profusion about her face, cheeks tinted pink with what Jack presumed was excited anticipation of the leave ahead.

"Good evening, Jack," Claire plumped herself down in one of the rattan chairs with a sigh. "Have you noticed how hot and steamy the weather is becoming? Most of the wives and their children are already preparing to flee to the hills, so I had better get a move on about booking our passages to England."

"Already done, my dear," Jack removed the pipe from his mouth and smiled. "I shall be accompanying my family on this trip. I have four months leave due, and I mean to take it all on this occasion."

Without amusement, he watched the colour drain from his wife's face. The unexpected news of her husband's company was evidently an unpleasant surprise. Clenching the stem of the pipe between his teeth, Jack waited for Claire's reaction.

"But…but Jack, how can you take such a long time away from things?" she tried to control the tremble in her voice. "The children were…were so looking forward to a few months on the farm."

"Rubbish!" Jack's answer was robust. "Only Diana and that other child like going there, because they can ride all day long and enjoy mucking out stables. No, this time we will be visiting my family in Scotland for a few weeks, and then we'll see. Italy might be a good choice to spend a month or so."

"I…er…I don't know what to s…say," Claire stammered faintly, her shock obvious. "A trip up to Scotland sounds quite ghastly. It's a long way to travel after the journey back to England, and the weather there is known to be dreadful."

"My parents are anxious to meet my wife after all this time," Jack was unperturbed by his wife's remark. "Since my younger brother blotted his copybook by impregnating a local crofter's daughter, it seems I'm back in favour. Besides which, we can visit one or two preparatory schools for William, since he'll be off to boarding school next year."

"*Sahib, Memsahib, makan* is served," the *bearer* silently appeared on bare feet. "Shall I bringing *mem's* drink to dining room?"

"No, please take it away," Claire stood, her mind whirling. "If you would excuse me, Jack, an incipient migraine seems to be its way so I had better lie down."

Forcing a smile that did not reach her eyes, Claire hurried back to her bedroom and shut the door. *Christ!* She pressed clenched hands against her mouth. Jack's decision to accompany her on leave was *catastrophic*! In light of their bitter parting the previous year, she knew it was imperative to spend as much time as she could with Ratty, if she wished to preserve their relationship.

Although they had since exchanged loving letters, Claire sensed from the tone of the last one that Ratty was at the end of his tether. During the summer months that they would soon be spending together, he was adamant that Claire must decide, once and for all, where her future lay. Further procrastination was intolerable.

Lying sleepless on her bed under a slowly revolving fan, Claire's mind drifted back to the last night she and Ratty had spent together. The two of them had made passionate love, all the more poignant as she was due to leave the next morning. Raising himself on an elbow, his expression enigmatic, Ratty lit two cigarettes and handed one to her.

"My sweet girl, do you realise I've been waiting almost seven long years for you to join me permanently?" Dragging at his cigarette, he blew out a stream of blue smoke. "This uncertainty can't go on, you know. I need you, Claire – permanently – not just for a couple of miserable months each year."

"Ratty!" Claire sat up in alarm. "I've explained the existing situation."

"No." his voice was firm. "No more prevarication, no more reasons why you are still Jack MacLeod's wife. Enough is enough. For God's sake, you haven't even started proceedings to obtain your freedom, have you? Do you think I enjoy feeling like your 'fancy-man', waiting for when the Calcutta climate becomes too hot for you? I do have some pride, you know."

"Don't! Oh, please don't say things like that, Ratty darling. You know how much I love you, but my hands have been tied…"

"By next summer, Claire, I shall expect you to be well on the way to becoming a free woman," he said firmly. "Like any other man, I want a wife, a stable home, and who knows, maybe even children. And, I want you, my darling heart – *you*!"

Panic-stricken, Claire had nevertheless forced the matter to the back of her mind once she was back in the hectic whirl of Calcutta society. For some obscure reason, it never seemed the right moment to broach the matter of divorce to her busy and often preoccupied husband. As time went by, the urgency lessening, she had been confident that once back in his arms, she could talk her darling Ratty round for another year.

Until those disquieting letters from him had begun arriving…

And now? Christ, it was an unmitigated disaster! With Jack directing operations, and spouting off about trips to Scotland and Italy, it was highly unlikely she could even visit France. How to get a message through to Ratty…who had no telephone? What could she tell him anyway? That she and her husband were going on leave together with their family? Claire was certain he would despise her moral cowardice.

Weepy and distraught, Claire found herself inexorably herded on to the liner with Jack and the children. Close proximity to her husband in the relatively confined space of the cabin became anathema, and she angrily rebuffed his amorous advances early on in the voyage. When it should have been Ratty, it seemed indecent – even gross.

Deeply annoyed, Jack left her largely to her own devices. The children spent most of the day in the ship's nursery, so Claire had plenty of time on her hands to brood on the disastrous blow fate had dealt her. Why had she not gritted her teeth and taken the plunge in asking Jack to release her? Charles Rattigan was the man she loved to distraction, so why was she unable to entirely commit herself? Was she so materialistic that a luxurious existence with a husband she came close to disliking...somehow seemed preferable? A cold voice from within provided an uncomfortable answer.

Quite simply, Claire was unprepared to live as Ratty's mistress in the likelihood that Jack would refuse a divorce. And even if he agreed to such a thing, how would she tolerate existing on charity doled out by the skinflint brother? In effect, she would exchange her cherished position in society as Jack's wife...for that of a nonentity, the unofficial other half of an impoverished artist. And what was that saying her mother was so fond of whilst persuading her to accept Jack MacLeod?

"Love flies out of the window...when poverty walks in through the door."

Over the following four months of the leave, no opportunity to slip away on her own presented itself to the distraught young woman. The weeks in Scotland dragged on interminably, and she was hard pushed to pretend enjoyment of Scottish 'delicacies' of black pudding and haggis that her beady-eyed mother-in-law put on the table. Just being aware of the origin of these items Jack gobbled with such relish was enough to turn one's stomach!

Diana and Timothy were fully occupied riding the grandfather's Highland ponies, and Claire rarely saw them during the day. Daphne set her teeth on edge, grumbling about being bored and refusing to eat anything except bread and butter – and sweets, of course. William's whining that rapidly developed into a tantrum when crossed, caused her to burn with shame upon catching her father-in-law's disapproving glare.

Distracted, she wondered what might be going through Charles Rattigan's mind when she failed to arrive as he was expecting. If only she had been able to send him a message! But Jack was there, watching, the proverbial albatross around her neck.

However, the family did not travel to Italy as originally planned. Diana had a bad fall from a pony whilst jumping a ditch. The pony lost its footing, the girl failed to extricate her feet from the stirrups and was lost to sight under the wildly struggling animal. Jack's father rushed to drag the terrified animal out of the ditch, and away from the injured girl beneath. It took three men to carefully lift her on to a makeshift stretcher to carry her back to the house.

Brand new riding boots had to be cut away from Diana's rapidly swelling legs, their destruction causing her to burst into floods of tears. Claire could scarcely credit it was not the pain she was clearly suffering that made her elder daughter break down, but the ruination of her cherished boots!

Necessarily, the family remained in Scotland for the rest of Jack's leave. The search for a preparatory school was put on hold for the moment, but Claire managed to obtain a list of leading establishments to peruse at a later date. When the time came to board the ship back to India, a pale Diana was still confined to a wheelchair.

Almost glad of the distraction of looking after her injured daughter, the voyage passed without incident for Claire. When they arrived in Bombay, she was determined to pay a visit to Naomi Bernstein at her new shop, in case a letter from Ratty had arrived for her. She would justify the need to spend a night on the grounds that Diana needed time to recover from the voyage, before embarking on a lengthy train journey.

The liner finally steamed into Bombay Harbour, dropping anchor some distance away from the quayside. A procession of small ferries bobbed beside the ship, ready to take disembarking passengers to shore. Almost unaware of intense heat and the pungent stench of the harbour waters, Claire could scarcely contain herself until she and her family were back on *terra firma*.

Ignoring her husband's disgruntled exclamation over the need to spend the night in Bombay, Claire booked her family in at the Taj Mahal Hotel. First settling the children in the suite, she informed Jack she was going to briefly visit an old friend.

The hotel doorman summoned a taxi, and Claire instructed the driver to take her to the new shopping mall in the elegant heart of the city. Meeting with immediate success, Naomi's shop now occupied a large expanse of the mall. The lady herself was there, and delighted to see Claire ushered her into her private quarters, ordering a pot of tea from a passing uniformed *bearer*.

"Claire dear, I know you have just returned from leave in England, but you look exhausted," Naomi exclaimed, her black boot-button eyes critically surveying the young woman. "Those dark shadows tell me you aren't sleeping well. Why?"

A distinct feeling of *déjà vu* swept over Claire, and her eyes filled with tears. All those years ago, Naomi had given sound advice to a much younger and ridiculously ingenuous version of herself. Pulling herself together, she described her inability to spend the summer with Charles Rattigan. And why. She now feared he might assume she had changed her mind about him, in light of her inexplicable absence.

"I couldn't even send him a letter without Jack noticing! I kept imagining poor Ratty meeting train after train, thinking I had just missed the thing, waiting for me to arrive. He told me in his last letter that he was sick and tired of a situation where he was only doled out a few months of my company. Either I ask Jack for a divorce, or...or..."

Her self-control dissolving, Claire sank into a nearby chair. Naomi regarded her with a touch of impatience. Did Claire truly imagine that this situation, maybe ideal to her, could continue on an indefinite basis? Was she that naïve? Couldn't she see how unfair it was to both men in her life?

Jack MacLeod was perhaps not the most exciting or imaginative of men, but he was kind, and allowed Claire every luxury and freedom to do as she wished. But that was not enough for this girl, who also wanted grand passion from life.

Naomi sighed. A letter from the chap in France had arrived two months ago. A relatively flimsy affair, compared with the crammed envelopes she was accustomed to forwarding on to Calcutta. In her view, that did not bode well. Walking over to her desk, Naomi withdrew the letter and handed it to Claire without a word.

Her face breaking into a relieved smile, Claire lovingly passed her fingers over the paper and pressed it to her lips. Thank God! She would waste no more time, but write to him at once with an account of the disasters that had befallen her. Slitting the envelope, Claire drew out a single sheet of notepaper, her eyes skimming over the elegant handwriting.

My dearest Claire,
In light of your failure to join me over the summer, I must accept your decision to remain another man's wife. Although I understand your reasons, perhaps you might have written

to inform me of the fact? Just not to come is an act of rank cowardice. But now, at least, I can get on with my own life.

Due to the unexpected death of my brother in a hunting accident, I shall shortly be leaving France to sort out family affairs. Edward had no legitimate children, so I have become Duke of Hartington, and along with the title, there is the responsibility of my family's estate. Not much time to spend in France, but I plan on keeping on the cottage for a few weeks each summer.

Our time together was an unforgettable era in my life, Claire, but it seems that all good things must come to an end. Good luck with the rest of your life, my dear.
Charles

White to the lips, Claire stared at the letter in her hand, the words dancing before her eyes. Ratty had ended things between them. Definitively. The very thing she had most feared. Numbly, she glanced across at Naomi.

"It's finished. He's had enough. Oh Naomi, what have I *done*? How am I to go on without him? His older brother has been killed out hunting, and he's now become duke with all that family money and vast estates in England. He's even signing himself now as 'Charles!' Naomi, I could have been his wife...*his Duchess*! How does that measure up with my worry over losing an exalted position in Calcutta society? But I still have William, Ratty's son and heir...except he's unaware of the boy's existence."

"Claire, you must admit to have treated him rather badly, you know," Naomi told her bluntly. "For years the poor man begged you to obtain your freedom, but you constantly prevaricated. You must have realised he wouldn't wait forever?"

"I know...oh, I *know*!" Claire was almost wringing her hands. "Here, read it," she thrust the letter at Naomi, "and tell me if you think there still may be a chance?"

Glancing over the brief letter, Naomi looked across at Claire. "I really can't say one way or the other, my dear," she said gently. "This man has been hurt, and is determined now to turn his back on what might have been. I think you must accept that. Write to him if you wish, but allow Charles time to re-establish himself with his estranged family. You would not wish him to think your interest has been re-piqued simply because he now has a title?"

"I'm sure you are right," Claire muttered dully. "I must sound horribly mercenary, but having access to money would help me to gain custody of my children."

"You also have to tell him about his son, Claire, and explain why you have kept the child's existence secret from him." Naomi looked at Claire in exasperation.

"Dear girl, you *must* learn to face reality. As regards the children, there are four of them to consider. Do you know for certain that Charles, in his new situation, would be willing to take them on? Would his family be content to see that happen? Aside from the probability that your husband is unlikely to release them to you."

Claire looked up at her friend, pain clear in the vivid eyes. "No, I know nothing about any of that," she whispered. "Charles always told me he would welcome my children, but that was before he inherited the title. As for Jack, I realise he would battle to keep the children – except Timothy, of course."

"Timothy *must* be counted as one of your children, Claire," Naomi said firmly. "No question of that, I hope?"

"Of course, but Jack continues to ignore his existence. William goes to school next September, so God alone knows what will happen then."

"You will just have to work on Jack to ensure that little boy goes to school with your son," Naomi replied with a frown of concern. "If not, I imagine he could continue his education in Calcutta."

Claire stood up, her untouched cup of tea now turned tepid. "I don't know much about anything at the moment, but I had better get back to the hotel before Jack starts a hue and cry. I don't think I can stand any more drama today!"

"All I can advise is that you take time to *think* matters through before you act, Claire. No snap decisions you may live to regret. Try hard to remember that, my dear."

Chapter Twenty-Three

Upon her return to Calcutta, Claire sank into a depression, almost equal to that over the death of her brother. She ate little, flew into tempestuous rages, wept uncontrollably for hours at a time and refused to leave her bedroom. The children were bewildered, especially William who was unused to his mother barely registering his presence.

Diana's injured legs recovered completely, and she thankfully resumed riding her horse every morning before school, glad to escape the gloomy atmosphere in the house. Disturbed by her mother's all-too-audible weeping in the bedroom, Daphne whined and gave trouble at meal times with demands for only cake and sweet biscuits.

Exasperated by the display of inexplicable grief, Jack sent for Christina. The young woman came quickly, alarmed by her brother-in-law's account of her sister's condition. Clinging to her fiercely, Claire haltingly confided to her the devastating loss of a man who had loved her for years...and the reason why.

Christina sensibly resisted the temptation to remonstrate with Claire. Instead, she hugged her, and talked of reassessing the situation once she was back on her feet.

"Carry on like this, and you'll lose your looks," Christina told her sister, fully aware of the effect that would have. "Scrawny people seem so much older than they actually are, don't you think?"

"What?" Claire glanced up at her sister. "I'm not that thin, am I?"

"Not far off, so get yourself up and we'll have lunch out on the veranda, shall we? The girls are at school, and the little boys have had theirs in the nursery with Sadie, so we can eat in peace and quiet."

It was the beginning of Claire's return to normality, and her natural insouciance slowly reasserted itself over the following few weeks. Christina once attempted to persuade her sister to visit their mother, but Claire remained inflexible.

"There is no way in hell that I am going to expose myself to another tirade of abuse," she declared, "to provide that bloody Sonia with entertainment."

Christina sighed, but wisely let the matter drop. She would remain in Alipore with Claire until she was fully recovered, and capable of taking up Jack's entertaining schedule. Then she would return home to help Minette in the house, since they now only had one *ayah*, old Mailie having recently succumbed to heart failure.

Although Seenta, Maile's younger cousin, was fortunately in good health, Christina wanted to prevent her stubborn but increasingly arthritic mother from attempting tasks that could cause her pain. Teaching Maths at the local boys' college took up her mornings, but she quietly undertook household jobs in the afternoons. Upright and always dictatorial, Minette had little to say by way of thanks for her daughter's efforts. Frederick, however, made sure Christina knew her assistance was appreciated.

Frederick had once suggested that Sonia might do something constructive to help out now and then. But the lazy creature pleaded inherent 'weakness', and was vigorously supported by Minette – to his intense irritation.

Over the next months, Claire wrote several times to Ratty at his French address in the hope he might be there, but her letters went unanswered. It was therefore with great joy that she happened upon an old newspaper bearing an account of the unexpected demise of the late Duke of Hartington on a hunting field in Surrey. *Surrey*! It was a clue to where Hartington Milford, the duke's family seat might be located. Claire felt closer to discovering her beloved's whereabouts...at long last.

Jack was insistent that eight-year-old William should start at boarding school at the beginning of the autumn term. Despite disgraceful behaviour whilst on leave, Claire tearfully declared her son to be far too young to manage such a major change alone. Unwilling to provoke a further depressive episode in his wife, Jack agreed she should remain in England for the boy's first term and the subsequent holiday in December.

Claire was jubilant.

Beechtrees, a small preparatory school in Sussex, was the final choice for William, and Jack set about renting a house in Eastbourne for Claire. Diana and Daphne would be sent to boarding school at a convent in Cornwall, not far from the farm where they spent their summer months.

It was now time for Claire to persuade Jack that the two boys should go to boarding school together. If Timothy accompanied him there, it would make the transition from home that much easier for William, and he must surely recognise that fact.

One evening, Claire and Jack were sitting beside the pool after an excellent dinner, and it seemed an opportune moment to broach the subject of the two boys attending boarding school together.

"Jack, I'd like to talk to you about Timothy going to school with William," Claire began, "*Beechtrees* takes them at six years old, and—"

"No, Claire! If you are about to suggest that I pay two sets of boarding school fees, you are gravely mistaken," Jack's tone was uncompromising. "I thought to have made myself clear on this point at the outset of your madcap scheme."

"Jack, how can you be so hard?" Claire was at her most beguiling. "William would find boarding school life so much easier if his friend was with him."

"*Friend?*" Jack laughed incredulously. "You're not trying to tell me William *likes* that child? For God's sake, Claire, the boy loathes the sight of him!"

"Nonsense," Claire said briskly, "all children have minor spats from time to time, but it doesn't mean they aren't attached to one another."

"Ever since you introduced that boy into the house, William has consistently told me how much he hates him. By going to boarding school, the poor chap will finally be freed from that incubus."

"*Incubus?* What a hateful thing to call a small boy." Claire struggled to control her temper. "Timothy is a child that everybody takes to, unlike…" her voice trailed to a halt, always reluctant to criticise her son.

"Then you had better find someone else to look after him, because I will not. It was sufficient to have him foisted on me during this last leave. *No more.* I mean it, Claire!"

Horrified, Claire stared at her husband. Now what? Her plans had been falling neatly into place, but this turn of events was an unmitigated disaster! How could she take Timothy to England, when there would be no school to send him to? And from what the miserly fellow was saying, he would refuse to even pay for the boy's passage. Going to school in Calcutta was not an option, since she would no longer be there herself.

"What…what am I to do with Timmy then? I'm staying in England for a few months, mostly for William's sake, but also to settle the girls in their new school."

"Search me," Jack answered shortly. "It's not as though you didn't know the day of reckoning would eventually come. I'm afraid you have to manage things by yourself."

"Please, Jack," Claire tried one last time. "I'm begging you to change your mind, because I simply don't know what else to do for the best."

"No." Jack was definite. "Now may we change the subject please?"

The weeks flew past and Claire still had not found a solution to the problem of Timothy. It was imperative that an arrangement must soon be made, for it was now only ten days until she and the children were due to sail. In utter desperation, she made up her mind and made a telephone call.

A week later, trunks and suitcases were packed and stood in a neat pile in the hallway. It was Saturday afternoon, and Claire called the children together for a trip into town for some last minute shopping, and then on to *Firpo's* restaurant for ice cream. Diana at fifteen, and thirteen-year-old Daphne arrived in the hall with dragging feet, hating the idea of shopping or being enticed by ice cream. William and Timothy, however, were hopping about with excitement at the prospect.

Claire and the children piled into the Daimler, and the driver set off towards the city, unexpectedly turning off towards the district of Ballygunge.

"Mummy, where are we going?" Diana asked with a frown. "I thought we were going to town?"

"We are," Claire answered shortly. "I just have to go somewhere for a few minutes."

Turning in through the high gates of the Loretto Convent in Ballygunge, the car came to a halt in front of the building. Telling the children to wait for her in the car, Claire rang the bell and then followed the nun who answered it inside.

Diana watched the driver open the boot of the car, and lift out a large suitcase that he deposited by the entrance. Another load of outgrown clothes for the poor, she thought resignedly. Why Mummy had to do it now when they were sweating away in a hot car, God only knew.

"If Mummy doesn't come back soon, I'm getting out," Daphne announced irritably. "I'm starting to feel all sweaty and itchy."

"She said to stay in the car," William told his sister importantly, "and when I tell her you were disobedient, I expect you'll go without ice cream."

"Shut up, William!" Diana barked. "Tattle-tale-tits have their tongues slit!"

"I'm going to have chocolate ice cream," Timothy piped up, unwittingly defusing the atmosphere. "What kind do you want, William?"

"I'll have a scoop of vanilla and *two* scoops of chocolate," William declared, casting a black look at his older sister.

"God, you little greedy-guts!" Daphne exclaimed in disgust. "You really are...oh, here comes Mummy at last! Maybe now we can go."

Emerging from the convent in the company of two nuns, Claire walked over and opened the car door. "Boys, come and say hello to Mother Ignatius and Sister Raphael."

William and Timothy obliged with alacrity, and went to stand shyly by their mother. Taking Timothy by the hand, Claire wordlessly handed the unsuspecting child over to Sister Ignatius. Bundling her bewildered son back into the car, she got in, slammed the door shut, and instructed the driver to leave at once.

The two girls stared at their mother – appalled.

"*Mummy*! Don't do this...oh, please God, *no*!" Diana choked, staring out of the rear window in agonised horror. "Stop...*stop* the car at once!"

Breaking free from the nun's grip, Timothy was running after the moving car, his freckled face screwed up in terrible distress. "*Mummy, don't leave me*!" he screamed frantically. "*Mummy, please, please don't leave meeee*..." the child's small legs suddenly gave way, and he tumbled over into the dust.

Scrambling to his feet, he once more evaded the clutches of the nun who was chasing after him. His dusty face streaked with tears, Timothy howled like a wounded animal for the mother who was abandoning him. The nun caught up, and picking up the distraught child, walked slowly back towards the convent.

Diana and Daphne were now openly crying. Kneeling on the back seat, sobbing, they stared out of the rear window, watching the little boy they loved as a brother disappear from their lives. Turning to again beseech her mother to go back, Diana noticed the self-satisfied expression on William's face.

"Don't you *dare* look smug, you repulsive little beast!" she yelled at her startled brother. "Pity Mummy can't give *you* away instead...Timmy is worth ten of you."

"Don't attack your brother like that!" Claire snapped. "William is your own flesh and blood, remember. Timothy was only—"

"Maybe so, and more is the pity!" Diana was not to be stopped. "I cannot believe you abandoned Timmy as if...as if he was some pie-dog you were fed up with! Didn't you *hear* him crying for you, Mummy?" the girl's voice broke.

"I absolutely agree with Di-Di," Daphne bravely spoke up to her sister's surprise, as she was usually too intimidated to challenge her volatile mother. "Poor Timmy didn't realise you were meaning to dump him like that. Jolly cruel, if you ask me."

Claire flushed scarlet with fury over her daughters stinging remarks. What the hell did they know about anything? Was she expected to sacrifice the carefully engineered opportunity to gain her freedom...the *only* chance she would have to rescue her relationship with Ratty? What other choice was there? None...thanks to the skinflint father of these judgemental girls.

"How *dare* you criticise me about something you know nothing about?" she ground out furiously. "Timothy is not a member of our family, and only came to live with us to keep your brother company until William went to boarding school. It was always intended that he would go back..."

Claire's explanation sounded thin and grossly inadequate, even to her own ears. A rush of unexpected guilt further inflamed her against the accusing faces of her daughters.

"Poor little boy, cast off as if he was a worn out old shoe," Diana inexorably continued. "It wouldn't surprise me if Daffy and I are next on the list to be dumped."

"Don't be ridiculous!" Claire blustered angrily. "Daphne and you are my own daughters."

"Neither of us have mattered since that revolting son of yours was born," Diana's distress caused her to cross the line of discretion. Resentments that had festered for years now spilled out in a torrent.

"The nasty piece of work you and Daddy worship...always takes precedence over Daffy and me. God, he even gets more pocket money than we do! As for myself, I bet you would have preferred it had I been born dead. You've always hated me. For all we know, you might already be concocting a plan to get rid of us two. Why not? You have proved yourself callous enough to do so."

Shaking with rage, Claire leaned across and delivered a stinging slap across Diana's pale face. Shocked, but dry-eyed, the girl sat motionless. Infuriated by her defiance, Claire slapped her again and this time with the back of her hand, her rings opening up a gash in Diana's cheek. Still the girl did not move. Crying with fright, Daphne cringed against her elder sister.

Long minutes ticked by.

"Do you know, I shall never, *ever* forgive you for that," Diana addressed her mother almost conversationally. "Just you wait, one day I'll have my revenge, and then you'll be sorry." The girl's eyes were like blue glass against her white face, blood trickling down a reddening cheek to soak into the collar of her frock. "At least Daffy and I now know where we stand."

"Oh, for heaven's sake, you shouldn't make me angry by saying such nasty things about poor William." Belatedly, Claire understood there had been an adverse shift in her relationship with Diana. Not her intention. She began once again. "Your little brother is only—"

"Oh, don't bother to explain. Maybe you don't care a fig for us because Daffy and I look a bit like Daddy...you're always fighting with him. As for your darling William, well, he looks like someone else," Diana's lips twisted sardonically. "And I wonder who *that* might be...?"

Shocked, Claire tightened her lips and glanced away, her reaction not going unnoticed by both her daughters. Diana grinned humourlessly, recalling an identical reaction when she had mentioned William's odd appearance years before.

"I'll thank you not to malign your unfortunate brother yet again, Diana," Claire said abruptly. "Your impertinence is astounding, and I'll have to think about whether or not to tell your father."

"Tell him what you please," Diana's tone was indifferent. "But I imagine he will want to know more about it, don't you think?"

Daphne stopped crying to look at her sister in frank admiration. She and Diana had often discussed the anomaly of William's strange appearance. They had come to the conclusion their brother resembled that fellow in France with the dog, who made their mother blush and giggle like a schoolgirl. It had been a possibility for them to titter over together.

Diana had actually voiced that very suspicion – if somewhat veiled. Daphne waited in awful fascination for their mother's infuriated reaction. It didn't materialise, but the tension inside the car was palpable.

"Well, what's done, is done," Claire broke the awkward silence. "I suggest we forget about shopping, and go straight to *Firpo's* for ice cream. What do you think?"

"How you can think of eating ice cream after seeing poor Timmy screaming for you, is beyond me," Diana declared scornfully. "Makes me want to puke."

"Me too," Daphne agreed. "I want to cry whenever I think about our little Timmy."

"Well, I want ice cream!" William sulked. "Mummy said we could, and—"

"Shut up, William!" Daphne said sharply. "You're piggy enough as it is."

"And *you* can stop siding with Diana against your brother!" Claire barked. "Driver, go home please, I've had more than enough of you girls."

Arriving back at the house, Claire stalked off to her bedroom and slammed the door behind her. Sadie took charge of a stormy-faced William, and from the sadness on her face it was clear she knew what had happened to Timothy.

As soon as their mother had disappeared, Diana and Daphne ran outside to ask the driver to take them to Camack Street. Both were devastated by what had happened to Timothy, and badly needed the comfort of their aunt and grandmother.

Early the following morning an *ayah* woke Claire with the information that her mother and sister were waiting for her on the veranda. Guessing the reason for the unusual visit, the young woman deliberately took her time to shower, make up her face, and put on a fresh *peignoir*. Thanks to Diana's loose mouth a battle might be ahead, she thought, but she intended to defend herself in a robust manner.

"*Maman?*" Claire sauntered into the veranda where Minette and Christina were sitting, glasses of *nimbu pani* on the rattan table in front of them. "To what do I owe the pleasure of your company so early in the day?"

"There is no doubt in my mind that you are aware of why we are here," Minette icily told her daughter. "I mean to discover the reason for your disgraceful abandonment of that poor little boy yesterday. Self-obsessed you have always been, my girl, but that episode of undiluted cruelty has taken me by surprise."

"I'm not answerable to you for my actions, mother dear," Claire replied haughtily. "Nor to you, Christina, so you can drop the holier-than-thou expression. I have my own reasons for what I did, one of which was that Jack refused to send the boy to boarding school with William. My dear husband declared he would no longer finance Timothy in any way at all. Is that reason enough for you?"

"Unless my memory deceives me, I seem to recall Jack warning you about this eventual outcome," Minette said reflectively. "But no, you were grimly determined to have your own way so you ignored his advice. Not to mention bamboozling poor Freddie into your scheme. And, as it turns out, at the expense of that poor child."

"Could you not have brought Timothy to us at Camack Street?" asked Christina, not far from tears, having been very fond of the redheaded little boy. "We would have cared for him whilst you were away in England."

"I have no idea about how long I shall be away," Claire casually lit a cigarette and fitted it into her jade holder. "Certainly over the Christmas term and holidays...perhaps even longer. Depends on how well William settles into his new school."

"You still could have asked us," Christina stated obstinately. "*Maman* and I would have found a way to resolve the problem, even if we took him on permanently."

"For Christ's sake, drop the bloody subject, will you?" Claire snapped. "I have arranged for the boy to be sent back to the orphanage in Kalimpong, and that's that."

"Nasty piece of work you are turning out to be, Claire O'Hara!" Minette stared disdainfully at her daughter who was unable to meet her eyes. "Just wait until the word goes round Calcutta about the dreadful thing you've done to a defenceless six-year-old child. Decent people will shun you, and even those fair-weather friends of yours are likely to be conspicuous by their absence."

"And I suppose you intend to propagate the tale with much embellishment," Claire muttered sullenly. "Enjoy yourself, do!"

"I have no intention – or need – to do such a thing," Minette retorted frigidly. "It stands to reason that people familiar with members of your family will ask questions, and discover the disgraceful answer. I bid you goodbye, Claire...my regards to Jack."

Christina followed her mother from the veranda, pausing to look back at her sister. "Claire, I have the strongest feeling that – sooner or later – you will bitterly regret the terrible thing you did to that child. Do as you would wish to be done by, remember."

Chapter Twenty-Four

Subsequent to the upsetting interview with her mother, Claire closed her mind to the matter of Timothy, and concentrated on the journey ahead. Jack made no comment regarding the boy's sudden absence in the house, and neither did Claire choose to enlighten him. In light of her mother's remarks, she cancelled all social engagements before her departure to avoid the possibility of being snubbed.

Passing through Bombay before boarding the ship to England, Claire hesitated over contacting Naomi Bernstein. She uncomfortably recalled Naomi's sharp remark that Timothy must be considered a member of Claire's family. How would she explain the fact that the boy was no longer with her? And Naomi, generally kindness itself, would not mince her words. Better to let the dust settle, Claire told herself. People would forget all about it when the next scandal exploded on the scene.

The sea passage to England was less than memorable for Claire. The girls were distant, and William grizzled and whined constantly over being sent away to school. In order to gain respite from the disagreeable atmosphere, Claire employed one of the stewardesses to supervise the children's evening meal. In this way, she would at least have the evenings to herself, dressed to the nines, and enjoy a little adult conversation.

Claire disembarked from the liner on to Southampton quayside, pleased that the early autumn weather was still fine and warm. A chauffeur-driven car was waiting outside the Customs shed, and she and the children were soon on the road to the furnished house in Eastbourne. It was a journey of several hours, with a stop for lunch to give everyone the opportunity of stretching cramped legs.

It came as a pleasant surprise to Claire when the car drew up in front of a graceful one-time vicarage, surrounded by immaculate lawns. Staffed by a housekeeper, odd-job man and gardener, the two men hurried forward to help the taxi driver with the unloading of a substantial quantity of luggage from the car.

Emerging from the house to greet the newly arrived family, Mrs Briggs, the housekeeper, turned out to be a capable-looking woman with a sweet smile. Looking about her, Claire thought what a delightful refuge it was, where she and her darling Ratty could eventually reconcile and plan their future together.

But the children must first be installed in their respective schools. William would be going in a week's time, and five days later the girls would be off. And in light of their hostile attitude towards her, Claire decided not to accompany her daughters to Truro, despite it being their first term at the convent. Assuring herself they were old enough to manage on the school train, she hastily suppressed a *frisson* of guilt.

William began his school term at Beechtrees every bit as dramatically as Claire had been dreading. Bawling and struggling shamefully, the outraged boy found himself firmly led away by a master to be dealt with behind closed doors. A tearful Claire was invited by the headmaster's wife into her sitting room, and offered a glass of sherry.

"Don't worry about young William, Mrs MacLeod...he'll soon settle in with the other boys in his year," the lady briskly told her. "It's a big change in his life, but he will adapt to life at Beechtrees, you can be sure of that."

"But he looks so...so *little* to be going to boarding school!" Claire wept. "It's breaking my heart, but his father insists."

Two glasses of sherry later, Claire returned to the house where Diana and Daphne were waiting impatiently for their lunch.

"Went well, did it?" Diana enquired sarcastically, noticing her mother's still-watery eyes. "I'm sure William positively charged into his new school, yelping with joy."

"I can do without your stupid remarks, thank you, Diana MacLeod!" Claire snapped, her eyes starting to fill once again. "In my view, William is far too young and sensitive to manage the draconian life of a boarding school."

"*Pshaw!*" Diana snorted derisively. "It will be the making of him to learn a little discipline, and he might even stop howling for his mother."

"If he does something so wet, other boys are bound to duff him up," sniggered Daphne with satisfaction. "I daresay he'll learn jolly fast how to behave."

"We'll see how *you* manage when it's your turn to go, you nasty piece of work," Claire snarled. "You're also a spoiled brat, remember!"

"Oh, for heaven's sake, Mummy!" Diana heaved a theatrical sigh. "Daffy and I are hardly in the same category as your darling son. Bet you anything our Willie toddled off with his pockets positively stuffed with pocket money!"

"I told you time and again *not* to call William by that stupid name, Diana!" Claire's temper was fraying. "If you can't keep a civil tongue in your head – leave the table."

Diana grinned at her sister, but said no more. She was hungry after all.

To her daughters' disgust, Claire continued to mourn the loss of her son over the following few days. Diana overheard her on the telephone to *Beechtrees*, begging to speak to him, and maybe take him out for the weekend. The headmaster was firm. William was settling in well, and it was far too disruptive to consider a leave out so soon. And no, boys were not allowed to take telephone calls.

Frustrated, Claire turned her attention to finding out where Ratty's family seat was located. It came as a pleasant surprise that Hartington Milford turned out to be no great distance as Claire had earlier feared, merely involving a half an hour trip by train. Elated, she dreamed of the reunion with her beloved, and his joy to see her again having imagined she was lost to him forever. It would also be exactly the right moment to tell Ratty about the existence of his son. Claire felt excited as a young girl.

It was soon Diana and Daphne's turn to leave for their school, and Claire sent for the same taxi that had taken her to *Beechtrees* to take them to the station. Clad in their new uniform blazers, the girls were taken aback to discover their mother had no intention of accompanying them. Deposited at the station, they followed groups of similarly attired schoolgirls to climb into carriages labelled for their school

Doors were slammed, the guard waved his green flag, a hooter blasted and the train pulled out of the station amid clouds of steam and metallic clanking. The girls' final destination would be Truro, and on to the Convent of the Sacred Heart.

Alone in the house at last, Claire began making plans to travel to Newby, the village closest to Hartington Milford. Once there, she decided to somehow arrange a 'chance' meeting with Ratty. Not that easy. Perhaps the best idea would be to put up in a hotel in the village, and then take matters from there.

There was indeed a hotel in the centre of Newby, and Claire booked a double room for the night. Packing a small suitcase with a change of clothing, she was glad she had bought a new nightgown whilst in

Eastbourne. A diaphanous affair, it was very pretty and seductive...not that she expected to wear it for long!

The morning of her departure, Claire brushed out her dark hair to frame her face, knowing Ratty preferred it to the shorter fashions of the day. Slender, perfectly made up and dressed with casual elegance, she set off on her longed-for mission. Soon now, she would see her darling man, to reassure him of her love and definitive commitment.

Newby turned out to be a delightful village, most of the houses possessing thatched roofs that included the hotel where Claire was booked to stay. Having registered herself at the hotel reception desk, she decided to explore the village where she discovered a post office, bakery and grocers around a marketplace. On the far side was an antique shop displaying silverware, jewellery and vintage glasses behind mullioned windows.

Intrigued by a Georgian silver salver in the window, Claire entered the shop to ask the price. As she waited to be served, she was startled to hear a familiar voice exclaim.

"*Claire?* Good Lord, whatever are you doing in this neck of the woods?"

Whirling, Claire looked straight into the brown eyes of the only man she had ever loved – Charles Rattigan, Duke of Hartington. Every pre-rehearsed speech vanished from her mind, and she stood there tongue-tied, her vivid eyes sparkling with joy.

"Ratty!" Claire found her voice. "Is it really you? How wonderful to see you again! As the children have gone to boarding school, I—"

"Boarding school already?" he interrupted her with a laugh. "Time really does seem to fly. I suppose I should soon be looking at..." he broke off as a noticeably pregnant young woman with strawberry blonde hair wandered over to join them.

"So there you are, darling," Ratty placed a proprietary arm about the newcomer's shoulders. "I'd like you to meet Julia, my wife. Claire is an old friend who used to spend her summers in France. I gather she's been putting her children into school."

The young woman smilingly extended a hand to Claire, who stood as if turned to stone. "How nice to meet you, Mrs...er?"

"MacLeod," Ratty supplied. "We should arrange to get together sometime and catch up, although I admit our own news is rather self-evident!" he glanced affectionately at his wife's swelling stomach.

"Yes, that would be nice," answered Claire mechanically. "When is your baby due, Lady Hartington?"

"Oh, please do call me Julia. The baby? Not for another six weeks, which is just as well since the nursery is still being refurbished – a whole month late. Workmen can really be the limit with their everlasting need for tea breaks."

"Why don't we pop over the road to the pub and have a spot of lunch together?" Ratty enquired. "The White Lion is renowned for its roasts."

Marshalling her shattered senses, Claire smiled at the man she adored to distraction. "Thank you, but no," she finally managed, "I've arranged to meet friends for lunch in...um...Broughton." Claire thanked God to have noticed the name of a station where the train had briefly halted.

"Maybe another time? Goodness, I must run or I'll miss my train... lovely to have met you both, and good luck with the baby."

Before either Ratty or his wife could answer, Claire hurried from the shop. Once she was certain to be out of sight, she bolted back to the hotel and up to the bedroom, flinging herself on the bed to give way to a storm of agonised misery, her cries muffled by a pillow. An hour later she regained a semblance of self-control, and rolling over on her back brooded over the incident in the antique shop.

How *could* Ratty replace her so quickly – he who had sworn eternal devotion? God, just hearing him call that simpering woman 'darling' had been as a dagger in her heart! Not only had he married the creature, she was also expecting his baby. But it was Claire's William who was Ratty's *first-born*! Except he was unaware of his son's existence – who by rights, should be his heir.

Why was life so bloody, bloody cruel? Claire's face burned, reflecting how close she had come to humiliation by flinging herself into Ratty's arms. Especially when the usurping wife had suddenly put in an appearance. Had she done such a thing, it didn't bear thinking about and made Claire cringe with mortification.

She now reflected on what she had so nearly sacrificed for the illusion of renewing her relationship with Charles Rattigan. Why, she had even toyed with the idea of asking Jack for a divorce before leaving Calcutta! Had she done so, she would have lost everything – *everything*! Now, at least, she still had a life to return to in India.

Unexpectedly – undesired – an image of Timothy's freckled little face sprang into Claire's mind, a stark reminder of her own ruthlessness in order to pursue her lover. Tears of shame filled her eyes and trickled down her cheeks, realising she would never forgive herself for that cruel act of sheer self-interest.

Hours later, she pulled herself together with an effort. It was the definitive end of an era, and the entire business must now be firmly relegated to the past. With a sinking heart, Claire realised she was truly alone for the first time in her life. The three children were in school, and Jack and Christina were in India.

The sense of lonely isolation did not sit well.

The following morning, Claire left the hotel early to travel back to Eastbourne, anxious not to risk running into Ratty and his ginger-haired wife. The pair had been the cause of enough embarrassment and pain to last her a lifetime.

Back within the security of the Eastbourne house, Claire retired to her bedroom and remained there for three days and nights...to the consternation of Mrs Briggs. Meals on trays placed outside the bedroom door remained untouched. Perhaps Mrs MacLeod was ill? She mentioned maybe calling a doctor, when she heard the bedroom door upstairs open and then close. Hurrying into the hallway, she was relieved to see the young woman descending the staircase, fully dressed and made up, only the vivid eyes seemed somewhat shadowed. She must be missing the children, the housekeeper thought with relief.

"Telephone for a taxi for me please, would you, Mrs Briggs? I'm going to stay at the Savoy Hotel in London for a few days."

After the taxi had vanished down the drive, Mrs Briggs went upstairs to tidy the bedroom and change the sheets on the bed. Upon emptying the bathroom waste bin, she was astounded to discover a transparent black lace nightgown, clearly unworn but tossed away. Tutting to herself with disapproval, Mrs Briggs imagined the item must be an unwanted gift, being quite unable to envisage the elegant Mrs MacLeod wearing such a depraved-looking garment.

William's letters home to his mother revealed the boy was settling in well at his school, announcing with pride that he was being considered for a cricket team. His end of term report indicated excellence in History and English, well beyond that of his age group. Claire was delighted and proud of her son.

In faraway India, Jack was pleased with the transformation of his son from milk-sop to regular schoolboy, for it was plain that William was maturing at last. Claire had told him in a letter that when she collected William at half-term, the boy had forbidden her to kiss him in front of other boys. Over the school holidays, however, it was clear that William's hatred of his elder sister remained unchanged.

The two girls were glad to back in Eastbourne for Christmas, their new school being unpopular with both. The nuns had been scathing over the quality of their clothing relative to that of other pupils, and neither were they reticent over expressing their opinion in front of other girls who took their cue to mock the MacLeod girls.

"Rich, over-indulged British Raj children," was an expression the two girls heard far too frequently. "Waited on hand and foot by a house full of servants," was another. Their handmade black leather shoes were confiscated, replaced by stiff black lace-ups chafing their feet until painful blisters appeared.

Brassières had also been taken away and replaced with tight-fitting Liberty bodices, causing Diana's full breasts to be painfully squashed inside the hated item of underwear. Daphne grizzled about having to get up before the bell, in order to manage the bodice's tiny buttons before getting dressed for breakfast. Both girls loathed the school food. Initially concerned by her daughters' vociferous complaints, Claire decided to put it down to being new girls. In time, everything would improve, she felt sure. At least William was happy...

Upon her return to Calcutta the following September, Claire was stunned to receive a letter from Naomi Bernstein, indicating she was severing their friendship. She was certain no explanation was required as to the reason why. A similar letter arrived from Sunita, Claire's *Maharani* friend. She, too, wanted nothing more to do with Claire, for what she had done to little Timothy was unforgivable. Panic-stricken, Claire visited the convent in Ballygunge in an effort to seek information about the boy's whereabouts. Maybe she could take him back?

"Timothy is no longer your concern, Mrs MacLeod," Mother Superior was frigidly blunt. "You abdicated that right when you abandoned the boy. I bid you good day."

Claire retreated to her home, distraught to have been condemned by Naomi and Sunita, the two people who meant a great deal to her. As if she wasn't already heavily burdened by remorse! She wondered if Christina might come to stay with her for a while? Recalling the last occasion she had seen her, Claire gloomily supposed not.

As for her husband, he seemed not to notice that Timothy had vanished from his home. Claire ground her teeth in frustration. She was being blamed for abandoning the boy, but nobody seemed to realise the fault really lay at Jack's blasted door!

Nevertheless, she was sensitive to covert criticism from friends, so she involved herself exclusively with her husband's business entertaining. She did not extend invitations for private dinners, cocktail, tennis or swimming parties as she had in the past – fearing the humiliation of rejection. Feeling herself to be a social leper, she longed for the winter season to be over so that she could return to Eastbourne.

The devastation she had suffered at Charles Rattigan's hands continued to fester in Claire's mind, blaming his faithlessness for her present difficulties. Had it not been for his sake, she would never have returned Timothy to the orphanage. And the bloody man hadn't wasted any time before replacing her, had he? Maybe his ginger-haired wife would present him with a gaggle of useless girls? My God, how *that* would serve him right! His true heir was William, now brutally deprived of his inheritance. One day, Claire would see to it that Charles Rattigan received a well-deserved come-uppance...

The following May, Claire sailed for England, thankful to get away from the hostility she sensed in people about her. It would be wonderful to see William again after such an age, and her girls too, of course. And how fortunate it was that Jack had taken the house in Eastbourne on permanent lease.

Upon arrival in Eastbourne, Mrs Briggs welcomed Claire with genuine warmth. The housekeeper had become fond of the sometimes over-solemn lady and her exuberant children. They would all be spending the summer holidays here at the house, and she understood the father, whom she had yet to meet, would be joining his family at a later date. Pleased, she dragged out a pile of cookery books, intending to compile a list of delicious meals for the family.

William was the first to return, and Claire stood excitedly outside the front door as the taxi turned into the driveway. The car door opened and the boy almost fell out, a lock of dark hair flopping over an eye, and clutching a battered cricket bat. Claire could scarcely credit the transformation in her son who stood before her, grinning, warm brown eyes dancing – the image of Charles Rattigan.

Seeing his mother's eyes fill with tears as she advanced, arms outstretched, William swiftly disentangled himself from the intended hug to offer her a grubby cheek to kiss. Swallowing her hurt, Claire followed her son inside where he greeted Mrs Briggs with a demand to know what was for tea, as he was starving!

The two girls arrived three days later. Claire had sent a taxi to meet them at the local station, and walked outside as the car drew up. Daphne was the first to get out, slender if decidedly grubby, and her hair had been badly cut. Diana then emerged, and Claire gasped in horror. She had always been a well-built girl, but never fat. Now, her face was as round as a full moon, her body ungainly with extra weight she had put on. The coppery hair was lacklustre, her expression morose.

"Darlings, lovely to see you both!" Claire pulled herself together and went to kiss her daughters. "My goodness, it's been such a long time, hasn't it?"

"Yes, not far off a year." Diana's answer was curt. "We were beginning to wonder whether you were ever coming back for us."

"Darling, don't be silly, you knew exactly when I was due to return," Claire replied.

"Mummy, we *loathe* that school!" Diana declared without preamble. "The nuns are mostly horrible, and they love poking fun of us because we live in India. All the girls now make monkey gestures and grunt every time they see Daffy or me."

"Girls do tend to tease each other dreadfully," Claire began. "Why, when I was—"

"I bet your teachers didn't encourage it, though," Diana interrupted, "and you should hear what happened to poor Daffy."

Claire glanced at her younger daughter, whose face was turning scarlet. "Doesn't matter," she muttered, "I...I don't want to think about it any more."

"One of those damned nuns wouldn't let Daffy go to the lavatory after lights out," Diana was not to be deterred, "so the poor thing had an accident in her bed during the night. In the morning, she reported what had happened to the nun in charge who made to stand with the wet sheet on her head in front of everyone during Assembly."

Horrified, Claire put an arm around Daphne's shoulders and the mortified girl burst into tears. What the hell were those black-clad witches thinking of, to subject a young girl to public humiliation of that kind? Her daughters would not be returning to such a dreadful institution. Claire's own experience of nuns had been in Simla, with those of the Loretto Order over several years. A group of kindly women, they would never have allowed such a cruel thing to take place.

"Don't cry, darling!" Claire reassuringly hugged the shaking shoulders. "Neither of you will be going back to that place, I promise. You obviously have to go to school, but we'll think of something else."

"What's going on?" William asked curiously as he joined the group in the drive. "Why is Daffy bawling?"

"Mind your own business, Willie!" Diana snarled. "And you're a fine one to talk about bawling. Remember when I scrubbed cabbages out of your ears last holidays?"

"Daffy had a…a very nasty experience at school," Claire explained before her son could retaliate. "Neither of the girls will be returning to that convent in Cornwall."

"Mother, have you noticed how jolly fat Diana is now?" William was out for revenge. "You should have seen the huge slices of buttered bread and jam she scoffed at the farm, as well as tons of cream and sugar over everything."

Storming into the house, Diana tried to shut her ears to her brother's jeering laughter. It was true she had enjoyed the crusty loaves Mrs Trevellian had baked each morning, spread thickly with freshly churned butter and home-made jam.

The pounds had rapidly piled on, and she had the embarrassment of telling the nun in charge her school uniform no longer fitted. Cackling derisively, the woman had told her that they didn't stock uniforms 'big enough for cows'. Despite her many sporting activities and vile school food, Diana only managed to shed part of the weight she had gained. And now she was obliged to suffer ridicule from her toad of a brother!

Claire lost no time in composing a letter to the convent, informing them of her decision to withdraw her daughters immediately – and why. She also wrote to Christina, describing the disgraceful incident at the girls' school and both girls' unhappiness there. She was now contemplating sending Diana and Daphne to school in France, and would she be interested in accompanying them as *loco parentis*?

Christina's reply was immediate. She would be delighted. Uncle Emile happened to be in Calcutta when Claire's letter arrived, and he had suggested a good school near Périgueux in the south-west of France. It was not far from his home so Christina was welcome to lodge there if she wished, and it would be a pleasure to see something of Marguerite's granddaughters.

Claire was relieved that affairs were working out satisfactorily for a change. Since Christina would be spending holidays in Eastbourne, holidays at the farm would no longer be necessary so Diana's diet and weight could be supervised. Guiltily, Claire was relieved her own freedom was not to be curtailed by maternal responsibilities. Meanwhile, there was Jack's arrival for her to contend with, and her heart sank. Before she left Calcutta, there had been heated exchanges over her continued refusal to acquiesce to his sexual appetite. Claire fervently prayed he accepted her decision.

Chapter Twenty-Five

Five years flew past with astonishing swiftness, during which Claire continued to spend seven months in Calcutta attending to Jack's social obligations during the cold weather season. The remainder of the year she would spend in Eastbourne, with an occasional foray to the warmth of the Côte d'Azur. Once or twice, Claire had been tempted to revisit the farmhouse in Juan les Pins, where she and Ratty had lived a halcyon existence. But the memories were still too painful. Nevertheless, she hoped her erstwhile lover hadn't shown excessively bad taste by taking his wife there on holiday.

Diana was now studying at Oxford University in England. Highly intelligent, she had no difficulty in separating a hectic social life from attending lectures, and putting in hours of study for her degree in French. Years of unpalatable canteen food had seen Diana lose the excess weight she had gained in Cornwall, to emerge as a well-built but attractive young woman, filled with exuberance, her hair a riot of coppery curls.

Returning to Calcutta over the long university break, Diana attended tea dances at the Saturday Club, eventually accompanied by Daphne. For her twenty-first birthday, Jack presented his thrilled daughter with a chestnut thoroughbred mare by the name of *La Gabelle*. Riding her beautiful horse, Diana subsequently took part in regular early morning paper chases, followed by an enormous breakfast for all participants.

Daphne had also left school, but was vacillating over her intended career, everything suggested seeming far too dull or boring. Dances and parties were much more fun! At eighteen, Daphne was an exceptionally pretty girl, slender, her shining fall of hair the identical shade of copper as her sister's. Vivacious – often flirtatious – she was the life and soul of every party she attended.

Now in his second year at Haileybury, a well-known public school in England, William continued to shine in sports – cricket, in particular. His studies in the Arts indicated excellence, and it was understood he would try for Oxford University to read English and History. Every time she saw her son. Claire was seized by a *frisson* of amazement that he should so closely resemble his biological father. And not for the first time, she thanked God that Jack had never met the man!

It was on one of Claire's brief summer visits to the south of France that she invited William to accompany her. It was over the half-term holiday, and delighted to be free of his bossy elder sister, he accepted with alacrity. The weather on the Côte d'Azur was sublime, and they both spent much of each day on the beach in Cannes. Not wanting to expose herself to the sun's damaging rays, Claire managed to procure a beach umbrella. Sitting in its shade, a Thermos flask containing a cool drink at her side, she would riffle through newspapers or magazines.

Four days into the delightful interlude, she was watching William playing quoits on the sand with other young people. The fourteen-year-old was now very much a young man, his voice deepening, a faint shadow appearing on his chin. From years of sporting activities, his body was well muscled and attractively tanned. Smiling with maternal pride, Claire's eyelids fluttered and she dozed off in the warmth of the sun.

"Good God!" A familiar voice startled her awake. "Is this *déjà-vu*... or what?"

Shading her eyes, she looked up into the eyes of the man she had once adored to distraction. Except for a touch of distinguished greying at the temples, Charles Rattigan was unchanged, his brown eyes crinkling with laughter over Claire's discomfiture.

"Ratty? Well, I suppose it's not surprising to see you in this neck of the woods. On holiday with your family, I imagine?"

"Yes, Julia is at the hotel with our two girls, Amy and Cora," he replied with a smile. "Amy is seven and Cora is five."

"Only two children, Charles? I remember you wanted a squad...at the very least!"

"Yes, just the two. Julia miscarried a boy three years ago, and she was ill for ages afterwards with severe depression. The doctor advised against further pregnancies. But believe me, those two little monkeys keep everyone on their toes! What about your girls, Claire? They must be so grown-up now."

"Yes, they are. Diana is completing her degree, but Daphne is still—"

"Mother?" William came up, out of breath and perspiring. "Game's over, so I thought I'd come and see what you were up to. Chatting to strange men, I see?" the young man remarked with a cheeky grin.

"Darling, this is Charles Rattigan...an old friend from long ago.

We were just catching up on each other's lives a little."

"Good to meet you," William held out a sandy hand. "You must tell me what my mother was like as a young girl…er…is something wrong?" he glanced from his mother to the man who stared at him as if stunned. Smiling uncertainly, William turned to his mother.

"Look, I'm just going to have a word with François over there, that chap with the goatee beard. He's an art student in Toulouse. Won't be long. Good to meet you, Mr Rattigan."

William dashed off to join his friend, and Claire looked down at her folded hands, a smile of satisfaction on her lips. Had she desired revenge for being cast aside, this was definitely a step in the right direction. Charles, Duke of bloody Hartington had no male heir, but now he had come face to face with his own son. And judging by the shocked expression on his face, he was fully aware of the fact.

Excellent!

The man gazed for a long moment after the retreating form of his son. Unsmilingly, he looked down at Claire. "You never told me. Why?"

"And what good would that have done…at the time?"

"I had a right to know, for Christ's sake!" Charles burst out, visibly upset. "That young fellow is my son…*mine*! Had you not prevaricated endlessly over your blasted divorce, I would have had the joy of watching him grow up. Instead, another man has enjoyed that privilege. What you have done to me is unpardonable, Claire."

Abruptly getting to her feet, Claire's eyes flashed blue fire. "I am not asking you to pardon anything at all, Charles Rattigan! That last summer, I had no means of letting you know of the disaster that effectively exploded my plans to join you in France. But you…you couldn't even wait to hear from me! Instead, you canter off and marry some other girl in my place. How the hell do you think that made me feel?"

"I waited nearly seven years for you."

"When you encountered me in that antique shop, I was coming to find you. All three children were installed in boarding school, and I was free to claim my freedom…and happiness. I also intended to tell you about William. But my darling man was already more than one step ahead of me! Not only was he now married, but in possession of a heavily pregnant wife." Claire drew in a ragged breath, remembering the terrible hurt. "No, you have forfeited any rights you may once have had where William is concerned. Go away, you faithless man…go back to your ailing wife and daughters."

Collecting up her possessions, Claire called to William who waved and indicated he was on his way. Without a further glance at the stupefied man, she set off towards the stone steps leading to the esplanade.

"I'll never forgive you for this, you know!" Charles called after her.

"Believe me, I have never forgiven *you*!" Claire threw back over her shoulder.

Her triumph in striking back beginning to fade, she was unexpectedly left with a fleeting sadness over what might have been. She also noticed she no longer thought of Charles Rattigan as 'Ratty'. That person no longer existed. Straightening her shoulders and lifting her chin, Claire consigned the love of her life to the past.

On a misty Saturday Calcutta morning in November three years later, Diana MacLeod led La Gabelle into her loose box and closed the door. Satisfied after an exhilarating gallop round the inside track on the racecourse, the mare had cooled off after being hosed off by a *syce*, and settled down to enjoy her bucket of feed. A net bulging with hay hung nearby.

Diana stood, watching the horse eat, but her mind was drifting elsewhere. She had important news to impart to her father, and was unsure of how he might react. With a gusty sigh, she left the stables and walked quickly towards the house to join the family for breakfast on the veranda.

Still in her *peignoir*, Claire was sipping a cup of tea and smoking a cigarette. Jack sat at the other end of the table, invisible behind a newspaper aside from puffs of blue smoke occasionally billowing into the air. Daphne also sat at the table, absorbed in sorting out which party invitations she wished to accept from a pile by her plate. On the other side of the table, William was wading through his fourth slice of toast and butter, a book open at his elbow.

"Morning all!" Diana plumped herself down in a chair and poured herself a cup of tea. "Daddy, I just want to tell you that Peter Lalinski would like to see you this evening. He…um…wants to ask you if he can marry me," she finished in a rush, her cheeks pinking.

"What?" Daphne looked up blankly. "Rubbish, he can't be! Peter's had his eye on me for weeks, Diana."

"Daff, don't be silly," Diana stirred her tea. "Peter has never had anything to do with you. In any case, I thought you were seeing Frank

301

Wellings these days? I know he's taken you out to dinner enough of times."

"Oh, that was just to make Peter jealous!" Daphne replied airily. "I knew the silly chap was secretly getting up his courage to ask me out, and I thought Frank's attentions would be just the job to get him going."

"Must have been jolly secret then," Diana laughed, "because we've been seeing each other almost every day since we met six months ago."

"I don't believe you!" Daphne's face flushed angrily. "Why would a good-looking chap like Peter prefer you...when he can have me? I mean, just look at you, Diana! Fat, filthy and stinking of horse!"

"Daphne!" Claire quickly intervened. "That's a dreadful thing to say to your sister – apologise at once!"

"*Apologise*?" Daphne shouted, leaping to her feet. "Why should I apologise, when the sneaky thing is trying to pinch my boyfriend behind my back?"

"For God's sake, Daffy," Diana said patiently, "You know perfectly well that Peter is not – has never been – your boyfriend."

"He is...oh, he *is*!" Daphne burst into tears. "You'll soon see how the land lies at the Saturday Club this evening, that's if you haven't already swallowed him whole!" the girl added spitefully and then rushed off, sobbing loudly.

"That went well, I must say!" Jack emerged from behind his newspaper. "I'm sure young Lalinksi would be flattered to know my daughters are fighting over him."

"No need to fight, Daddy," Diana spread butter over her slice of toast. "Daff is just being silly. Peter has never given her a second glance...she's not his type."

"So this Lalinski fellow actually *wants* to marry you?" William asked in apparent incredulity. "Once he sees your true colours, though, I bet he'll run a mile!"

"I can do without your pathetic remarks, Willie," Diana retorted, knowing how her brother hated the nickname. "Besides, it's none of your damned business."

"So, tell me about this chap, Di-Di," Jack enquired. "According to your sister, he's nothing less than God's Gift to women?"

"Absolutely!" Diana brightened. "I agree he's jolly handsome, but nice with it."

"And his credentials...apart from being God's Gift, that is?"

"Peter is a captain in the British Indian Army, and a member of the

Calcutta Light Horse," Diana replied with unconscious pride. "You'd approve of him, Daddy, I'm sure! Before coming out to India, he was a tea broker in London."

"Hmm, sounds a steady enough fellow to me," Jack mused. "I take it your mother knows him, so what does she think?"

"Excuse me, I happen to be present at the table so I can be asked directly," Claire remarked sarcastically. "I've met Peter several times, and he seems a sound chap with a good future ahead. If he wants to marry Diana, he certainly has my blessing."

"What an accolade...and from one who knows," Jack grinned at his daughter. "So I'm to meet your young man this evening?"

"Yes, he's popping in for a drink before we go on to the Saturday Club dance."

"Good. I shall subject him to a third degree as to his intentions," Jack teased his daughter, "which I trust are strictly honourable?"

"Of course they are, Daddy darling," replied Diana, her eyes dancing.

With a resigned sigh, Claire made her way to Daphne's bedroom and found her younger daughter lying on the bed, a pillow over her face. Peering from behind it, Daphne emitted a pathetic sob for her mother's benefit.

"Less of the theatrics, if you don't mind, Daffy," Claire briskly told her younger daughter. "You and I know perfectly well that Peter Lalinski has never shown an interest in you. Frankly, I find it hard to understand why you, surrounded by young chaps at every party you attend, should seek to ruin things for Diana."

Daphne sat up, the pillow cast aside. "I don't care about those others, Mummy," she said sulkily. "Peter and I get on like a house on fire, he was just too shy to ask—"

"*Daphne*!" Claire interrupted sharply. "You will not spoil things for your sister this evening by creating an atmosphere, do you understand? If you are planning on flinging yourself at that young man, the end result is likely to be your own humiliation. I assume you would not care for that?"

"It's not fair!" Daphne's expression was mutinous. "Why would Peter prefer a great carthorse like Diana...when he could have *me*?"

"Probably because he sees you as a spoiled little besom, and I have to admit you give a fair imitation of being precisely that on occasion. Remember to behave like the lady you imagine yourself...or you will regret it. Bitterly."

Peter Lalinski arrived at the MacLeod residence, armed with a corsage of white blossoms for Diana, and a large bouquet of flowers for Claire. The *bearer* showed him into the sitting room to wait, where a fan slowly turned overhead to his relief. He was already hot around the collar at the thought of the interview ahead with Jack MacLeod.

The door opened and Diana came in, and Peter's jaw dropped in delighted amazement. The tennis-playing, horse-mad hoyden had vanished, and instead a vision in black lace stood before him, a shy smile on her face. Glowing pearls hung from her ears, echoed by a double string about her neck, the black lace gown providing a perfect foil for Diana's cap of coppery curls.

The door opened once more to admit Claire, followed by Daphne whose mouth drooped sulkily. Peter shrugged inwardly. The difference between these two sisters was like chalk and cheese. Admittedly, Daphne was a very pretty girl, but he could never be bothered with the skittish shenanigans she indulged in with her band of admirers. Praise God, his Diana was incapable of that kind of nonsense.

Jack MacLeod made a brief appearance to invite the young army officer into his study. As the door closed behind them, Diana nervously asked the *bearer* to bring her a gin and tonic. Surely there was nothing that her father could object to in Peter? Still, the wait was rather nerve-wracking…

Fifteen minutes later, Jack and Peter emerged from the study. The young man grinned his success to Diana, whilst Jack put an arm about his elder daughter's shoulders to give her a brief hug. Claire smiled, kissed Diana, and sent the *bearer* to bring out the bottle of chilled champagne she had organised earlier in the day.

A glass of champagne in her hand, Daphne stood by herself in the background. Used to being the centre of attention, she fumed over being relegated to a back seat whilst her porky sister took centre stage. Maybe when Peter noticed how gorgeous she was looking tonight…

Wearing an apricot silk evening gown, her hair an auburn halo about her face, neck and ears adorned with gold jewellery, Daphne was undoubtedly very attractive. But the young army captain didn't give her a second glance. His eyes never left his new fiancée's face as he slipped a diamond engagement ring on her left hand. Sick with envy, her mother's dire warning nevertheless resonated at the back of Daphne's mind.

The following morning, Claire and Diana were at the breakfast table on the veranda when Daphne sauntered in, yawning, to join them. Jack had departed earlier to play a round of golf. Leaning over to pick up the teapot, Diana's engagement ring sparkled in the morning sunlight, and catching sight of it the younger girl's lips tightened.

"I didn't think much of the Saturday Club dance last night," she said to nobody in particular. "There wasn't a single chap there worth talking to, in my opinion."

"Well, I thoroughly enjoyed myself," Diana took a sip of tea and grinned. "But then I only danced with Peter, as he wouldn't allow anyone else to dance with me."

"Horrid to have someone be so possessive, I'd have thought," Daphne remarked. "Watching you dancing together, Peter seemed to be rather shorter than you."

"As a matter of fact, he isn't," retorted her sister, the glow of happiness dying from her face. "Do remember I was wearing high heels, but thanks for mentioning it."

"Well, I shall make sure I am able to wear any height of heel with the man I decide to marry," Daphne said, brushing toast crumbs from her lap. "Couldn't stand to have people sniggering and thinking I look ridiculous."

"All supposing someone asks you," Diana replied, unmoved. "And he'd have to be happy to fade into the background whilst you flirt outrageously with other fellows."

"Oh!" Daphne retaliated furiously. "Don't worry, I'll find myself a husband who will be terribly handsome, wealthy and above all – *tall*!"

"Have I missed something?" William walked into the veranda. "Having a sisterly cat-fight are we?"

"I'm off to change," Diana rose to her feet. "Peter is picking me up at ten to go for a sail across the Hoogly."

"All I can say is that Peter Lalinski must be a very brave man to be taking you on, Diana," William slathered butter on a slice of toast. "Better get the wedding ring on quickly...before he finds out what you're *really* like!"

"What a hoot!" Daphne snickered. "Especially on the wedding night, when you are obliged to undress and display all that flab."

"Enough!" Claire interceded before Diana decided to exact physical vengeance on her siblings. "That's enough nastiness for one day, thank you. This is Diana's special time, so neither of you are to spoil it for her."

Glancing at her mother in astonishment, Diana departed, leaving her brother and sister gazing after her, open-mouthed over the unusual support of her elder daughter. But nothing could detract now from the older girl's clear happiness.

The date of the wedding was set for December. There were to be only two bridesmaids, Daphne, and Diana's best friend, Freda Clarkson. The marriage ceremony would take place at the great cathedral where Jack and Claire had made their vows many years before. The wedding reception would, of course, be held at the MacLeod home. Peter had managed to obtain sufficient leave to go on a brief honeymoon, after which he would be obliged to rejoin his unit in Burma.

The morning of the marriage between Diana MacLeod and Peter Lalinski dawned relatively cool and fine. The bride gazed into the cheval mirror in her bedroom, nervously twitching the long Brussels lace veil attached to a circlet of tiny white blossoms perched on her burnished curls. Subsequent to weeks of strenuous dieting, Diana had lost sufficient weight to fit into her form-fitting taffeta and lace bridal gown. Blue eyes sparkling with happiness, her lips tinted rose, she looked beautiful.

Daphne was sulkily slumped in an armchair, uncaring of crushing the primrose taffeta bridesmaid's dress she wore. Freda, the other bridesmaid, covertly glanced at the girl in growing concern. Surely she wasn't intending to cast a shadow over her sister's wedding day by indulging in a tantrum of some kind?

"Daphne, get up from there this minute!" Claire walked into the room. "For God's sake, just *look* at your dress…it's creased to hell!"

"So what?" replied the girl morosely, nevertheless getting to her feet. "It's not as though anybody will be looking at me, will they?"

"I will not allow you to ruin things, Daphne MacLeod!" Claire snapped. "What impression will be given if one of the bridesmaids appears to be wearing the next best thing to a dish-rag?"

Daphne shrugged. "If I don't care, why should anyone else?"

"Now you listen to me, my girl!" Claire was incensed by the girl's careless attitude. "Get out of that dress, and ask the *ayah* to run an iron over it. The car will soon be here to pick up the bride and bridesmaids, and should you not be ready when it arrives we will leave without you. Diana will simply have one bridesmaid – Freda."

Daphne opened her mouth to argue – then closed it again. Judging by her expression, it was clear her mother meant business. And she didn't want to miss the wedding, even though she only had a minor role to play. With a theatrical sigh, Daphne flounced from the room, shutting the door behind her unnecessarily hard.

Festooned with white ribbons billowing in the breeze, the bridal car arrived, a posy of white flowers attached to the figurine on the end of the bonnet. Diana settled herself on the back seat, her mother beside her, helping to arrange yards of veiling on the car floor. The bride's bouquet of white flowers and green fern lay in Claire's lap, to avoid possible staining of Diana's gown. Freda took her place on a small flip-down seat opposite, but there was no sign of Daphne.

Just as Claire leaned forward to instruct the driver to leave for the church, the front door flew open and she came running out, her dress now immaculate.

"You were going without me," panted the girl in outrage, "I would have missed the wedding, and you wouldn't have cared!"

"Get in and be quiet!" Claire ordered. "And if we had left, it would have served you right, you ridiculous girl."

Waiting for his bride inside the great cathedral, the young officer was looking remarkably handsome in army uniform. Far from displaying last minute nerves, Peter was anticipating his bride's arrival with joy. Since he had decided he wanted to marry the intelligent and exuberant Diana MacLeod, he had not swerved from his purpose. And now, the day had come when she would finally become his wife.

Organ music swelled into Elgar's *Pomp and Circumstance* that signalled the bride and her entourage had arrived at the church. Glancing eagerly towards the doors, Peter saw Jack MacLeod slowly advancing down the aisle, his elder daughter on his arm, her face partially concealed by a lace veil.

Drawing level with the bridegroom, Jack took his daughter's hand and symbolically gave it into her bridegroom's for safekeeping. Facing one another, the young man lifted the veil from his bride's face, and a radiant Diana looked into her future husband's blue eyes. Both made their responses, and then vanished into the vestry to sign the register.

Smiling with happiness, the newly married couple walked slowly down the aisle to Mendelssohn's *Wedding March*, and then out through the cathedral's great doors where the bridegroom's fellow officers honoured them with swords held high overhead. Peter and Diana Lalinski were then summoned to pose for official photographs.

Waiting to be included in a family group, Claire stood beside her husband, recalling the day she had been married in this same cathedral. Her naïve little head had been filled with entirely unrealistic dreams – as she had learned in the most brutal manner. She glanced up at Jack, wondering if he was also thinking of their wedding? No. Her husband was earnestly speaking to William, the young man he thought to be his son. Claire's lips twisted cynically. If only he knew...

The reception went off well, and bride and groom eventually departed to the station in a beribboned car. Their wedding night would be spent in a railway carriage on the way for a week's honeymoon at the beach resort of Gopalpore.

Claire sighed and turned back to the house. Throughout the years, she and her elder daughter had rarely seen eye to eye, but she sincerely hoped Diana would fare better than she had in the marriage stakes. Peter clearly adored her, and that was a good start.

Chapter Twenty-Six

The morning after the wedding, Jack and Claire were having breakfast together on the veranda. William and Daphne were still in bed, having extended the previous day's festivities by going on to a nightclub with a group of young people. Stirring her tea, Claire glanced at the back of the newspaper her husband was reading.

"Jack, could you *not* read at the breakfast table for once?" she asked irritably. "I thought we might discuss the events of yesterday, since it's not every day a child of ours gets married."

"What is there to discuss?" Jack answered from behind the newspaper. "The whole thing was a raving success as events organised by you invariably are."

"That's not what I meant at all. I thought we might exchange incidents, views, that sort of thing."

Jack carefully folded the newspaper and laid it on the table. "Frankly, there isn't a great deal I wish to discuss with you these days, Claire. As you are forever harping, you lead your life...and I mine. Not very satisfactory, but there it is."

Claire flushed uncomfortably. What exactly was Jack inferring? Was it possible he knew something about Charles Rattigan? Impossible...or was it? This was dangerous ground, and she must tread carefully.

"Actually, I was astounded to see such a change in *Maman* yesterday," Claire casually remarked. "For a moment I hardly recognised her, until I spotted Sonia sitting there. For God's sake, did you see what that girl was wearing? More suited to a six-year-old—"

"Claire, must you always be so bloody critical of others?" Jack said sharply. "And I'm not surprised you found your mother changed, since you haven't bothered with her for years! I don't suppose you even know that Frederick has been hospitalised with some blasted wasting disease. He's been diagnosed as being terminally ill."

Claire blanched. Uncle Freddie in hospital? Soon to die? *No...please God, no!* Frederick had always been there, an invincible rock upon whom her entire family had depended at one time or another. She cringed inwardly, not having noticed the dear man hadn't been at the wedding yesterday. No wonder Jack was angry.

"I didn't know," Claire said quietly. "There was so much going on, that I—"

"No. That's the trouble with you, my dear, self-absorbed to a degree."

"Why, thank you, Jack!" Claire snapped sarcastically. "Believe me, living with you is not far distant from living alone, I'll have you know. No time for me, permanently preoccupied, it's little wonder I've had to develop a sense of self-reliance."

"*You*...self-reliant?" Jack laughed without humour. "Having been taken care of for your entire life, I doubt you know the meaning of the word."

"How dare you! I've often worked myself to a standstill dealing with your deadly dull business people and government associates."

"I certainly wouldn't argue that issue, but as a companion you are sadly lacking, Claire. You are rarely in Calcutta these days, and consistently refuse my advances in the bedroom."

"Perhaps you should ask yourself why, Jack!" Claire tone was icy. "No woman cares to be used as an item of gymnasium equipment for a man's physical exertion! Get on a bloody a horse, why don't you, or even a bicycle?"

"Take it from me, it's hardly a pleasure to make love to the next best thing to a blasted log!" Angrily getting to his feet, Jack picked up the newspaper. "If you need to make small talk, go and rouse Daphne or William out of bed. Not that they are likely to find your early morning conversation particularly riveting."

Turning on his heel, Jack strode from the veranda without a backward glance at his fulminating wife. He entered his study and closed the door, breathing heavily with suppressed temper. For God's sake, hadn't he always made sure the bloody woman had everything she wanted? Only to receive damn all in return, except for her faultless organising skills and glowing accolades that reflected well on himself.

For the umpteenth time, Jack wondered if Claire had some bloody man lurking in Europe somewhere? Maybe at one time, for he recalled how she used to live in happy anticipation of boarding the boat for England. These days she seemed preoccupied and even morose at times. No point in trying to ascertain why. Better just accept things as they were, and avoid unnecessary arguments if possible.

It was unfortunate that Claire had caught him on the raw just now, when he had been brooding over losing his eldest daughter. Nevertheless, he could console himself that his loss was to a man who thought the world of Diana. Jealous little Daphne would make certain she was not far behind, and she had the choice of most young bachelors in Calcutta. And William? Jack's expression softened. Yes, indeed, the young chap was a son to be proud of. An ardent cricketer, his university friends included poets, artists and sportsmen. No bad influences there. His boy should do well in life.

A week later, the newly-weds returned to Calcutta after their brief honeymoon. Peter immediately left for active duty in the Burmese jungles, and his disconsolate bride returned to her parents' home – an anti-climax after the excitement of the wedding.

Bored to tears with occasional tutoring of children in English and French, Diana was determined to find something more rewarding to do with her time. At a small dinner party she attended, she overheard other army wives complaining about the dearth of schools for their older children. As things stood, parents were obliged to send their children away to England to be educated after the age of eight, and were unlikely to see them again for a number of years.

Diana pricked up her ears. Why not start a school? After all, she had all the necessary qualifications. But not in Calcutta's filthy heat, but up-country somewhere, such as Darjeeling or Ranchi? Diana wished she could discuss the project with Peter, but he was not due back for another month. It really was a terrific idea! Maybe she should talk it over with her father...or even her mother? The young woman's eyes shone with enthusiasm for her new project.

Claire thought the idea of starting a school excellent, and suggested Kalimpong as a possibility. Not too distant from Calcutta, the hill station possessed a delightful climate that would be conducive to the wellbeing of children. Unable to leave Calcutta herself due a government convention she was organising, Claire suggested that Christina might be interested in accompanying Diana on an investigative trip up-country. The young woman telephoned her grandmother's home at once, and asked herself to tea.

Minette was delighted to see her granddaughter and hugged her to an ample bosom. She then listened carefully as Diana outlined what she hoped to achieve.

"*Chèrie*, what an enterprising young lady you are turning out to be!" she exclaimed in admiration. "Lucky Peter to have you as his partner in life. Have a slice of this lovely *gâteau*, darling…I made it this morning when I knew you were coming."

"Thank you, Grannie," Diana took the plate from her grandmother. "Now tell me, how is Uncle Freddie? Mummy told us he was very ill, which was why he couldn't come to our wedding."

Her faded blue eyes filling with tears, Minette swallowed convulsively before answering. "Freddie died a week ago, Di-Di. It was a blessed release because he was suffering a great deal of pain. But I…I miss him dreadfully."

"Oh Grannie!" Diana exclaimed, distraught. "And none of us knew! Why didn't you *tell* us what was happening, so we could have been there for you?"

"I couldn't bring myself to talk about it, *chèrie*. I've never been good at sharing personal things with others."

"But we're not just anyone, Grannie! We're your family, so of course we would have supported you throughout your grief."

"No." Minette shook her head. "Your mother and I have not spoken to each other for years. Freddie was my dearest companion, and private to me in the circumstances."

Diana remained silent, unable to refute her grandmother's bald statement. Mummy was so wrong to have ignored her own mother for years like that! Grannie had every right to haul her over the coals after that terrible business with Timothy. The young woman briefly wondered where Timmy had ended up. Had he stayed at the Kalimpong orphanage, or had he been farmed out to another family? Hopefully, to a family more reliable than her own had been.

Perhaps she should settle for Kalimpong as a suitable venue to start her school. An opportunity might present itself to ask after the redheaded boy, who must now be in his late teens, and she had always been very fond of him.

"Di-Di!" Christina hurried into the room, and kissed her niece. "*Maman* said you were coming, but I just had to finish correcting examination papers. Done now, so I can relax."

"Auntie, how would you like a trip up-country to look for a suitable property that I could rent for a school I mean to start? I thought Kalimpong would be just the job."

"Kalimpong is a lovely little village as I recall," Christina mused, "but, tell me more this school you are thinking about."

Diana quickly outlined her plan to start a school, so that parents could avoid being obliged to send their children away to be educated. There had been so many unhappy tales circulating, some children either obliged to live with less than welcoming relatives, or at dreadful 'holiday homes' that almost starved the poor things. If the response to her idea proved promising, she would look for a separate house where her pupils would sleep.

"Darling, the whole thing sounds wonderful, and it will take your mind off missing Peter so much. What fun! Term has just finished so I'm free as air to accompany you."

Diana beamed at her aunt. "Brilliant! We can have a lovely snoop around the Himalayan countryside, and locate exactly the right houses."

"*Maman?*" Christina paused to glance at her mother. "Will you be all right on your own? Di-Di and I can always go later."

"No, no! I'm perfectly happy for you to go with Diana…she shouldn't really be going on her own on a trip like this. *Non, ce n'est pas du tout comme il faut!*"

"Oh, Grannie!" Diana laughed. "That sort of thing went out with the ark! Girls do all sorts of things on their own these days."

"Certainly not girls from *our* kind of family," Minette assured her granddaughter.

Christina and Diana set off the following week for Kalimpong. Having expected an intensive search ahead for the right property, the *taxi-wallah* who drove them from the station to the hotel proved to be a fount of information.

"My auntee, she working for big Indian *sahib* who has many, many house in Kalimpong," the man confided. "One veree big one up on hill, near one not so, and also one bungalow empty since old ladee die."

"Can you come tomorrow and show us these houses?" Christina asked. "And how can the owner be contacted?"

"Tomorrow veree good!" said the *taxi-wallah*, wagging his head from side to side approvingly. "I ask auntee, mebbe she come too as she knowing *chokidar* looking after one, two, three house on hill."

On the drive from the station, they also discovered Kalimpong possessed a doctor, a bank and a market. Thanking the man, they registered themselves at a hotel on the village outskirts. The rooms were sparsely furnished, but the beds were comfortable and the two bedrooms shared a small bathroom.

"What a stroke of luck!" Diana exclaimed over a welcome cup of steaming coffee. "Wouldn't it be incredible if we need look no further than the *taxi-wallah's* houses?"

"Better not pin your hopes on such an unlikely event," Christina advised her niece, "as the odds against it must be very strong."

The next morning, the *taxi-wallah* appeared to collect his passengers in front of the hotel promptly at nine o'clock. A rotund Indian woman in a bright blue and gold sari stood beside him – the aunt – Diana assumed peering out through a window. Seeing Christina and Diana emerge from the front door, both salaamed politely and the *taxi-wallah* introduced his companion.

"This my auntee, she called Nina. She already made meeting with owner-*sahib* of three house on hill in one hour."

Nodding pleasantly to the woman, Christina and Diana piled into the back of the car, the aunt taking her place in the front. Her nephew started up the car, and drove through the village and up a narrow winding road for about half a mile. He then turned off into a lane and up a short driveway leading to a whitewashed bungalow.

"This one is bungalow," announced the *taxi-wallah* unnecessarily, and then pointed up the lane. "Two big house up there."

The taxi continued its way along a somewhat overgrown lane, up a slope and around a corner. It stopped abruptly, jerking its passengers forward uncomfortably, the driver having taken his foot off the clutch too quickly.

"Look up there, *Mem*...one big, big house for you!"

Jumping out of the taxi, Diana gazed at a house octagonal in shape, semi-enclosed verandas encircling its two storeys. The roof was slate tiled, and from a distance appeared in reasonable condition. Sweeping lawns surrounded the property, sadly overgrown by brambles and weeds, and a set of rickety wooden steps led up to a front door hanging off its hinges. Quickly touring the huge reception rooms on the ground floor – Diana was jubilant!

This enormous house could not be more perfect for her purpose.

"Now we go looking at other house, *Mem*," the *taxi-wallah* broke into Diana's happy daydream. "Not too far away from this place."

The second house turned out to be a slightly smaller edition of the first, its large rooms easily lending themselves for conversion into dormitories.

In a happy daze, the two were driven back to the bungalow where a tall, rather thin individual was waiting on the small veranda. Plump Nina chattered excitedly in Hinde, indicating the gaunt man was the owner of all three properties.

Two hours later, Diana and Christina went back to the hotel, everything having been signed and sealed to their satisfaction. The rental of all three houses turned out to be reasonable, and would run from year to year as Diana wished. Even the bungalow suited requirements, containing three bedrooms, bathroom, a small kitchen outside of which was a sizeable vegetable patch.

The owner promised to send workmen to mend the damaged steps and front door, and a *mali* to attend to the garden wilderness. 'Auntie' Nina declared herself willing to help the *memsahibs* move into the bungalow, and would later find suitable *ayahs* to work on a permanent basis.

Thus Hilltop School was born, and the boarding house was christened Hillside.

Over dinner that evening, Diana decided to return to Calcutta the following day to pack up her possessions and order text books and stationery to be boxed up for transport. She also intended to inform army personnel that a new boarding school in Kalimpong would be opening its doors in two months time. Ambitious, but Diana was determined to fulfil the timetable.

Christina offered to remain in Kalimpong to oversee necessary work on the houses. She would live in the bungalow, and go for relaxing walks – she informed Diana, who was unsure about her aunt being left all alone. She was finally persuaded when a tall bearded Sikh presented himself at the hotel with the information he was the house owner's personal *chowkidar*. He reassured her he would see to it that the 'old *mem*' came to no harm. Reassured, Diana took the train back to Calcutta.

Jack and Claire were both at home when Diana's taxi drew up outside the house. Anxious to impart her wonderful news, she quickly made her way to the veranda, where the *bearer* told her they were having drinks. Jack's eyes lit up to see her, and even her mother smiled with pleasure and offered her a cool cheek to kiss.

It was only then that Diana noticed a tall, startlingly handsome young man was also present, who rose politely to his feet. But before he could be introduced, Daphne appeared and clung possessively to the young man's arm.

315

"Diana, may I introduce my fiancé, Robert Mackenzie?" she purred. "Daddy has just agreed to our engagement, but the wedding won't be until next year."

"Congratulations!" Diana grinned at the man destined to be her brother-in-law. "And now I've got brilliant news to tell you about my future school."

"What?" Daphne pouted. "I think it's more important to discuss our engagement party at the Saturday Club next week! Rather more interesting than listening to you boring on about some stupid school."

Annoyed, Jack watched the joy die from his eldest daughter's face. Trust the jealous little madam to throw cold water over her sister's achievement. Turning to Diana, he deliberately ignored the younger girl's snide remark. "Come on Di-Di, tell us about your trip up-country and whether you've found a suitable property yet?"

Gratefully, Diana gave him an account of the Kalimpong adventure and the marvellous success she and Christina had in discovering perfect houses for the school. After tying up loose ends and buying necessary equipment, she intended to spend as little time as possible in Calcutta before returning to Kalimpong.

"Peter will soon be back for a week or two, so we can both go to Kalimpong and settle into the bungalow properly...so exciting!" she enthused, and then glanced at Claire. "Mummy, how would you like to come up-country with us for a change?"

Lighting a cigarette, Claire fitted it into her holder. "I really think I might...after Daphne and Robert's engagement party, of course," she hurried to add, noticing her younger daughter's immediate glower. "A week or two of cooler air will do me good, and I'd very much like to see the houses for the school."

"Auntie Christina wanted to stay on in Kalimpong, and living in the bungalow where she's very well-guarded by a huge Sikh *chowkidar*!"

"I can just imagine how that must appeal to independent Chrissy," Claire laughed. "I only hope she's not trying to convert him."

"That's settled then," Diana turned to her sister. "Now, tell me how you and Robert came to meet?"

"At a party," Daphne looked mollified. "It was love at first sight, wasn't it Robert?"

The big man grinned. "Of course, dear girl...quite the best way to fall in love," he answered in a soft Scots accent. "Daff has told me a great deal about you."

"I bet she has," Diana retorted dryly. "And none of it flattering I'm sure."

Ten days later, Peter Lalinski returned to his ecstatic wife, and the two of them went to the beach for a few days to enjoy each other's company. Upon their return, the organisation of school equipment packed into wooden boxes began, to be later loaded into the train's luggage van for departure to Kalimpong. Suitcases filled with warm clothes and blankets followed, and the two Lalinskis and Claire finally boarded the train for the journey up-country.

Upon her return, Diana was relieved to see Christina looking rested and happy, and she certainly had not wasted her time. Walking up the lane to Hilltop with Peter, her mother and aunt, she was astonished to see the whole property was already spick and span. Neatly stacked desks and chairs filling a lower veranda was also a surprise, and new blackboards were propped against a wall.

Down the slope at Hillside, Diana discovered twenty-five beds waiting for allocation to dormitories. Watching her niece's delighted reaction, Christina grinned with undisguised pride over her many achievements.

Energised by the cool scented air, Claire and Christina walked down to the village each morning, returning from the post office with carrier bags full of letters requesting bookings for start of term. Three Anglo-Indian teachers were recruited, and Mrs Potts, a buxom Englishwoman, who recently lost her husband to malaria, gladly accepted the position as Matron for Hillside. Two young half-caste women were employed as her assistants, and preparations for the school's opening progressed apace.

Peter's furlough came to an end, and tearful Diana saw her husband off at the station, knowing she would not see him again for several weeks. Anxious to distract herself, Diana bought herself a mountain horse that she named *Thomas*. Glad to have a physical outlet, she rode early each morning before walking up to Hilltop.

Inevitably, Christina was obliged to return to Calcutta in time for the new term at the college where she taught Maths. Before leaving, however, she promised Diana she would consider terminating her post, returning to teach at Hilltop School.

It was Claire who took over the running of the bungalow, walked down to the village to do necessary shopping, and planted out the vegetable garden in which she took a proprietary interest. It was the first time that she and her eldest daughter were obliged to rely on one another, and it resulted in a softening of attitude in both women.

Tired of weeks of sea travel each year, Claire told her husband on the telephone she intended to remain in Kalimpong for the entire hot weather season. After a pause, Jack said he would join her for a few days, and probably bring Daphne with him. His younger daughter was presently in a deep sulk, having been forbidden to accompany Robert Mackenzie on a business trip to England. In Jack's view, it was not done for an unmarried girl to travel with a man, fiancé though he might be.

Hilltop School opened on schedule and progressed on oiled wheels, and a listing of boarders to oversee at Hillside was given to Matron Potts. Herself a powerhouse of energy, Diana organised morning sporting classes, but had no intention of abandoning her early morning ride. Cantering along dew-drenched pathways threading their way along hillsides dotted with firs always set her up for the day ahead.

The summer months passed, and the school was a burgeoning success. The quota of pupils was almost full, and requests for future admissions poured in. Further members of staff were employed, and mornings resounded to the cries of excited children enjoying games of rounders or cricket. Even Claire, who was disenchanted by the younger generation at the best of times, watched the development of her daughter's school with immense pride. Headstrong child Diana had once been, but she was now channelling that same determination to excellent use.

Jack and Daphne arrived to spend a week at the bungalow recently re-christened *Bon Ami*, and in order to allow them a bedroom, Diana decamped to Hillside, returning only for the evening meal. It wasn't long before it became obvious that Daphne was wildly envious of her sister's success.

"I'm thinking of enrolling in teacher training college," she announced at dinner one evening, a week after her arrival. "Then I might start a kindergarten in Calcutta."

"Whatever for?" Claire asked in astonishment. "Calcutta is already full of infant schools. Besides which, it would also be unlikely that parents would entrust their offspring to an untried young person such as yourself."

"Oh! Why do you *always* have to put me down, Mummy?" Daphne exclaimed, on the verge of tears. "I want to do something that fits in nicely with Robert's day."

"Well, find something else," Jack muttered in exasperation, fork halfway to his mouth. "Must you emulate Di-Di's every move?"

"I don't!" Tears trickled down Daphne's cheeks. "Diana always, *always* has everything her own way, whilst I—"

"Oh, *do* stop that rubbish, Daff," Diana had heard enough. "Remember all those years I spent swotting at university in freezing cold England, whilst you were gadding about to parties in Calcutta? Don't complain, I beg you."

Daphne leaped to her feet. "One day I'll surprise you all, you'll see," she shouted. "And it will put your wonderful school into the shade, Diana. I bet you're green with jealousy of my Robert...he's better looking and *much* taller than Peter Lalinski!"

Diana shrugged. "You're joking, of course? I'm happy to admit Peter is nothing like that chap you're so proud of, since I'd lay a winning bet our Robert is quite a flirt on the quiet," she added with an evil grin.

Weeping noisily, Daphne rushed from the room. With a resigned sigh, Claire put down her knife and fork and followed her out. Really, Daphne should have outgrown this ridiculous sibling rivalry, she thought crossly, and she intended to tell her so. But Diana's jibe over her sister's choice of husband resonated. Was her eldest daughter's remark perceptive, or merely retaliatory? It was true the handsome Robert Mackenzie had a certain air about him...

A week later, with a heartfelt sigh of relief, Diana saw her father and sister off at the local station. During his stay at Bon Ami, Jack had seemed unusually morose, and she noticed he had gained a few superfluous pounds. As for Daphne, she could do without her daily histrionics and flouncing! Mentally washing her hands of the irritation of past weeks, Diana happily settled down to running her school.

One morning, the young woman awoke to a surge of nausea, making her spring out of bed and run to the bathroom. Breathing deeply, she sat on the floor, hoping it would pass. Then another wave of nausea seized her, and Diana hurriedly leaned over the lavatory bowl to be violently sick.

"Diana?" Claire appeared in the doorway in concern. "I heard you vomiting...what can you have eaten to upset you like this?"

"Oh God, I can't think what it could be!" groaned the afflicted girl. "We ate the same thing last night and you seem to be all right. Help me up, Mummy...I can't ride this morning, but I've got to get to school."

"Don't be ridiculous, you can't go up there in this condition. Go back to bed, and I'll tell Miss Tyler to arrange for somebody to take your class. If this is a bout of incipient dysentery, you are going to need medicine so I'll walk down to the village and find that doctor. What's his name... Dogshit?"

Diana grinned in spite of herself. "*Dikshet*, Mummy...Doctor Dikshet."

The good doctor duly presented himself in his rattletrap car, and gave the pale-faced Diana a thorough examination. Finally, he stood back and laced his fingers together across his waist-coated midriff. "No dysentery, madim," pronounced the doctor. "I am telling you there are no symptoms of nasty infection. It is now early for telling, but mebbe madim can expect a little *baba* in few months time."

"*What?*" Diana gaped in horror. "I simply can't have a baby at the moment! What will happen to the school, and I'm planning so many new things for next term. Having to cope with a baby would be a dead bore.... impossible, in fact."

Doctor Dikshet stared in consternation at his distraught patient. He had thought to impart glad tidings to the young lady, who should be happy to be giving her husband a child...maybe even a boy. Instead, she is almost weeping...

Hauling on her dressing gown, Diana hurried into the sitting room where her mother stood next to the window, smoking a cigarette. Claire had recently decided to abandon her long jade holder for a smaller and more convenient model. Now she swung round in alarm at Diana's precipitate entrance.

"What is it? Nothing serious, I hope?"

"It's the *worst* news!" Diana's eyes swam with panic-stricken tears. "It seems I may be pregnant! How can I manage a baby, for God's sake, when I have a school to run?"

"Good gracious, maybe I'm going to be a grandmother!" Claire laughed in relief. "For a moment, I thought you had something really horrid going on there."

"It's not funny, Mummy!" Diana wailed. "And now I'm going to be sick again!"

Watching her daughter vanish into the lavatory, Claire was aware of a presence in the doorway of Diana's bedroom. "Madim, may I talk with you a moment?" the doctor advanced timidly into the room. "Your good dotter must be nicely tekking care of herself, so *baba* be good big size…but definitely she *not* to putting on plenty weight. That veree bad for dotter's health."

"Don't worry, Doctor…er…Dikshet, I'll keep an eye on what she eats," Claire reassured him, impressed that the doctor had evidently taken note that Diana struggled with weight gain. "But I'd like you to come up and check on her once a month before she goes to Calcutta for the birth."

"You dotter not having *baba* in Kalimpong?" the doctor looked surprised. "So veree hot in Calcutta-side!"

"No. My daughter's husband is in the army, so he would want the baby to be born within reach, supposing he isn't off somewhere in Burma. I daresay an army doctor will oversee the delivery."

"I see," nodded the doctor. "Well, goodbye Madim, I coming back in one month."

Diana's worst fears were realised when morning sickness dogged her life every day over the following four months. She burned with resentment that the inconvenience of the coming infant would effectively put paid to plans of offering riding lessons, and weekly cross-country runs. It was all Claire could do to restrain her from riding in her condition, and the young woman railed angrily against the enforced inactivity.

Two items of good news made Diana smile, however. Christina was soon to arrive, and would take over the running of the school whilst Diana was in Calcutta for the birth of her baby. That was certainly a load off her mind. And Peter, newly returned from active service, was delighted by the news he was to become a father.

Chapter Twenty-Seven

Claire and Diana left Kalimpong earlier than was strictly necessary. Final arrangements for Daphne's wedding required organising, and the bride's mother and sister were expected to join in pre-wedding celebrations. Disgruntled over her ballooning stomach, Diana refused to attend any such parties, threatening tears if pressed. The wedding itself would be unavoidable, but she was damned if she would make herself a butt for 'beached-whale' jokes.

Albeit reluctantly, Diana had been persuaded to allow the newly married couple to honeymoon at Bon Ami in Kalimpong. Christina said she was happy to decamp to Hillside to allow the bridal pair complete privacy. And so it was settled.

The day of the Daphne and Robert's wedding finally dawned. The bride was a vision in white satin, a large satin bow on her pageboy fall of auburn hair securing a long veil. Excitement tinted her cheeks rose, and she held a large bouquet of yellow and white flowers. Claire thought she had never seen Daphne look so exquisite. She only hoped the young Scotsman she was about to marry would take good care of her...

Diana appeared, wearing a navy blue and white spotted dress that went some way towards concealing her bump. Also in Calcutta for the event, William was now very much a man-about-town. Gazing at her handsome dark-haired son, Claire's heart contracted with pride. That faithless Rattigan could have had William as his heir – had he not been in such a hurry to replace her. *Bah*! Let him stew with his sickly wife and puny girls, and the title could go to some distant male relative or other.

In choosing her bridal gown, Daphne allowed nobody to advise her in any way. Everything to do with her ensemble *must* be her own choice! It was therefore with wry amusement that Claire noticed her veil was easily twice as long as Diana's had been, and that she would be preceded by flower girls strewing petals before her, and a bevy of six bridesmaids following behind. And what of that towering wedding cake she had seen arriving at the house? Claire sighed. Daphne was forever in competition with her older sister. Would she relax this eternal vigil now that she was marrying the man of her dreams? One must hope so.

The reception over, the newlyweds spent their wedding night at the Grand Hotel on Chowringhee – an extra wedding present from Jack MacLeod. The following day, they would take the train to begin their honeymoon in Kalimpong. William also sailed for England the next day, to take up a posting with the British Navy.

As Diana's pregnancy crawled towards its end, her temper was short, crying over nonsense, and depressed over her heavy breasts and thighs. To everybody's heartfelt relief, Peter returned on furlough, and immediately defused the tension by comforting his tearful wife with assurances that he loved 'a good armful'. Affectionately calling her *Winnie*, Peter said she reminded him of his adored Pooh Bear. The pet name stuck over the years that followed.

The baby's delivery date came and went, and still there was no sign that the infant was ready to arrive. Diana's temper frayed further, and her parents were everlastingly grateful for their son-in-law's presence. At ten o'clock one morning, contractions began and Diana was whisked off to the army hospital.

Her possessions having been installed in a private room, the apprehensive young woman was wheeled into theatre under the supervision of Colonel Gough, surgeon and obstetrician. Labour was protracted throughout the day, but Diana was eventually delivered of a baby girl at eight o'clock that night.

Gazing at the squalling morsel of humanity, the new mother burst into tears, having convinced herself she was expecting a boy. Even his names had been chosen! Taking his distraught wife in his arms, Peter whispered that he had secretly hoped all along for a little girl, just like his darling Winnie…

Diana insisted on discharging herself from the hospital the following day, arguing that she had herself been born at home…so where was the risk? Besides, her mother would be there to help. Sighing, Colonel Gough reluctantly agreed.

The baby was named Susanna. Soon after arriving home, the infant set up a wail to be fed, and having settled herself in a rocking chair, Diana undid the flap of the nursing brassière she was obliged to wear.

Feeling the warm nipple brush her cheek, Susanna grasped it in her tiny mouth and began sucking with enthusiasm. Moments later, she began making small unhappy sounds before releasing the nipple, and starting to howl. The nipple was returned to her mouth and the baby resumed sucking, snuffled, opened her eyes and began bawling. Exasperated, Diana looked down at the screaming baby, not knowing what to do next. Why had the hospital midwives not prepared her for this? She had, however, been warned by her grandmother not to spoil the baby, and begin as she intended to go on from early in the child's life. Perhaps the baby was not hungry enough? Re-hooking her brassière, Diana put the screaming baby down in her bassinet cot. She would wait for half an hour and then try then again. For God's sake, her breasts were heavy with milk!

"Diana?" Claire looked round the door. "Why is Susanna screaming like that? Isn't she due for a feed?"

"Yes, but for some reason she won't suck properly. I tried again, but she threw her head back and began screaming."

"Maybe she's thirsty?" Claire frowned. "Give her to me, and I'll give her a little drink of glucose water."

The small face screwed up in distaste to have a rubber teat introduced into her mouth, but a moment later the infant began sucking avidly. Once the ounce of glucose water was finished, she immediately fell asleep.

Claire gently laid the baby back in her bassinet, covering her lightly with a fine cotton-knit shawl. Gazing down at her, she smiled. It had been a long time since she had held a baby in her arms. And what a lovely baby she was, her head covered with fine red-gold hair and a birth weight of nearly eight pounds. A good start to her little life. Claire quietly left the room.

Twenty minutes later, Susanna awoke and began to cry. Once again, Diana offered her breast to the infant. Sucking frantically for a few moments, the baby released the nipple to begin screaming. Crying with frustration, Diana almost threw the baby back into the cot and left the room.

Hearing the *fracas* in the bedroom, Claire hurried in and picked up the scarlet-faced, hysterical infant. Once again, she fed Susanna a few ounces of glucose water, and again the baby drifted off to sleep. Returning the sleeping child to the cot, Claire went to find her daughter.

Diana was sitting on the veranda, her face tear-streaked and angry. "That bloody child just won't feed!" she burst out. "I tried to feed her but she *again* rejected my breast after only a few sucks."

Claire was silent a moment unsure of what to suggest. There was nothing wrong with the baby's physical ability to suck...that had been ascertained by a midwife shortly after birth. And the glucose water had gone down the hatch without a problem. Despite her heavy breasts, was it possible that Diana didn't have any milk? But Claire knew she would have to tread carefully where her prickly daughter was concerned.

"Have you thought of giving her a bottle?" Claire suggested at last. "When I gave her a drink of glucose water, she drank that without a problem."

"Grannie said no bottles," Diana's reply was definite, "or the baby could refuse the breast permanently. She'll feed when she's hungry enough."

Claire looked askance, but said no more. It was not her baby after all, and Diana had every right to decide what was to be done. She only hoped the little thing fed properly the next time she was put to the breast.

It was not to be.

Over the next four days, the house resounded with the baby's screaming, together with yells of rage and frustration from her mother. How fortunate it was that Jack was away for ten days in Delhi – Claire thought feelingly. She fed Susanna glucose water, but it was no longer sufficient. It was clear the baby was desperately hungry, but Diana steadfastly refused to give her a bottle of milk.

It was on the fifth day that matters came to a head.

Heavily asleep, having spent most of the night trying to comfort the screaming infant, Claire awoke to complete silence. Alarmed, she leaped out of bed and hurried to Diana's bedroom to check on mother and child. To her horror, Susanna lay glassy-eyed in her cot, immobile, a tinge of blue around the slack little mouth and making weak mewing sounds.

Diana was nowhere to be seen.

Her heart pounding with fright, Claire picked up Susanna whose head drooped terrifyingly to one side. Holding the infant close to her body, she rang the army hospital with an urgent request to speak directly to Colonel Gough. He came immediately to the telephone, and Claire gave him a succinct account of what had transpired since leaving hospital. The baby had not managed to feed at all, and her condition was now serious.

"I'll be at your home in fifteen minutes," the doctor told her. "But in the meantime I would like you to prepare a bottle of formula for the infant – just two ounces – and see if she will take it."

"But what about Diana, the baby's mother?" Claire asked in desperation. "She's so set on breast-feeding her baby...it's that which has been the problem."

"Do what you can for the infant, but you may leave that young lady to me."

Her hands shaking with fear, Claire made up two ounces of powdered milk in a feeding bottle. Cradling the infant in the crook of her arm, she sat on the edge of her own bed. Shaking out a drop of milk from the teat, she gently moved it against the baby's slack mouth. Susanna remained disinterested. Swallowing convulsively, Claire was deathly afraid it might be too late. Again, she rubbed the milky teat against the baby's mouth. The eyes flickered, and then a little tongue flicked out. Resisting the urge to push the teat into the child's mouth, Claire waited. The tiny mouth opened and Claire allowed a few drops of milk to fall on the infant's tongue. Her lips closing on the teat, she made an effort to suck – then stopped. Tense with apprehension, Claire held her breath. Another suck… then another…and another! Slowly but surely, the baby drank the two ounces of milk.

"What the *hell* do you think you are doing, Mummy?" Diana charged into the bedroom, her face scarlet with fury. "How *dare* you feed that stuff to my baby?"

"If you were unable to see the poor mite has been slowly starving to death, you need your eyes tested," Claire told her daughter sharply. "She's had two ounces of milk, but with great difficulty as she's so weak."

"You have no right to do whatever you want with my child," Diana yelled furiously. "Grannie was quite clear about not—"

"Did you not hear what I just said about the condition of your baby?" Claire rose to her feet, the infant asleep against her shoulder. "I'm not going to argue with you, Diana. Colonel Gough is on his way, maybe he will explain things better than I can."

"Colonel Gough?" Diana hesitated. "Why is he coming? For God's sake, it was only a matter of time before the baby gave in and accepted the breast!"

"Time was something Susanna simply did not have, you foolish girl. Your child was not far off the point of death, and may still not be out of the woods."

A commotion was heard in the hall, and the *bearer* announced that Colonel Gough had arrived. Ignoring her furious daughter, Claire went to greet the doctor and told him she had succeeded in feeding two ounces of milk to the infant. She then directed him to the bedroom, where Diana was still fulminating against her mother.

"Now then, my girl," Colonel Gough closed the door behind him. "What's going on here for heaven's sake? I gather your baby hasn't been feeding?"

"I don't know why Mummy sent for you," Diana burst out, "Susanna is an obstinate little tyke but she was beginning to give in...until my mother interfered!"

"Diana, you must accept the fact your baby is in a serious condition," the doctor said gently. "Five days without food is a very long time in an infant's life, you know."

"But I *tried*...I tried so hard to feed her, Colonel Gough," Diana burst into tears. "But she just kept on screaming and screaming until I thought I would go mad."

"I'm sure you did, my dear, but your mother was quite right to call me. The situation had to be resolved, or you would have lost your child. And it was I who told her to give the baby a bottle. By the grace of God, she was still strong enough to suck."

"But Grannie told me it was unwise to introduce a bottle when breast-feeding, which was why I—"

"Let me have a look at your breasts, Diana. It may be that the problem lies there."

"I doubt that since they are heavy with milk, as you'll see," the young woman disrobed. "See what I mean? Plenty in there for one tiny baby."

Carefully examining Diana's breasts and nipples, Colonel Gough straightened and put a comforting hand on her shoulder. "It's true your breasts are heavy, but they do not contain milk, my dear. During your pregnancy, you put on a considerable amount of weight, which would also have increased their size."

"What? If I don't have milk now, it's because that bloody baby refused to feed and it dried up," Diana dissolved into tears once more. "You can't know how it feels to be rejected by your own baby!"

"Susanna hasn't rejected you...what an odd idea," the doctor frowned. "And there is no question of the baby being the cause of your milk drying up, since it is unlikely there was any in the first place. Had you remained in hospital for a few days as I advised, this condition would have been immediately noticed. Diana, I want you to accept that the situation is neither your fault nor the baby's. Occasionally, this does happen."

Diana stared mutinously down at her hands. She *did* have milk at first...she knew she had! If the baby hadn't made all this fuss, the milk

would still be there. People would think she was a failure as a mother...
unable to feed her own baby!

"Young lady, you are not a failure in any way whatsoever," the doctor
read her mind with singular accuracy. "But I want you to promise me that
Susanna stays on the bottle, as it's essential for the baby's very survival.
Do I have your word, Diana?"

"Yes, I promise," she mumbled, "but Mummy will have to get on
with that, as I'm heartily sick of the whole business."

Colonel Gough nodded, and left the room. Claire was sitting on the
veranda, waiting to speak to him. The baby lay asleep in her arms, pink
beginning to tinge the pale little face. Glancing up in apprehension, she
relaxed to see him nod and smile.

"That unfortunate young mother has no milk in her breasts, in spite
of their size, Claire. I've explained the situation to her, and although
it's understandably difficult for her to accept, she has promised not to
make further attempts to breast-feed. I believe it would be in everyone's
interests if you took over the baby's care for the time being, and allow
your daughter to rest and recover her strength and spirits."

"Of course, Colonel Gough, I'm happy to do that," Claire smiled
gratefully up at the doctor. "But I need guidance about how much and
when I should feed Susanna."

"Without weighing the child, it is clear she's lost a frightening amount
of her birth weight. I recommend you feed her little and often for the first
two weeks: two ounces of milk per feed. I'll pop in from time to time to
see how she's progressing."

A month later, Susanna was pronounced well enough to travel to
Kalimpong. Still somewhat frail, she was nevertheless slowly gaining
weight. Diana was desperate to return to her school, worried by comments
her sister had casually dropped upon her return to Calcutta.

"I made one or two changes in the school whilst I was in Kalimpong,"
Daphne had airily told her, "but for the better as I'm sure you will
agree."

"*What* changes?" Diana grated through clenched teeth. "You were in
Bon Ami for your honeymoon. You had no business to interfere with the
running of my school."

"Well, one or two of the staff were getting too big for their boots, so
I put them on probation...on reduced salary, naturally."

"You really are the bloody end, Daphne! How dare you throw your weight around and penalise my carefully selected staff. What else did you do, for God's sake?"

"Nothing much. I did wallop a boy who was pinching strawberries from our patch." Daphne glanced guiltily away. "Horrid child, I thought."

"What did Christina think about all this? Not a lot, I bet."

"A bit nonplussed, I suppose, but she's over cautious about everything."

Subsequent to the exchange with her sister, Diana could scarcely wait to instigate damage control in her school. She was feeling much better in herself, and resolved to resume riding her horse as soon as possible. The only fly in the ointment was the care of the baby...lots and lots of time-consuming care, from what she had seen.

Meanwhile, Jack MacLeod was feeling unwell, being consistently plagued by dizzy spells and conscious of thirst that nothing seemed to quench. He had visited the doctor who mumbled about diabetes, but tests were required to confirm that diagnosis. Maybe later. Nevertheless, Jack wanted to speak to his eldest daughter about her odd attitude towards her baby. Which he did...and in no uncertain terms.

"I've noticed it's your mother who takes care of your child, Diana. I would have imagined that to be something you would want to be doing yourself?"

"Mummy thinks she does things so much better, so who am I to argue?" Diana retorted, piqued by the unexpected criticism. "Must be the novelty, since she used to park us off on nannies all day long."

"Happy though I am to look after Susanna, I didn't imagine you would abdicate all responsibility towards her," Claire put in sharply. "You spend no time at all with your little girl."

"For Christ's sake, the child's too young to know who the hell is taking care of her!" Diana snapped. "Criticism, and even more criticism...that's all I ever hear from you these days, Mummy. Just because I don't – have never wanted – to spend my days looking after a constantly grizzling infant, and handling hundreds of dirty nappies."

"Don't exaggerate, please." Claire retorted. "Susanna rarely has a dirty nappy since I pot her before and after a feed."

"That's *exactly* what I mean! I have a school to run, so there's no chance in hell that I'll be chasing about with a bloody potty in one hand. I'd employ a nanny, except there isn't enough room in Bon Ami. I'll have to find an *ayah* to look after her."

"An *ayah*? For heaven's sake, an *ayah* can't take care of a fragile little thing like Susanna, who needs constant care."

"Well, if the baby's welfare is so close to your heart, Mummy, then you'd better come back to Kalimpong!" Diana shouted. "Then you can make certain your darling granddaughter is being looked after to your entire satisfaction."

With a frown of concern, Claire watched her eldest daughter flounce from the room in tears, unusual in Diana. It was true she worried about what would happen to Susanna once she was no longer under her personal care...but go back to Kalimpong? What would Jack have to say about that, with the busy cold weather season about to begin? She discovered the answer to that when they were having dinner that same evening.

"I saw the doctor a few days ago about dizzy spells I've been having, and this vile thirst that comes and goes," Jack casually told her. "He suspects diabetes, but can't be sure of what stage until tests have been done. Nothing to worry about, I daresay."

"Diabetes? Isn't that too much sugar in the blood or something?" Claire raised her eyebrows. "With all that whisky and beer you consume each day, not to mention your love of iced cakes, it wouldn't be surprising if that was the direct result."

"Claire, can you not make an effort to be pleasant?" Jack asked, annoyed. "Diabetes can be highly unpleasant in an advanced stage. I'm not feeling particularly well, so I can do without you making it into something self-inflicted."

"Oh, stop being over dramatic, Jack," Claire lit a cigarette and fitted it into her holder. "Actually, I want to discuss Diana's suggestion that I return with her to Kalimpong to look after Susanna until she is stronger. As you heard, the general idea is to employ an *ayah* of some kind. Not even a proper nanny."

"Do whatever you want, as you generally do, whatever I might think."

"Must you wallow in a sea of self-pity, Jack? If you don't want me to go, all you need do is say so instead of passing snide remarks."

Yawning, Jack stood up. "I'm going to bed. Now that British Government personnel have transferred to New Delhi, the new capital of India, I'm no longer obliged to do as much entertaining as before. Since I'm accustomed to being abandoned for months when you vanish to Europe, I daresay I'll manage with an efficient secretary."

"Fine, I'll tell Diana tomorrow. Goodnight, Jack."

Chapter Twenty-Eight

Once back in Kalimpong, Diana and Claire settled down to their individual routines. Both women were invigorated once again by the freshness of mountain air and peace and quiet. Christina had been delighted to see them, but had loudly complained about her other niece, who had supposedly been on her honeymoon.

Neither did Daphne's new husband meet with Christina's approval. Not long after their arrival, he had taken up the habit of vanishing down the road into town for hours at a stretch. In her jaundiced view, the man could only have been up to no good! Claire frowned, having heard snippets of gossip regarding her new son-in-law's continued philandering. Christina continued the tirade, telling them that during her husband's absences, Daphne found herself at a loose end and had amused herself by constant interference in school matters.

Susanna continued to thrive, but Claire sadly recognised the baby girl was unlikely to achieve much in the way of chubbiness. Prone to colic, the baby would scream with pain which only carrying her upright against a shoulder seemed to help. If left to cry, she would struggle to breathe, and even momentarily lose consciousness. The first time it happened, a terrified Claire sent for the doctor. Arriving in his ramshackle car, Doctor Dikshet reassured her that the condition was not life-threatening in itself. Nevertheless, he advised it would be better to avoid the spasm by not allowing the baby to cry for long. She would probably grow out of it in time, possibly by the time she was two.

As the bouts of colic receded, Susanna fell seriously ill with measles. For weeks Claire lived in a darkened room with the sick baby, constantly on the alert in case she cried, and feeding her tiny quantities of milk in the hope she did not vomit it back up. Sitting for hours in the dark, she reflected on the novel experience of caring for this frail little mite – despite having had three children.

It was also the first time in her life that Claire felt truly needed by a helpless human being, and thanked God she had agreed to come to Kalimpong, for it was unlikely the baby would have survived otherwise.

Not because Diana was deliberately negligent, but she was preoccupied with the running of Hilltop School, and might not have recognised the needs of a sick child.

Slowly, very slowly, Claire's vigilance paid off, and Susanna began to show signs of recovery. Thin to the point of scrawniness, the ten-month-old baby girl managed to stagger about on her matchstick-like legs. Possessing a mischievous grin, her favourite occupation was to fish in handbags placed on the floor by her grandmother's friends who were absorbed in a game of bridge. Seizing a 'trophy', she would giggle and scoot off as fast as she could to her nursery. Caught by her grandmother, a still giggling Susanna would relinquish what she had pinched without a struggle.

Claire adored the naughty little imp.

Just as the child began to regain some weight, she succumbed to a bout of whooping cough. Once again, Claire slept next to Susanna's cot so that she was ready to take her in her arms, to massage the arching little back until the terrible whooping had passed. In what seemed like hours, Susanna lost the small amount of weight she had gained.

Claire received a telephone call from Jack. His diabetes had developed rapidly to an advanced stage, and the dizzy spells were more frequent and prolonged. Reluctantly, he admitted to have largely ignored strictures imposed by his doctor on consumption of sugary foods. He was now on a stringent diet, designed to radically lower the sugar in his bloodstream. He had also received a dire warning that should he stray from it, he would risk having insulin injections for the rest of his life. Advised to take life more easily, he was also supposed to take up gentle exercise. Hearing this, Claire snorted scornfully, knowing her husband had abandoned any such thing years ago. Now, his only form of exercise was the short walk from his car to the bar at the Saturday Club.

"Do you want me to come back to Calcutta, Jack?" she asked, dreading the answer. "Of course, I will come if you need me."

"No. I'm telephoning to say that I'm going on a recuperative cruise for a couple of months. Concentrate on my health. Possibly to South Africa, where I can tie up a few loose ends for the company whilst I'm there."

South Africa. That woman. No, Jack was probably past that sort of frivolity, besides feeling unwell. "I see. When do you expect to be back?" Claire asked.

"Can't say at the moment. I've dropped all government duties, so

I only have the company to think about. I may even take early retirement unless I feel a lot better."

From the tone of his voice, Claire suddenly realised her husband was terrified of his own mortality. "Isn't that rather drastic?" she asked curiously. "What on earth would you do with yourself all day?"

"I'll cross that bridge when I come to it," he replied shortly. "When I know what my plans are regarding a return to India, I'll send you a telegram. Give my love to Di-Di, and a kiss for little Susanna."

The telephone went dead. Replacing the receiver, Claire was aware of a surge of relief that she wasn't obliged to abandon her little granddaughter. With luck and a following wind, Jack would not be back for a couple of months. With a lighter step, she went to see if Susanna had woken up from her afternoon nap.

A pony was bought for the little girl when she was fourteen months old. Every morning a *syce* would arrive, leading a tiny Shetland by the name of Tinkerbell. Claire would bring Susanna out and place her into a ring saddle, specially designed to prevent the child from slipping off. Thrilled, she would lean forward to wrap skinny little arms round the pony's neck, before being led off down the path for half an hour. Photographs of the child and pony were taken, and Diana even evinced an interest in perhaps taking her daughter out riding when she was a little older.

Bedtime was invariably unpopular with Susanna, who would energetically resist being put down in her cot. To avoid uncontrollable crying which might result in that terrifying loss of breath, Claire would sit with the child, telling her stories in a soft voice until her eyes fluttered closed. She would then stay fast asleep through the night until six in the morning, when she was put in her highchair for breakfast.

As soon as Susanna's molars began to push through, Claire's nights were disrupted by the child waking and howling with pain. Generally, she would be the first to hear and hurry to pick her up. One night, however, it was Diana who was out of bed first.

"You've had a drink and sat on your pot, so now back to bed you go," Diana put her daughter down in the drop-side cot. Immediately, Susanna scrambled to her feet and holding the cot sides, began to bawl.

"Come on, lie down at once and go back to sleep!" Diana told her crossly. "It's the middle of the night, for God's sake."

"Don't worry, I'll deal with her," Claire appeared at the nursery door. "I know just what—"

"No, Mummy," Diana prevented her mother from picking up the howling child. "Susanna is ridiculously spoiled, thanks to you. A little discipline will do her no harm."

"You know how badly she's teething, Diana," Claire tried to keep her voice level. "She's in quite a lot of pain with those back teeth coming through."

"Always some pathetic excuse for her, eh? Sick or having a horrid dream, and now it's teething! That little tyke gets her own way because you consistently pander to her."

"Diana, be reasonable!" Claire said in desperation. "You know quite well Susanna's prone to this or that, and she's been so very ill on occasion."

Scarlet in the face, the child's howls were reaching a crescendo. Diana furiously faced her mother and pointed to the door.

"Go back to bed, Mummy, and leave me to deal with my own child."

Unwillingly, Claire backed away and went to fetch her cigarettes from the sitting room. Lighting one with shaking hands, she walked out to the small veranda.

Susanna continued screaming for several minutes…then there was sudden silence. Tensing, Claire waited for her to cry again. Silence. Unable to bear it, Claire threw her cigarette into a flowerbed and ran back into the nursery just as Diana pushed past.

"That bloody child plays to the gallery like a past master," she threw over her shoulder. "You've taught her a fine sense of theatrics, if you ask me!"

Susanna lay writhing in her cot, blue round the lips, wide eyes starting from her face as she struggled to breathe. Frantic, Claire picked up the child as the small body arched with the effort trying to draw breath, then with a gasp she sucked air into her lungs and began high-pitched screaming.

The hysterical child in her arms, Claire boiled a kettle and added hot water to cold in a tin bath until it was pleasantly warm. Peeling off the sweat-sodden nightgown, she gently lowered the baby girl into the water. The screams soon became sobs, and then stopped altogether. Gazing up at her grandmother through tear-filled eyes, Susanna hiccoughed, and attempted a watery smile.

The water now cool, Claire lifted the child out of the bath and wrapped her in a towel to begin drying her. It was only then that Claire noticed a red handprint marking Susanna's small bottom. The child wasn't yet two, she thought disgustedly, yet Diana was determined to 'discipline' her in this way.

Sitting in the dark, she cradled the little girl, humming tunelessly until she fell into an exhausted sleep. Lowering her into the cot, she covered her with a shawl and went back to her own bedroom, praying the child would not wake again. Claire was unable to sleep, agitated that Diana had raised a hand to the frail little girl. Before falling into an uneasy doze, she resolved to tackle her daughter in the morning.

"So what if I smacked the little wretch," Diana demanded, a slice of buttered toast halfway to her mouth. "I could see she was having me on, even if you couldn't."

"Don't be ridiculous, the child could scarcely breathe!" Claire retorted. "How can a little thing in her condition be capable of pulling a fast one?"

"I'm not going to discuss it, Mummy," she declared loftily, getting to her feet. "If I think Susanna needs it, I shall smack her whether you like it, or not."

"I never thought you capable of unkindness, Diana, so why—"

"*Unkindness*? How dare you talk to me about unkindness after what you did to Timothy? Do you ever think about that little boy who used to call you *Mummy*, and the agonised bewilderment he felt when you dumped him? Not to mention the hefty slap across my face you delivered when I dared mention such a thing."

Claire flinched, but remained silent. The terrible sin she had committed against that child was never far from her mind, and Diana was cruelly rubbing it in. But maybe she deserved it? What she had done was inexcusable. There was little she could do now to atone for it, except to take care of her waif of a granddaughter to the best of her ability. Fighting tears, she rose without a word and left the breakfast table.

Further altercation was avoided by a visit from Peter Lalinski. Her face alight with joy to see her husband, Diana appeared to forget about 'disciplining' her unruly child. It crossed Claire's mind to wonder how Peter would regard his small daughter, now that she was on her feet and speaking?

Largely preoccupied with his wife and her school, he showed a vague interest in watching Susanna ride her pony. Aside from that, his only other remark was that she was far too skinny, and wouldn't it be a good thing to fatten her up with a big bowl of porridge each morning? Claire smiled, but said nothing. It was all she could do to cajole her granddaughter into eating a few fingers of toast and butter for breakfast.

A week later, Peter went back to Calcutta and life resumed normality. Christina was rarely seen, having met a clutch of nuns in the village with whom she tended to spend most of her free time. Peter had brought a pushchair from Calcutta for Susanna, so Claire began taking her granddaughter for a daily walk along myriad pathways through the hills. The fresh air was lightly perfumed by wild flowers growing in profusion in the warm June sunshine, and after an invigorating stroll, she would find a convenient rock on which to sit and enjoy a cigarette or two.

Early one Saturday morning, a tearful Christina came hurrying into the bungalow, barely able to speak in her terrible distress. Alarmed, Claire led her to a chair in the sitting room, gently sat her down, and poured her a cup of tea from a brown teapot.

"Chrissy darling, what's the matter? Are you ill?" Claire put her arm about the shaking shoulders, whereupon Christina dissolved into tears once again.

"It's *Maman*. Our mother is dead, Claire," Christina sobbed. "And nobody was with her at the end. She died in her office, sitting in her old chair, gazing out of the window as she always did. She...she never got over Uncle Freddie's death, you know."

Claire blanched, unable to prevent hot tears stinging her eyes. Her mother had always been a significant presence in her life, be it adversely or not. "Who found her, Chrissy?" she asked at last. "And what's happened to Sonia?"

"It was Sonia who found her, and she went screaming out through the gates into the middle of the street," Christina swallowed convulsively. "It was lucky she wasn't run over, and that a passing car stopped and took her home. Needless to say, she's completely hysterical, and keeps on calling for her mother. Of course, I'll have to go back to Calcutta and attend to her, as well as dealing with *Maman's* affairs."

"I...I can't go, Chrissy," Claire tentatively began, "you see, there's little Susanna..."

"No, that's fine," Christina was aware of the strained relationship between Diana and her small daughter. "I'm not sure what to do about Sonia, but I'll put the nursing home on the market. Perhaps even our old home."

Tears falling down her cheeks, Diana sat silently, grieving for the grandmother she had genuinely loved. However unlikely, she hoped Daphne and Robert would see to it that Christina had whatever moral support she needed when dealing with Sonia and tying up their family affairs.

Six months had flown past before it occurred to Claire that she had not heard from Jack. Surely his cruise could not have lasted this long? Perhaps he had fallen seriously ill? Concerned, she rang the house in Calcutta to find out if there had been any news from him. The *bearer* answered the telephone, and informed her the office had sent a message that *Sahib* would be home in a month. Relieved, Claire waited to hear from her husband, wondering what to do should Jack order her back to Calcutta.

It was not the expected telegram that arrived for Claire, but a letter written from South Africa. So he had missed her enough to write, she thought in surprise. Despite Jack's lack of imagination and pedantic conversation, she was nevertheless grateful for the security of his steadfastness in her life. Lighting a cigarette, Claire settled herself in a chair on the veranda and opened the envelope.

My dear Claire,

This is not easy letter for me to write, and perhaps unpleasant for you to read. However, what I have to say is important, so bear with me.

As you are only too aware, many years ago I fell in love with a married lady, Anne Winterton. For reasons that are obvious, we were obliged to break off our liaison and go our separate ways. She remained in her marriage, and I returned to Calcutta to marry you. I realise our marriage may have been a disappointment for I was never able to offer you the romantic love a young bride has every right to expect. I apologise for that.

When I set off on a cruise to try and regain my health, upon arrival in Durban, I discovered Anne's husband had died two years ago. She is now free to remarry...but I am not. Which is why I am asking you to be generous and release me from our marriage, that I may spend my remaining years with the woman I have always loved.

Naturally, I will take care of you financially, and perhaps you will want to buy a property in France where I know you feel at home? Give it some thought and let me know. I have cancelled the rented house in Eastbourne since it is unlikely either of us will be using it again.

Due to my chronic ill health, I have made the decision to take early retirement. As things presently stand, I shall leave India for good in around two years time. I suggest you remain in Kalimpong for the time being, as I shall be requiring the Calcutta house for myself. In any event, I know you have little Susanna to look after. What do you want done with your personal possessions? Please let me know as soon as possible and I shall have them packed up and sent to you.

I wish you the very best for the future, Claire, and hope you can find it within yourself to understand, and perhaps even forgive me.
Jack

Her fingers numb with shock, Claire replaced the letter in its envelope. Arbitrarily dumped by the very man she had thought to count on! Dry-eyed, she wrapped her arms about herself, and began rocking back and forth. Suddenly aware of tension in the atmosphere, Susanna abandoned the cardboard box she was playing with, and toddled over to lay a curious hand on her grandmother's knee.

Both men in her life had wanted to see the back of her. First it had been Charles Rattigan who had wasted no time in replacing her. Now it was Jack – the most reliable of husbands – anxious to replace her with that raddled South African hag! Reading between the lines, Claire was certain he wanted to install that damned tart in their Calcutta home. *Bloody nerve*! She'd see them both in hell first.

Insidiously, it permeated Claire's initial outrage that she now faced a future entirely alone. How could this have happened at this late stage in her life? What, in God's name, had she done to deserve this? Unconsciously seeking comfort, her arm went round the small figure who was gazing up at her with trusting eyes. Was this frail little girl the only person who truly loved her? Claire doubled over, gasping with the pain of such a terrifying admission – even to herself.

"Any letters for me?" Coming up the steps of the veranda Diana halted abruptly, noticing her mother's pallor and beaten expression. "Mummy, what's happened? Is Susanna..."

"Susanna's fine," Claire answered jerkily. "It's your father. He wants his freedom so that he can marry his old tart in Durban, and means to bring her back to Calcutta."

Diana gaped at her mother. Daddy...with a *tart*? Never! Mummy must have got it wrong, he'd never do such a shabby thing to his family. Smiling mirthlessly, Claire watched the changing expressions on her daughter's face. Diana was evidently finding it hard to believe.

"Read the letter for yourself. Your dear father has thought it all out to his satisfaction. Happy ever after – he and that woman – violin music softly playing."

Taking the letter, Diana scanned the contents with tightening lips. Finally, she folded the flimsy paper and rammed it back in the envelope. "I would never have believed it of Daddy, I must say. But if he intends to import that woman to Calcutta, can you imagine the scandal it would provoke? Daddy has always been overly conscious of guarding his precious reputation, so he can't have thought it through properly. I imagine he's trying to cover all eventualities, as well as avoiding confrontation and possible rows."

"The stark fact is that he wants to be rid of me, his wife of twenty-odd years. Diana, I don't know what to do or where to go, and I'm afraid of being alone for the rest of my life." Claire's voice shook.

"Have you ever met this woman?" Diana asked curiously. "And when did Daddy begin this liaison with her?"

"During our engagement, he went on business to Durban and had a prolonged fling with her. And yes, I met her a long time ago whilst on holiday in South Africa. In fact, I had something of an altercation with the bloody woman, and then had the shock of my life when your father fiercely took her side. I found that hard to forgive."

"Damned if I'll allow dear old Daddy to get away with this scot-free," Diana exclaimed fiercely. "I'll write and ask how he imagines your friends would view his mucky little affair, not to mention those government types he cultivates? I wonder what the company boss in Durban would think about Jack MacLeod screwing the widow of a company director...for the second time around?"

Diana grinned evilly. "And now that the Winterton woman's husband is conveniently dead and gone, he plans on taking the poor fellow's place! Does he think his precious son would accept the replacement of his mother? After reading my letter, I daresay good old Daddy will be hastily re-thinking plans to bring that woman back to Calcutta."

In spite of her outrage, Claire felt cheered by her daughter's support. It was true that Jack had always put tremendous store by what others thought. But where she was concerned, the very thought of living with a man who was trying to rid himself of her was abhorrent, and probably unacceptable.

"I don't think I can live with your father after this," she muttered. "I'm sure I would continually feel he was hankering after that South African creature."

"*Pshaw*!" Diana snorted. "She'll rapidly vanish into the mists, if Daddy reacts to my letter as I imagine he will. You have plenty of time to think about it, Mummy, but do try to keep an open mind."

Later that morning, Diana sat at her desk writing three letters. One was to her father in South Africa, the other to Christina and the third to Daphne. She felt it only right that the family should know about her father's attempt to divorce her mother, and for what reason. She also outlined what she intended to do about it. Christina would be shocked, Diana knew, for her aunt had always been fond of her brother-in-law. She would leave Daphne to drop a line to William and let him know the score.

Daphne telephoned a few weeks later, having just received a letter from William who was dying of anxiety in case his London friends heard scandalous gossip about his family! There had been no mention of his mother, not even an enquiry as to her state of mind. Daphne had replied furiously to the letter, tearing strips off her egotistical brother. Diana shook her head. Selfish toad thought of nobody but himself – as always.

Far away on the outskirts of Durban, Jack and Anne Winterton were sitting at the breakfast table on the patio of their recently purchased property. Diana's letter lay open between them. Shock had rendered the pair speechless, having assumed their future together was assured. However, Diana Lalinski's attack on her father seemed to have thrown a very large spanner in the works.

Anne fought to suppress the black rage consuming her, wanting to blurt out her fury against Claire's interfering bloody daughter! Jack's arrival in Durban had been fortuitous for Anne, her husband having disinherited her subsequent to the discovery of further dalliances on her part. His wealth had been left to their sons, who were not demonstrating the slightest inclination to share it with their mother. Anne had been obliged to move from the palatial home where she had lived for many years, to take up residence in a small town apartment.

With Jack MacLeod's unexpected arrival in Durban, it was an ideal opportunity to attempt to change her downturn in fortune. It had not been difficult to re-ignite her ex-lover's desire for she was still an attractive woman, without a single grey hair on her head thanks to the attentions of an excellent hairdresser. Subsequent to a month of delirious happiness, Jack had declared a desire to marry her, and that they should look for a house outside the town where they would eventually spend the rest of their lives together. A beautiful property with an enormous garden on the rural outskirts of Durban was their mutual choice, which Jack had immediately purchased, and the two of them had promptly moved in together.

He then wrote to his wife, asking for his freedom.

Whilst waiting for Claire's answer to the letter, Anne had been gently pressurising Jack to allow her to accompany him back to Calcutta. To her private irritation, he had been surprisingly reluctant, being unwilling to provoke gossip. She stepped up the pressure, telling him that idle gossip should be of little account since they would shortly be married. Hating the idea of being parted from her, Jack had begun to waver.

Out of the blue, the letter from Claire's blasted daughter arrived.

"So what are you going to do, Jack?" Anne broke the silence. "You aren't going to kowtow to this young woman's ridiculous demands, are you?"

Jack was silent, stunned that his Di-Di should have written to him in such a condemning vein. 'Tawdry affair' had hit home. 'Taking up with a woman of loose morals whose husband had conveniently expired' – that also did not go down well.

Then came the threat.

Unless their father abandoned his disgraceful liaison, Diana and Daphne would see to it that everybody in Calcutta and even Delhi was made aware of it. Jack MacLeod, that fine upstanding citizen, would be seen by all to have a smutty side to him. Think of the *shame* – Diana advised – his impeccable reputation forever besmirched.

"Jack?" Anne's voice broke through his dismal reflections. "Darling, you can't mean to dance to your daughter's extremely unpleasant tune, surely?"

"It's not as easy as that, Anne. I've lived and worked in India for the best part of my life, building up a circle of friends and associates who are important to me. Should I be seen to ignore the existing code of morality either here or in India, my reputation would be in shreds. How am I to live with that?"

"But you would have *me*, my darling!" Anne's voice rose in desperation. "After all these years apart, we have a heaven-sent opportunity to be together. Don't condemn us to a future of solitary lives without one another."

"I cannot ignore this, Anne," Jack turned agonised eyes to the woman he had always loved. "Knowing my daughter, she will carry out her threat to the very last detail, and I can't face ending my career in India under a cloud of condemnation and shame."

The woman sitting opposite tightened her lips. "Go on then, abandon me! For heaven's sake, you don't know if that spiteful little wife of yours will have you back."

"My only hope in this catastrophic situation," Jack replied, "is that should Claire refuse to consider a reconciliation, I would then be free to lead my own life as I wish. But for the moment, I must return to Calcutta immediately – alone."

Chapter Twenty-Nine

Sitting out on Bon Ami's veranda, Claire gazed unseeingly across the valley, an unread newspaper open on her lap. A few feet away, Susanna sat in her wooden playpen, engrossed in building an unsteady tower with a few coloured building blocks. On occasion, she glanced up to see if her silent grandmother might be lost in admiration of her efforts.

It had been two months since the bombshell from Jack had blasted her world to smithereens. It now appeared he was returning to India with the intention of reconciling with his wife. Under the circumstances, however, the prospect did not fill her with joy.

"Told you!" Diana had chortled, waving her father's letter in the air. "At the end of the day, taking on his bloody South African tart was less important than losing his much-prized reputation!"

Claire had smiled, wishing she could feel more elated than she did. She still loathed the idea of living with a man who had been intent on rejecting her. And he only wished to reconcile under dire threat! Jack had already returned to Calcutta, and telephoned to say that after dealing with outstanding office matters, he would be travelling up-country to Kalimpong. A recent telegram indicated he was now on his way.

The day after Jack's arrival, Susanna fell ill with a sore throat and fever. Doctor Dikshet was duly summoned and diagnosed a severe case of tonsillitis. He strongly advised removal of the child's inflamed tonsils that poisoned her system. If neglected, it would hamper her growth. Attending to the sick little girl left Claire no time for marital discord or discussion.

Once the urgency of Susanna's condition was lessening, Claire was able to notice her husband seemed to have aged in the year since she had seen him. He had lost a considerable amount of hair, and there was an expression of dull resignation in his eyes. She wondered grimly if the reason for that was because he was being forced to give up his tart? If so, he could go straight to hell! She had endured being second best to that man for the very last time. Tension in the bungalow started to escalate.

The unannounced arrival of Peter Lalinski served to redeem the atmosphere, and Diana was overjoyed to see her husband. The two of them went off after supper to sleep at Hillside, only returning to Bon Ami for an evening meal. Jack was genuinely pleased to see his easy-going officer son-in-law, having heard disturbing rumours about Robert Mackenzie's increasingly profligate ways, although Daphne appeared oblivious to her husband's alleged activities.

One morning when Jack had taken himself off for a walk, Peter took the opportunity of talking privately to Claire. Diana had told him her mother was steadfastly refusing to consider taking back her husband. The slight Jack had inflicted on her had gone deep, and Peter knew Claire to be a proud woman.

"Have you decided what your answer will be to Jack's offer of a reconciliation, Claire?" he asked, lighting a cigarette. "It seems quite genuine to me."

"How am I to know that?" Claire demanded. "It wasn't long ago that he was determined to be rid of me."

"A stupid mistake, I'm sure. He hadn't thought things through as he should, but from what she has told me, Diana soon put him right."

"Yes, but with threats and menaces," Claire retorted dryly, lighting up a cigarette herself. "A nice way to begin one's marriage again, I'm sure."

"Of course, the alternative would be to demand a divorce, but that would allow the South African floozy to benefit enormously," Peter remarked casually. "Jack must be considered a wealthy man, and his retirement provident fund must be sizeable."

Claire sat silently, exhaling a stream of blue smoke. Money. At the end of the day the whole thing boiled down to money, she cynically reflected. It was true that she and Jack could live extremely well on the retirement fund, probably better than if she struck out on her own. Being alone was a frightening prospect, as she had never managed her life entirely by herself. From the time she became Jack's wife at the age of nineteen, she had depended on him to pay bills and sort out occasional difficulties. Taken him for granted, perhaps? Nevertheless...

Holding his breath, Peter watched the changing expressions on Claire's face, hoping to God she would accept her husband's overtures. Although fond of his fiery mother-in-law and appreciative of the care she took of Susanna, Peter was guiltily aware he did not want the responsibility of her future welfare. Diana felt the same reluctance.

"I suppose I could think about it," Claire conceded eventually. "To tell the truth, Peter, there is nothing I would like more than to scupper that bloody tart's ambitions."

"Absolutely!" Peter pressed home the advantage. "You could even make it a condition that you choose the country of your retirement."

Peter sensibly let the matter drop, and walked over to the playpen where his small daughter was cuddling the teddy bear he had given her. Looking up, Susanna treated her father to a wide smile displaying a full set of pearly teeth.

"Susa loves new teddy," she told him. "An' I'm havin ice ceem for supper!"

For the moment, the tonsillitis seemed to have receded. Sweet little thing, really, he thought, and a damned shame Diana seemed unable to communicate with her own daughter. Maybe when she was a bit older…

Jack used his time in Kalimpong to make his peace with Diana, the daughter to whom he had always been close. Wisely, he made no attempt to excuse himself or explain his motives in wanting to reside in South Africa. He spoke mainly of the medical condition that was prompting him to cut short his career, both in business and government. Privately, he was agonisingly conscious of Anne, waiting and hoping for his return.

Finally, Jack could procrastinate the matter no longer. Inviting himself on a walk with Claire and Susanna in her pushchair, he broached the subject of reconciliation to his wife. Part of him hoped Claire would tell him to go to hell: but the other part wished to resume a steady if unexciting lifestyle and be rid of any suggestion of scandal.

"Why, Jack?" Claire reaction was brusque. "Why would you want me when your floozy of yesteryear is waiting patiently for you in Durban?"

"I made a mistake," Jack suppressed a surge of annoyance to hear Anne referred to in derogatory terms. "A mistake that I'm anxious to put right."

"I wonder if you realise the extent of the insult you dealt me, Jack? No woman cares to be classified as being ready for the rubbish bin."

"You could never be classified as that, Claire," Jack answered. "Bear in mind you had been absent from my life for months and I suppose I was lonely."

"I see." Claire looked slightly mollified. "Can you promise me that you will *never* do such a thing to me again?"

Jack sighed resignedly. "Yes, my dear, I can promise you that."

"One more thing, Jack. I want to live in France after we leave India."

"France it is, then. I will look into suitable areas, but much of the country is devastated by German occupation, you know."

"I don't want to live anywhere in the south, Jack. I…I don't care for the influx of tourists during summer months. Maybe somewhere along the Brittany coast?"

"Brittany might well be the most ravaged area of all, but we'll see."

"That's settled then," Claire said neutrally. "That marriage-breaking creature in Durban is in for a nasty shock," she unwisely added with an air of satisfaction. "I'm certain she's been looking forward to the life of Old Riley on your retirement fund."

Jack glanced across at his wife, the expression on his face akin to dislike. "Allow me make something clear to you, Claire. I will not…repeat *not* tolerate a continual stream of denigration against Anne Winterton. It may seem odd to you, but she happens to love me for myself. My decision to remain married to you will be a devastating blow."

"Don't presume to tell me what I can or cannot do!" Claire flared, her tone causing Susanna to look up in vague alarm. "If you are so concerned for the woman's delicate feelings, then clear off back to her!" she flung at him, then stormed off down the path towards the bungalow, her eyes glittering with fury.

If she was to have that woman rammed down her throat every five minutes, Jack could bugger off back to his damned tart! She would find a competent lawyer in Calcutta to handle the divorce, who would also ensure she received sufficient alimony to lead a reasonable lifestyle.

Jack followed behind at a distance, his face tight with anger, only rigid self-control preventing him from taking Claire up on her suggestion. By the time he came within sight of the bungalow, cold common sense returned. He simply could not allow himself to be labelled an out-and-out cad that would stain a reputation and image he had cultivated throughout his entire career. A future with Anne must be relegated to the past, and he would force himself to forget what might have been.

Diana was dismayed to notice the icy atmosphere between her parents. Peter had told her that Claire was considering taking back her husband, so something disastrous must have subsequently occurred. Frost between the two persisted over the following days, until a drama from another quarter served as a distraction.

Susanna was ill again, with very badly infected tonsils.

Doctor Dikshet was summoned, and he was emphatic that the child's condition must no longer be ignored. If she was to thrive, her tonsils must be removed as soon as possible. In light of this pronouncement, it was decided that the moment the existing crisis had abated, Susanna would be taken to Calcutta. Being the child of army personnel, she would be admitted to the British Military Hospital for the operation.

A week later, Claire and Jack set off on the train to Calcutta with their pale and decidedly skinny granddaughter. Diana and Peter would follow in a few days time, after Hilltop closed down for the holidays. Jack's driver brought Christina to meet them at Howrah Station, and she helped carry the child's equipment and possessions to the Daimler parked outside. Grizzling miserably in Claire's arms, Susanna was exhausted by the stress of travelling, whorls of sweat-darkened hair sticking to her face.

Walking into the house she had left more than a year ago, Claire was seized by a feeling of surrealism. How close she had come to losing her home, and everything in it besides! She still secretly believed her husband had intended to install his whore in her home, the thought bringing a flush of fury to her cheeks. God, the woman must be devastated to have lost her ageing Piggy Bank lover!

Susanna was fed, settled and cooler under a slowly turning fan in the old nursery when Claire quietly shut the door behind her. In her own bedroom, she stripped off and had a shower before changing into fresh clothes. Sitting out on the veranda with a glass of *nimbu pani*, she began to reflect on Jack's long silences and dour demeanour. Hardly an enticing prospect for the future, she thought gloomily, but at least there was time to opt for a divorce after all.

Depressed, Claire gazed round the garden in which she had taken such pride, but there was little sign of its former glory. Creeper and weeds crowded once-immaculate flowerbeds, and tufts of grass pushed through cracks in the tennis court. The swimming pool lay empty, only a puddle of brackish water remained at the deep end. She supposed Jack had dispensed with most of the staff before departing on his cruise.

There were only a few servants still working in the house. She supposed it wasn't worth employing more servants, since one way or another they would be leaving the house for good in only a few months.

Her mind focused on the problem constantly niggling at the back of her mind. What would become of little Susanna when she left? Diana still found the child irritating, and had little patience to deal with her all-too-frequent illnesses. Who would take care of the toddler? Notice when she was off-colour? Comfort the night-fears that too often seemed to plague her? Her eyes pricking with incipient tears, Claire needed a shoulder to lean on, but Jack was nowhere to be seen.

Two days later, Diana and Peter arrived at the house in time to accompany their small daughter to hospital. Frightened by the strong smell of antiseptic, Susanna began to howl despite the comfort of her grandmother's arms, the screams escalating when the surgeon, Major Simms, attempted to examine her.

Diana regarded her small daughter with distaste. "How a scrawny thing like that can produce such ear-splitting howls is quite beyond me!"

"Well, a distinct advantage is that Major Simms has no problem looking down Susanna's throat," grinned her husband. "Besides, she'll soon be under, and won't remember a thing about it."

"Mrs Lalinski, I'll arrange for a bed to be made up for you next to your daughter, so that she sees you upon waking from the anaesthetic. I want her to remain as calm as possible to avoid exacerbating the soreness of her throat."

"Oh!" Diana looked at Peter in frustration. They had been planning to go with friends to the cinema, and then on to the Saturday Club for a nightcap. It now seemed she was expected to stay with this noisy little monster. Unless...? Diana glanced questioningly at her mother.

Claire nodded. "I'll stay with Susanna, so off you go and have lovely evening. Just let your father know what's happening. I'll give you a ring when she's properly *compus mentus* again."

The next few days were difficult for the little girl, who did not understand why her throat was so painful and became worse if she cried. Ice cream fed in small quantities by her grandmother was all she was able to swallow. As she slowly improved, Claire was eventually allowed to take her home to Alipore. Jack was there when they arrived, showing genuine concern for his small granddaughter, who took a clear liking to the big man with a pipe.

"This is your Grandpa, darling," Claire explained. "Can you say *Grandpa*?"

"*Graddy*!" Susanna said triumphantly. "I like my Graddy."

"Grandpa...*Grand-pa*," Claire enunciated. "Try again?"

"Graddy," Susanna repeated obligingly. And so Graddy it was.

Diana appeared a little later with Peter, and both thanked Claire for saving the day with Susanna. Throwing her tennis things on a chair,

Diana went over to her daughter who was sitting on the floor playing with an array of toy farm animals.

"Feeling better are we, sweetie?" she bent to give her a kiss. "No excuse now for giving trouble over food, eh?"

Startled by Diana's naturally loud voice, Susanna scrambled to her feet and ran to her grandmother, peeping with scared eyes from behind Claire's skirt.

"For God's sake, what's the matter with her *now*?" Diana exclaimed in annoyance. "Come here, Susanna, Mummy wants to talk to you."

"*No!* Stay with Mama...wanta stay with Mama!"

Stiffening, Diana stared at her mother with hard eyes. "So you've taught *my* daughter that you're her mother? Not good enough, Mummy, I won't have it."

"I most certainly haven't passed myself off as her mother," Claire denied heatedly. "Susanna needed to call me something, so I tried to teach her Grandma...which somehow evolved into Mama. Much the same way that Grandpa became Graddy. Don't worry, I've no secret plan to steal your child."

"But she doesn't bother to call *me* anything, does she?" Diana said suspiciously. "Anyway, why is she whingeing...or is it now an ingrained habit? And why won't she come to me, her own mother?"

"Probably because you can't speak without bellowing," Claire was losing patience. "And she wasn't whingeing just now, only playing with her farm."

"Ridiculous!" Diana snapped. "The cunning little tyke is playing to the gallery as always. She must learn to do what she's told. Susanna, come to Mummy – *at once!*"

"Diana, she's only just come home from hospital, do let her—"

"I *said*, come here, Susanna, and don't encourage her, Mummy!"

Her eyes wide with fright, the child shrank against Claire as her mother seized her none too gently by an arm. "Do what you are told for once, will you? I'm sick and tired of the histrionics we've all had to put up with from the day you were born."

Struggling vainly to free herself from her mother's grasp, Susanna opened her mouth and screamed at the top of her voice. Drawing a ragged breath, the child prepared to scream again when her mother's hand came down hard on her bottom.

"Don't you scream in my face, you bloody little tyke," Diana shouted, incandescent with jealous rage. "You will do what you're told – *understand*?"

"For God's sake, Diana..." Claire was on her feet, but not fast enough to prevent another hefty wallop descending on the howling child's bottom.

Her back arching, Susanna's mouth opened wide as she fought to catch her breath. Claire's heart sank. What did Diana think she was doing? She had been hoping the child's stress-triggered breathlessness had all but disappeared, but now her body started to buck, her eyes bulging with effort. Suddenly she went limp, a dead weight, hanging by an arm in her mother's grip.

"*Susanna*!" Diana shook the child, whose head flopped back and forth. "Stop this nonsense at once, or I'll—"

"Winnie, let her go." Gently detaching his wife's hand from the skinny little arm, Peter caught the child as she fell to the floor. "Susanna's not pretending, darling. She's out for the count. Let Claire take her, she knows what to do."

"Oh Peter, I can't stand it!" Diana burst into tears, and turned to lean her face against her husband's chest. "I can't cope with constant rejection from my own child! She's *my* daughter – *mine*, dammit!"

"Never mind, sweetheart," Peter soothed, "I'm sure it's unintentional. Look, why don't you go and have your shower? Remember we're having dinner with Colonel Boothby and his wife this evening."

Still sniffling, Diana left the room, and Peter handed over his small daughter to a horrified Claire, who hurried from the room with her burden. How was she to leave this frail little thing to the tender mercies of an over-impatient mother, who was also free with her hand? It did not bear thinking about...

Diana chose to ignore Susanna over the following days, for which Claire was deeply thankful. Subsequent to the altercation with her mother, the child was inclined to dissolve into tears upon simply hearing her voice. But time was running out, Peter would soon be rejoining his regiment, and Diana would return to Kalimpong.

With Susanna.

One evening, Claire put her granddaughter to bed, and then went out on the veranda to join the family for a drink before dinner. Taking a puff of his pipe, Jack made an announcement with a slightly embarrassed air.

"I've just been advised that I'm in line for a peerage in recognition of services to the British Crown. Can you imagine it? Lord Cameron MacLeod...*ridiculous*!"

"Daddy, that's wonderful," Diana smiled. "I must say, the honour is richly deserved after all the years you put in."

"Good Lord, that means I shall be Lady MacLeod," Claire breathed, a genuine smile of joy on her face for the first time in months. "What a hoot!"

"I shall decline, of course." Jack chose not to notice the outrage on his wife's face. "I've no intention of adding a handle to my name that immediately increases the cost of anything I want to purchase."

Claire glanced over at Diana and Peter, who were still gaping in astonishment over Jack's statement. She wasn't the only one to think he must be losing his mind.

"But wouldn't it be an insult to refuse such an honour?" Claire asked faintly. "No, Jack, you must be pulling our legs."

"As a matter of fact, I *do* mean to refuse it, my dear. It would be ridiculously pretentious for a man such as myself to masquerade as a lord. Plain Jack MacLeod has always been good enough for me, and will do so in the foreseeable future."

Sick with disappointment, it crossed Claire's mind to wonder if her husband would be this obdurate had his tart been in line to become Lady MacLeod? At last she would have attained the title she merited through her own lofty French ancestry that had been denied to her. And now it was happening again...

The day before Peter left for Burma, he and Diana found Claire in the bathroom kneeling beside the bathtub, where Susanna was floating two yellow plastic ducks in the bathwater. Seeing her mother enter, the child froze, her mouth turning down as if threatening to cry.

"For pity's sake, why must she look at me as if I were the devil incarnate," Diana exclaimed crossly. "Mummy, Peter and I want to discuss the possibility Susanna going with you to France. I have a school to run, she's a such a demanding child, and I simply can't be doing with all the endless clap-trap she seems to need."

Getting to her feet, Claire stared incredulously at her daughter. Did Diana really mean it? For Susanna she would put up with Jack's morose attitude, and even overlook his unconcealed glee that he had scotched her chance of acquiring a long-desired title. Searching her eldest daughter's face, she could scarcely believe that to all intents and purposes, the little girl was being given over to her. Glancing over at Peter, she saw him nod his agreement.

"We know how much you love Susanna," Peter told his mother-in-law. "And it would be a weight off Diana's mind to know she was being properly cared for. Besides, you seem to be the only one able to handle her," he added with a rueful smile.

Claire's face broke into a beam of sheer joy. "Of course, I'll take her to France with me! Who knows, her health might improve in a different climate."

"Whew!" Diana blew out her cheeks in relief. "That's settled then. Peter darling, hadn't we'd better change for the Marchants' cocktail this evening?"

Lifting the child out of the tub, Claire enveloped her in a towel and settled herself on the bathroom stool. As she dried the skinny little body, she planted a kiss on top of the fair head.

"Just think, you're soon going to be a little French girl, darling...what fun!"

Returning home that evening, Jack found Claire beaming, her eyes shining with happiness. Discovering the reason for his wife's improved demeanour, he mentally shrugged. If looking after Susanna would keep her pleasant and distract her from dwelling on his sins – so much the better. Besides, he rather liked the little thing.

The following morning, Peter left to rejoin his regiment and two hours later Diana caught the train to Kalimpong. Before leaving the house, she glanced at her small daughter, unsure if she should attempt to kiss her goodbye. Seeing the child's eyes widen she decided to leave well alone, and went outside to the Daimler that was waiting to leave for the station. Claire followed her down the steps into the driveway, Susanna in her arms, waving until the vehicle vanished round the corner.

The house and some of the furniture was sold, the remainder going to Daphne and Robert for their new home in Burdwan Road. Jack and Claire's personal effects were packed into steamer trunks, and orange boxes filled with Susanna's paraphernalia. The big house looked empty and forlorn, except for prospective buyers wandering through the echoing rooms.

Jack, Claire and little Susanna took the train to Bombay, where they were booked to stay at the Taj Mahal Hotel for two nights before boarding the liner for Southampton. Upon arrival, Claire and Susanna were to stay at a hotel for a few days whilst Jack went up to London, to obtain details of his new posting as British Consul in northern France. Still not in very good health, he was thankful the position was not onerous, his presence at the Saint Malo government offices being required only twice a week.

During an interim period in France, Jack had arranged to rent a house on the outskirts of Dinard, a small market town on the Brittany coast. A short ferry journey across the water from Saint Malo, it was said to possess long sandy beaches and was also relatively free from bomb damage. He idly wondered if any English people had remained there during the war? No linguist, he had no desire to learn to speak French.

During his stint as British consul, Jack had every intention of investigating the possibility of purchasing a house on the island of Jersey. No great distance from France, it was the largest of the Channel Islands, possessed English-speaking doctors, and in any case he preferred to buy property on British soil. However, he had been given to understand the islands had only recently been freed from German occupation, and he had no real idea how bad the conditions were there.

Claire had always enjoyed her stay at the Taj Mahal Hotel. The first time had been a long time ago as the guest of Emile, her mother's kindly uncle, who she supposed must be dead by now. At the reception desk, Claire noticed with surprise that Jack had not reserved a suite, but had merely booked a double room with the addition of a cot for Susanna. One of the hotel *ayahs* had been employed to baby-sit whilst Claire and Jack went downstairs for dinner, and the child was fast asleep before they left the room.

Elegant in coral chiffon and gilt sandals, Claire's spirits soared as they were ushered to their table, having noticed admiring glances from gentlemen at other tables. It really raised her spirits to know she still merited that! Casting a covert glance at her husband, she sighed inwardly, seeing his unreadable expression. Maybe now they had Susanna, of whom Jack was clearly fond...could she be a catalyst for them to start afresh?

The meal was excellent and Claire sat back in her chair, a cup of coffee in her hand. Jack was smoking a cigar, a glass of fine brandy on the table in front of him.

"This is a wonderfully luxurious hotel, Jack, expensive, but worth every penny," Claire remarked with satisfaction. "I shall miss coming here from time to time."

"Make the most of it, my dear, because we'll have to watch the pennies from now on," Jack's reply was dry. "*Economy* is a word you will become very familiar with."

"What?" Claire looked blank. "Penny-pinch? Come on, Jack, I'm well aware you have a substantial retirement fund to invest, not to mention proceeds from the house sale and Daimler. We should be able to live very comfortably on the income from that."

"Not exactly. Having abandoned Anne, I felt morally obliged to remit half my provident fund monies to her by way of compensation. In addition, I gave her the deeds to the property I purchased at a time when we intended to make a home together."

"*You did what?*" gasped Claire incredulously, colour draining from her face. "So you've handed over sacks of gold and a bloody great property to that tramp, who was only after your money in the first place? How could you be so bloody stupid, Jack?"

"I was not prepared to leave the poor woman flat," he retorted, angered as always by gratuitous denigration of his lover. "I can't imagine why you begrudge her money and a home, when you've managed by hook and by crook to claw *me* back?"

"*Tcha!*" Claire almost spat. "Your ridiculous vanity leaves me breathless! Don't you realise the woman is probably laughing all the way to her bank, with every intention of buying herself a handsome young swain...thoughtfully funded by an ageing idiot?"

"That's enough!" Jack hissed through clenched teeth. Controlling himself with an effort, his grin was not dissimilar to a snarl. "For most of your life, my dear Claire, you've enjoyed everything money could buy. I shall find it amusing to see you having to go without. Watching what you spend. You've made your bed – so now you can damned well lie on it."

Standing up, Claire stared at her husband, her eyes cold. "Your unrelenting spite towards me is horrifying, Jack. Undeserved, since it was not I who betrayed our marriage. I shall never forgive you for this – *ever.*"

Picking up her bag, Claire swept towards the dining room doors. Her eyes stinging with unshed tears, she went up to the bedroom and paid off the *ayah* who was sitting by a sleeping Susanna. Eyelashes fluttering against cheeks flushed pink with sleep, the child turned over with a sigh. Looking down at her, Claire's heart contracted with love. Here, at least, was someone who truly loved and needed her.

As for Jack, that bloody bastard who had deliberately cheated her of the comfortable retirement he knew she expected...how she *detested* his sneering face! Hopes of the fresh start she had earlier been nurturing now made her burn with humiliation, and she mentally castigated herself for not knowing better.

Claire's eyes hardened. The die was cast. Live together they must, but she was not obliged to speak to him unless strictly necessary. See how he enjoyed living with a wife who didn't trouble to hide her dislike. For the moment, she would sleep as far away from him as possible in the blasted double bed in the bedroom.

Jack was conspicuous by his absence over the remainder of the stay in Bombay, reappearing an hour before it was time to board the ship. Dumping his possessions in the cabin, he disappeared once again without speaking a word, leaving Claire frustrated and angry at the lack of courtesy towards her.

A siren screamed and the ship shuddered as its engines burst into thunderous life. Crewmen shouted, gangways were hauled up and thick ropes were thrown back on deck to be coiled by a waiting seaman. Edging away from the quayside, the great vessel slowly made her way towards the harbour entrance, escorted as always by a flotilla of tugboats to ensure her safety until she reached open sea.

Holding Susanna's slightly sticky little paw, Claire stood in the stern to watch the ship's departure. Unexpectedly, she was gripped by a sense of isolation and misery and blinked furiously to prevent treacherous tears from trickling down her face. Taking her thumb from her mouth, Susanna looked up at her grandmother in sudden alarm.

"Mama?" she asked. "Mama's crying?"

"Crying?" Claire put a hand to her cheek, finding it wet with tears. "No darling, it's just the wind making my eyes water."

"Oh!" Susanna nodded, and resumed sucking her thumb.

Patting her face with a handkerchief, Claire gazed at the rapidly diminishing shoreline, certain she would never see India again. What had once seemed an exciting start to a new life had now been reduced to a depressing prospect. Condemned to live with a man she utterly despised, she was also expected to develop cheese-paring ways in order to maintain a bare minimum of lifestyle. Claire smiled grimly. In fact, she and her granddaughter were not unalike – both of them cast aside as flotsam and jetsam.

Life's rejects.

For little Susanna's sake, she would make the best of things and devote herself to giving her the most wonderful childhood she could manage. After such a miserable start in life, her waif of a granddaughter deserved to eventually become a confident, happy and healthy young girl, looking forward to a bright future ahead.

As regards herself, Claire expected nothing more. Except that perhaps in the fullness of time, she would come to forgive herself for Timothy...

COMING SOON:

Susanna

The third book of the 'Merencourt Saga'

Susanna leads a happy, carefree childhood in France with her grandparents but upon the reappearance of a hostile and critical mother she doesn't know, seven-year-old Susanna is abruptly torn from the security of her grandmother's home. During the years of misery that follow at boarding schools, she becomes the victim of intense bullying and knows little happiness... except with horses.

Thinking to escape her mother's control at last, the eighteen-year-old girl plunges into marriage with a cold and emotionless man she scarcely knows. Subsequent to the birth of two children, a deeply unhappy Susanna flees her marriage. Through the betrayal of her own mother, she loses custody of her beloved and very young children.

Meeting and marrying a good-looking pilot, Susanna looks forward to a bright future at last. Delirious with joy to find herself pregnant with her third child, she is ordered by her husband to abort the baby. Appalled, Susanna refuses. The subsequent consequences of her refusal become close to intolerable.

Can this girl, seemingly born under a malevolent star, ever find the happiness and serenity she rarely knows but desperately seeks? Does she possess the courage to battle the courts to regain custody of her children? She is soon to discover whether or not she has what it takes to survive...

CPSIA information can be obtained at www.ICGtesting.com
Printed in the USA
LVOW13s2150241113

362675LV00001B/256/P